We were nearing the end play. Three hours' worth of adrenalin was racing through my body and my mind was a volcano. I strode down to the edge of the stage and boldly surveyed the first-night audience. Then I began the epilogue with which Shakespeare, speaking through Rosalind, hoped to win some applause:

'It is not the fashion to see the lady the epilogue; but it is no more unhandsome than to see the lord the prologue.'

A smattering of premature cheers broke out among the feminists – it was the early 1970s, women's lib had taken off in Cambridge. I nodded my approval but held up my hand to stay their enthusiasm. Still in the character of Rosalind, I continued the epilogue.

It was a good audience. News of our unusual production had spread in advance and every seat was sold for every performance. I hoped a lot of those seats would be filled by Londoners, preferably critics. As the epilogue neared the end I could feel the excitement rising again – the whole audience was dying to applaud. I turned and began to saunter back upstage, throwing the last lines over my shoulder with a mixture of confidence and modesty. Then, still as Rosalind, I turned back for a low curtsy.

The curtain fell. The audience broke into thunderous applause.

In the privacy behind the curtain Jas flung his arms round me. 'Rosie, you're bloody brilliant! How do you do it?' I hugged him hard and there was no difference between Rosie and Jas, Rosalind and Orlando, as the curtain shot up, exposing all four of Shakespeare's couples in amorous bliss. All eight of us stared in mock surprise at the disappearing curtain and at the audience. The audience roared with laughter.

We had rehearsed this too, and the rest of the curtain calls, doing it all in character. It was a neatly choreographed performance of its own in the Tyrone Guthrie manner, designed to leave the audience on a high right to the end. It worked. The whole little ADC theatre seemed to lift off its foundations and float away on the euphoria of both cast and audience.

And then cast and audience were mingling as friends began to fill the tiny backstage area. There were hugs and kisses and extravagant praise which to outsiders always sounds phoney but isn't. We were awash with love and relief and gratitude and it was as real as anything in real life.

1

For me, 'real life' had consisted almost entirely of the ADC from the moment I'd arrived in Cambridge eight months before. I had no time for punting on the Cam or lounging around The Backs with boyfriends, even less for champagne parties given by the offspring of the idle rich. The ADC was as good a training as most drama schools and I was determined to make the most of it. The official title – Amateur Dramatic Club – was misleading. There was nothing amateur about it. Hundreds of students like me were using it as a back door into the profession, and with so much talent to choose from, standards were high. What's more, it was the busiest drama group in Cambridge, more like a repertory company, putting on several productions each season.

Well, that was what I wanted: to get as much experience as I could in the shortest possible time. I worked like hell to prove my worth and at the end of the year landed my first big role: Rosalind in *As You Like It*.

Love at first sight: the role, the play, Shakespeare himself. It would have been a wonderful experience even as a conventional production, but the thing that set us alight and later lifted the theatre into the skies was the director's vision. This was not, he said, a facile comedy, a pleasant little romp through Arcadia. The Forest of Arden was no pastoral idyll full of sighing lovers. Each of the characters who fled to it did so in danger of his or her life. It was the court life that had been idyllic, and the characters had been banished from it into the brutalities of the forest where they had to battle against a hostile climate, wild animals and starvation. The final happiness of the eight lovers was earned after long struggle. This was, he said, a dark, harsh play, only emerging into the light by stages as it reached for its ending.

Accordingly, we began it on a dark, bare stage dressed in dark, plain clothes, with lighting only just sufficient for visibility. As the play progressed, we and it gradually took on light and colour until finally bursting into the radiance of the happy resolution. Once we'd talked through the text, our version seemed so obvious we couldn't understand why it hadn't been done before. I suppose it was our conviction of the rightness of what we were doing that made it such a strong production. That, and Jas, my Orlando.

Jas was a third-year student. He'd been in nearly every Cambridge play during those three years, including those done by the prestigious Marlowe Society. No one doubted he would become a professional actor. He was tall and angular like me, with a leprechaun's face, madly expressive eyebrows and a body so oddly jointed that he could turn himself into anything he chose by an infinitesimal adjustment of his limbs. Even his colouring seemed designed for drama. He had longish dark hair and beady black eyes which could switch in a fraction of a second from piercing to impish, from sly cunning to affection.

Five minutes after meeting Jas I knew two things for certain: one, that he was homosexual, and two, that he would be a very dear friend for life. There are no explanations for that kind of thing other than the inadequate word, 'chemistry'. Well, we had it, and it was probably the chemistry between us as much as any talent of mine that landed me the role of Rosalind. From the moment we started reading together at audition, the casting was obvious.

I loved working with Jas. There was in him a sense of barely-suppressed explosiveness which was perfect for our vision of the play. Orlando was doubly enraged – by ill-treatment from his brother and by the threat to his life which forced him to leave the court. Rosalind, too, had good cause for anger. Her father had been unfairly banished and now she, too, was threatened with death unless she left. When the two future lovers met up in the Forest of Arden, a sense of violence born of injustice underpinned their wooing and made their flashes of tenderness all the more poignant. And when Rosalind, disguised as a boy, undertook to cure Orlando of his love for Rosalind, there was real bitterness in her diatribe against love, stemming from her disillusionment with all human relationships. These were tough, gritty lovers who had good reason to fight against the love which came to them unasked and unwanted.

It may or may not have been relevant that both Jas and I had been rejected as children. It may have been our own suspicion of serious relationships that spoke through the lovers in the Forest of Arden. Or it may simply have been good acting, Jas's vigour bringing out unexpected depths in my own performance. In any case, we did these scenes for real. We could feel the tension among the rest of the cast and the audience. It wasn't surprising, then, that the resolution into the light after the long, dark struggle brought a sense of overwhelming relief to us all.

So there we were, awash with it, still clinging to each other as well-wishers poured backstage and engulfed us in an ocean of good feeling. I suppose we were all waiting for the one person who mattered most. In my case, it was a barmaid.

My friendship with Belle wasn't as surprising as it might appear. Belle was also an actress, 'resting' (cruel euphemism) between jobs. She'd graduated from the Central School of Speech and Drama some years before but had never quite made it into a good career. Part of the fault was her appearance. She looked like a medieval kitchen wench plonked into twentieth-century London: a big blowsy blonde with big extravagant gestures and a passion for gaudy clothes. Casting directors took one look at her and cast her as . . . a medieval kitchen wench. Unfortunately, there weren't all that many plays with medieval kitchen wenches and so Belle, finding herself out of work more often than in, drifted back to her home town, Cambridge, and took a job as barmaid at the Criterion.

The Cri, a slightly disreputable pub, was full of students who considered themselves alienated by student life. I'd been taken there by Jas and had found myself watching the barmaid with increasing curiosity. Finally I realised what it was: she was playing a role, and doing it beautifully. She was the gutsy medieval barmaid with a heart of gold but an iron fist, should anyone get out of order. At the end of the evening, when she came round to collect the glasses, I looked her straight in the eye and said, 'RADA?'

A burst of gutsy laughter. 'Clever you! Actually, it was Central.'

From then on Belle became one of my closest friends. My father would have had a fit. Apart from the prestige, the thing he liked about Cambridge was 'the contacts, my dear, the contacts. Cultivate them.' And here I was, with my best friends a barmaid and a homosexual.

Finally I saw her making her way towards us, a cross between a ship of state and a gaudy parrot. 'Belle!' I called.

A jam of people suddenly parted like the Red Sea and through it whooshed Belle. She flung her ample arms round both of us.

'You were *unspeakably* good, *both* of you, *all* of you!' she cried, her big face glistening with excitement. 'God, I can't *wait* to see the reviews! Even a *critic* must see what you've done!'

We burbled mindlessly while all around us the crowds surged. Then they started to thin. 'Look, Belle, Tony's giving a party – why don't you come along?'

'I'd love to, but –'

'Heaps of people will be crashing – anyway, you're my guest.'

'Ros, I'd love to, but Brendan's waiting outside with a student.'

'A what?' Belle's husband taught Land Economy at the university and it was a standing joke that most of his students had more money than brain. I couldn't imagine any of them coming to see a play.

Belle laughed. 'I know, but this one's different. He's really bright.'

'Well, bring him along! Seriously, it's not that kind of party – Tony'll be delighted! Please come, Belle. Personal insult if you don't.'

It took ages to change out of costume and clean off the worst of the make-up in what passed as a dressing-room. As Jas and I left the theatre, already a sense of anti-climax was beginning to descend. Acting was like a drug; it kept you high, performing incredible feats for as long as needed, and then suddenly dropped you just when you craved a little reward for your efforts. We all knew it, and yet we always tried to keep the high going.

Little knots of people were waiting outside. Ours was easy to find. Brendan was in appearance a perfect match for Belle: a big red-haired Irishman as extrovert in his gestures as his wife and equally warm and welcoming. He enveloped me in an extravagant bear hug. Only when he released me did I notice the student. Dark-haired and dressed in dark clothes, he merged with the night until Brendan brought him forward and said, in his remains of an Irish accent, 'Rosie, lass, here's a brand-new fan for you!'

The speech would have bombed from anyone else, but Brendan had a special licence. He could say anything. You couldn't take offence from a man so full of goodwill towards the human race.

I leaned towards him now and said in a stage whisper, 'Does he have a name?'

Brendan clapped a hand to his forehead. 'Isn't it just the like of me! Ros Rawlinson, Jas Molyneux. David Farleton.'

We shook hands all round and laughed. Whoever he was, his obvious affection for Brendan and Belle made him an instant friend of mine. Even so, there was something about him that made me uneasy. It was only when we reached Tony's house and were absorbed into the party that I began to see what it was.

He wasn't absorbed into the party. No way. While

everyone else was brightly dressed and chattering with that suppressed hysteria which follows a first night, David Farleton stalked the party like a dark, sombre Hamlet ranging restlessly through the corridors of Elsinore. I don't think he meant to. He just wasn't the sort of person who could fit in, least of all in a setting so flighty as this.

Put simply, he was the most extraordinarily intense person I'd ever met. We, too, could be pretty intense in our acting, but with us it was an inward directed thing: searching our own souls to uncover the essence of the character we were playing. David Farleton seemed indifferent to himself. He seemed to be looking outward, trying to make sense of the world, if only that small part of it now contained in Tony's house.

This lack of self-interest extended to his appearance. He was astonishingly good-looking – the tall, dark and handsome cliché carried to extremes – but I don't think he knew it. He had masses of near-black hair, but it was raggedly cut and had had no more than a brief encounter with a comb. His eyes were also black and stared with such steady force that many people turned away, disconcerted. He probably didn't realise he was staring or that other people were watching him with fascination. He seemed almost to regard himself as invisible. This was all the more striking in someone his size. From his big, strong features right down to his feet, he was an imposing figure, to say the least. But while Brendan and Belle had large gestures to match their size, David Farleton was curiously self-contained, a still, calm centre in the vortex of the party. I found myself watching for each small gesture, each tiny change in facial expression, much as one watches a subtle actor.

But actor he was not. It was clear even then that he knew only one role: David Farleton. The multitude of conflicting personalities that most of us harbour within ourselves had in him drawn together into one large, strong, unified whole. The word that came to mind – and it was an odd one – was integrity. Not only in the moral sense but in every other way. David Farleton was a perfectly integrated human being, the inner and outer man combining to form something complete. That completeness in turn gave him force, as if he were a man driven by some private vision and looking only for an outer world in which to accomplish it.

He wasn't likely to find it in us. Our own vision, that which had held the play together, had vanished as soon as the curtain went down. We were now a motley group of excitable magpies, awaiting the results. Stephanie, the woman who played Celia, had a brother in the West End. His own play was opening that night and he planned to wait for the first editions. He'd promised to phone us if he found anything in them about us. This is what we were waiting for with such pleasure and dread. Belle had spotted at least two London critics in the audience and had seen them speed off before the curtain calls began – to phone in their copy, we hoped.

Meanwhile, we made merry. I felt rather responsible for David Farleton – after all, it was me who'd brought him here – so I kept an eye on him. It wasn't difficult. He radiated a quiet sense of presence, wherever he was. Mostly he was with Brendan and Belle, the three of them often chatting with actors Belle knew from the Cri. Brendan (who'd done amateur theatricals in his time) and Belle were perfectly at home among us; David, though not, seemed contented enough. At one point he laughed at something someone had said and I was startled to see the heavy, broody face suddenly transformed. The delight he expressed was almost childlike in its innocence, wholly unexpected in a man like that.

Later I saw him temporarily stranded and went up to him. 'I didn't think you practical people went in for the theatre,' I smiled.

He turned that dark, sober gaze on me and said very seriously, 'Brendan told me it was a play about trees.'

My first impulse was to laugh but it occurred to me that he might mean it. 'I hope you weren't too disappointed,' I said cautiously. Even before the words were out I saw the corners of his mouth begin to rise and realised how badly I'd misjudged. 'You are rotten!' I cried.

At that point someone whisked me away for an urgent consultation which turned out not to be the least bit urgent. When I returned to the main room, the first thing I saw was David, patently waiting for me. I went up to him again.

'But you're right,' he said, as if I hadn't been away. 'I don't think anyone else from Land Economy was there.'

'No one else has Brendan twisting their arm,' I suggested.

'Their loss,' he said.

'What *is* Brendan like as a teacher?' I asked. 'Somehow I can't imagine him in a classroom, at least not teaching something . . .' I trailed away.

'As boring as Land Economy?' he smiled. 'You're right, it is boring – except for Brendan. Everyone else is half a century behind the times. Brendan can see the future. He should have been promoted, he should be running the department.'

'Strong stuff,' I said.

'He's a strong person.'

Tony erupted into the room. 'Anyone know shorthand?' he yelled.

A quaint question for a bunch of actors but, amazingly, someone did: Lala, the girl who'd played Audrey, got up and followed Tony into the hall. I looked at my watch. Just gone three. If there was to be a phone call, it would be soon. Through the half-open door I watched them scrabbling around for paper and pencil. When it was found and placed by the phone, they returned. Dozens of eyes had watched this small drama. It was like those awful few minutes before the curtain goes up, the tension growing by the second.

When I turned back, David Farleton had been reclaimed by Brendan and Belle. I didn't mind. I felt too nervous to concentrate on a conversation. And yet, to my surprise, I missed his presence. I wanted to sit quietly with him, waiting for the phone, neither of us saying a word. I wanted to soak up his steady calm.

And, in a strange way, I did. From then on, I was aware of him watching me all the time. At one point he smiled across at me, so reassuring that I could feel the tension fall away. I smiled back and felt us linked, two quiet centres of calm in a room that was rapidly reaching a new pitch of hysteria. A strange image flitted across my mind: the room a tropical forest filled with bright, twittering parrots while beneath the trees sat two quiet animals unaffected by the chattering which surrounded them.

And then, silence. The phone had rung. Tony and Lala rushed out to answer it through a room gone hushed. Maddeningly, she turned her back to us as she sat down and began to scribble. It was only the positioning of the chair and table, but nothing could have increased the drama more than that uncommunicative back. Jas was beside me. I felt his hand groping for mine and I squeezed it hard for comfort.

It was the longest phone call I've ever not heard. When finally it finished, Lala came to the doorway and gave the victory sign. A small tentative cheer. Then she began reading. I missed the first words – I was listening too hard to hear. Finally the words began to come through the mist: '. . . and new interpretations have become more clichéd than the conventions they displace. But on this occasion new ideas are matched by a total vision which pulls the play together. The interpretation is devastatingly simple, so obvious that seasoned directors will be hating themselves for leaving it to the ADC to uncover.'

By this time Jas and I were leaning against each other. I don't know who was propping up whom. We didn't dare look at each other.

The review continued with a few quibbles, none of sufficient magnitude to disrupt the rapt attention. Then came the individuals, beginning with Jas. I held my breath. It's not true that actors hate each other. We're fiercely partisan, above all to those with whom we've slogged through weeks of rehearsal and the terror of the first night. If some git of a critic had failed to see what Jas was doing, most of us in that room would have seriously considered catching the first train to London to gun him down.

We needn't have worried. 'Oh, Jas,' I whispered. 'Well done!'

'Shh. You're next.'

'. . . beautifully matched by the aptly named Ros Rawlinson. With her boyish figure and clear, fresh face, she makes the transformation into Ganymede more convincing than any I've seen. There's a powerful sense of male solidarity between the future lovers in these scenes. But the moment she casts off her disguise and re-emerges as Rosalind, one marvels that this deliciously feminine creature could have fooled us for so long. Further, she accomplishes her chameleon changes without any of the embarrassing trickery of many more experienced actresses. This is subtle acting indeed and in time may well turn into great acting. Ros Rawlinson is a name worth watching in the years to come.'

There was a stunned silence. Then the cheering broke out. Jas hugged me. A few foolish tears plopped over the edge and began to make their way down my cheeks. I could hear affectionate laughter, feel a handkerchief wiping them away. Before the next lot could form, I shushed everyone so we could hear the rest of the review.

It was wonderful. Yes, there were criticisms, but they were fair ones, and already I could feel my mind cranking into action again, saying yes, we should try it this way or that way for the next performance, yes, that bit wasn't as good as it could be.

But it was too much to take in just now, and my mind, so overwrought, finally gave up the ghost. The rest of the party passed in a haze; the late hour, the wine, the strain of the performance, the euphoria, the thrill of that wonderful review – all of it closed in on us now. We, the lovely butterflies of the evening, were packing up our wings in happy exhaustion. It wasn't long before we were drifting towards the door. More hugs and kisses, clumsy now with fatigue.

I have no memory of leaving the party. All I remember is being outside again, in a Cambridge dawn which felt incomparably fresh and clean and untouched. And then another touch, also fresh and clean: David's hand, or rather, two fingers, laid feather-light on my cheek and shaking just a little. And David's face, slightly misty above me, or perhaps it was the mist rising from the Cam which veiled those strong features and made them seem so suddenly gentle. His voice, too, was veiled in softness, barely audible and, like his touch, a little shaky as he whispered my name.

2

The gates were magnificent: heavy black wrought-iron bars lightened at the corners by a tree-like pattern branching gracefully towards the centre. The massive stone pillars holding them were equally impressive. On the top of each was a stag's head inclined slightly towards the gates. When I looked again I saw that the patterns I'd taken for branches were in fact echoes of the stags' antlers. The whole effect was simple but grand and deeply harmonious. There was a sign, surprisingly modest, on one of the pillars:

FARLETON HALL

Farleton Hall. Oh, my God. How could I have been so stupid? I thought back over the few weeks I'd known David. All the signals had been there, if only I'd had the wits to read them correctly. His clothes, well-worn and slightly shabby, but good. His voice, quiet and yet clearly audible above those of other people, the voice of a man who'd always been listened to. All his physical gestures – spare but telling, strong but graceful, a man with good reason to feel at home in his body. Above all, that sense of being a calm, still centre of stability in the vortex surrounding him. Even his diffidence, which I'd misread, took on a new meaning. It was the modesty of a man who doesn't want – doesn't need – to draw attention to himself. The attention had been there from birth, not only his but also centuries of Farletons before him.

It was a new David Farleton I watched get out of the car and open the gates. Behind me Brendan and Belle had suddenly gone quiet, and I realised that they, too, were unprepared for what they were seeing. Surely Brendan must have had some idea? Evidently not.

As the gates swung back, the land beyond opened out into a broad grey-green sweep of parkland. It was raining, a soft, warm midsummer rain. It had rained much harder as we'd driven north in the luxurious old Saab, but as evening approached, the sky had lightened into one of those sumptuous mosaics of silver and grey lit from within by a hidden sun. The rain coming down now formed a silver gauze curtain through which the land seemed more mysterious.

David returned to the car, drove through, then got out again to shut the gates. Even the clang of metal on metal was discreet, like the quiet patter of the rain on the car roof and the muted baas of the sheep scattered about the parkland. The sheep, too, blended into their landscape; even they were silvery-grey against the green of the grass and trees. It was a picture of timeless grace, elegance and calm.

And David, returning again to the car. Grace, elegance and calm. I sneaked a sideways look, wondering if his face would reveal how he felt at this quiet display of his wealth.

Nothing. He didn't seem to notice it any more than he noticed the rain. I tried to imagine what it was like to be born into all this, and failed. Even the richest of my schoolfriends had had nothing so grand. It made me realise how narrow my life had been until now.

It also made me realise how little I knew David. We'd barely seen each other since the first-night party; he was taking his finals, I was finishing the play's run. Every night I'd looked for him in the audience and found him. I'd wondered then how he managed to get tickets – the play was sold out. Now I knew. Money.

There had been white roses, too, for Rosalind. Jas had been amused. 'If he can afford a bouquet that size . . .' he trailed off.

'And just what are those three dots supposed to mean, Jas?'

He leaned forward and said in a stage whisper, 'A rich

backer! Seriously, Rosie, it's just what we've been dreaming of: someone rich enough and keen enough to finance a transfer to the West End. How about it? Twist his arm?'

'Why, Jas, I had no idea you were so mercenary!'

'Ah, but for Art!'

'Shh. Your cue's coming up.'

It never crossed my mind to mention it to David. If I imagined anything at all, it was a doting mama who sent him a nice allowance to 'Enjoy yourself, you're only young once.'

As the opulent parkland slid by, I realised that he probably could afford to be our fairy godfather. But a West End transfer was the last thing on my mind. Everything had changed since that strange Cambridge dawn in which he'd touched my cheek and whispered my name. I still threw myself into the play, but the moment the curtain went down, my only thought was that David would be there, waiting for our ritual late-night coffee before we went our separate ways. I was crazed with eagerness to see him. I didn't give a damn what the critics said. David's was the only opinion that mattered. All the hugs and kisses of friends backstage meant little compared with the moment when David reached across the table and put his hand on mine. It was the only physical contact we'd had in our few brief meetings, and yet I felt as if we'd been lovers all our lives.

I still don't know how it happened. There was no moment of realisation, no flash of insight which illuminated the sky with the neon-bright words 'I love him'. And yet, it happened so quickly – within the space of those few hours after the play – that the absence of a thunderbolt still amazes me. All I knew was that before the first night of *As You Like It*, David Farleton didn't exist. After it, he was the centre of my life.

So I wasn't too surprised when he asked me to come up to Yorkshire with him 'for a few weeks . . . or better still, the whole summer . . .' It was inconceivable now that we would ever be apart again. What *is* surprising is that I never saw it in terms of 'Come and meet the family', with all that that implies. I never saw it in any terms at all. I simply didn't think. I was young, an unstable whirl of emotions that had never had anything to anchor them to earth. I had no core, nothing to hold together all the fragments and form a coherent whole called Ros Rawlinson. Even my name wasn't mine.

And then, suddenly, the whirlpool stopped and there was David. I'd never met anyone like him before. He seemed so sure of himself, seemed to know exactly who and what he was. It was hard to believe he was only two years older than myself. It was as if already he had a lifetime of experience packed into that big calm body. I wanted to be a part of it – both the body and the lifetime that had formed it. I saw him as a god, an all-knowing deity with the power to give coherence and meaning to my own life. Had I been older and more experienced myself, I would have seen how unfair I was being towards him. And if he had been as all-knowing as I thought him, he would have seen beneath my sham self-confidence to the insecure child it concealed.

Instead, we proceeded in state down the long drive: Ros Rawlinson, beautiful, talented actress-to-be, radiating confidence in the arrow-straight career ahead of her; and David Farleton, handsome young scion of an ancient family, about to begin his own clearly mapped future as guardian of that heritage. I don't think we meant to deceive each other, but at that age I suppose we all feel we are the one outsider in a world full of people living happy and meaningful lives. We hope, foolishly, that by pretending to be one of them, we will grow into the role and become it.

And Brendan and Belle? All I knew was that David had a piece of derelict woodland and wanted Brendan to give his opinion on how it should be managed. Brendan had agreed, and Belle had taken some time due to her from the Cri to come along and make a holiday of it.

I looked round, wondering where the woodland was, but there was nothing derelict about the landscape passing by the car windows, just acre after acre of serene parkland.

And then, suddenly, a glimpse of heaven, or so it seemed to me. Far ahead, flickering slightly through the green filigree of trees, was a shimmering silver mirage. Farleton Hall. I caught my breath, scarcely believing what I seemed to be seeing. It was as if a piece of that luminous rain-washed sky had, at the touch of a magician's wand, coalesced into stone, the kind of stone elves might use to build a fairy castle. I suppose it was an effect of the strange evening light, but the building seemed to float above the land, a pale lustrous vision, not quite real.

As we drew nearer, I could see that part of the ethereal effect was carefully planned. Farleton Hall was beautifully proportioned, an eighteenth-century triumph of the neo-classical search for perfect harmony. It was a large building, and symmetrical, but any sense of heaviness was dispelled by the delicacy of its windows and the decoration of its roofline. Despite its size it seemed light and airy, and wonderfully placed in a landscape which was itself light and airy and open. It was a place for being weightless and free. I felt giddy just looking at it.

The car pulled up on the gravelled circle in front of the house. A shallow flight of stone steps led to a large front door flanked by two equally large windows. Behind them I glimpsed movement. Then we were out of the car, climbing the steps, breathing the unbelievably clear, fresh air. We arrived at the door just as it opened to frame the shape of a woman.

I had to smile. The doorway was so big, the woman so small. She was smiling, too. She must have been about sixty, but she was one of the most beautiful women I had ever seen. Her hair was the same silvery grey as the house, untouched by blue rinse and cut in a short, practical style with just enough natural curl to give it softness and grace. Her face was the colour and texture of fine parchment, all the wrinkles delicate small ones which only added to her beauty. She wore a pearl-grey silk dress which gleamed with every movement. But, as if all this lightness were too much, her eyebrows and lashes were defiantly dark and framed a pair of jet black eyes which were unnervingly youthful and sharp.

'David!' she cried.

A moment later, big David had engulfed this tiny woman in a bear hug, lifting her right off the ground. The strength of the embrace surprised me. The landscape and house and woman seemed so elfin-light that the physicality of their relationship was unexpected. Also, David had been so reticent with me. I felt, unfairly, rather jealous.

Not for long. We had scarcely entered the hall before the warmth of David's mother engulfed us, too. The staff had assembled there to greet the young master on his return from Cambridge. There was Mrs Noble, who had been David's nanny and was now housekeeper and companion to Mrs Farleton. There was her husband, who served as valet and chauffeur and just about everything else. There was their son – gardener and handyman – and his wife Melinda who did the cooking and some cleaning.

The nine of us were dwarfed by the hall. It had been designed to impress, and did. Here, too, everything was serene and harmonious. A pale marble floor continued in a magnificent staircase which branched at a landing before rising to a gallery which surrounded the entire hall. Two huge marble fireplaces stared across the empty space at each other. Windows at the front of the house and from the back of the gallery flooded the hall with light. The only dark touches were a few pieces of furniture – Jacobean chests, tables and chairs – sparsely arranged around the walls. The lack of clutter was refreshing, the effect elegant.

Several doors led off from the hall. When the greetings were over, the staff dispersed and the five of us moved through into the drawing-room. Here the elegance diminished a little, with comfortable but well-worn chintz sofas and chairs making it a room one could live in. The carpet was worn, too, and the wallpaper faded. A fire burned brightly, competing with the light coming through a row of windows along one side. The sun was still trying to penetrate the opalescent sky; a touch of gold lurked among the silver.

'Do come and sit by the fire,' said Mrs Farleton. 'This house is so cold. David calls it the winter palace and sometimes I think he's right. It has no notion of summer. It was built by frost giants and they left their mark.'

We sat down. Here, too, the furniture was sparse but good and arranged in a way which increased the sense of spaciousness. Everything about the room, the house, its setting, was so *right*. As I sank into my chair, I could feel my past slipping away from me. It was almost physical, as if layers of confusion were falling from my body and leaving me clean and whole, as fresh as the rain-washed sky. I wanted never to leave this room. It was as if this peaceful house had been waiting for me to come to it all my life. I was meant to be here. Fifteen minutes after my arrival, with a man I'd met only a few weeks ago, I belonged. I sighed deeply with contentment and smiled.

Opposite me, Mrs Farleton smiled back. Did she guess my thoughts? Probably not. In her high wing-backed chair, she, too, had been transformed. She seemed much larger and grander than the little person framed in the doorway, and there was a firmness to her features that I hadn't noticed before. A formidable woman, despite her size.

David was pouring the drinks. As he handed me my whisky, our fingers touched. Instinctively, I avoided Mrs Farleton's eyes. She would be watching me closely and those bright black eyes would miss nothing. I wondered what David had told her about me, what reason he had found for bringing home an actress he'd known only a few weeks. He'd told me nothing about his home and mother; perhaps he'd told her nothing about me. Very possibly he brought home so many friends that this occasion wouldn't strike her as having any special meaning.

And perhaps it didn't. I looked at David. He'd served everyone else and now paused with his own drink in front of a window. He seemed to have forgotten our presence. The conversation slowed and died as, one by one, we noticed his abstraction. I wondered what was happening beyond the windows to capture his attention so completely. From where I sat, I had a good view. The rain had nearly stopped and the light was clear, whisking away the silver veil to reveal the sharp green contours of the countryside, miles and miles of it, uninterrupted until it came to a long whaleback hill far to the north. Before setting out, I had looked up David's home on a map ('Kirkby Langham,' he had said. Not 'Farleton Hall.') and knew that the North York Moors began only a few miles from it. Presumably that was the whaleback: the beginning of the moor, outlined against the sky. But that didn't explain the intensity of his gaze, let alone the frown that had appeared on his face.

The silence had stretched too long to be ignored. I looked at Mrs Farleton for an explanation.

She was sitting quite still, no longer the tiny *grande dame* but a sad old woman staring down at her wrinkled hands. 'I'm sorry, David,' she murmured.

He turned abruptly from the window and smiled at her. 'It's not your fault. You did what you thought best.'

It was the first hint I had that something was wrong at Farleton Hall.

3

After drinks, Mrs Farleton showed us our rooms and then, at Belle's request, the rest of the house. It was laid out in an orderly manner with two wings extending from the central hall and gallery. A square block at the back, reached by a green baize door hidden in the shadows beneath the staircase, contained the kitchens. The entire west wing was closed down, the shutters fastened tight, the furniture dust-sheeted and ghostly.

I felt sorry for the west wing, sad that any part of the marvellous building should be unused, but the remainder was ample. Everywhere we went, our footsteps echoed through the big rooms, all of them high-ceilinged and as light and airy as the great hall, all of them furnished with the same quality and sparseness. It was wholly unlike anything I'd seen in stately homes open to the public. There the rooms were crowded with an accumulation of possessions, diminishing the specialness of each and substituting for it a sense of history, of generations of rich magpies unable to resist a costly trinket. Here there were only large pieces carefully placed to display their qualities. The few smaller objects which stood on them were also well-chosen and in keeping with the austere beauty of the house. In a similar manner, the few touches of colour – a tapestry, an Aubusson rug, a painting – seemed to gather to themselves all the light of those big windows and glow with unexpected richness. The effect was stunning, and I said so.

Mrs Farleton laughed. 'How kind you are to make a virtue of our necessity. I may as well admit the truth: we sold many of the contents after my husband died. Taxes, repairs. We kept the larger pieces because few houses have space for them these days and so they sell badly. But

I rather agree with you; the sparseness does have a kind of elegance. It suits the winter palace. And here' – she opened a big double door – 'is the Long Gallery.'

We stepped inside. It was the barest of all the rooms so far and in striking contrast to them. While everywhere else in the house the walls were pale to catch the light, the walls here were panelled in dark oak. Above them was an oak ceiling, below an oak floor. The walls and ceiling were beautifully carved, as were the two massive oak fireplaces. The floor, though plain, consisted of boards two feet wide at least. The darkness was offset by the tall windows which virtually covered the whole of one long wall, but even so the effect was rather sombre.

'It has marvellous acoustics,' Mrs Farleton was saying. 'It's the classic shoebox shape, like the best concert halls, and all the wood resonates. Do give it a try – perhaps one of Rosalind's speeches?' She smiled and gestured towards one end of the room.

I laughed. 'It's a bit awesome for an amateur like me. Belle, how about you?'

'You rotten old thing – you just want to show me up!'

'No, seriously, I'd like to hear.'

Belle cocked her head, thinking. Then she whirled towards the end of the room in a flurry of multi-coloured skirts. 'All right then, which of my kitchen wenches shall it be? No, wait – I used to be a rather fetching Second Witch in the Scottish play. Can you bear it?'

We urged her on, and in a movement surprisingly graceful for a woman her size, she settled herself before an invisible cauldron and began stirring:

> 'Fillet of a fenny snake,
> In the cauldron boil and bake;
> Eye of newt and toe of frog,
> Wool of bat and tongue of dog,
> Adder's fork and blind-worm's sting,
> Lizard's leg and howlet's wing,
> For a charm of powerful trouble,
> Like a hell-broth boil and bubble.'

It was uncanny. Even in that short speech, Belle had transformed the role and lifted it above cliché. Her witch *was* a kitchen wench, carefully stirring her brew and recalling the recipe in a reflective voice. The effect was far more sinister than the usual cackling hag. And Mrs Farleton was right about the acoustics. Belle's housewifely whisper filled the big room, clearly and without distortion.

'Wonderful! Wonderful!' Mrs Farleton applauded, Brendan and I applauded, and I warmed even more to David's mother for appreciating Belle's talent.

'Has the room ever been used for plays?' I asked.

'Only by the children. The usual sort of thing: rainy afternoons when all the Welsh cousins were staying. It was they who loved playing at theatre – David and Hugh were being brought up to be "manly" and had to be dragged into it by the girls. I think they rather enjoyed it, though they pretended not to.'

I pictured the happy muddle of Farleton Hall in the days when whole families descended for weeks. The children racing around the huge rooms. Riding their ponies across endless land that was theirs. Playing in the streams and woods, making a nuisance of themselves on the farms. It was all so remote from my chilly childhood. How lucky David had been, and to have a mother like this, too. Even before she did her flit, my mother had hardly noticed my existence except as an object to clothe and feed and get off her hands as soon as possible. She would have scorned childish theatricals, though not the place they were held in. She would have filled this house with overdressed people and empty chatter.

The three walls not occupied by windows were filled with paintings. 'Are these the Farletons?' I asked.

She nodded. 'The rogues' gallery, all in chronological order – the Farletons were very particular about their history.'

I noticed her use of the past tense but said nothing. We began a tour of the room.

'The earliest ones aren't here, of course – people didn't think of portraits in those days. They only get going with the Tudors and even then there are gaps.' She smiled ruefully. 'Rather awful, most of them. The Farletons had a better eye for architecture than painting.'

I didn't have such a good eye for painting either, but even I could tell that these were nothing special. Face after wooden face stared out, the painters putting most of their meagre skill into the expensive clothing and jewellery and background objects. Only towards the end did they begin to improve. I stopped in front of one of the last. It was larger than most and showed a blond, blue-eyed man, rather fleshy and florid. The face was on the surface rather jolly, a typical country gentleman, but there was beneath it a hint of arrogance bordering on cruelty. The rather old-fashioned term 'degenerate' came to mind.

Belle peered at the painting. 'Looks a bit of a womaniser.'

'He was,' said Mrs Farleton. 'He was my husband.'

'Oh, God, I'm sorry,' said Belle.

Mrs Farleton laughed. 'Don't be. Full marks to you for noticing. Not everybody did, even when he was alive.'

We passed quickly to the next. There was no mistaking the subject: Mrs Farleton. The painting gave no hint of her size. A rather grand and extremely beautiful woman gazed out into the room. A mass of black hair coiled about her face and emphasised the blackness of her eyes. She was wearing a simple dress of dark blue velvet. The portrait was conspicuous for its lack of ornament, only the lovely face and a single beautiful ring: a huge emerald in a setting so ornate that it seemed at odds with the rest of the painting. The picture was clearly done by the same person who had painted her husband. Here, too, he had managed to capture something beneath the surface. Despite the calm and dignified pose, there was something restless about the hands, and the eyes held a curious combination of impatience and amusement.

'I didn't want the painting done,' she explained. 'I hated sitting still for so long. He did much of it from photographs but insisted on several sittings as well. I'd just discovered a circle of standing stones on the moor and was deep into archaeology. All this portrait business seemed a waste of time. After all, I'm not even a Farleton.'

Again this distancing of herself from the family so richly displayed on the walls. It was inconceivable to me that someone should wish to stand apart from all this, wilfully turn herself into an outsider.

She was watching me closely and with a hint of the same amusement as in the portrait. 'I'm afraid I have little taste for family history. Nor,' she added, 'does David. It's a pity that Hugh wasn't the elder. He cares much more about his heritage.' Then she shrugged and led us from the room.

And yes, there was a gong summoning us to dinner. The sound rolled through the vast half-empty rooms to meet an echo of all the gongs that had sounded in the past, back to the Tudors and, Mrs Farleton had implied, further back still.

I'd had quite a job of it to dress for dinner. David had given no hint that he lived in a place like this, and I'd brought with me casual clothes suited to countryside walks. Luckily, long skirts were in fashion for everyday wear and I'd included a light woollen one in amber which I'd thought looked vaguely countrified. Now I was busy trying to de-countrify it with a long-sleeved white blouse and an amber necklace. I put my hair up too, trying to smooth its obstinate strawberry-blonde waves into a sleek coil. Little curls at the temples kept escaping. Then I closed my eyes and out of years of habit invented a role for myself.

You are the Honourable Rosalind Rawlinson, daughter of a prominent lord. You are known not only for your beauty (legacy of your adored French mother) but for your wit and intelligence. You have every intention of remaining single – for ever, if need be – until a man worthy of your respect can be found. Meanwhile, you are carving out a modest niche in the world of French literature as . . . let's see . . . a translator of obscure medieval plays. But you have more traditional tastes, too, and have just returned from a day's hunting . . .

Oh, shit. They don't hunt in the summer, do they? I shut the door on my ignorance, amending the last bit to 'from a pleasant ride on your father's estate'. Then I opened my eyes.

There she was, the Hon. Ros. Tall, slim, with the upright posture of the born rich. Her features sharp, clear and delicate beneath the thin peaches-and-cream skin: the fine nose, the small, pointed chin, the nicely-etched mouth. Above all, the eyes. Whatever role I chose to play, the eyes remained the same. They had always been my best feature. They were true green, a rare enough colour even without the peculiar faceted effect which made them seem like peridots shining out of an ivory face. They caught the light and in good moods sparkled (in bad, they glittered). I suppose it was the odd colouring – light green, ivory, just a hint of blush – which gave my face a slightly exotic look. On the first day I'd met Jas he'd stared into my eyes and said, 'Rosie, you'll have to go into films. Your eyes are wasted on the stage.'

I didn't want to go into films. Sullen cameras were no substitute for a real audience, and I disliked the permanence of it all. Far better the ephemerality of the stage, where there was always the possibility of the performance growing, getting better and better and better.

I also didn't want to go down to dinner. There was something wrong here, and I couldn't pin it down. It certainly wasn't Mrs Farleton. Already I adored her. The warmth of the greeting between mother and son had been for real and had extended to us all. There was no doubt that she was delighted to have us here. Nor was there anything formal or fearsome in her manner. She had the genuine charm of a woman who looks outside herself for interest. She was wholly unpretentious. Probably she would realise her son's thoughtlessness in failing to tell us about the grandeur of Farleton Hall. Very likely she would dress down to make us feel more at home, and would succeed.

No, there were other, smaller things that made me feel something was going on beneath the surface. That extraordinary little exchange between mother and son in the drawing-room was only part of it. David had been absent during the tour of the house. Nothing strange about that, I suppose, except that he'd made a sarcastic remark about the estate manager's 'conspicuous absence' before striding off to find him. It wasn't like David to be so uptight about one member of staff failing to show for the returned-heir ritual. He simply wasn't that vain. Clearly there was enmity between them, and yet the estate seemed to be well-managed.

In all of this I felt like – and was – an outsider. Brendan's presence was straightforward: he was being consulted about the piece of woodland, and Belle was simply accompanying him. My own presence was more anomalous. Did Mrs Farleton suspect the strange closeness that had grown between her son and myself in the last few weeks? If so, she gave no sign. She treated me with the same simple friendliness as Brendan and Belle. I felt uneasily like an imposter, playing the role of casual friend when I knew I was much more than that.

Well then, better the role of the Hon. Ros. After a final glance in the gilt mirror, I swept out of the room to obey the gong.

4

It was very late when I discovered I'd left my handbag downstairs. Heaven knows why I was so keen to retrieve it – it held nothing of significance. I suppose it's some primitive instinct women have, never to be parted from their handbags. I wondered wryly, as I slipped on my dressing-gown, if cave women had had some equivalent of a handbag.

I felt no shyness at all as I padded along the corridor, around the gallery and down the splendid staircase. Mrs Farleton had said we must make ourselves entirely at home, everywhere except behind the green baize door where the staff lived their own lives and were embarrassed by any intrusion. Nor did I try to tread lightly as I approached the drawing-room where I knew my handbag lurked. My hand was reaching out for the door knob when I heard the voices.

'I'm sure he's up to something, Mother.'

'But did you *find* anything? Was there anything in the estate records?'

'Nothing. That's what's so odd. They appear to be in perfect order, almost too perfect. I didn't find him either – I'm sure he's avoiding me. He might have some notion of why Brendan's here.'

I could hear the smile in Mrs Farleton's voice. 'Then he must be a mind-reader. I don't. What does a piece of woodland matter to Simon Lowther?'

'It's not just the woodland. I want Brendan to have a good look at the whole estate.'

'Mr Lowther won't like that. Meddling. He might take it from you but not from a stranger, let alone a Cambridge academic.'

'I know. It helps that Belle and Ros are here. It makes it look like an ordinary houseparty.'

I felt myself stiffen and a surge of blood rush to my face. Was that why I was here? Just a front to cover up whatever was going on? For the first time I almost disliked David. I also stopped feeling guilty about eavesdropping. If he was being disingenuous with me, why shouldn't I listen to find out more?

But the talk swiftly moved away from me. 'Brendan's one of the best brains I've ever met,' David was saying. 'You'd never guess it from that jolly Irish manner, but he is. If something's going on, he'll find it. I can't sack Lowther on a suspicion. I need some pretty serious evidence.'

'Sack!' There was a long pause before Mrs Farleton continued. 'Nobody is ever sacked at Farleton Hall. It just isn't done. Even your father knew that much.' I thought I heard the smile return to her voice as she went on, 'Do you remember what a ghastly cook Melinda was? And look at her now. All I did was send her on a *cordon bleu* course. She only needed to learn. If I'd sacked her, I might never have found a cook as good as the one she's become. That's how we've always done things here.'

'Lowther would never go on a course. If he did, he wouldn't learn a thing. He's set in his ways, and his ways are my father's. Between them they've ruined the estate.'

'I don't know how you can say that, David. You can't blame Simon Lowther for your father's debts.'

'Not that, perhaps, but other things. Like advising you to sell those farms.'

'Ah . . .' A long sigh. 'David, I *am* sorry, but it –'

'It wasn't your fault.'

'That's not what I was going to say. It *was* my fault. I should have known the tenants were cousins of his. And I should have known that whatever one does, one never sells land. Anything but land.'

'He should have known, too, and did. I think if Brendan does a little digging he'll find the whole estate's been run for the Lowther clan for years.'

Mrs Farleton sighed. 'Well, if you do find out, at least use some tact when you talk to Mr Lowther. It's not your strong point.'

'I'm not going to talk. I'm going to sack him.'

'David, he may be a little old-fashioned, and he may be keeping an eye out for his family's interests, but it's not easy to find good estate managers these days. You've only just left Cambridge. You can't possibly take over the whole estate overnight.'

'I know that, Mother. That's why I brought Brendan.'

There was a long silence. In it I heard the tick of the clock in the hall and the sound of someone – presumably David – pacing inside the room. Then he spoke again.

'I didn't want to tell you until I'd talked to Brendan, but perhaps you'd better know. It's not just the woodland or his advice on the estate. I'm hoping . . . I'm hoping that if he likes what he sees, likes it enough . . . I'm hoping he might become the new manager.'

I caught my breath. Clearly Brendan had no more idea of what was being planned for him than I did of my own position here. Again I felt a twinge of dislike. David really was an autocrat. Imperious and scheming.

'David, why on earth should a Cambridge don throw away his life on an insignificant little estate in Yorkshire?'

'He's not really a don. He's been passed over for promotion several times and yet he's the best of the lot. I think he's getting impatient. He might be ready for a change.'

'I'm sorry to sound anti-intellectual, David – we had enough of that from your father – but academic theory is one thing, running an estate is another. Even if he agreed to come, he has no more experience than you do.'

'That's one thing I did learn at Cambridge. Academics aren't as ivory-towered as people like to think. Least of all Brendan. I've known him three years, Mother. He could do the job, I haven't the slightest doubt of that. The only question is whether he'll want to.'

'And Rosalind?'

I stepped away from the door as if I'd been scalded.

Absurdly, I looked round to see where I might conceal myself if either of them should suddenly open the door. Not much hope in a hall as bare as this.

'And how long have you known *her*?' Mrs Farleton continued.

The clock ticked madly, hiding any footsteps that might be approaching the door.

'Three weeks.'

'And what part is she to play in your scheme of things?'

A long, long pause. I closed my eyes, dizzy with the abruptness with which I'd taken centre stage in the little family drama I shouldn't be hearing. David said nothing and Mrs Farleton continued: 'She seems a nice enough girl, David, but I think you should realise that a place like this can have quite an effect on someone so young.'

And now he did speak. 'Ros isn't like that,' he said softly.

'And you know what she's like? After three weeks?'

Another long pause.

'David, I don't want to interfere. But you must also realise that someone in your position doesn't have a private life, not like other people do. You do understand that?'

'I don't want to discuss Ros.'

Mrs Farleton sighed. 'Ah, David, I really have made a mess of my life. I married the wrong man for the wrong reasons and got what I deserved. Then I neglected my sons, who made me think too much about my marriage, and dashed off to play amateur archaeologist instead of trying to become close to you – it's true. I know you love me in your way, but there's always some barrier. I can go only so far and then the door's shut on me. Then –'

'Mother, that's not –'

'And then I commit the worst folly imaginable and sell off your land to pay your father's debts. And now I start interfering in your love life –'

'Mother –'

'It's true. *Mea culpa*. Well, I won't interfere any more. I won't even try to persuade you not to sack Mr Lowther.

Farleton Estate is yours. You must do as you see fit.'
I heard the rustle of silk and fled up the stairs.

The next morning the sun swept the clouds clean out of the air and installed itself in a pure blue sky. The effect on Farleton Hall was startling. No longer a silver palace floating on a grey-green sea, it had turned itself into a honey-gold concoction outlined firmly against the bright green land and azure sky. It looked strong, lusty and sure of itself.

Shortly after breakfast we left for the uplands. Mrs Farleton declined to come with us; she was meeting a builder about repairs to the church tower in Kirkby Langham. I hadn't realised that Farleton Hall was the centre of the whole of Langhamdale and the market town which served it. It seemed a strange and wonderful thing, to a person as rootless as myself: generations of Farletons quietly overseeing this large and diverse community. I almost wished I could go with her instead of trekking up to the derelict woodland Brendan was to inspect.

We went in the Land-Rover. It felt awfully upright and stern after the luxury of the Saab. I was relegated to the back with Belle – David wanted to point things out to Brendan as we went along. I wondered if that was symbolic. I had fulfilled my function: a smokescreen to hide David's scheming. Now I could take a back seat, literally.

A few miles beyond Farleton Hall, the flat vale ended abruptly in a steep wooded slope. From there the road snaked up through the trees in a series of hairpin bends until it reached the top of what seemed like a second plain, this one perched high above the dale.

'Keldreth,' David explained. 'This is the upland part of the estate. What's left of it. My father sold off the two farms to the west to pay his father's death duties. Then my mother sold off the ones to the east to pay off part of his. All we've got is the woodland in the middle.'

Brendan was staring at David. 'It's not entailed?'

'No. There's no title, remember? We're just plain old country squires.'

'Even so . . .'

'Yes,' said David abruptly. 'My father was an ass. Irresponsible. He only cared for show. Rather than touch a single one of his trinkets in the Hall, he sold the land.'

'Irresponsible asses are common enough,' said Brendan. 'But your mother . . .'

'Not an ass, but under the influence of our estate manager. You begin to get the picture?'

'Well enough, Davey lad, well enough,' said Brendan softly.

From the lip of the plain called Keldreth, the land dipped very gradually into a gentle fold which ran from east to west. The road went down to it through a dense green tangle of trees which hung over the road and turned it into a claustrophobic tunnel. Through the open windows came the dank scent of rotting wood. The road seemed to be rotting, too, a potholed track overgrown with weeds and threatened at both sides by encroaching brambles. Derelict. Everything about Keldreth was squalid and derelict, a sad contrast to the beauty of the floating palace below.

Then, abruptly, a crossroads. A signpost which some car had obviously run into teetered at an angle and announced, on weatherbeaten boards and in paint scarcely visible, that to the left were Cappelrigg and Graegarth, to the right some other properties with equally odd names. Straight ahead was a pair of rusted gates, a mockery of the ones at Farleton Hall. These hung sadly on their broken hinges. The once-elegant pattern of stags' antlers was broken, and if there had ever been stags' heads on the gateposts, they'd long since disappeared. There was only a rotting wooden sign:

FARLETON LODGE
PRIVATE

David and Brendan got out to open the gates and have a look at some of the trees nearest the road. Brendan was shaking his head when they got back into the Land-Rover.

They didn't even bother to close the gates again after we'd driven through. The road, distinctly uninviting to trespassers and thieves, was security enough. It all but disappeared after the gates, becoming nothing but two rutted tracks almost obliterated by weeds. Broken branches and brambles brushed the sides of the Land-Rover.

I felt under attack, pulling my own sides in against the intruding tangle, and was relieved when, suddenly, a huge clearing appeared to one side, finally letting in some light. Then I saw that it was as derelict as the woodland. It had obviously been felled and never replanted. The space had been colonised instead by sickly scrub, dock, nettles, thistles, and yet more of the ubiquitous brambles which made me think of triffids.

'Whisht,' said Brendan softly. 'You'll be telling me now that this is the *good* bit?'

'More or less,' said David.

'I begin to see the truth of the epithet you place on your sire, Davey, lad.'

David stopped the Land-Rover. He looked at Brendan. 'So that's it. Any hope?'

'There's always hope, boy. Given a few minor aids. Like several decades and a heap of money big enough to bury Midas.'

'What would you do?'

Brendan gazed long and hard at the desolation before replying. 'To be sure, the easiest is to clear-fell the lot and start from scratch – draining, roads, culverts, finally the planting. But . . .'

'But?'

'But something in my guts screams out against it. There must be a *few* good stems hidden among this trash. You'd need a detailed survey by an expert, and that's more cash just for the privilege of being told you've got a mess. Then, if there *is* some gold among the dross, years of selective clearance and endless underplanting as you go along. A real heartbreaker, Davey. I could strangle your father.'

A weak smile from David. 'The gout got him first.'

'How could he *do* this to an innocent piece of land?' Brendan moaned.

'Pheasants,' said David. 'They like the mess. Nothing else does.'

'All for the fun of killing a few dumb birds. The times we live in, Davey. It's enough to make a body despair of the human race.'

'You're human, Brendan.'

'The peerless wife might dispute it,' said Brendan.

Belle roared with laughter. It was the first time the men had taken notice of us during the whole drive. It broke the spell enough for David to start up the Land-Rover again. Despite myself, I was beginning to be interested in the arcane discussion. I looked at the woodland more closely as we bumped along the track. If I squinted and used a huge amount of imagination, I could almost see how it might have looked once. It must have been rather lovely, a cool green haven rather than the threatening jungle it now was.

I was so preoccupied with turning the clock back that I barely noticed when the Land-Rover stopped again.

'All out,' said David.

We got out of the Land-Rover. And stared.

We were on what was once a graceful apron of gravel in front of the most absurdly delightful building I'd ever seen. 'What on earth?'

David came round and stood beside me. He put his hand on my shoulder. I shivered with pleasure at the rare contact. The long cold drive through the sunless jungle, the hurtful exclusion from his company – all of it vanished under the warmth of his hand and the warmth of the sun which beamed down into the clearing. The house smiled, too, I swear it did.

'Farleton Lodge,' said David. 'My great-great-or-whatever grandfather built it in the early nineteenth century. He started to build a folly, then decided it would be more fun to build one to live in. From then on it just grew and grew. I don't think it had an architect – no architect would design such a lunatic thing.'

It was built in the same material as Farleton Hall but there the resemblance ended. This stone hadn't had its surfaces smoothed, would never be able to gleam silvery. It was knobbly rough natural stone right up to the absurd crenellated roof and foolish little turrets and towers that seemed to sprout at random. The windows were random, too, plonked all over its surface in unexpected places and forms. There were tall lancet windows, oriels, medieval casements, elegant Georgian sashes. The whole history of windows was cheekily displayed on the face of this ridiculous building.

A sound of rushing water could be heard as we walked round the side and through one of the huge archways which connected two extensions to the rear of the house. A crumbling stone wall at the back completed a cobbled courtyard. From the back the house was even weirder. The compendium of windows continued and finally exhausted itself in a big stained glass extravaganza which was totally out of place – assuming anything was in place in such a strange building. The two extensions were equally whimsical, one of them looking like a Greek temple and the other a clutter of medieval outbuildings all stuck onto each other in a merry hodgepodge.

I went to the dry-stone wall and peered over. Beyond was an overgrown garden with a little pool at the centre. Behind it was the most spectacular backdrop imaginable: a high cliff looming straight up with a waterfall tumbling over the edge and making its way into a stream that fed the pool. The cliff face itself was almost another garden, studded with wildflowers whose seeds had just drifted into all the little crannies and decided to stay.

'God, the potential!' said Belle. I'd been so enchanted that I hadn't heard her approach. 'Wouldn't I just love to get my hands on that garden!'

I nodded. 'The whole place. It seems awful to neglect it.'

David called across the courtyard. 'Coming in?'

We joined the men and together entered a rather gloomy room at the back which David said used to be the gun room. David knocked on an inner door. A middle-aged woman opened it and beamed at him, beamed at us all. The housekeeper. I'd noticed already how much the staff liked 'Master David', all except the mysterious Simon Lowther who was avoiding him.

We had barely entered the kitchen when Belle cried, 'What a marvellous room!'

A huge whitewashed room flooded with light from equally huge windows at the back, it was ringed with an assortment of sideboards, dressers and shelves crammed with preserves. In the big inglenook an Aga chugged away in front of a cheerful rag rug. Beside it were two ancient but obviously comfortable chairs. In the middle was a magnificent oak table and some chairs. A room to be lived in, and very likely the housekeeper did.

David introduced us to Mrs Jowett. Clearly she was expecting us – a big cast iron kettle was steaming on the Aga, there was crockery on the table and a plate of home-made biscuits. Mrs Jowett fussed about, making the tea, urging us all to sit down. As we did, a man entered.

'Master David! It's good to see you back!'

Mrs Jowett served the tea – it must have been the only place left in England which hadn't heard of coffee for elevenses. David scowled at the four teacups and saucers. 'Mrs Jowett . . .'

Sheepishly, Mrs Jowett fetched down two more cups and saucers. Cautiously, she and her husband sat down at the table with us.

'Now, tell me how those brats of yours are doing,' said David.

The whole scene was surreal. I couldn't match this easy-going David who sat at a kitchen table, chatting to the caretakers, with the squire who had presided over the sumptuous dining-room of Farleton Hall last night. Were they really the same person? I looked closer, studied his expression and the subtle movement of muscles on that big, handsome face. The muscles were relaxed, his smile had more warmth and spontaneity.

The youngest 'brat', John Jowett, had just finished

school and started working on his bachelor uncle's farm, Cappelrigg. The older, Denise, was doing a catering course in Scarborough. From there the conversation moved on to the parents and I deduced that the Jowetts lived rent free at the lodge and were paid just to keep it from collapsing entirely. It was, apparently, Grade One Listed, which didn't surprise me in the least, though Farleton Hall was by far the more beautiful building. Clearly the lodge was too much for one middle-aged couple to manage. I wondered why Mrs Farleton hadn't sold off the lodge instead of the farms, sold it to someone who had the time and money to look after it.

After the tea, Mrs Jowett showed us the whole house. The oddly placed windows were explained: 'Mad William' – David's early Victorian ancestor – had been miffed because he couldn't plant a maze (something to do with the wind) and instead turned the house into an indoor maze. There was no ground floor, first floor and so forth. Instead, random bits of stairs led to rooms at all levels, capricious bits of corridor led to unexpected places. I was lost before we even started.

Lost but enchanted. Mad William had designed each room thematically, and although most of the furniture was under dust sheets, the exotic nature of the rooms (Moorish, Renaissance, Russian, Chinese) showed through. As room after crazy room displayed its dimmed delights, I thought that if I owned Farleton Estate, I would sell the lodge to someone who would restore it. I would use the money gained by the sale on Farleton Hall, remove the dust sheets there, open it up to throngs of friends and relatives, let it live again.

David was staring at me.

I could feel the blush which I'd spent years learning to control creep up into my cheeks. I hoped he couldn't read my mind. If I owned Farleton Estate, indeed! Why would David Farleton marry a penniless would-be actress? I admit that the thought of marriage had flitted through my mind during those hectic weeks in Cambridge, but that was before I knew about the estate.

And then, a sense of mourning for what could have been. And suddenly I resented his wealth. If only he'd been an ordinary person, even a *small* landowner, we might have had a chance. I had misread more signs than those which should have told me he was a wealthy squire; I had also misread the feelings I imagined he had for me. I was indeed a temporary smokescreen, part of a party of people brought here to mask David's business activities. How could I have been so stupid, so naive?

I had no place here, that was the truth of it. And I never would. I thought back to that exhilarating first night of *As You Like It* – the euphoria, our success, the wild applause, the crazy party, that wonderful review. I wished myself back to that night, this time obliterating David. If only I hadn't met him. How wonderful it must be not to know he existed. My future had been neatly planned until that night, and I had looked forward to it with gusto. It was still there, of course, but now I would return to it with a huge gaping chunk ripped out of my soul.

We were in the Scheherazade Room. It was a beautiful room and I hated it. I stood by the window, looking down into the courtyard where nothing was happening. Behind me I heard the others beginning to leave, ready to go on to the next room. Let them. I didn't want to see the damn house. I was rooted to the floor, paralysed by grief and anger.

'Ros?'

David came and stood beside me. I wished he would go away.

'Ros, is anything wrong?'

Full marks for perception! But don't think I'm going to let you into my mind ever again. I turned round and flashed him a sparkling smile. I let the hard green brilliance of my eyes play over him and dazzle him.

'What on earth could be wrong?' I smiled. I listened to the innocent waterfall of my laughter wash over him. Then I took his arm, raised a mischievous eyebrow, and together we left the room.

5

We had lunch at the lodge. This time Mr and Mrs Jowett seemed more reconciled to sitting at table with their employer. The meal was lovely: home-made rabbit pie (part of Raymond Jowett's job was to keep the rabbit population down so that whatever seedling trees managed to squeeze through the undergrowth wouldn't be eaten off).

The conversation was good, too. The informality of the lodge enhanced the holiday spirit felt by everyone except me, but even I managed to contribute to the table talk. It wasn't too difficult. Well, what was my training in acting for if not for occasions like this? All I had to do was avoid looking at David. My life was threatening to become as overgrown as this land; I needed to clear a straight path through it again, get back to the night before David entered my life. When people fell into holes, they climbed out of them again, assuming they hadn't broken a leg. So if I had stupidly fallen in love, the obvious solution was to climb out of it again. I hadn't broken a leg, only a heart.

After lunch, the Jowetts returned to their work and the rest of us went for a walk through the forest. Though equipped with wellies, we had no protection above calf level against the hateful brambles. Over and over again we had to turn back, try somewhere else. If it wasn't the brambles it was tree trunks – some inexplicably felled and left to rot, others snapped off by the wind. Covered with ugly fungi and oozing the pervasive smell of rot which drowned out the normal woodland scents, they repeatedly blocked our path. But even the jungle was preferable to the desolate areas which had been felled and forgotten, leaving the tatty scrub and weeds to take over. The ground squelched beneath our feet.

'Holy Mother of God,' said Brendan. 'Jesu Christus.' 'Our Father in heaven.' Calling in the entire Holy Family as witnesses to the destruction of Farleton Forest.

Why on earth hadn't Mrs Farleton sold this mess instead of the farms? Probably because no one would buy it.

I didn't care. I was letting go, and it felt good. As long as I didn't look at David.

By the time we got back to the Land-Rover, we were hot, sweaty, tired and criss-crossed with a network of thin red lines where the brambles had had their way. Belle and I were silent, she looking mournfully at her shredded skirt, I brooding on the success so far of my campaign to fall out of love with David.

We had just got out of the Land-Rover at Farleton Hall when the door opened and David's mother came down. I expected amusement at the sight of her raggle-taggle guests, but her face was set and anxious. We were all in a clump, so it was impossible not to overhear her words to David: 'Mr Lowther is back. He wants to see you.'

Dinner was late. Brendan and Belle had no idea why, but I did. David and the invisible Mr Lowther were closeted in the estate office for the rest of the afternoon and well into the evening. That could mean only one thing: that the confrontation which David had threatened was now taking place, earlier than expected and without the preparation he had hoped to bring to it.

Mrs Farleton knew, too, but she didn't know that I knew. Once again I felt the falseness of my position. The intruder who knew too much.

Mrs Farleton was the perfect hostess, filling in the hours so gracefully that Brendan and Belle probably suspected nothing. Once we'd washed and changed into decent clothes, she gave us a tour of the gardens. The roses were coming into bloom and flooded the walled garden with their scent. There was mock orange, too, and a few lilacs that had delayed their flowering to compete with the others. The kitchen garden was also a treat: cordoned fruit ripening on sunny walls, rows of lusty young vegetables gleaming green in the evening light.

But already I was noticing the signs. Some of the roses were a little too lank, there were more weeds than there should have been. Bits of garden wall had crumbled. A gutter sagged at the back of the house. How long before Farleton Hall went the way of the lodge? More than ever I thought David should sell the lodge, pay more attention to his own house. Well, it was none of my business. His prolonged absence was giving me the respite I needed to harden myself against him.

So I was unprepared when, just as we were finally sitting down to dinner without him ('Melinda will keep his dinner warm.') he lurched into the room and my heart lurched with him.

I hardly recognised him. He was still wearing his mud-smeared and bramble-torn clothes, and his hair was a wild black tangle framing a pair of black eyes that spat anger. He looked like a lunatic freshly escaped. We gasped aloud, all of us, just like in a bad film.

Mrs Farleton recovered first. In a voice as smooth as her blue silk dress, she said, 'I'm sure dinner can wait while you change.'

David ignored her. He thumped himself down in his chair and called for his soup. Melinda looked decidedly nervous but David took no notice. He didn't notice any of us. He spooned the scalding liquid into his mouth as if oblivious of it and everything else. It was the most appalling display of bad manners. I felt sorry for Mrs Farleton. She didn't even try to cover up for him. Silently she sipped her soup. Silently we all sipped our soup while the tension rose. It crackled in the air above us. How long before it broke?

David's spoon clattered to rest in the empty bowl. He looked up for the first time. He looked at each of us in turn, a hard, frightening look, leaving his mother until last. Then he smiled. It was a hard smile. Once again I pictured a lunatic climbing over the asylum walls and come to terrorise the neighbourhood. Finally, still smiling, still staring at his mother, he spoke: 'I sacked the bastard.'

A sharp intake of breath from Mrs Farleton. 'David, I don't think this is the time or place –'

His fist crashed down on the table. 'This *is* the time and the place!' His head jerked round and the full strength of that eerie smile was fixed on Brendan. 'Brendan. Will you take over the estate?'

Brendan shot back in his chair like a passenger caught out by take-off in a creaky old aeroplane. The chair screeched in protest. Brendan's jaw gaped open, but for once the gift of the gab deserted him.

David spoke again. 'I'm asking you to become my estate manager.' His voice was just a fraction softer. It should have melted the tableau around the table, but didn't. Four seated statues stared at the intruder, waiting for his keeper to come and take him away. I couldn't believe this was happening, not at Farleton Hall.

Then something extraordinary. David's head suddenly sank into his hands. His hands covered his face. I couldn't see his expression but his arms were shaking.

Freed from his awful gaze, the rest of us finally started to thaw. Brendan looked furtively at Belle, Belle looked at Mrs Farleton, Mrs Farleton looked at me. I looked at the crumpled giant in his chair and, to my dismay, had a desperate desire to rush over and fling my arms around him. It was absurd, but I wanted so much to comfort him, hold that big unruly head against my breast and whisper soothing words. The succession of Davids reeling before my astonished gaze that day had bewildered me. I had no rational thought left.

Finally he lifted his head from his hands. The face was ten years older, but gentle. He looked at his friend and tutor again. 'Brendan, I'm sorry. I didn't mean to . . . I'm sorry.'

A weak smile from Brendan. 'Don't be talking like that, Davey. You've had a hell of a day, seeing the peerless mess of that woodland. It'd take a saint not to break down with the woe of it all. If it'll make you feel easy, I'll accept your apology, but there's no need to offer it. What are friends for?'

David bowed his head. Then he smiled, and for the first time that evening it had some warmth in it. 'I should have taken it slower. Trust me to be such a bloody oaf.' Then he sighed. 'And Mother's right. Why should you give up a decent job at Cambridge to bury yourself in this dump? I had to ask you, Brendan. Even if I put it so badly. But there'll be no hard feelings on my side if you turn it down. I –'

'Turn it down? But I thought . . .' Brendan shook his head as if to clear the muddle inside. 'Davey, I didn't know you meant . . . I thought it just came out of the mouth before it paid a visit to the brain. You'll not be telling me you were *serious*?'

'I haven't been fair to you. I should have told you what I was thinking months ago. The fantasies. That some day you would come up to Farleton Estate, take it over, help me turn it into something . . . something . . .' He trailed off, lost in his own vision.

'You *were* serious? You *are* serious? Davey, let me get this straight: *are* you asking me to become your estate manager? Because if you are, bedamn, I'm going to jump at the offer, the goodwife willing, and that's a fact.'

There was a long pause. When David spoke again it was barely a whisper, as if he didn't dare hope. 'You would do that, Brendan? Give up a secure job at Cambridge to come to this godforsaken place? Work yourself into the ground for a piece of land nobody gives a damn about except me?'

Brendan laughed and shook his head. 'No. I would give up a lousy job and for the first time ever have a chance to do something worthwhile with my life. Davey, I'm weary to the eyeballs with trying to drum a little sense into those deadheads down there. I might as well be talking to a tree trunk as try to change their ways. Sure, a few of them open their ears five minutes and take back an idea or two – a bit of cosmetic fiddling here, a token gesture there. But you're the first student I've ever had with both guts and brain. Davey, when I think of all those lonely acres up there just pining for a little TLC . . .' He turned to Belle. 'What about it? How does it strike your eardrums? Playing barmaid to a pair of crazy visionaries in the wilderness of Yorkshire?'

She put her hand on Brendan's and grinned. 'Where my man goes, I go.'

Brendan roared. 'What kind of talk is that from the terror of the Criterion? She that's bounced men out of the pub like ping-pong balls? Woman, I expect you to have a brain of your own and not traipse after me like a meek little spouse.'

'Another crack like that and I'll bounce you out of the dining-room. I come with you because I want to. God, never to see another of those smirking faces at the bar! But I'd better warn you, David: I don't know one end of a chainsaw from another.'

David smiled slyly at Brendan. 'My new manager will take care of everything.'

So there it was. In a few whirlwind minutes, all the twisted little lives in this domestic drama were straightened out and given the fairy-tale ending so appropriate to this floating palace in which we sat. David acquired the perfect estate manager. Brendan was given the work he'd always longed for. Belle would have a fresh start and the pleasure of seeing her adored husband happy at last. Even Mrs Farleton seemed pleased. She seemed to have resigned herself to David's authority. Very likely she was relieved no longer to have the responsibility, and it was clear that already she had a high opinion of Brendan and his chances of making a success of the estate.

Yes, everybody happy.

Oh, have I left someone out? Silly me.

Yes, silly me, sitting at table and then in the drawing-room while everyone else talked excitedly of the future. Silly me, trying to be happy for the happy people, fixing a magnanimous smile on my face while waves of other people's happiness washed over me. I didn't begrudge, God knows. I loved these people, delighted in their delight. I only wanted to share.

But there was no place for me in all this. The realisation which had first hit me that afternoon strengthened with every minute that ticked by during that tormented evening. If only I could have packed my bags and left, bestowing my useless blessing on everyone else. But something else had happened that evening. In that gut-churning moment when I'd longed to comfort David, I'd understood that all my work at freeing myself from his spell was wasted. I loved him. Had loved him from that first Cambridge dawn. And loved him even more after seeing the crack in his protective armour this evening. I couldn't leave him and I couldn't stay.

When finally the evening ended and we dispersed, I stood before the mirror in my room and stared at the wretched person reflected there. Who or what could I turn myself into to make David love me? I listed the possible roles, one by one tried them on.

But something was wrong. The person in the mirror didn't budge. Each role I suggested slipped off her like the waterfall behind the lodge slipped down the cliff face, scarcely touching its surface. Not even in the privacy of my room could I make her do my bidding.

It was the first time my ability to act had failed me, and that shook me almost as much as my love for David. What if by succumbing to David's magic I'd lost my own? If the one thing I relied on to salvage my life now failed me, the abyss that opened up was complete.

I don't know how long I stood there, frozen by shock, and I don't know either how I got to the bed. All I remember is suddenly being there, flung across it in an empty heap, sobbing hysterically.

It all came rushing back to taunt me: the childhood I'd never had, the sense of belonging which had always eluded me. I'd scarcely seen my parents when I was young. Their sole interest had been making and spending money. They'd lived abroad most of the time, returning to London for brief periods to buy a bigger investment flat. Once they'd installed me in it they were off again. Each of my successive 'homes' had been supplied with a new housekeeper resentful of her employers' daughter, the rootless child who had nowhere else to go during school holidays.

The rest of the time I'd been packed off to boarding school. School had been my real life, the only place in which I had a chance of belonging. The teachers had taken more interest in me than my parents had and I'd got on well with the other girls, too. I used to imagine myself into their lives and conjure up an image of the person they wanted me to be. Then I would turn myself into that person. They'd been for real, those performances; I'd genuinely wanted to *be* all these people.

That had been my first experience of acting. From there it had been an easy step to the school plays. No one was surprised when I announced my intention to become an actress.

No one except my parents, they who knew me least of all. My mother had by then gone off to Australia and married another businessman who wanted nothing to do with me. As for my father, he'd been the first real setback to my career. He'd been both derisive and outraged at the prospect of his daughter being an actress. A prestigious marriage, that's what he wanted out of me, that's what my face was for: a trap to ensnare the husband who would take me off his hands and give his own status a boost. I certainly wouldn't find him in the penniless ranks of young actors. He'd made it clear that he would withhold all financial support if I went to drama school, and because his income was so large I had no hope of getting the grant I would need. On the other hand, it would be ridiculous to approach the provincial reps with CV and photograph straight out of school. *What* CV? With what for an Equity card?

Slowly I had realised that university was the only answer – several of them offered degrees in drama. But my father said no to that, too. In the end, a sympathetic teacher had told me to try for Cambridge. If I worked like hell I might get in to read French and German. Then I could spend most of my time in the drama companies which so many of my predecessors had used to learn their craft and gain the coveted Equity card.

The only thing to mar my joy at being accepted had been my father's satisfaction. He didn't give a damn about academia, but the status – oh, the status! I'd listened coldly to the long-distance voice at the other end of the telephone line as he told me how right he'd been to talk me out of 'all that theatre nonsense'. He'd never taken the slightest interest in me before. Only now, when he could boast of 'my daughter at Cambridge' to his rich chums abroad, did he want to know me. How much more so if I did become famous? 'My daughter, the famous actress.' Once I was famous he would forget 'all that theatre nonsense'. The smug satisfaction would merely change direction. 'Aren't you glad I talked you out of drama school? All those wonderful connections you made at Cambridge that got you where you are. You wouldn't have had any of that without me.'

That was when I decided to change my name.

As if by magic, other things seemed to change, too. It had been a happy year – hard work but happy. At last I'd begun to have a sense of belonging. I hadn't expected to be loved – I had no experience of that – but at least my life was beginning to have some meaning.

No wonder, then, that David had entered my life with such unexpected force. And now he was about to leave it again. Those three weeks had been an illusion after all.

Someone knocked at the door. I hiccupped on a sob, horrified that it might be Mrs Farleton. Then the sobs broke through again.

A second knock. Even Belle, I couldn't face even her, not now.

The door opened. My eyes were awash, I couldn't see who was there. Nor could I control my crying, no matter how hard I tried. Something had irreparably broken at that moment when my real self stared back at me from the mirror. I had no defences left and no strength even to hide the fact.

'Ros?'

David's voice. If anything had the power to shock me back to my senses, it should have been David's voice. But the sobbing from the stranger who was me only increased.

'Ros, what's wrong?'

A swift movement, the sudden sag of the bed as he sat down and leaned over my hysterical form. 'Ros. Rosalind. Rosie.'

I heard the familiar incantation of my names with bitterness. I didn't want to be that person, anyone but her.

Then I felt his arms lifting me up, my body being folded gently against his chest. His big hand that I loved so much was stroking my hair, his deep bass voice was murmuring over and over, 'Rosie, Rosie, Rosie, tell me what's wrong, please tell me.'

If I'd had a scrap of rational thought left I would have laughed at the reversal: I, who had a few hours earlier wanted to comfort him, was now being comforted by him. I had reverted to that small child who had wanted, wanted, wanted, but never been wanted in return. That child had, in misty years almost forgotten, turned to the father who was the greatest rejector of all and had stupidly clung to him for comfort, stupidly whispered, 'I love you, Daddy, please don't leave me.' The time between then and now had vanished along with my defences, and I heard the same child whispering, 'I love you, David, please don't leave me, please, I love you so much.' The censor who should have silenced those words had gone, leaving me shameless. We'd both lost our defences that evening, David and I, both exposed great gaps in our armour. Now it was my turn and I felt no shame, only a desperate need to say the truth. I didn't give a thought to the consequences, didn't have a mind to think with, didn't care about anything except my own words which were the first truthful words I'd said for years.

'Rosie, Rosie.' His grip tightened, he was clinging to me as much as I was clinging to him. 'Rosie, I'll never leave you, it's you who'll leave me, and I won't be able to bear it, I know that now.'

For a long time we just held each other and whispered our foolish words, barely hearing each other, two parallel tracks failing to meet. Only gradually did the fog begin to clear and his words penetrate my mind. It was beginning to function again, but what it was telling me was so incredible that I couldn't believe it.

Something similar must have been happening to David, because finally he whispered, 'Do you hear what we're saying to each other, Rosie? Do you hear? Does it mean that it's possible after all? That we can stay together after all? Does it mean that? Tell me, Rosie, fast, don't leave me longing and hoping if there's nothing to hope for.'

I stared, not understanding. It didn't make sense, and yet there was no doubting his sincerity. 'David . . .'

'Rosie, will you stay with me? Would you really give up everything and stay with me? Could you really bear to do that? I'd do anything to make you happy if you married me, Rosie, anything.'

I still didn't understand, not quite. I couldn't possibly be hearing these words. Some decent part of me which had also been exposed that evening wanted to help him, make possible his retreat from the rash words. 'But David, I . . . you . . .'

'You and I – we could be happy together, couldn't we? I know it's a terrible thing to ask of you, to give up your career and bury yourself in this godforsaken place. But I'd try to make up for it, Rosie, I really would.'

To give up . . . to bury yourself . . . The words echoed from a few hours before. David, speaking to Brendan, apologising for the fantastic offer he was making. I touched his face. 'David . . . what you just said . . . to Brendan, too.'

'What?'

'To Brendan, when you asked him to stay here. Don't you remember? "Would you really give up your future to come to this godforsaken place?" David, why do you do this to yourself? What are you apologising for? Do you really not understand? Do you really think you're so impossible to love?'

He wasn't interested in my questions. His mind was on a single track and that was me. 'Do you really love me, Rosie?'

'Of course I love you. Isn't that obvious? Hasn't it been obvious every minute of these three weeks?'

'And would you really marry me, Rosie?'

'David, how can you doubt it? Isn't that obvious, too?'

'Rosie!' The cry of joy burst from him. Then I was engulfed in his arms again.

6

If that evening was a whirlwind, the next few months were a cyclone, the events spinning by in such a jumble that it's difficult to reconstruct what happened. I'm not even sure of the order, but one of the first things must have been our announcement to David's mother.

She took it well. She embraced me with what felt like genuine warmth and said, 'I'm so glad!' I still felt shaken by the speed of things. If it was difficult to comprehend that David loved me, it was even more difficult to believe that Rhiannon (as she now insisted I call her) could welcome an insignificant actress into the family, but there was never the slightest sign of regret in her manner. Perhaps the sight of David's happiness overruled any misgivings. Perhaps she remembered her own half-hearted marriage, deficient in love from the start, and was truly glad that David's would be different.

Whatever the reason, the outsider who for two days had occupied such an ambiguous position was now wholeheartedly welcomed into the family.

I reeled under the joy of it all. Rhiannon was the mother I'd never had. I adored her. In the days that followed, she began to acquaint me with the running of the house, preparing me to become mistress of Farleton Hall. I listened attentively but had no desire to usurp her position. I was happy simply to be there, and to be loved.

To be loved. It was the most extraordinary sensation. I didn't realise until then just *how* starved I'd been of love. Now, suddenly, I was wrapped in wave after wave of this wonderful thing. I was a child unexpectedly plucked from the orphanage and set down in a fairy-tale kingdom whose inhabitants wanted nothing more than to give me everything I longed for. I felt almost ill with the excitement of it all, the starveling suddenly let loose at the feast table and eating myself silly. Surely my body was too small to contain so much happiness? Surely I would burst, or some hidden trickster would pop out of a cupboard and whisk it all away again? But the feasting went on, day after day, growing ever more sumptuous. As well as Rhiannon, there were Brendan and Belle. We would all be living and working together in the future, and their delight in their own good fortune shed an extra exuberance over mine.

And David? It's impossible to convey the bliss of those first few months. Though we maintained the decorum of two separate rooms for Rhiannon's sake, there was no question of David sleeping in his after that first amazing night. We could hardly bear to be apart even when he used it to change clothes or shave. We felt like twins who'd been separated at birth and had now found each other at last. All the old myths – hermaphrodites, two halves seeking each other and coming together in the perfect union – all of it was true; night after night we experienced it, marvelling at the wisdom of the old sages and storytellers who had told our own tale thousands of years before we were born.

As for the armour, the gaps which had been ripped out that night to allow us to find each other were no longer sufficient. We abandoned our armour altogether and came to each other naked at last. We loved wholeheartedly and with our whole bodies, and during the brief periods when our sated bodies were separate our minds fused together and we talked as one person.

It was uncanny how alike we were. We had each put on a disguise to cover two childhoods that had run parallel to each other for years. Only the disguises were different: mine an ambitious extrovert determined to make a career to compensate for the loveless child beneath; David's a quiet introvert, occasionally surly, occasionally erupting into helpless rage because he, too, had never been allowed to be himself as a child. Well, now he could, and so could I.

Oh, the relief of not having to act! I told him everything

and he loved my naked mind as much as my naked body. And I listened to him with the same absolute love. How could I not? What I was hearing was the same story as mine, differing only in detail. True, his mother at least loved him, but his father had been as scathing towards him as mine was towards me.

'He despised both his sons,' said David. 'I was a stupid, impractical dreamer and Hugh was a drip and neither of us was fit to take over the estate, he said. "If only I'd had a *real* son." The times he said that to us. He didn't even try to hide his disgust.'

'I hope he's writhing in hell,' I said furiously. 'How *could* he not love you? Probably he was jealous. He knew you were worth a thousand of him. He knew that as soon as you grew up and people started to know you, they'd adore you and despise him.'

'My sweet Rose,' he smiled. 'Are you sure he wasn't right? That I am a stupid, impractical dreamer?'

'You're a brilliant, forceful visionary.'

David laughed. 'Now I know what it feels like to be rescued by a knight – are there female knights? – in shining armour.'

'No more armour,' I said firmly. 'That's all in the past. The future begins right now.'

When it came to the wedding, however, David fulfilled his father's words, became the impractical dreamer.

'Can't we just get a licence and go to the Registry Office next week? There is one in Kirkby, isn't there? Must be.'

Rhiannon looked at him over the half-glasses she used for reading – we'd been working on the invitation list. The look was eloquent, but David refused to see it.

'Well?' he demanded. 'We don't want a lot of fuss, do we, Ros?'

Rhiannon sighed, took off her glasses and set them down on her writing table. Then she looked up at her hulking son glooming the doorway of the morning room. 'David. The tenants. The estate workers. The good folk of Kirkby. How would they feel if the heir to the estate just scuttled off to a Registry Office like some fly-by-night? We're woven into the fabric of this community, David. Cut one thread and the whole falls apart. Your fiancée has more sense than you; she understands these things, don't you, Ros?'

I nodded.

David glared.

Rhiannon continued. 'Further, I do think you should take some interest in your own wedding. If you don't, you'll complain that we've conspired behind your back. Isn't that right, Ros?'

I nodded.

David glared.

Rhiannon continued. 'Is it such an onerous thing, providing a happy day for the community? Do you begrudge other people a share in your own happiness? Ros doesn't, do you, Ros?'

I shook my head.

David glared.

Rhiannon sighed. 'Well, if you're not going to help us, go away. You irritate me, hovering in the doorway like that. Go. Shoo.' She flicked a hand towards her son.

He left.

After this, I felt worse than ever about the thing I'd been bracing myself to tell Rhiannon. I'd been trying to find openings for several days but without success. I would have to do it now, and with no graceful way in. I looked down at my hands.

'Rhiannon, you've been so good to me, I feel awful about what I have to say. But I do have to say it. I hope you'll listen and try to understand.'

My parents, of course. And so I told her the story of my childhood, the same story I'd told David. I was honest in the telling, not disguising my bitterness at all. The only thing I left out, as I had with David, was the one factor that infuriated me most: my father's triumph. He'd made it quite clear that he hoped I'd meet and marry one of those fabled rich young Cambridge men, notch up another success for Daddy. I'd had no intention of doing such a thing, and now I'd done it. I pictured him at the wedding, the fat little toad waddling about with his champagne glass, his red face gleaming with sweat and satisfaction, his smug smile as he ingratiated himself with the gentry to whom he would now be connected by marriage. 'Didn't I tell you?' he would smirk at me between hiccups. 'Wasn't I right?' I felt sick at the thought. No way. No way could I stand either of my parents being there on that of all days. They wouldn't have the faintest appreciation of what David was really like. All they would see was the august family going back to the Normans, the thousands of acres of land, the fine house, the wealth and influence. I liked these things, too, I don't deny it, but to me they were just a bonus, a backdrop which paled to insignificance compared with the beloved figure always in the foreground of my mind.

Rhiannon listened with quiet patience. When I finished, she said nothing. I waited, terrified that in one awful outburst I'd ruined my relationship with this wonderful woman. I couldn't bear the thought that this gift which had come so unexpectedly might be whisked away again. But still less could I bear the vision of my parents sullying that gift.

Finally she spoke. 'Is it really so important to you, that your parents be excluded?' Her voice was soft and surprisingly gentle.

I nodded miserably.

'Do you really hate them that much?'

I nodded again.

There was another long silence. Then she said, in a voice so quiet I almost didn't hear, 'I think I understand.'

I felt my heart leap involuntarily.

Rhiannon continued, almost in a whisper. 'David hated his father like that. I tried to be the peacemaker – between David and Hugh as well for that matter. All it did was make all three of them resent me. David and Hugh forgave me in the end – they realised that I meant well. But their father never did.'

She stopped speaking and looked out of the window for

a long time. I didn't know if she was remembering those days or trying to think how to persuade me to change my mind. Then she got up and began to pace the room.

'Parents have to earn their children's love,' she said slowly. 'Earn their respect. My husband and I failed, too. I can hardly chide you for not feeling anything towards your family.' She stopped by the window. 'Strange, how alike you and David are in that way.' She opened the window further. The scent of Albertine roses came into the room, their apple-green sweetness a contrast to the sour confessions within. 'My marriage was a sham,' she said. 'My own wedding day was an empty show. My fault. *I* at least was old enough to know better.'

She turned suddenly and faced me. 'I don't want yours and David's to be the same.' Then, incredibly, she smiled. 'Thank you, Ros. You've given me a chance to make amends. Don't look so worried, my dear. We'll find something to tell the guests – not quite the truth but not quite a lie. It'll be all right. You'll see.'

I could have wept with gratitude. I could have flung my arms round my compassionate mother-in-law to be. Then, remembering that I was no longer the repressed child who had to hide my feelings beneath a role, I did both.

Brendan and Belle left. They had to give notice on their jobs, wind up their affairs, organise the moving of their possessions to Yorkshire.

While they were gone, Rhiannon and I re-organised the house. We had decided to divide it up, unofficially, into three separate units: David and I in one set of rooms, Belle and Brendan in another, Rhiannon in the ones she'd occupied since the old squire's death. However much I loved Rhiannon, David and I had to have a life of our own, and Belle and Brendan would feel the same. So would Rhiannon.

David took no part in these preparations either. 'Ros, I'm not a male chauvinist pig, truly I'm not, but . . .'

'But this is women's work, right? Okay, Tarzan, get back to your jungle. Let the chimps do all the work.'

He looked worried, always slow to see when I was teasing. 'You do understand, don't you, Ros? I just can't get interested in houses.'

'I had noticed. I'm surprised you don't sleep up a tree.'

'Don't mock. I can't help it. It's the land that matters to me, always has. I don't care where I live, as long as you're there.'

'I'm here, Jungle Boy.' I kissed him. 'Go back to your forest.'

It wasn't just the forest, though. He was getting to know all of his land, the lowland farms included. Every day he went off to see some farmer or other and inspect the drainage and fences and things like that. I was proud of him, even if I couldn't share his excitement about the land. He was taking his duties seriously, hoping to repair the damage done by his father and the dubious Mr Lowther. We were all of us filled with hope. It was the beginning of a new era and we were the ones who were going to bring it about. I felt strangely moved when he pulled on his muddy wellies and got into the Land-Rover to go and deal with some arcane estate matter. It was going to be a beautiful estate, a model estate, mile after mile of lovely farmland and forest, happy tenants, smug sheep and cows, and at its centre, the dreamy silver palace of Farleton Hall, waking up from its long slumber like a sleeping beauty, soon to be filled with life and gaiety again, the doors flung open, the lovely rooms thronged with happy people. Sometimes I thought it was me who was dreaming. Could this really be happening? Was it possible to be so happy?

'Sometimes,' I whispered to David in bed one night, 'I think I'm going to wake up and it'll all be gone and you'll be gone and I'll be back in Cambridge or London and I won't be able to bear it.'

'My foolish Rose.' He took a rose from the vase on the bedside table and tucked it into my hair.

'It'll wilt,' I said.

'There are more. There'll always be roses for my Rosie.'

I smiled, thinking of the white roses he'd sent me at the ADC. In the time measured by mortals, so recent. I remembered the scene between Rosalind and Orlando about the different speeds of Time. Orlando saying, 'I prithee, who doth he trot withal?' and Rosalind answering, 'Marry, he trots hard with a young maid between the contract of her marriage and the day it is solemnized: if the interim be but a se'nnight, Time's pace is so hard that it seems the length of seven year.'

David's voice, whispering in my ear, tickling. 'What are you thinking about?'

'I wish we were getting married tomorrow.'

'Why not tonight?' He pulled me closer and turned out the light.

I stood before the portraits of Rhiannon and her husband. All around me people scurried, readying the Long Gallery for the concert, but I was hypnotised by the portraits. Or rather, Rhiannon's. The old squire I hardly noticed – he bore no resemblance to his son. Rhiannon, by contrast, was clearly her son's mother, both stamped with the wild dark beauty of the Welsh. In Rhiannon it was tempered by the curious mix of dignity and impishness which made the portrait so compelling.

David's arm landed on my shoulders. He who had been so reticent in Cambridge was now so openly affectionate that I marvelled at the transformation. All these years he'd been waiting for someone to unlock him and set him free. And I, most fortunate of women, had happened to be that person.

'Beautiful, wasn't she?' said David, nodding towards the portrait.

'Still is.'

'True. She's aged wonderfully.' He scrutinised my face with the mock-serious look of a painter by his canvas. 'So will you.'

'Are you really thinking that far into the future?' I teased.

'Of course.'

'When shall we have ourselves done?'

'Done?'

'Immortalised in paint – isn't that the phrase? Should we add a pair of youthful, impetuous portraits to the rogues' gallery, or should we wait until we've mellowed to show off our tremendous dignity? What says my squire?'

He scowled. 'You don't seriously want us to go in for all that empty pomp?'

I laughed. 'Hath not old custom made this life more sweet than that of painted pomp?' I couldn't resist. Lines from *As You Like It* often came to mind these days. It was hard not to see us as Orlando and Rosalind.

'Exactly,' he said.

'Don't be such a spoilsport,' I laughed. 'Of course we have to have them done; it's just a matter of when.'

Oblivious of the people moving about us, he took my face in his hands and looked at me so seriously that I felt apprehensive. 'Ros, I hope you don't mean it. I thought we were done with all the empty pomp. We're going to transform the estate – you and me and Brendan and Belle. There's no place in it for portraits, don't you see? That's exactly what we're trying to get away from – all the hollow show that disguises the rottenness beneath.'

'David,' I said tentatively, 'you're not seriously blaming a few old portraits for –'

'Not blaming, of course not. But look at those two.' He nodded towards the last portraits. 'The biggest of the lot. And my father was the biggest fraud of all the Farletons. I didn't want to tell you yet, but what I've been learning from the farmers isn't good. The estate's even worse than I thought. Brendan's in for a shock when he gets back. It's nothing but a pretty crust covering the mess beneath. The land, the trees, the buildings – even the Hall itself – it's all been quietly rotting beneath its surface for decades. Nero fiddled while Rome burned. My father had his portrait painted.'

'All the more reason to have ours done,' I smiled. 'We'll be the ones who put it right again, and ours will be the portraits our descendants will respect. You've made up my mind,' I laughed. 'We must have ourselves done while we're young and fresh, to show how energetic we were to do all that we're going to do!'

David shook his head. 'I don't think you understand. We're not doing these things for our descendants. We're finished with all that "heritage" nonsense. We're doing it for the land itself. Any future Farletons worth anything will realise that's exactly why we didn't have ourselves painted – that we threw off the old regime to begin the new.'

His words chilled me. They were the words of a fanatic. 'Visionary' I'd called him. There was a thin line between the visionary and the fanatic. All the more reason for David to be firmly grounded in his tradition, to prevent him from flying off into the frightening no-man's-land of . . . the word 'madness' sprang to mind. I pushed it away, but the memory returned of that evening when he'd burst into the dining-room like a freshly escaped lunatic. Of course he wasn't mad. But there were, I suddenly realised, areas of his mind I still didn't know.

I sighed. The stubborn set of his chin told me it was useless to argue today. There would be a better time and place. I must be patient and wait for it.

In any case, things were beginning to get hectic. Tonight Farleton Hall was being opened to the public for the first time since my arrival here. What Rhiannon had neglected to tell us during our tour of the house was that the Long Gallery with its wonderful acoustics was regularly used for concerts. It was Rhiannon who had initiated them, not long after her husband's death and in defiance of his memory. While he had staged feasts and balls for neighbouring squires, Rhiannon preferred the company of more interesting people. Talent rather than status. Quality rather than show. Now, people who'd never seen the inside of the house which dominated their landscape were allowed entry for the price of a ticket, the proceeds going to charity.

'In the beginning most of the people who came were just plain nosy,' Rhiannon had said. 'But once they satisfied their curiosity, they became more interested in the music. These are happy occasions, Ros. I do hope you'll enjoy this one. I'm sure you will.' She hesitated, then went on impetuously, 'Ros, forgive me if I'm being an interfering old mother-in-law, but I'm so anxious that the concerts continue, that you'll take them over when I'm gone. It's not the "traditional" use for the room, but one has to start new traditions if the old are to have any meaning. And this one means a great deal to me.'

'Of course the concerts will continue. They're a lovely idea. I hope there'll be even more "new traditions" like it in the future.'

Rhiannon looked at me for a long time, very seriously. Then she sat down on a carved oak seat – we were in the rose garden – and said, 'I owe you an apology.'

I was astonished. 'You? Whatever for?'

'This is going to be a difficult confession, but I'm getting old and I want to clear my accounts before I go.'

'Nonsense!' I cried. 'You're not old at all! And if you "go" much before you're ninety, I'm going to be very angry with you!'

She laughed, then grew serious again. 'You make me even more ashamed. You see, when David brought you here, I thought you were just dazzled by Farleton Hall. I was afraid that you didn't – couldn't – really know David. After all, you'd only known each other a few weeks. It all seemed rather sudden. I'm afraid I thought the worst.'

'A flighty little golddigger out to marry above my station. I know. I overheard.'

A stunned silence. 'Overheard?'

'That first night. I left my handbag in the drawing-room and came down to fetch it. I overheard you talking with David.'

'Ros, I'm so ashamed.'

I laughed. 'Don't be. There's a lot of precedent: actresses and dancers and chorus girls. You were right to be suspicious. And you were also right about my being dazzled. I was, and am. But I'm also dazzled by David. I wouldn't care if he were the penniless son of a road sweeper.'

'I can see that now. That's why I wanted so much to confess, to make things right with you.'

I smiled. 'That makes two of us. I've felt terribly guilty about eavesdropping. Even more after you were so good about our engagement. I wanted to tell you then, but I'm more cowardly than you. Truce?'

Rhiannon laughed. 'Truce. I'm glad you're marrying David. I think you have some notion of just how difficult he can be. I hope you'll be strong enough to curb some of his wilder ideas.'

'About tradition, for example?'

'Yes. I understand his passion to reform the estate, and he's right, of course. But he's likely to throw out the baby with the bathwater. Not all traditions are iniquitous. He has a violent need to destroy everything his father stood for. I understand that, too. But David's not very subtle. I'm afraid he won't be able to distinguish the good from the bad traditions.'

'Like the concerts. Don't worry. The concerts will continue, even if I have to throw him into a dungeon for the duration.'

I would, too. It was a marvellous evening. For the first time I saw what Farleton Hall must have been like in the past: thronged with people, the Long Gallery filled with music. There were a lot of people, far more than one would expect for the dead month of August and a pair of unknown locals who were only students at the Royal Northern College of Music.

I was beginning to learn just how cunning Rhiannon could be. 'People have come to see *you*,' she whispered between pieces. (Our engagement had just been announced in the *Langhamdale Gazette*.) 'I knew they would,' she continued. 'It seemed a good way to get a big audience for the young ones. They need to get used to big audiences – a part of their training. You don't mind, do you?'

'Of course not. If they don't mind sharing the limelight.'

The music began again: Schubert's second A major sonata for violin and piano. I've heard it many times since, performed by some of the most famous musicians in the world, but never again has it sounded so enchanting as on that first magical evening when Farleton Hall came to life. And whatever else has happened, and however much my world has changed since those innocent days, I will always love that piece more than any other. As the sunny, warm-hearted music filled the beautiful room, I leaned back and breathed perfect happiness.

It was impossible, but there it was: one perfect little clearing in the midst of all the mess called Farleton Forest. A bright green oasis filled with a different kind of sunshine and warmth and song than Schubert's. Nature's Long Gallery.

I smiled at my lover. 'Did you know this was here?' I whispered.

He shook his head and gripped my hand. 'This is how it could *all* be,' he said, his eyes glittering with the desire of Nature's devoted servant.

'Then it's *ours*,' I breathed. 'Yours and mine alone. Our discovery. Our secret.'

I drew my lover down with me, onto the warm dry carpet of wild bedstraw foliage. All around us the forest rustled with the secretive noises of small birds, graceful little swags of sound festooning the trees. There were no flowers to break the green-gold festival, but the air was sweet with a thousand unseen scents.

We were sweet and golden, too, my lover and I. The sun burrowed into our naked bodies and lodged there, giving out its light through a translucent veil of skin. We glowed: with the sun and with the fresh green passion of early love. No one had ever loved as we loved, of that I was sure. We were the centre of the universe. It was our two bodies alone that kept the earth spinning and us spinning along with it.

That was when it happened. A strange sense of heat which had nothing to do with us or with the sun pried open my sleepy eyes just at the moment when he stepped into the clearing. A stag, a golden stag, burnished from the tips of his antlers right down to his delicate little hooves. I blinked, but he was still there, no figment of my imagination. The clearing was so still and David and I so still at the centre of it that the stag was unaware of our presence, or, if aware, unafraid. Perhaps the smell of love is different from the smell of the hunter. In any case, he stood there long enough for me to drink in his beauty and imprint him on my memory for ever.

He was exquisite. Someone had carved him out of magic, using a wand for a chisel. His clear, flawless outline glowed against the intense green of the forest, dazzling my eyes. I couldn't believe it was a trick of the light, a stronger-than-usual ray of the sun turning him into myth. He really was gold, gleaming with a brightness so vibrant that it almost hurt my eyes. I had to blink again.

Whether it was that or something else that startled him I don't know, but suddenly he moved his head with its majestic crown and looked straight at me. His eyes were gold, too: hard, imperious nuggets with no warmth in them at all. I shivered.

That was it. His head swung in a single violent arc, his gilded antlers shooting sparks in every direction. Then he was gone.

'Rosalind,' said David as we walked back through the trees, 'there are no deer in Farleton Forest.'

'David, I saw him.'

He stopped, took my face in his big work-roughened hands and smiled at me. 'You see a thousand golden visions in that lovely head of yours. That's why I adore you.' He kissed me.

I should have been satisfied with that, but I couldn't relinquish the vision which I knew was real.

'If there were any deer, you would know it,' he said. 'They're not the pretty little Bambies you think. Those gilded antlers would have shredded every sapling in the forest. That "chiselled forehead" would have chiselled the bark off hundreds of trees to mark its territory. Deer are killers, Ros. Don't wish one on us. We've got enough to cope with as it is.'

That night, Rhiannon died.

7

ROSIE STOP PHONE IMMEDIATELY
IMMEDIATELY STOP JAS

I read the telegram a second time and a third, wondering if the Post Office had made a mistake or if the repetition was his quaint way of underlining the urgency. Probably the latter. Perversely, it provoked in me a bolshy lethargy. *I will not be rushed.*

I put the telegram down and looked round the morning room. My morning room. I'd been rushed into that, too. It seemed only minutes ago that I'd arrived at Farleton Hall as a gauche young student, awed and bewildered. Now I was its mistress. The Mistress of Farleton Hall. I shook my head with disbelief and out of the motion shot the memory of Jas's face. Dear Jas. How could I punish him for my own confusion? I picked up the phone.

'Jas. Rosie. What's with this stuttering?'

'Rosie! Thank God! I've been clutching the phone all day trying to squeeze a ring out of it. I was terrified you might have one of your bolshy fits and go silent on me. Where the hell have you been? Do you have any idea what a devil you were to track down? It was *hours* before I remembered that white rose guy of yours and twigged and then I had to wave a gun around Senate House before they'd divulge his address and I still wouldn't have got it if an old flame of mine hadn't been working there. How could you do this to me? Flit away without a word to your nearest and dearest? You don't deserve the stupendous news I'm about to present to you.'

I waited. 'Well?'

'Show a little enthusiasm, loved one. This is It! The Breakthrough! The Miracle!'

'Give me a clue. Animal, vegetable, mineral?'

'All three. Sweetheart, it's happened! The rich backer! He lives! Rosie, darling, *we're going to the West End!*'

I should have been used to absorbing shocks by then, but wasn't. 'What?'

'We're opening at the Fortune Theatre in a fortnight, poppit, so put on your skates and get your ass down here immediately, immediately! We've had a hell of a time summoning all from the four corners and you're the last piece of the jigsaw, so get Sir White Rose to hire you a helicopter – rehearsals start on Tuesday! Don't worry about a thing, I'll sort everything out at this end – I've got a great landlady with a spare room, so just get yourself down here, fast! A drag, commuting between Cambridge and London for the duration, but you've got to do it, we're counting on you!'

Slowly my mind digested the news and even more slowly conjured up a picture of the devastation I was about to inflict. 'Jas,' I said cautiously, 'it's not that easy. Everything's changed. It's a long story – promise you'll be patient?'

'Tell me all the stories you like when you get here, just get here!'

'Jas, I'm not going back to Cambridge,' I said. It was horribly blunt, but I had to cut through his excitement somehow.

'Fine! Their loss – though you'd be a fool to drop out altogether. Take a year off, great, just catch the first train down here!'

'Jas, I'm sorry. I can't. Please don't be too angry, please try to understand. I can't come to London. I can't be in the play.'

Now it came: the stunned, disbelieving silence. Finally, 'I didn't hear that, Rosie. You didn't say that.'

'I'm sorry, Jas. Now will you listen?'

Another long silence. 'Speak.'

'I'm married, Jas.'

'This is no time for jokes.'

'It's no joke. I'm married. He of the white roses. I'm Mrs David Farleton now.'

This time the silence was so long I wondered if we'd been cut off. Finally, 'So? Use whatever name you like on the programme.'

'Don't you understand? I've got a husband to look after. I've got a bloody great house to run. I can't just whiz down to London. By the way, I do think you might have the grace to congratulate me.'

'Congrats. I'll buy you a bottle of bubbly when you get here.'

'You haven't heard a word I've said.'

'I've heard. Look, I deplore your haste in fettering yourself at such a tender age. I deplore the difficulties you're making for your career. But if that's what you want, fine. But you're not seriously telling me that White Rose intends to chain you to the marriage bed for the rest of your life?'

'His name is David.'

'Fine. Tell Sir David that if he doesn't let you go I'm coming up there to strangle him with my own fair hands.'

'He's not a monster.'

'Then what's the problem?'

'Me. I love him. It practically kills me to be away from him during the hours when he's working. Do you really expect me to leave him for weeks, maybe months? All for the sake of some silly play-acting?'

Bad move. Tactless. That silly play-acting was the single most important thing in Jas's life. It had been in mine, too, but no longer. It had no meaning now. I didn't want it. I wanted to be with David, every minute of every day and night.

'Ros. I don't believe I'm hearing this. You're not seriously thinking of giving up acting? After reviews like those? Now? With a big fat West End plum clutched in your tiny hands? Ros, grads of famous drama schools struggle for years to get what's being handed to you on a plate. Ordinary mortals have to push through the slime of two-handers in dingy pubs, a spot on the Edinburgh Fringe nobody comes to, a stint of rep in Skegness if they're really lucky. Years and years of it before they get this. I think my ears must be out of order. You can't be saying that.'

'I'm sorry, Jas. I am.'

Another long silence. 'Rosalind, you are stark raving mad. Further, you are the most selfish bitch in the universe. Think. Just think. Two weeks we have. Two weeks to train up a new Rosalind for that play. To train up some half-baked idiot nobody wants to see. Think what you're doing to the rest of us. This is *our* big chance, too.'

'Oh, God.'

'Am I getting through?'

'You're getting through. Jas, I feel terrible. I'm sorry. I didn't realise.'

'Ros, *you can't let us down*. All right, give up a brilliant career if you must. But *after* this show. *Please*.'

'He's right,' said Belle.

'I know. That's what makes it so awful.'

We were in the dining-room, the four of us huddled at one end of the huge table. The table seemed twice as big without Rhiannon. How had such a small person taken up so much space? The whole house had doubled in size with her absence. I missed her terribly. I felt like a dwarf suddenly called on to run a giant's house. The giant's winter palace, she'd called it.

'How long is it likely to run?' Belle asked.

For a moment I thought she meant the house. 'Oh, the play? Impossible to tell. It's West End, commercial, so as long as people keep buying tickets, I suppose.'

'They usually transfer just for the summer, not this close to term,' she mused. 'Odd to take a Shakespeare to the West End, too. You'd think there was enough at the RSC and the National.'

'Apparently there hasn't been an *As You Like It* at either for years.'

'Still odd. Who's the bricks and mortar?'

'The what?' said Brendan.

Belle smiled indulgently at her husband. 'The backer. Producer, theatre owner, whatever. He who's putting up the money.'

'Some eccentric,' I said. 'Jas says the guy's got a bee in his bonnet about the other two having a monopoly. He wants to show them that other companies can do Shakespeare just as well.'

'Risky.'

'Yes. I don't suppose it'll last long, just long enough for the backer to make his point.'

'And the ADC to chalk up a triumph,' said Belle. 'We're back at the beginning. Jas is right: it's a chance of a lifetime.'

'Don't,' I said.

Now I knew how children felt in those tug-of-war divorces. On the one hand, Jas, my dearest friend and ally for that whole wonderful year with the ADC. On the other, David, who had whisked away that year and given me a new life full of new excitement. There was a monstrous irony: I was being given *too* much. The greedy child had finally reached saturation point. I should have been the happiest person alive. I had a wonderful husband, a magnificent house and two dear friends to help us turn the estate into paradise. I also had a once-in-a-lifetime opportunity to break into the big time with my career. I should have been shooting through the ceiling with joy. Instead, I wished the floorboards would swallow me up, relieve me of having to make this awful decision.

David had said nothing so far. I was waiting for him to speak. I wanted to know his thoughts without prompting. Finally I could wait no longer. 'Well? What are you thinking?'

'I'm thinking,' he said slowly, 'that if I were Jas, I'd be hating David Farleton.'

'Nonsense,' I lied.

'I'm also thinking that if I were you, I'd be hating David Farleton, too.'

I sucked in my breath.

He smiled sadly. 'I was afraid this would happen. This or something like it. Putting you in an impossible position.' Then he looked directly into my eyes. 'Never mind Jas. What about yourself? How are you going to feel, a few years from now, when you look back and remember how you gave up a chance like this for me? And how will I feel, being the monster who ruined your career?'

'David, it's not like that. I don't want it any more – isn't that clear by now?'

'You might not want it now, but what about the future? The nagging at the back of your mind, the what-if, the what-might-have-been?'

'David's right,' said Belle. 'Anyway, it's not an irrevocable step. It's just one production. It might not lead anywhere. But you'd feel awful if you didn't have a go at it. Think of the excitement, Ros! To have had that wonderful experience!'

It was Brendan who came to the rescue. Dear practical Brendan. 'I'm thinking there's no performing of a Sunday, am I right?' He turned to David. 'Myself and the wife can keep things ticking over up here for the weekends. Sure, it's a hell of a trek and all and not the greatest way to start a marriage, but it's got to be better than this almighty mess we seem to be getting into. And much as I hate casting aspersions on Rosie's talent, truly this run can't last for ever? Not with being Shakespeare and all that competition from the subsidised? How about it, Rosie? Give your man a ticket every Saturday night and call it a deal? Three for opening night – don't think you'll shake off your fan club that easy!'

From that moment, until the train pulled out of York station, I clung to David as never before. I didn't understand why I felt *such* desperation. It was out of all proportion to the situation. After all, the play would probably fold in a few weeks; it wouldn't kill me to be away from David that long. True, there was an incompleteness about our marriage which this premature absence emphasised. We'd had no honeymoon, barely even had a wedding. All the lovely plans had died with Rhiannon and the cloud of her funeral had hovered over what there was: a tiny private ceremony with Brendan and Belle the only witnesses. After that we'd plunged straight into estate matters made even more complicated by Rhiannon's death. Sometimes I wondered if I was married at all, if the wedding had been a dream, a figment of my imagination like (David insisted) my vision of the golden stag.

And then, that night, I dreamt about him, a detailed re-run of that moment when he'd stepped into the clearing. The dream made even stronger the terrible contrast between his gilded beauty and the hard, cold glance of his golden eyes. There was no doubt that, vision or reality, this was a mythic creature with all the awesome power of a primitive god. It should have made me flee the forest in terror.

Instead, the dream-Rosalind rose from her green couch, left her lover and floated unresisting towards the creature. Strange things were happening. The birdsong faded, an ethereal tinkling as of tiny fairy bells took its place. The cool green freshness of the clearing was fading, too, with every step I took becoming warmer, as if the stag radiated some unearthly heat from his own body.

Then, as I approached, something stranger still. The stag's head dissolved and in its place a face began to form, a human face, every bit as beautiful as the stag's but with the cold eyes now mournful. In the dream I didn't even marvel, took for granted the thought that came to me: 'Why, this is no stag at all but a fairy prince some witch has turned into a stag.' Immediately I knew what I had to do. Just as in a fairy tale, I need only step up to the lovely sad creature and kiss him for the spell to be broken and the prince to become a prince once more. So clear was this directive that I barely heard when David, from somewhere far behind me, seemed to wake and murmur softly, his voice still blurred with sleep, 'Don't, Ros. Don't.' Slowly I drifted on, not heeding the voice. Only a few more steps now.

Then a sharp rustling noise behind me as David sat

up. Now his voice was clear. 'Rosalind! No!' This time I stopped, startled by the horror in his voice.

In that moment of hesitation, the stag/man looked deep into my eyes and I knew everything was lost. By hesitating I had failed him and failed myself. The face dissolved again, turned back into a stag's head, its antlers such a bright gold that I shielded my eyes from the blaze.

Then I saw that the antlers were coming towards me like a forest of golden swords flashing in the sun, lashing out at me. I stepped back and tried to turn round, meaning to run back to David, but it was too late for that, too. I'd become rooted to the spot – literally. My naked arms, raised in self-protection, began to twist into the limbs of a tree, my bare feet to dig their roots deep into the forest floor. My arms were covered with leaves now, lovely fresh gleaming green leaves, but I had no time to admire my new foliage because the stag was coming closer and closer, his breath hot and the fire of his antlers hotter still.

Then I saw the first leaf singe at the edges and curl over onto itself and I understood at last the form my punishment was going to take. I tried to open my mouth, meaning to call out to the stag, 'Wait! I *will* come to you!' But trees have no mouths, and just as my attempt to return to David had failed, so now this other attempt was doomed. More leaves were burning now, and now for the first time I felt the fire bite into the bark of my arms.

'Don't! Ros, don't cry!'

I awoke sobbing to find myself in David's arms, his mouth close to my ear. 'Don't cry, Ros. Rosie, wake up, it's all right, I'm here, don't cry.'

It took me a long time to disentangle the David who had his arms round me from the David in the dream, and when I did I only cried harder. 'I'm staying here, I'm not leaving you, don't make me go away,' I said, over and over until finally I wore myself out and lay back against the pillows exhausted while David stroked my hair and tried to comfort me.

'Do you want to tell me about it?' he said at last. 'It was a nightmare, wasn't it?'

I nodded.

'Would it help if you told me?'

I hesitated, then remembered that it was that very hesitation which had turned me into a burning tree.

And so I told him. He listened more patiently than he might have done, given that he didn't believe I'd seen the stag at all. When I finished, I had to ask, though some other part of me cringed from knowing.

'David, *are* there any legends about a golden stag? In your family, I mean?' I hesitated again, this time with more reason. The pain of Rhiannon's death was so fresh, I didn't want to hurt him. 'I mean, it seems so extraordinary, seeing that stag in the clearing the day before . . . I know she had a weak heart, but even so, the coincidence . . . And now, just before I leave . . . David, I don't want to go to London.'

A long silence. 'I don't want you to go.'

'Then why, for God's sake, am I doing this crazy thing?'

In that moment it seemed so clear to me. All I had to do was phone Jas, grovel my apologies and stay here with David. Jas would never forgive me, nor the others in the company, but did that matter so very much? My place was here now, now was the time to cut the last tie with my past.

'I suppose,' said David, 'it's a matter of honour.'

The clear lovely moment of escape was over. I nodded dumbly.

'I suppose, too,' he went on, 'that I'm hoping . . . well, hoping this will be the end of it. That everything will be different now, that the magic of the theatre will be gone and you'll come back to me knowing you've made the right decision. That there'll be no gnawing doubts in the future.'

'There aren't any now,' I said gently. 'I've never doubted my decision and I never will. I'm only going because of, well, honour.'

Dawn was creeping towards the windows. An invisible sun caught the branches of a tree outside and pushed its shadow slowly up the wall of the room. Grey branches, grey antlers. I shivered. The daylight which should have dispelled the nightmare only brought it closer.

'David, I have to know. About the stag.'

He sighed impatiently. 'There's nothing to know. Dozens of coats of arms have stags on them; ours is no different. It's not even gold, it's a perfectly ordinary heraldic stag, and if it worries you so much you should see why I want to dump all this heritage business. It's just a load of troublesome baggage and now it's even giving you nightmares.'

He turned towards me, a reassuring smile forming on his lips. Then he saw the wall. He stared, and slowly he began to laugh. 'Rosie, my lovely impossible dreamer of dreams. Look – there on the wall. There's your stag.' He got out of bed and shut the curtains. The stag disappeared.

8

'Rosie!'

'Jas!'

He hugged me as best he could – I was bristling with luggage. I'd brought a lot with me in the perverse hope that it wouldn't be needed, that the production would fold after a week or two and I could go home again, duty done.

'That looks hopeful,' he said to the luggage.

'Well, it's going to be a long run, isn't it?'

'That's up to you. Tony says our bricks and mortar's crazy about you, wouldn't go ahead unless you stayed on as Rosalind.'

I looked at him in surprise. 'You didn't tell me that.'

'Didn't want to exert undue pressure.'

'Liar. You said I'd be "the most selfish bitch in the universe" if I didn't come. That's not pressure?'

'Ah. Yes. Well. I got a little carried away on the phone. Panic, you know. Oh, all right: I behaved badly. Very badly. Forgive?'

'Forgive.'

There was no chance to say more as we lumbered through the crowded concourse weighed down by suitcases. I kept bumping into people. In the few months I'd been away, the personal space around me had increased; I'd lost my ability to judge distances. I felt like a foreigner in my own city.

Outside King's Cross it was raining. That much at least was familiar. But this was a different grey from the soft grey-green which enfolded Farleton Hall. I'd become used to tall green trees standing still. Here there were short grey people scurrying about. I felt dizzy as I watched the taxis zoom in, zoom out. Finally our turn came. As I clambered into it I thought fleetingly of the Land-Rover.

'So who's my admirer?' I asked.

'Head of a big chemical firm, believe it or not. One of those sad types who craved the arts but got shoved into business by Daddy. Familiar?'

'Awfully. Poor sod. Do we meet him?'

'Probably not. Tony did his Temperamental Director on him, told him he would brook no interference, whatever the money. Rather risky, but Tony's no fool. B and M was eating out of his hand after that. Funny how people like their artists temperamental. Me, I'm just a friendly little homebody. Grovel, grovel.'

I snorted. The taxi stopped, clamped into the eternal traffic jam which is London. Beside us a bus spread a big red wall across our vision. The colours of London, grey and red. 'Who's paying for the taxi?' I asked suddenly.

Jas's leprechaun face took on an offended look. 'Would I ask a lady?'

'I meant, our frustrated thespian? Or have you mugged an old lady? It's been a while since your bank balance ran to taxis.'

He smirked. 'Friend.'

'I see.'

'Friend's paying for dinner, too. And a night out at the opera – *Der Freischutz*.'

'Why this access of generosity? I mean, to finance your rave-up with a lady friend?'

'Ah. Well, actually, he doesn't know about you.'

'Thought not.'

'And . . . ah . . . well, it's a sort of compensation. I wanted to give you a good night out to compensate for . . . well, you'll see.'

I saw. The bedsit raised its fusty grey brows and eyed me wearily: yet another in a long succession of rootless people making do before they moved on. It was all there. The junk shop chairs with their springs poised for attack. The all-purpose gate-legged table, its top pitted and stained. The Baby Belling whose crusted surface someone –

probably Jas – had tried to excavate in search of the original enamel. The yellowed sink countless men had peed into because they couldn't face the freezing corridor to the communal loo. The decrepit sash windows with their unique ability to jam and rattle simultaneously. The dusty curtains, the threadbare carpet. The ancient single bed in which David and I would make love.

'Not exactly Farleton Hall,' said Jas nervously.

I walked over to the sink. At least it had a plug. The cupboards had been cleaned out, the crockery didn't look too bad. In fact, I now saw that the whole place, however dowdy, was surprisingly clean. Someone had tried hard. No, not exactly Farleton Hall but, 'I've seen worse,' I smiled. 'What about yours?'

He pointed to the ceiling.

'The attic?'

He nodded.

I frowned, suddenly suspicious. 'Let me see.'

It was ghastly. At least my room had a modicum of comfort to counteract the dinginess. Jas's room was just plain squalid. I looked at the skylight. I'd met that skylight before, or its relatives, in the bedsits of Cambridge friends. In summer it dripped melted tar; in winter, rain. On the table beneath it, a pile of clothes still on their hangers had been dumped in haste. The rain dripped down on the shabby leather jacket I'd seen him wear so often in Cambridge.

I closed my eyes. 'You've given me your room,' I said. 'Don't lie.'

I opened them again to see his face suffused with guilt. 'Oh, Jas, how could you?'

I burst into tears.

Covent Garden. Dress Circle. Front row, middle. Our seats could hardly be more choice. 'Friend has a Friend in Box Office, right?'

'Friend *is* Box Office.'

'Ah.'

All around us the monied classes glittered and gleamed.

We glittered and gleamed, too. No one would guess we'd emerged a scant hour ago from a grotty terrace in Fulham. The term 'yuppy' wasn't invented yet, but that's what we looked like, its 1970s equivalent. Acting, of course. Actors knew how to make the best of their clothes, use them to climb into a role.

There were real actors, too. A few seats away was Ralph Richardson. I gave Jas a discreet nudge and swivelled my eyes towards the source. Jas looked. His own eyes tried hard not to pop out on stalks. We stared at the god in wonder. How innocent we were beneath our finery, as innocent as David and I in our rural paradise.

The lights dimmed, the conductor appeared, the house hushed, the music began, and all acting ceased except on the stage. I didn't know Weber's opera at all, only that it had a famous overture and an equally famous scene in a wolf's glen. I didn't even know it was set in a forest, let alone that the main character, Max, was a forester. My heart lurched on his first appearance, and though he bore not the slightest resemblance to David, from that moment on I identified totally. I *was* Agathe, she whom Max so loved that he entered into a pact with the devil to win the shooting contest and the woman who was its prize. And when, during the contest, he shot the white dove and the white-clad Agathe collapsed on the stage, I felt my own body crumple.

'You all right?' Jas whispered.

I snapped back to reality. 'Of course. Shh.'

The applause at the end was thunderous. It had been a wonderful production: highly stylised, a bravura display of artifice. The producer had judged shrewdly; through the blatant unreality the truer reality that lay beneath shone more brightly than it would have done in a more naturalistic setting. As I applauded the soprano who'd sung Agathe, I felt a twinge of envy. I wished I could sing. If I'd gone to drama school instead of Cambridge, singing and dancing would have been part of the course. Not to this standard, but at least I'd be able to manage if a part in a musical came up. As it was, I'd have to struggle.

Perhaps I should splurge, have private singing lessons. Dancing, too . . .

I shook myself. What on earth was I thinking about? I'd given it up. This wasn't my world any more. From now on, once our run was over, I would be a spectator like any other.

Another twinge.

I swept it away and joined the surge of audience now turning its back on the stage and making its way out of the building.

'That's it, Rosie,' Jas whispered, though no one was bothering to eavesdrop. 'Our theatre!'

We were on Russell Street. In front of us rose the Fortune Theatre, now disgorging the last of its audience.

'Just think,' he said, his voice awed. 'In a week or so that'll be us – not the audience but inside, on the stage! Doesn't it make you want to whoop with joy?'

I laughed, touched by his excitement. His sophisticated veneer was so thin, the childlike enthusiasm beneath so strong that it seemed like some impatient animal always eager to burst its fetters. It was, I knew, the thing that made him such a stunning actor: people sensed the energy crackling beneath the surface. I was glad I'd come. David was right. It would have been monstrous to deny Jas his chance.

I turned round and looked across the street. The stage door and the famous colonnade of the Theatre Royal, Drury Lane. One of the biggest, oldest and most famous theatres in London. The two theatres in such proximity were comical, the lion and the mouse.

Jas, undaunted, put his hand on his chest in a melodramatic gesture worthy of Garrick himself. 'Today, the Fortune. Tomorrow . . . the world!' His arm shot out to indicate the location of the world. An indignant passer-by barely escaped decapitation.

I laughed. 'I like the Fortune better. Sweet.'

Jas nodded sagely. 'From little acorns . . .'

'. . . large clichés grow. Come on, you need a drink.' I clamped his arm before it could do more damage.

He beamed at the people around him. 'Little do they know that the two lunatic obstructions they're now swearing at are about to become the greatest theatrical team of the twentieth century! Years from now these people will be settling down with their cocoa and slippers in front of the telly. They switch it on. The screen bursts into life. Two faces shine out. The great Jas Molyneux! The stupendous Ros Rawlinson! They (I refer to the cocoa-fiends) blink, look furtively at each other. "I say, Nicky, haven't we seen those faces before?" Nicky nods. "Sure of it. Wasn't it . . . hey! . . . I remember! . . . that little theatre on Russell Street, whatsitcalled . . . outside, remember? Those kids outside. Chappie nearly had my head off, remember?" Their heads bob in unison, in awe. "Just think, Sylvie: if only we'd known then . . ."'

Two teenagers giggled past. They stared at Jas. One of them shook her head. 'Crazy.'

'Quite,' I said. 'Come on, Jas. Save it for the first night.'

The champagne fizzed. 'I'll buy you a bottle of bubbly when you get here,' he'd said, and he'd kept his word. But there was nothing celebratory about his face across the restaurant table.

'How could you do it, Rosie?'

'Easy. I love him.'

'Love. Bah, humbug.'

'Don't let Friend hear you say that.'

'That's different.'

'No, it isn't.'

'Is. I'm not marrying him.'

'Humph.'

'Don't humph me, Ros. Marriage is a serious commitment.'

'I'm a serious person.'

'You're hardly out of nappies.'

'Thanks.'

'Him too.'

I was getting annoyed. I'd spent the whole of our dinner describing the last few months, assuming that at the end of it Jas would see how obvious it was that I should marry David. But it hadn't happened. Even to my own ears the events leading up to it sounded unreal.

'You don't have a single thing in common,' he said. 'Admit it.'

'Not true: love.'

'Love! If you say that word once more I'll pour this over your head.'

'You old Scrooge. What have you got against love?' I ducked out of range of his glass. 'Jas, people are staring.'

'So they should. One of the most gifted actresses of her generation trades in her Equity card for a seat on the parish council. Honestly, Ros! How could you do it?'

'We've been here before.'

Jas sighed. 'I suppose there's a rep in York.' He made a face. 'From the West End to York. Wow.'

'Jas, I'm not going to York. Or any other rep. Or any other theatre. I thought I made that clear. I've only come down to do you a favour. Frankly. You and the rest of the company. After this, finis. Please, can we finish our dinner in peace?'

A church basement in Kentish Town. Or Streatham. Or anywhere. Back to earth with a bump. My head still blurred with champagne, I stumbled through the mis-named 'run-through' on this, our first day of re-rehearsal.

'Ros.' Tony's voice dripped with ill-concealed sarcasm. 'Ros, you've just walked through a tree.'

'Have I? Sorry.' I looked down at the network of coloured tapes stuck to the floor. Among them a few improvised props pretended to be the Forest of Arden. 'Are you sure? I thought that was the path.'

He pointed. '*That's* the path. All right? Try again.'

I continued my stroll through the forest, accompanied by my cousin Celia, alias Stephanie. Then, in the middle of a short speech bewailing my love for Orlando, I dried. Mid-sentence, no warning.

'What's got into you?' said Stephanie.

'Sorry. Just a bit hungover. It'll be –'

'– all right on the night?' said Tony. 'Not at this rate, it won't. Ros, you're scaring the shit out of us all, you know that, don't you?'

'Sorry.'

'Sorry, sorry, sorry,' he mocked. 'That what you're going to tell the audience? They're not paying to hear you say you're sorry.'

'Leave her alone,' said Jas. 'She's just out of practice. For God's sake, it's only the first day. What's got into *you*?'

Tony grinned sheepishly. 'Panic. All right, *I'm* sorry, Ros. Let's break for coffee and try another scene after.'

But it wasn't all right. I'd never dried before. A good memory was one of my strong points. It meant I could learn my lines more easily than most, clear my mind for the serious work of getting into the character.

The stage manager handed me a mug of Nescafé. I cupped my hands round it gratefully. It was the only warm thing in the room. Behind me an ancient radiator clanked like a whole chorusful of prisoners in chains. I put a hand on it. Stone cold.

'Full of sound and fury, signifying nothing,' said Jas, scowling at it from beneath his black bushy eyebrows. Then he folded his lanky body to squat beside me and stared into my face, his own full of concern. 'You're shaking, Ros, and it's not just the cold.'

I shook my head.

'Missing Sir White Rose?'

I nodded.

'Poor Rosie. I'm a swine, making you come down here. But you see how it is. We need you.'

I nodded.

'Come on, drink up. Then we'll do some breathing exercises to clear out the cobwebs.'

The first technical, still in the unspeakable church basement. By now there were ice cubes circulating through the radiators. The room was arctic. Two hairy spheres lurked in what the tapes on the floor told us were the wings: Jas and I, ten sweaters each. On stage, so to speak, Jaques was delivering one of his most amusing speeches. The audience, a row of bored technicians, slouched in their chairs and watched through hooded eyes. Now and again they yawned, scribbled a note in their copy of the script, and sank a little further into their chairs. Their equivalents at the ADC had been part of the company, had been as enthusiastic as the rest of us. These – professionals – had seen it all. They made no attempt to conceal their dismay at having to work with a bunch of Cambridge kids instead of the greats.

'RIP,' Jas whispered, nodding towards the sound engineer who gave every appearance of having died in his chair.

'Not quite,' I whispered back. The engineer's half-open mouth wheezed a gentle snore. 'Still alive.'

Jas sighed. 'So much for the thrill of the West End.'

'Cheer up. We haven't got there yet.'

I didn't want to tell him, but I was pleased with the boredom of it all. I now knew why I'd been drying up; I'd been resisting getting involved. Once or twice a twinge of excitement had whizzed me back to the old days and I didn't want to go there. I wanted to do my duty and go home, my peace of mind intact, unruffled by what I was giving up.

No problem. I watched with gratitude as the sound engineer snored on. I was almost annoyed when the head of lighting jabbed him in the ribs and he woke up.

Jas left my side and waddled on to the stage: Orlando the penguin, his nose blue with cold. I suppose he couldn't see his feet through all the padding. In any case, he tripped over a dead potted plant which was supposed to be a tree.

Life at last. The technicians sprang up in their chairs and applauded.

'Remember this moment, Rosalind my love.' Jas's voice,

trained to reach the back of the highest balcony, rang out portentously in the cold clear air. Then he opened the stage door with a stage flourish and gestured me in. 'Your first West End stage door,' he announced, his eyes misting over with fake tears.

I'd given up saying, 'And my last.' Jas refused to accept my decision. I suppose it was his way of coping with my rejection of his world. Did he think David a phantom? Did he envisage a magic carpet which would whisk me daily between Yorkshire and London so I could continue the career he seemed so determined I should have?

I nodded nervously at the Cerberus guarding the stage door and went in.

The building was full of people, some of them ours, some not. Ours were in the minority. Even a stranger could pick us out by the bravura we pasted over our quaking hearts as we strode through the corridors, pretending to belong. 'Where the hell are the dressing-rooms?' someone muttered. Someone else shrugged.

At home, David and Brendan would be striding through the forest, talking and laughing and planning the revolution. Belle would be in the kitchens – she'd broached the green baize, the staff adored her. Probably she was standing by a cooker with Melinda, the pair of them giggling over some joke or other. What on earth was I doing here?

'Upstairs,' said a frizzy-haired old woman, without seeming to open her mouth.

We trudged up the stairs. There were a lot of them. 'Tents on the roof?' I suggested.

At last we arrived and, oh God, there it was, one of those unwelcome twinges as I opened the door to my dressing-room. My dressing-room. Well, ours. Two mirrors told me I was sharing this broom cupboard. Steph, I hoped. At least she was thin. I peered at the costumes squashed together on the clothes rail. Rosalind and Celia.

Steph squeezed through into the room, her eyes aglow. I smiled at her, feeling decades older than she who played my cousin. Marriage does that to you, ages you overnight in a nice way, makes you feel protective towards those who were your peers only a few months before. Steph was hysterical with joy at this début. I didn't want to be the wet rag, so I cranked myself into gear to exude the excitement to match hers. Oddly, it wasn't so difficult.

Dress rehearsal. We crept out on to the stage, costumed and made-up, like a troop of children strayed timidly into a territory they know is not theirs.

I looked round the stage as if I'd never seen a stage before. The ropes and wires, wheels and weights, staircases, ladders up into the flies. On the stage, the set itself, newly erected the night before. In the middle, Tony, reassurance at last. We gathered round him like moths round a light, hoping for a little warmth in these hostile surroundings.

He gave. The pep talk was brilliant, finishing with the words so familiar to anyone who'd ever worked with him at the ADC. 'Just relax, enjoy yourselves. If you do, the audience probably will, too. And don't worry if you make a Godawful mess of it today. Remember, "Bad dress rehearsal, good show."'

It was a lousy dress rehearsal. The results of the sound engineer's kips were manifest. Ditto the lighting. Ditto the props. The set, sparse though it was, was a disaster. So were we. As we blundered through the play we'd done so well in Cambridge, I consoled myself with the thought that it didn't matter, not really. I hoped the others did, too. After all, many of them were still at Cambridge. They still had their academic work, other plays at the ADC. There would be other chances, too, after they'd graduated. It wasn't the end of the world if we flopped. Not really.

I managed to convince myself right up to the end. Then, after we'd rehearsed the curtain calls, a weight which had been hovering at the top of my brain suddenly crashed down through my whole body.

Bad dress rehearsal, good show. Maybe. But there were limits to the cheery old saying. We'd gone beyond them.

The play was going to flop. It had no life in it. We were just going through the motions, zombies all.

'It'll be better with an audience,' said Jas.

'Sure.'

'Ros?'

'Jas.'

'I hope it's not going to be *too* bad. I hope we haven't dragged you here for nothing.'

I smiled, feeling a hundred years old, and patted his arm. 'Of course not.'

But I was glad I'd kept my old name, glad no Rosalind Farleton would appear on the programme.

First night. I peered through a chink at the wall of faces. One of them would be David's. He'd driven down with Brendan and Belle. I hadn't been able to see him yet, hadn't belonged to myself all day. I was simply part of a machine being oiled and polished at the last minute in the hope that it would run smoothly despite all the ominous signs. Well, miracles happened, and no one believed more fervently in miracles than actors did. It kept us sane.

I wandered back to the dressing-room, rigid with terror. Steph was there, likewise petrified. Why did we do it?

Tony came in. He was doing the rounds of the dressing-rooms, trying to cheer us up, take us out of our individual panics and mould us into a unified troop. If anyone could do it, he could. He had charmed us into brilliance at the ADC. I felt a lot better after he'd left, and I think Steph did, too.

The Tannoy crackled: 'First call for Act One beginners.' The actors doomed to begin the play – Orlando, Adam, Oliver – padded past, seeking the stairs. I heard Jas's voice trying to reassure the others. He didn't sound too convincing.

Several years later it seemed, the Tannoy went quiet. Then, amazingly, the first words of Orlando's first speech rang out. Act One scene one. It had begun. It was really happening. Up until then, I'd gone through the motions, half-believing we were kidding ourselves. It was a fantasy.

At the first call on the Tannoy our make-believe would crumble and we'd wake up in our own beds. April Fool! I shook my head incredulously and looked at Steph. She was as bug-eyed as me. 'It's for real,' she whispered.

I nodded. Our first West End appearance. Those were real people out there, paying real money to see us act. Please God, don't let me faint, don't let me be sick. I looked at Steph. For her, this could be the most important moment of her life. She'd graduated this year. She needed this success to launch a career that mattered desperately.

Suddenly I saw how selfish my own panic was. I didn't need anything. Out there was David, and when this run was over he would whisk me back to Farleton Hall and my own real life.

I touched Stephanie's arm and cocked my head towards the Tannoy. 'Listen,' I said. 'You hear? It's going well, it really is. How about some breathing exercises?'

We breathed our bodies into submission while listening to the play unfold on the Tannoy. Mercifully, it wasn't long before another voice superimposed itself, calling up the actors for scene two. Rosalind and Celia.

'Come on, Coz,' I smiled. 'This is it.'

My legs felt like rubber as we went down the stairs, but no way was I going to let Stephanie know. She needed to believe in my own confidence to supplement her own.

Jas was in the wings, dripping with sweat but grinning. He gave us the thumbs up.

Celia and Rosalind strolled out on to the lawn of the Duke's palace. There was no time to think, no time to inspect the wall of faces. The lights beamed down on us and through the dazzle I heard Stephanie's first words: 'I pray thee, Rosalind, sweet my coz, be merry.'

And I was. The miracle was happening. The audience was doing its time-honoured thing and injecting adrenalin into our veins. The zombies were springing to life at last. I knew now that the dress rehearsal had done its work. I also knew that during the previews we had all of us hung back just a little, not meaning to but not yet pushed to the pitch which only the first night could bring. After the first few moments of terror subsided, a new person rose from the ashes. Ros Rawlinson was gone. In her place stood Rosalind, daughter of the banished Duke. I had nothing to worry about because I didn't exist any more. Only Rosalind existed, reaching out to the audience to tell her tale. There was no question of drying up or stumbling or breaking the magic which cupped us in its hands. The good fortune of the Fortune Theatre smiled upon us. We could do no wrong.

The applause was warm-hearted. Through it rang a few cries of 'Bravo! Brava!' from faithful friends. I glowed. We had brought to life the sights and sounds a long-dead genius had engraved on the page. It was a miracle, the nightly taken-for-granted miracle that our training had taught us to perform. I felt newly humbled. Never before had I felt it so strongly, that sense of being a handmaid to someone's vision. It was a privilege above all others, to be allowed to serve Shakespeare's vision. All the hard work, the disappointments, the fears – all of it vanished, swept aside by the applause which told us we'd served our master well.

It was a night of miracles: some genie pushed aside the walls of our tiny dressing-room. Into it poured a thousand people at least, engulfing us in a warm wave of love. But I wanted just the one, the dark anarchic head which would loom above the others.

Finally I saw it, side by side with another: a honey-gold head which, in the strange unnatural lighting of the dressing-room, gleamed like burnished gold. I shivered involuntarily, despite the sudden increase in temperature seeming to radiate from the gold. Then I blinked and the second head was gone and David alone was making his way towards me. A moment later his arms were around me, the mouth I'd been longing to kiss was saying sweet things into my ear. Everyone else vanished. The centre of my universe had returned. I was home at last.

The magic of the Fortune was withdrawing, leaving just a cramped dressing-room strewn with discarded costumes, a jumble of make-up, the stale odour of sweat and perfume. Only one touch of the enchantment remained: David's roses, a dozen white roses smiling between the naked light bulbs which surrounded my mirror. Two dozen, the mirror said.

I drifted towards them, suddenly desperate for their fresh scent to counteract the stifling room. The card that had come with them was there. I picked it up, wanting to read again David's words, the words that mattered most.

It wasn't David's card. His card had disappeared. In its place was another. This one was cream-coloured with words picked out in gold.

HANNO HIRSCH

Beneath the name was an address in Wigmore Street. That was all. No message, no explanation.

I saw again another flash of gold: the head which for a moment had been beside David's. And I knew with absolute certainty that it had been him. Some stranger had pushed his way into the dressing-room on the tide of well-wishers to deposit this horrid card. I clenched my teeth. As if I were some common chorus girl. How could he? Did he really expect me to obey the summons? My cheeks burned. The card burned in my hands.

I tore it up and threw it into the waste paper basket.

9

I leaned back in the comfortable old Saab and savoured the last miles of my homecoming. Home. It really was that. In a few short months Kirkby Langham and the countryside around it had embedded itself in my heart, displacing all the temporary stops in what now felt like a life of interminable wandering. Already the stop which had been my West End début seemed remote.

We were purring through the streets of Kirkby. It was dusk. The Christmas decorations, sparse and tatty, seemed infinitely more beautiful than Oxford Street's. Our car was well-known; several shoppers bending against the wind paused to wave at us. The simple gesture touched me more than all the applause I'd received at the Fortune. I waved back ecstatically. I was beginning to carve my little niche in Kirkby Langham. It seemed the greatest accomplishment of my whole life.

David had been quiet during the drive from London. That wasn't unusual. He was often abstracted, thinking of estate matters. It was a likeable trait. There was something solid and reassuring about that big handsome head quietly ticking over, going about its work. Because he'd been so quiet, I'd chattered to him about the theatre, filling in all the little details we'd never had time for when he came down for his brief weekends.

Those weekends had kept me sane, anchoring me to reality and preventing the magic of the theatre from taking over. It had been a genuine danger. Our run had been unexpectedly successful, and during it we'd had ample opportunity to rework our production. A big fat two-and-a-half month run, with two matinées a week, had been long enough to settle into, a real luxury. We'd used it well. By the end, the production was so beautifully polished that it was a wrench leaving it.

But that was 230 miles ago. Now, as the damp grey-green countryside slid past, I marvelled that I could have cared. This was where I belonged. London had shrunk to a distant pocket of dirt and noise. Here the land could breathe, and with every breath it seemed to expand further and further until it merged with the sky.

'So peaceful,' I murmured.

David glanced at me. 'I hope you won't be bored, after London.'

'Oh, ye of little faith.'

Even the broken-up bits of the road were becoming familiar. I anticipated them with a friendliness which would have surprised the council. I wondered if I'd be eligible to become a councillor. Perhaps there was some convention which excluded the lady of the manor. Never mind. There would be other things I could do to knit our band of four into the community. I wished I'd been here during the autumn. I might have been able to plan something for Christmas. Perhaps not, so soon after Rhiannon's death. Still, there was plenty of time. I was home now.

Home. The familiar wrought-iron gates appeared. I remembered how awed I'd been the first time I saw them. I'd never dreamed, last June, that they would become the entrance to my own home.

I frowned. Someone had plonked a huge noticeboard of some sort right next to the gates. A recent gale had blown it down, marring the grandeur of the entrance.

'The nerve! Presumably you've told whoever it is to clear up that mess?'

David was getting out of the car to open the gates – I couldn't tell if he nodded or not.

But it was too small a thing to annoy me for long. I breathed deeply as we went up the long lovely drive, becoming more excited by the minute. This was my real Christmas present: coming home. I couldn't wait to see Belle and Brendan, feel their warmth and love enfold me once again. Christmas at Farleton Hall. I still couldn't believe the incredible luck which had brought me here. I reviewed all the chance things, the little what-ifs that might have altered my future. If David had gone to Oxford instead of Cambridge. If Brendan hadn't singled him out among his students. If Brendan hadn't been married to Belle, if Belle hadn't worked at the Cri, if Jas hadn't brought me to the Cri, if Belle hadn't brought David to the ADC. So many terrifying possibilities.

I swept them out of my mind as I raced up the steps and opened the front door.

Something was wrong. Brendan and Belle were there, but looking like children caught with their hands in the biscuit tin. I hugged them both and felt their bodies relax. When I released them, the guilt seemed to have gone. Probably I'd imagined it. My imagination was hyperactive with having to imagine myself daily into the character of Rosalind. No more. Rosalind was gone, this time for good. I must learn to be myself again.

It was cold in the hall. I opened the door into the drawing-room. And stopped.

At the far end stood a huge Christmas tree. Its fragrance filled the room, its fresh green needles shone brightly against the faded furniture. From its boughs hung a million ornaments at least, glittering in the light of the fire. It was perfect, the Christmas tree every child longs for and never gets. My eyes glazed with the beauty of it. I drifted across the room in a trance, five years old and full of hope. This time the hope was fulfilled. The tree was still there, the pungent scent of its resin stronger than ever. On the boughs stood exquisite little candle holders with real candles in them. On Christmas Day they would be lit. We would gather round this miracle and exchange our modest presents. We would laugh a lot, eat a lot, get a little bit too drunk. Perhaps we would wander out into the park after lunch to breathe in the clean quiet beauty of our land. It had been a long wait to find my childhood. Long, but worth it.

Belle was by my side. 'Ros, I do hope you don't mind

too much. I know you would have liked doing it yourself – your first Christmas, too. But there just wasn't time. It took ages, it's all on such a scale; we really couldn't have got it done before Christmas if we'd waited. I hope you don't mind.'

'*Mind*?' I looked at Belle. Her face was anxious again. So that was it. The strained atmosphere, the guilt. They were embarrassed at having taken over my position, created the tree without me. They were afraid I would feel left out. Couldn't they see that for me that was part of the magic: the five-year-old child entering the room, unknowing, to be surprised by the tree Father Christmas had brought? '*Mind*?' The five-year-old's eyes were misting over. 'Belle, this is the loveliest surprise anyone has ever given me.'

'It's one of ours, of course,' said Brendan.

'Of course,' I said, smiling at his pride. Always a big man, he had taken on even more solidity with his new job. His red hair and blue eyes seemed brighter, more vivid. I could understand that. Happiness did that to people.

'Seems the old squire planted a stand of spruce years ago and then forgot about it. No thinning, no pruning, no brashing. Just abandoned the poor devils. To say the truth, we thought the lot would have to be cleared for pulp, didn't we, Davey? When we first saw them.'

We were having dinner. Melinda's cooking, always good, was heavenly after the scrappy meals I'd had in London. I was devouring my dinner like a starveling, content to let the conversation waft about me – estate talk, mostly.

'But myself and Davey took a closer look, and damned if those trees didn't start whispering among themselves. There was life in the poor things after all.'

Rhiannon's absence had diminished just a little during mine. The four of us didn't seem quite so stranded at the end of the table any more. She would have loved that tree. Most of the ornaments were antiques, some of them very old indeed. The Farleton Hall Christmas tree was always something of an event, David had told me.

'So we set about doing a belated thinning, selling off the tops as Christmas trees in Kirkby. Sure, it's a risk and all, with the rest of them exposed to the wind so sudden. Windthrow,' he explained.

I nodded sagely.

'We'll give them a couple of winters and if they're still standing, then we'll underplant.'

David had said little all evening. It was beginning to puzzle me. Normally he and Brendan chattered away about all the arcane details of the estate. Tonight Brendan was reduced to a monologue punctuated here and there by a remark from Belle.

'Beech, we're thinking,' Brendan continued. 'Beech and Douglas fir – they'll not be minding a bit of shade.'

A hint of strain had crept into the atmosphere again. I couldn't think why, unless it was Rhiannon. This was David's first Christmas without her. Perhaps Belle and Brendan were treading lightly, hoping not to stir up memories.

'Of course, we kept the best for ourselves,' said Brendan smugly.

'Of course. And it *is* a beautiful tree.'

'Myself and Davey, we're thinking that when we move up there proper, we'll look into the whole Christmas tree market. There'll be better species than Norway spruce. The market's right for a change. We could make a killing, going into pine or Noble fir.'

'The land's too wet for pine,' said David. It was practically his first utterance of the evening.

'For sure, unless we do some draining, which would be a good thing anyway. And we'll need some conifers for the good of the land – a nice sprinkling of needles to bulk up the soil texture.'

Belle had been watching me closely for some time. Now she spoke. 'You're taking it very well, Ros.'

I looked up in surprise. Needles, soil texture. 'Taking what well?'

She hesitated. 'Well, what we've done. We didn't take the decision lightly. We knew how upset you'd be. But there didn't seem any way round it.'

I put down my knife and fork and laughed. 'Belle. I thought we'd finished with that. I'm *delighted* you did the Christmas tree. Honestly I am.'

'Tree?'

There was a long silence. In it the slushy snow pattered against the curtained windows.

'Tree?' Belle repeated. She looked at David. David looked at his plate. His face was utterly miserable.

Something *was* wrong. 'David,' I said quietly. 'What is going on here?'

Silence.

I tried again. 'There's been something funny about the atmosphere from the moment I came home. What's going on?'

'Oh, David.' It was Belle. 'You haven't told her?'

Silence.

I stiffened. I still didn't suspect, but whatever was going on must be pretty serious. 'Told me what?'

Brendan groaned. 'Isn't this the nice state of affairs?'

'David,' said Belle. 'You had two hundred and thirty miles to do it.'

'Do what? Look, will someone tell me what's going on?'

Belle looked at David. He nodded. She turned to me.

'Ros, this isn't easy for me, and I can't think of any way to make it easier for you either.' She paused, took a deep breath and continued. 'Didn't you see the announcement?'

'Announcement?'

'By the gates.'

'Announcement of what? What's this all about, Belle?'

'Of the sale,' she said quietly.

I looked round, hoping for a smile which would tell me it meant nothing. 'But that's absurd,' I protested. 'There's hardly any furniture left.'

Belle shook her head. 'It's not the furniture.'

I stiffened. I tried to remember which farms were left. There weren't many. 'But no one's said a word.'

'We didn't want to . . . well, upset you. During the run. That's why. We didn't mean to go behind your back, Ros. It just seemed, well, best to . . .'

'You told me no one ever sold land,' I said accusingly to David.

The wind was rising, hurling the snow against the windows. I could hear the wind in the chimney, too. The room seemed suddenly cold, the electric sparks in my head the only oasis of warmth.

'It isn't land,' Belle said gently. 'I'm sorry, Ros.'

'Well, what else is there?' I tried. I must have suspected, but still I couldn't face it. The sparks were dying down, my head was growing as cold as the icy room.

It seemed a long time before Belle spoke again. When she did, the words were unambiguous.

'It's the house,' she said. Her voice came as from a long distance. 'I'm sorry, Ros.'

And still I tried. 'Well, damn it all!' I exploded. 'Tell them to put the fucking noticeboard where it belongs – at the lodge, not here!'

There was a stunned silence. I never swore, never used obscenities. The outburst shocked me as much as anyone else.

Belle's face was collapsing. She reached across the table and put her strong hand on mine. She held it hard. Her eyes were pleading. 'It's not the lodge. It's the house. Farleton Hall.'

We moved to the lodge at Easter. Looking back, I think that's the moment it all began: the long, slow death of our marriage. Not the move itself – by then I was too numbed to feel anything. No, it was that awful Christmas Eve when Belle's words short-circuited my life. From then on I was a zombie just going through the motions.

I'm still not sure why it felt like the end of the world for me. I honestly don't believe it was the status. I loved being the mistress of Farleton Hall, but it went much deeper than that. I loved the Hall itself, this great floating palace of light and beauty built by elves. No one could build another Farleton Hall, not with all the money in the world, not ever. There was something other-worldly about it which, when lost, would be lost for ever. Rhiannon had entrusted it to me. 'I'm glad you're marrying David,' she'd said. 'I think you have some notion of just how difficult he can be. I hope you'll be strong enough to curb some of his wilder ideas.'

I hadn't. I'd failed Rhiannon and failed Farleton Hall. She'd been explicit, too, warned me of David's passion to destroy everything his father stood for. I'd been too dazzled by love to see that the greatest of those emblems was the Hall itself. If I'd been older and wiser and less exuberantly in love, I might have read the signs. If I hadn't gone to London, I would have been there to prevent the disaster.

I still tried. From the terrible Christmas Eve right up until the moment the Hall was sold, I tried. Couldn't we sell something else? Why not sell the lodge instead?

Because no one would buy it without a huge chunk of land to go with it. We'd already lost too much land; now we would have the money to buy some of it back again.

Why did Keldreth matter so much anyway? Why not sell the lot and concentrate on the Hall and the lowland farms?

Because the public wouldn't accept turning prime farmland into forest. The whole point was to use land not fit for farming, remove the heavily subsidised hill farms from it and turn the land over to what it *was* fit for: trees.

Then let someone else do it! Sell the lodge and the derelict forest and let someone else play with it!

But that's all they would do: play. We know what needs doing. It's up to us to create a showpiece for the rest of the country.

Just who is this *we*, this *us*? Not me, that's for sure! You're lunatics, all three of you, you're all out of your minds! I feel like a warder in an insane asylum! Who do you think you are? Napoleon?

Calm down, Rosie. Let me explain.

You have explained! A thousand times! You're crazy! Hundreds of years you're destroying! A building that's irreplaceable! For what? For a bunch of goddamn trees! Anyone can plant trees! No one will ever build another Farleton Hall!

Rosie, it's not being destroyed. Someone else will take it over. They'll have the money to repair it, to look after it.

So would we if you sold that lousy dump in Keldreth!

Don't be childish, Ros. The lodge is a lovely house. You said so yourself.

I hate it! I hate it! I hate it! You're doing this just to spite me, to spite your father, to spite Rhiannon!

Rosie, that's not true, please listen to me.

I have listened! All I've heard is the babble of lunatics!

Farleton Hall was sold to a consortium. Farleton Hall was going to become Farleton Hall Hotel.

On the day the contracts were exchanged, I took the Saab and roared off. I have no idea where I went, no memory of the drive itself. All I remember is waking up and finding myself parked by the railway station in York. I sat in the car a long time, trying to remember what had happened and how I had got there. Then I tried to think where I should go.

Nowhere. There was nowhere for me to go. I'd dropped out of Cambridge. I'd given up my career. I'd abandoned my family, such as it was. I didn't even know where Jas was. I was alone again, one insignificant speck sitting in an old Saab outside York station.

That night they found me – David and Brendan and Belle, in the Land-Rover. God knows how they knew where I was. I never asked, they never explained. They took me back with them.

At Easter we moved to the lodge.

10

'Hello, Maid Marian?'

'Jas? Is that you?'

'None other. So how are things? How's your Robin Hood?'

'Jas. I demand an explanation. Where the hell are you? And where the hell have you been the last three years?'

'That long, is it?'

'Some friend you are.'

'Didn't you get my postcards?'

'What postcards?'

'All those picturesque missives recording for posterity my whirlwind tours of the world's cultural capitals.'

'Like?'

'Bromley. Basingstoke. Plymouth. Westcliff-on-Sea. No Skegness, alas. Such heights I have not yet attained.'

'Mr Molyneux. There were no postcards.'

'Ms Rawlinson. I *distinctly* remember buying those postcards.'

'And?'

'And I'm *quite* sure I wrote them out. Well, some of them.'

'And?'

'Well . . . it's not beyond the bounds of plausibility that I failed to locate a stamp merchant at the apposite moment.'

I had to laugh. It was impossible to remain angry with him for long. 'All right, forget it. So where are you now?'

'York Theatre Royal, no less. Which is the purpose of this phone call. Viz, I demand your presence at our gala opening. *Demand*, you hear?'

'Jas, that's marvellous! What's the play?'

'A whole season's worth, dear heart. The one in question being *Death of a Salesman*, with yours truly the eponymous.'

'That *is* wonderful! You really are doing well!'

'Kind of you to say, my dear. Given that the elusive RSC continues to elude.'

'In good time. I'm sure it'll happen.'

'Goddammit, Rosie, it's marvellous to hear you again! I've missed you terribly!'

'I've missed you too, Jas.' More than I dared admit. The past was rolling back to meet me across miles of telephone wire. 'But how did you know where I was?'

'There. You admit. You, too, have been remiss. Or don't they have postcards in Sherwood Forest?'

'Not a lot. Well?'

'I phoned your erstwhile home and demanded to speak to the lady of the manor. Some little snip informed me that you and your merry band had fled to the hills where you were engaged in robbing friars and donating the loot to Friends of the Hedgehog.'

'I'm sure the receptionist didn't say that.'

'In words less colourful, perhaps.' Pause. 'What *are* you doing up there?'

What indeed? I'd tried so hard, in the last three years, to put meaning back into my life. And in one brief phone call, Jas had ripped through my achievements and emptied it again. It wasn't his fault. It was mine.

It had taken me a long time to get over the shock of loss. Farleton Hall was now a thriving country hotel, but as far as I was concerned it was as thoroughly annihilated as if a fire had raged through it and reduced it to a mocking black skeleton. It was a skeleton, a corpse, and with its death something had died in me, too.

But I couldn't mourn for ever. All around me was a whirl of activity with myself the dead centre, exuding dissatisfaction. And so I'd picked myself up and invented a purpose. The land was David and Brendan's, the garden and kitchen were Belle's. That left me the rest of the house. I'd made an inventory of the crazy rooms and their even crazier furnishings. Then I'd set about restoring the lot. I'd had to force myself at first, working against my resentment that it wasn't Farleton Hall. But it was a charming house, an endearing muddle. It wasn't its fault that I couldn't love it.

And then the miracle had happened. I remember the moment precisely. I was in the Tudor Room, a big round one in the south-east tower. From it rose a circular staircase to a sleeping balcony above. I was on that balcony when David wandered in. I watched him look round, glance through a window and prepare to go. Then I spoke.

'Oh David, David, wherefore art thou David?'

His head jerked round and then up. Something in my voice must have alerted him that change was in the air. He smiled uncertainly. There was hope in his eyes. 'I'm afraid I don't know the next lines,' he said, a little anxiously.

'That's all right. Neither do I. But it is like a stage set, isn't it? All we need is a rickety ladder for Romeo instead of the stairs.'

'I suppose so,' he said slowly. Then, 'Ros, if you need money – you know, for doing up the rooms – it's all right, it's there.'

It was there because he'd sold Farleton Hall. But for the first time I felt the bitterness diminish a little. Poor David. He was trying. Up until then he'd resented spending anything on the house; everything went into the land, the trees. He looked so touching, standing down there in the big dusty room, his face upturned in hope. I remembered the night I'd sobbed myself silly because David could never love me, never want me. He'd come to me then and we'd whispered absurdities to each other and his face had taken on that frighteningly vulnerable look of hope and he'd said, 'Tell me, Rosie, fast, don't leave me longing and hoping if there's nothing to hope for.'

'David,' I said now, quickly, without thinking, 'I'm sorry I've been such a bitch. I think it'll be all right now. Don't you think?'

Again that uncertain smile. 'I'm sorry, too, Rosie. It's not your fault. I've been clumsy. Do you think . . . ?' He trailed off.

I smiled. 'I think we've had enough sorries. I think it's time to wipe the slate clean. What do you think?'

He was up the stairs in an amazingly short time.

From then on everything had changed. I stopped resenting the lodge, began to see it as a big rambling theatre, each room a different stage set, myself the stage designer. The restoration of the house which had begun simply as a project to pass the time now became my own obsession. And just as David's obsession with his forest was beginning to show results, so was mine with the house.

And now Jas, innocently dancing through my life again and with his light leprechaun words exposing the futility of my achievement.

I rose heavily from the kitchen chair and went through the rooms. It was nearly finished, my work. Each room was a jewel. Each room gleamed with polish and fresh paint, glowed with the vibrant colours of newly washed curtains, newly cleaned upholstery and rugs.

And each room was empty. We had no visitors, no one to open the door and exclaim in delight at what I had done. No one to sleep in the beds or finger approvingly a new lampshade or a cushion cover. The very thought of a visitor sent David into a sulk. Already the people of Kirkby Langham viewed us with suspicion.

We were starting to buy up parcels of farmland and turn it over to trees. The locals were outraged. Centuries of tradition gone just like that. I tried to explain. The land wasn't fit for farming, I said; it never had been. It had only survived because of massive public subsidies to hill farmers. It was time now to acknowledge nature's wisdom and return the land to the one thing it *was* fit for: trees.

No one wanted to hear and I soon stopped trying to make them listen. I also stopped trying to persuade David to open up the lodge for public functions.

'What do we want with a load of strangers poking their noses into our business?'

'They're not strangers, David. They're locals. You have some responsibility towards them. For centuries your family –'

'Spare me the heritage speech. I've done with that.'

And so the rooms stood empty, and with them myself, empty also. What had been the point of all this work if nobody used the rooms? I'd wanted to bring life and laughter back to Farleton Hall and I'd failed. Then I'd tried to bring the lodge back to life and failed again. My life had no purpose.

Somewhere down there in York, no doubt in one of the ubiquitous church halls used as rehearsal rooms, Jas and the others were huddled over their scripts, full of crazy hope and the touching arrogance of actors in search of the perfect performance. They would sweat over that text for weeks. At the end they would present their gift to the public. It wouldn't be perfect; it never was. In the audience even younger actors would be thinking: when I have the chance, I'll do it differently, better. And on it would go, the search for the impossible. The eternal poignant story of man trying to be god. Failing. Trying again. But they didn't fail, not like I had failed. However imperfect their performance, there would always be a few people it touched with magic, transforming their lives and giving the lives of the actors themselves a purpose.

I sank to the floor in the Scheherazade Room and wept.

I hugged the bony body I'd hugged so often before. 'Jas, you were marvellous! You really were! The RSC don't know what they're missing!'

'Yes, they do,' he said crossly. 'I've told them dozens of times.'

'Never mind – it'll come.'

'Humph.'

'And stop sulking. You've done bloody well – you haven't been out of work once in all these years.'

'True,' he smirked. 'I am bloody marvellous.' Then he

held me at arms' length – literally – and peered at me. 'And how about you, my Roslein? How is that bandit treating you?' He scowled through his bushy black eyebrows. 'Thin. You're too thin.'

I snorted. 'I've always been thin. I was born thin. Stop grizzling and come out and see him – he's in the lobby with Brendan and Belle.'

'Don't want to.'

'Why, Jas, I do believe you're jealous.'

'Of course I am. You're mine. I found you first.'

'If you don't make your peace with David, I'll never come and see you again.'

'You rotten little blackmailer.'

David was charming to Jas. Sometimes I forgot just how charming he could be when he didn't feel threatened by disapproving locals. We walked through the narrow streets en route to the first-night party. There were cars everywhere, taking their owners home from a night out at the theatre or a concert or a meal in some restaurant. Cars and lights and people all over the place, laughing and arguing and just being alive. I was surprised to see how much I'd missed urban life. I remembered the night after that ADC opening, when the five of us had walked through the streets of Cambridge on our way to another party. How much had changed since then.

The party was marvellous. Although I didn't know anyone except Jas, within minutes of our arrival I was moving happily among the other actors and talking shop. It was startling how quickly it all came back – the familiar patter, the terminology, the references to other plays, the exaggerated gestures and tone of voice. In a sense, I *did* know these people. They were my kind.

And when Jas introduced me to the director, I felt perfectly at home with him. Until Jas, apropos of nothing, suddenly said, 'Rosie's going to audition for us next autumn, aren't you, Rosie?'

11

'I don't like auditions. Auditions are humiliating.'

'So? What's an actor's life if not one long humiliation?'

'Exactly. I don't want to be one.'

'Yes, you do. You don't fool me.'

'I'm only doing this to humour you, Jas.'

'Okay. Humour me through this door and into this waiting-room.'

I sat down, majestic in my grumpiness. Two dozen other hopefuls eyed me suspiciously. They looked terrified. I felt terrified. Ridiculous, I told myself. I don't even want the job. Jas sat down beside me. I was the only accompanied person there. I felt like a lunatic with her keeper.

A door opened and a name was called out. Its owner shot to her feet and, face blanched, lurched into the room beyond. The door closed behind her.

'I could be doing some shopping,' I said irritably. 'Or having a peaceful sit in the Minster. How long am I going to have to hang around here?'

'Not very. Your CV may be small but it's spectacular. A West End lead. Not to mention those fabulous reviews.'

I waited. After several years, the door opened again and another name was called. Either there was another exit or the previous girl had been eaten by a minotaur within. Or by the auditioners. The woman calling the names caught sight of Jas and grinned.

'Who she?' I whispered when the door had closed behind her.

'Assistant stage manager,' he whispered back. He waggled his eyebrows. 'How much you want to bet you're called next?'

'I see. You've been pulling strings.'

'A tiny one. What are friends for?'

Sure enough, the next name was mine.

I entered a long room. At one end was a trestle table shrouded in gloom. At it sat several people – including, I [illegible] the director I'd met at Jas's first night.

[illegible] of the shapes at the table stirred. 'Well, what have you got for us?'

'Lady Macbeth,' I said. 'The sleepwalking scene.'

'Rather premature, don't you think?' said a dry voice.

My face reddened. I would kill Jas. I didn't need to subject myself to this.

A scrap of tired laughter. Then, 'In your own time,' a voice drawled.

I went to the other end of the room. I'd already lost the job through hubris. Lady Macbeth: the ultimate goal of every actress. And I had dragged her into a tawdry audition. I deserved the curse which accompanied the play. Why hadn't I chosen something less obvious? Too late now.

A filthy skylight illuminated me. I shut my eyes, tried my best to imagine myself into an unimaginable situation, then opened them and began. 'Yet here's a spot.' God, were there ever words so trite? 'Out, damned spot! Out, I say!' The horrid voice which waits in ambush inside every actor whispered 'Try Persil.' I stiffled a giggle. That's all I needed – to corpse at the start of an audition. I pulled myself together. 'One: two: why, then, 'tis time to do't.' On it droned. What had happened to the marvellous speech? How had words so ringing turned to dough in my throat?

The speech limped on to a dead close. I announced my second speech – Elvira from *Blithe Spirit*. Thirty seconds into it a voice from the other end of the room stopped me. 'Try it as if it were Lady Macbeth.'

I stared into the gloom, incredulous. 'I beg your pardon?'

'All right, Edward Heath then.'

'Imitations aren't my strong point.'

'Any way you like. Just differently.'

I started again. I sounded like Ros Rawlinson playing Elvira. At the end a tired voice said, 'Very interesting, thank you.'

The assistant stage manager directed me through another door. Outside Jas was waiting. I tried to smile. 'I'm sorry. A total balls-up.'

'Bet it wasn't.'

'I wouldn't mind for myself – I don't even want the job. But you probably gave them a hyped-up spiel and now they'll think the worse of you. Oh, Jas, I really am sorry.'

'Don't be so sure. These guys are shrewder than you think. Come on, let's have a coffee. Then we can sit in the Minster if that's your heart's desire.'

I looked at the letter. They must have made a mistake. They'd turned over two papers at once and typed out the wrong name. I picked up the phone.

'Jas, I think there's been a mistake. They've offered me a year's contract.'

'Of course they have.'

'There's no of course about it. I gave a crappy audition. They've typed out the wrong name.'

'Birdbrain. Look, I hate to puff up your ego but I should remind you that you're rather a brilliant actress.'

'Jas, that audition –'

'Do I have to spell it out? Ros Rawlinson on an off-day is still several megawatts above the nearest competition acting their hearts out. All right?'

'Your faith astounds me.'

'Not faith, dumbbell. Judgment. When do they want you to start?'

I told him.

'Great! See you then!'

Whoever the grey spectres of the trestle table were, they vanished as soon as I joined the company. I was surrounded by warmth, excitement and love. I felt like the prodigal daughter being welcomed back into the fold.

Life in rep was hectic and made even more difficult by the distance between my moorland eyrie and York, but I never felt tired. I had limitless energy. Not all of it went into the acting. There was plenty to spare when I got home and chattered to the others about the day's events. Perhaps I hadn't failed after all; the lodge *was* coming to life. True, most of the rooms still stood empty, but those we used were now crackling with life, each of us contributing.

Why hadn't I thought of York sooner? All those years I'd wasted, with a perfectly good rep on the doorstep. Well, a rather distant doorstep, but not impossible. Why on earth *shouldn't* I have a career, based on the reps within reasonable distance from the lodge? All right, so it wasn't the West End or the National or the RSC. So what? I was giving pleasure, doing what I was intended to do. At last my life had a purpose, and I think even David agreed it was a purpose as valuable in its own way as the work he was doing on the land.

It was a joyous year, in many ways a repeat of that happy year in Cambridge. Here, too, I had to prove myself, working my way up through a series of minor roles until I landed the plum of Lady Mary in *The Admirable Crichton*. What a wonderful role! Three completely different identities within the scope of a single play: the indolent snob of Act One, the tomboy on the island, and finally the mature woman who ends the play. The director was well pleased with my transformations. I didn't have the heart to tell him how easy it was.

The director wasn't the only one. The critics were well pleased, too. So were the audiences. The play became a smash hit, each night attracting people from further and further away. Once again there was talk of a West End transfer. I didn't care. I was simply enjoying myself. I didn't even want it to transfer. London had lost its appeal. I couldn't bear to leave David again, live the dreary bedsit life as I had for *As You Like It*. No, York suited me just fine. All I wanted was enough success to ensure a welcome from every rep in the north, and of that there was now no doubt. Already I was signed on for a second year at York – this time with no audition.

It might have happened, too, just as I planned it, if our run had been just a week or two earlier, a week or two later. If a London agent hadn't been travelling through just then. If he hadn't bought that newspaper, hadn't glanced at that particular review. If my name, a name he knew, hadn't been so prominent in it. If, if, if. If a hundred little ifs hadn't happened, my whole life would have been different.

Last night – of the play, of the season. Somewhere in York a big party was brewing. Somewhere else – backstage at the Theatre Royal – a series of mini-parties was preceding it, each dressing-room crammed with friends in no hurry to leave. Lady Mary was dividing her attention between her dressing-table, where she was trying to wipe the remnants of Lady Mary off her face, and her well-wishers who insisted on hugging and kissing her and telling her she was the greatest actress since Judi Dench, since Peggy Ashcroft, since Sarah Bernhardt, since –

'Flattery!' I laughed, taking another swipe at my make-up as Jas sailed in, fresh from his own mini-party in the dressing-room next door.

'Nay, do not think I flatter,' he quoted. 'For what advancement may I hope from thee, that no revenue hast, but thy good spirits?'

'What really flatters a man is that you think him worth flattering,' I quoted back at him.

The room which seemed filled to capacity was filling up further. How had I come to know so many people in just a year? Friends of the other actors had become my friends too, popping round from someone else's dressing-room to add their congratulations. Jas frowned as a particularly fat man – an uncle of our 'Crichton' – squeezed through the doorway. Jas signalled should he shut the door? I shook my head; the room was stifling.

If I'd let him shut the door would it have happened?

This time I didn't see him enter, my golden stag. But I

knew without thinking that he was there. I had my back turned, talking to David, when I felt the heat. Just as in the clearing in the forest. Just as in my nightmare before going to London. Just as in the dressing-room of the Fortune. I'd barely given him a thought since then, but now the years between seemed to shrink and I knew precisely what I would see if I turned round. I resisted. I didn't know who or what he was, only that three times he had come to me and each time I had felt the heat he radiated as something ominous. I will not turn round. I will not look at you.

I turned round and looked.

He was standing right in front of me, his golden eyes compelling mine to meet his. I shut my own in terror but too late. Behind my darkened lids the face glowed on, bringing with it the memory of the nightmare, that awful moment when the golden stag had taken on a man's face.

It was the same face.

The room had gone silent. I opened my eyes and saw nothing, just a burning golden circle as if I were looking into the sun. And then two voices. The first was Jas, anxious: 'Rosie, are you all right?' The second, a stranger's, deep and burnished like the sightless vista spread before me: 'Come to me when you're ready.'

I don't remember what happened after that, only that the intense heat vanished as suddenly as the golden glow and as suddenly as most of the people who'd crowded my dressing-room. I was standing in the centre of a room miraculously emptied of all but David, Brendan, Belle and Jas.

I shook my head to clear the remnants of the vision. Then I raised my hand – intending, I think, to brush the hair from my face, which was drenched in sweat. But there was something in my hand. I looked at it, surprised. It was a card, cream-coloured with gold lettering.

Jas took it from me and read it. He stared at the card, then at the empty doorway, then at me. 'Good God,' he said, his voice incredulous. He sat down abruptly, handing back the card. 'Well, well, well.' Then he smiled and studied my face as if he were seeing it for the first time. 'Well, well, well,' he repeated. 'I knew you were good, but even I never suspected . . .' He trailed off.

'Suspected what?' said David.

'So that was Hanno Hirsch,' Ja[illegible] said softly, then smiled at me again. 'Rosie, old girl, you've made it.'

12

'So who *is* Hanno Hirsch?' Hugh asked.

I turned to him gratefully. At last a topic of conversation that wouldn't have David and Hugh at each other's throats. The reconciliation I'd worked so hard to bring about was going disastrously wrong. What's more, it was ruining Belle's dinner. 'An actors' agent,' I explained. It wasn't a subject I would have chosen – even now, a year after that uncanny encounter in my dressing-room, my stomach lurched when I thought about him – but I couldn't afford to be fussy. I had to save this celebratory dinner somehow.

'So?' said Hugh. 'There must be hundreds. What's so special about this one?'

Belle came to the rescue, leaving me to quell my stomach in peace. 'He's rather mysterious,' she said. 'No one knows who he is. He avoids people.'

'In that profession?'

'Exactly. That's what's so uncanny about him. Most agents cultivate contacts. Hirsch locks himself in his office and lets the world come to him. Not very much of the world at that. The only people who've met him are his clients and a handful of the best directors and producers in the country.'

'So what's his secret?'

Belle laughed. 'Ah, well, rumour has it that he's made a pact with the devil.'

A forkful of venison stopped midway to Hugh's mouth. 'You're joking.'

'Well . . .' said Belle. 'No one's come up with a better explanation.'

I shivered. In the last year, I'd tried often enough to

come up with an explanation myself – not for his success but for the strange effect he'd had on me. The disturbing thing was that I'd felt it long before knowing who he was; otherwise I could have dismissed it as an unconscious response to the rumour. Not that that would have explained the other thing: the terrifying resemblance between Hanno Hirsch and the golden stag of my nightmare. I hadn't told anyone about that. I certainly didn't intend to now.

'But what does he do?' asked Astrid, Hugh's wife.

'Makes a star out of every single one of his clients,' said Belle.

Astrid's eyes opened wide. 'Every one?'

'Without exception,' said Belle.

'Some people just have an instinct,' I said. I had a vested interest in de-mystifying Hanno Hirsch.

'Sure,' said Belle. 'But a hundred per cent?'

'I expect no one hears about the failures, that's all,' said David. He'd hardly spoken during the meal. The sound of his voice, so matter-of-fact, was reassuring.

'I'm sure you're right,' I said. 'After all, if no one meets him, how can anyone know? He might have a whole string of failures on his cards.'

Belle shook her head. 'Not according to his ex-secretary. She's seen the files.'

'Ex?'

'She left – couldn't stick the atmosphere. She's the main source of what little is known about him.'

'Not very reliable,' I suggested. 'Probably an angry ex-mistress.'

Belle shook her head. 'Apparently he lives like a monk.'

'So how does he find his clients?' Hugh asked. 'If he never goes out?'

'Oh, he goes out,' said Belle. 'Just not very often, and then always to the right place. He seems to know exactly where a potential client is going to be. He slips into the theatre unnoticed. Then, if he likes what he sees, one of his calling cards turns up in the dressing-room.'

I shivered again, remembering the mysterious calling card at the Fortune Theatre all those years ago. I'd torn it up in indignation. And in ignorance. If I'd known then, if I'd responded, how different my life would have been. I was glad I hadn't known.

'And The Chosen One glides off to his office, never to be seen again?' Hugh smiled.

'Oh, they're seen again,' Belle laughed. 'Everywhere! That's the point. He doesn't take them on unless he's sure he can make them into stars.'

'Surely his clients talk about him?' Hugh persisted.

'Apparently not. I don't know if it's a part of their contract or what, but they never talk. Never.'

'But other people know they're his clients?'

'Oh, yes. And it gives them a sort of aura.' Belle laughed. 'I don't mean a supernatural one, just that everyone treats them as future stars. Which they become.'

'There you are,' said David. 'Self-fulfilling prophecy. There's nothing mysterious about it after all.'

Belle turned to him. 'But they're good – really good. And he sees it before anyone else.'

'Indeed and he doesn't!' said Brendan indignantly. 'Any fool could see our Rosie was good way back at the ADC. And how long ago was that, I'd like to know? It looks to me your devil's darling took his sweet time to discover her.'

I cleared my throat. 'Well, actually, he didn't.'

Everyone stared.

'Actually . . .' Why did I feel like a silly schoolgirl about to make a confession? 'As a matter of fact, one of those calling cards turned up at the Fortune.'

Silence. Then, 'The what was that?' said Brendan softly.

Belle was still staring at me. 'Ros, are you telling me you actually had one of his cards *before*? And you did nothing about it?'

'Well, actually, I tore it up.'

'You *what*?'

'Well, I didn't know who he was, did I? I thought he

was just some rich playboy looking to the chorus line for a bit of fun.'

'Jesu,' said Brendan. 'Now *there's* a story to add to the myth! One to our Rosie!' he laughed.

Belle wasn't laughing. 'I don't believe I'm hearing this. *You tore up his card?* Ros, do you realise? You could be top billing at the National or the RSC by now. All these years! If only we'd known!'

'We've been through this before: I can't possibly be an actress in London and a wife in Yorkshire.'

Hugh laughed. 'Surely El Diabolo can manage something as trifling as that. You know – magic carpet. Helicopter at least.'

'Don't be ridiculous,' said David. He was sounding irritable again.

As always, Belle to the rescue. 'Just one thing, Ros. *When* did you get that first card? Which part of the run?'

'First night.'

'You see?' said Belle triumphantly. 'How did he know to turn up at the first night before the reviews? Unless he'd been to the ADC. Which then begs the question of how he knew to turn up at a student production. You see? He's got some kind of inside information.'

'There you are,' said David. 'Inside information. There's nothing mysterious about that either.'

'But why doesn't everyone have it?' Belle persisted. 'What's more, he's always had it – even before he had time to build up any secret network of contacts.'

'How long?' asked Astrid.

'About ten years,' said Belle. 'He just arrived from nowhere. Two years later his list of clients had everyone reeling.'

'He must have been terribly young when he started,' I said. 'He didn't look all that old to me last year. Maybe thirty-five?'

Belle nodded. '*Wunderkind*, they called him. Even now.'

'He is German?' Astrid asked.

'No one knows that either.' Belle turned to me. 'Did

he have an accent, Ros? Do you remember? He did say something to you, didn't he?'

Come to me when you're ready. The words were branded on my memory, and yet, when I tried to conjure up that moment, it twisted from my grasp, melted away like a wisp of smoke. I could remember no accent, not even remember *hearing* the words, as if they'd been conveyed by some other means. Perhaps he hadn't spoken at all, perhaps I'd just imagined it.

I shook my head. 'I can't remember.'

'Good,' said David. 'Then we can drop the subject.'

Hanno Hirsch wasn't the only subject that had to be dropped during that awful visit by Hugh and Astrid, and it was all my fault. I'd played the Pollyanna, tried to bring about a reconciliation between David and Hugh without understanding the strength of the antagonism. They'd always been opposites, hating each other as much as they hated their father.

Hugh had been abroad when Rhiannon died. We'd tried to locate him in time for the funeral but failed. When finally he returned, he refused to believe how hard we'd tried to find him. As for our wedding, it had been so low-key and so soon after the funeral that we didn't invite anyone at all.

I should have left well enough alone, but working with the rep in York had revived my confidence. I was bursting with happiness and love. I couldn't believe the rest of the world didn't feel what I felt. Surely David and Hugh would love each other, too, if only they were brought together again in the right atmosphere?

During my second year at York, I wrote to him on impulse, inviting him to the lodge. His reply was brief, polite and negative. Then, a few months later, I learned that he had married – a Swedish pianist called Astrid. Taking a deep breath, I wrote again, this time to her.

Her reply was a delight, full of warmth and idiosyncratic English. We agreed that the brotherly estrangement was ridiculous. We agreed that two sensible women like us were just the people to bring about a reconciliation. 'Leave this on me,' she wrote. 'Hugh will come. I promise this!'

Come he did, along with his splendid wife, the summer my second season at York ended. The initial signs were good: the weather gorgeous, the lodge smiling in the sun, welcoming. As for Astrid, it was love at first sight for us all. No one could resist Astrid, no one. She was, like Belle, a large woman, every inch of her exuding goodwill. Strangely for a Swede, she was very dark, almost Slavic in appearance, with dark hair pulled smoothly into a knot from a centre parting which left her broad beautiful face free from clutter. Her eyes were large and black and luminous, her cheekbones high, all her features big and strong and certain. Even when serious there seemed to be an eternal smile lurking just beneath the surface, waiting to come out again. When it did, it dazzled. I adored her. Belle adored her. Brendan was wild about her. Even dour David succumbed. Not since the early days of our marriage had I seen him so relaxed and animated. Astrid was magic. As soon as she arrived, I wished I could keep her here with us for ever.

And Hugh? At first meeting, he was as delightful as his wife, though in a totally different way. Hugh was as fair as Astrid was dark, as thin as she was broad. He was tall and willowy, his body so flexible that he seemed to bend with every breeze, an odd little bobbing effect with a hint of the courtly bow. He was the more obvious heir to the estate. Rhiannon had thought so, too. Her words came back to me. *It's a pity that Hugh wasn't the elder. He cares much more about his heritage.* He even looked like his heritage, his features, like his body, all long and thin and stamped with the ancient line. Unlike Astrid, when he was serious he was very serious, with no hint of a lurking smile. His face then was almost frightening in its austerity. But when he smiled, as he did often in those first few hours, he had an impish, almost frivolous, charm.

'Ah, so *this* is the fair lady who has brought our wooden brother to life! Pygmalion in reverse, with Galatea breathing life into her creator! I like it, I do indeed! And such a lovely Galatea, too!'

I laughed. 'Wood is a living material, and warm. Not like the cold marble poor Pygmalion had to work with.'

'And wits about her, too!' he said in a mock aside to Astrid.

The aside, so like those in Shakespeare, made me feel at home. Very likely Hugh was a frustrated actor. How could I not warm to him? And how could David be so immune to his good nature?

David and Brendan were absent at the arrival. We'd had a row about it. There was some brashing that needed doing, David said. He couldn't neglect his work, hang about for an arrival which could be delayed for hours. Brendan tried to argue, but on occasions like this David's aristocratic arrogance came into play, silencing poor Brendan.

I put Astrid and Hugh in the Queen Anne Room. It was exquisite, right down to the graceful desk by the equally graceful sash windows I'd so lovingly restored. Astrid clapped her hands in delight. 'But so beautiful?' she exclaimed, her Swedish lilt tweaking her sentences up at the end, turning everything into a question.

Belle and I showed them the rest of the house. Astrid's joy seemed limitless, her exclamations more and more exuberant. So much so that it took me a while to notice that as Astrid's enthusiasm grew, Hugh's diminished.

'An amusing little house,' he said at the end, making one of his bobbing bows in my direction. 'And what wonders you've done with it. Considering.'

Considering?

'Ah, but Astrid, if you'd seen Farleton Hall! It was magnificent! Wasn't it, Ros?'

I nodded, despite some unease.

'But two houses is so silly, yes?' said Astrid winningly.

'But why did he have to choose this one?' Hugh turned to me again, suddenly earnest and rather forbidding. 'He could so easily have sold this one instead. Couldn't he,

Ros? A foolish bauble on the edge of these godforsaken moors. Madness, madness!'

He'd put me in an awkward position, inviting me to ally myself with him against David.

I think Belle sensed this. 'Come and see the stables,' she said.

The stables had been designed as a Greek temple: light, airy and full of the peacefulness characteristic of classical architecture. Like Farleton Hall.

'Like Farleton Hall,' said Hugh wistfully. 'Wasted on horses, don't you think?'

'Oh, I don't know,' I said. 'I rather like it.'

'Folly,' Hugh muttered. 'That's all it was meant to be. The Farletons, reduced to living in a folly.'

I winced. Some of the locals down in Kirkby had started to call it 'The Folly'. They meant, of course, our activities: turning farmland over to trees. But one or two remembered that the lodge had been built as a folly. It was a sore point with David. I hoped Hugh wouldn't use the word while David was present.

'This is our latest project,' said Belle, yet again changing the subject. 'We're buying a pair of heavy horses for timber extraction.'

Hugh's face twisted in a little moue. 'At least Mad William had *real* horses.'

'They're rather beautiful,' I said defensively. 'The Shires. I went with David to see some of them. I don't think they'll disgrace the stables.'

'You have a generous soul, dear lady,' he smiled.

'Not really. Just an open mind.'

'Touché!'

I laughed despite my annoyance, confused by the succession of reactions Hugh produced in me. Hugh wasn't nearly as malleable as I'd hoped. As for David, he was the most stubborn person I'd ever known. The signs which had at first seemed so hopeful were changing fast.

As we walked across the cobbled courtyard back to the house, Astrid and I lagged behind. She raised a dark eyebrow. 'We have the work cut out with us?' she said ruefully.

'We do indeed,' I replied grimly.

It was a ghastly weekend. All we could do was connive to keep the two brothers apart as much as possible. When they were together, no subject was safe. Even the weather, time-honoured trivialiser of conversation.

'Ah, those misty summer dawns,' said Hugh, long after dawn when we were breakfasting together. 'Do you remember them, Ros? Were you there' – 'there' being, as always, Farleton Hall – 'long enough to experience them? Exquisite!'

David shovelled a forkful of bacon into his mouth. 'You were never up that early.'

'And you were,' said Hugh. 'Virtuous as ever.' He smiled at me. 'I've never understood the virtue of early rising. In your profession, of course, it's quite impossible.'

Another occasion. Evening. Astrid playing the sturdy upright piano in the library we used as our living-room. Clever Astrid, knowing that conversation would be rude during her performance. After all, she was a professional, well worth listening to. Bar after bar of Chopin rippled up from the modest piano, entwining us all in its magic. Peace at last. Until a break between two Études.

Hugh: 'Lovely, my dear. Only you could make a piano like that purr.' He turned innocently to David. 'Whatever happened to that marvellous old Bechstein at the Hall?'

David (non-committal): 'I presume it's still there.'

Hugh (feigning astonishment): 'Dear oh dear! I suppose the pub pianist, or whatever they call themselves, tinkles his little tunes while the patrons stuff their faces. "Rose Marie" with your lamb chops.' He laughed. No one else did. He turned to me. 'Mother used to play it at Christmas – not as well as Astrid, of course, but tolerably. Christmas carols. Lovely big party, all the tenants and staff. Wonderful occasions. Wonderful.'

David (pointedly): 'Quite. Mother was no snob.'

Hugh (ditto): 'She didn't need to be; she had taste.'

Astrid announced her next piece. It opened with a loud flourish, drowning out whatever Hugh said next. My jewel of a sister-in-law.

But nothing could reprieve us for long. Over and over Hugh returned to his memories of Farleton Hall. So I was almost relieved when, during our last evening together, the subject of Hanno Hirsch was raised. At least he had no connection with Farleton Hall. Even Hugh couldn't manufacture one.

My relief didn't last long.

'How devoted you must be to this place,' said Hugh. 'To give up your career for it.'

We were having coffee in the library. 'I do believe in what we're doing here, yes. But I haven't given up my career.'

Hugh's smile was patronising. 'Provincial rep.'

'Some of the best stuff in the country comes out of provincial rep,' I said evenly.

'Yes. Comes out of. And goes to London. Say what you like about decentralisation, my dear, anything of real value finds its way to London sooner or later.'

'Ros doesn't have to prove her value,' said David. His voice was quiet, ominous.

'You mean,' said Hugh, 'that you don't want her to.'

'Rosie has been to London,' said Brendan. 'And come back.'

'A student production,' said Hugh. 'A transfer. One of those flukes – they happen from time to time.'

'It wasn't a fluke,' said Belle. 'Hanno Hirsch wouldn't have given her his card.'

'Ah, but that was a year ago. What would happen if you turned up at his office tomorrow?' he said to me. 'Would he remember?'

'He gave me his card twice,' I reminded him. 'I think he would remember.' Fatal, the pride of an actress.

Hugh's face brightened as if he'd just solved the world's problems. 'Well, then,' he smiled, raising his hands, 'come back with us to London! Confront the great Hanno Hirsch!'

I stared at Hugh. We all stared at Hugh.

'There's nothing to prevent, is there?' he asked innocently.

'But I don't want to go to London. I've done it, remember? I'm happy at York. I'm happy here.'

'Well, of course I realise that our modest house in Islington can't compare, but really, the flat upstairs is quite sweet and just longing to be used, isn't it, Astrid?' He turned to her before anyone could raise an objection. 'Don't you agree, my love?'

Astrid looked confused. However slow her English, she had a quick mind. She must have sensed that Hugh's hospitality was suspect, a means to sow discord between David and myself. 'But of course Ros must be free always to use the flat, and also everyone else! But also the rest of the house. You must come for visiting often!'

'I meant,' said Hugh patiently, 'that Ros should *live* in the flat for a while. Have a whirl at the big time. Put Herr Hirsch to the test.'

By now I had some inkling of what he was up to. 'I'm quite contented where I am,' I smiled. 'But thank you for the invitation.'

'Contented,' Hugh scoffed. 'Cows are contented. An actress of your calibre can't possibly be contented in a place like this. Unless,' he suggested, 'there's something else preventing you?'

'Well, I am married to David,' I pointed out. 'By and large, husbands and wives do live together.'

'Ah,' said Hugh. He turned sharply to David. 'So you're the impediment.'

David glared at his brother. 'Ros is free to come and go as she pleases.'

'Is she?' said Hugh.

'Of course I am. Now, can we please just drop the subject?'

But he didn't drop the subject. He kept returning to it, over and over, like a dog worrying a bone. By the end of the evening he'd manipulated us all into a corner from which the only escape was my acquiescence.

'All right,' I said at last, exhausted. 'I'll go to London for a week or two. Will that satisfy everybody?'

It wasn't a bad idea. I could take in a few plays and concerts, do a bit of shopping. As it happened, Astrid had a recital coming up. I could time my visit to coincide.

'And you'll meet Hanno Hirsch,' said Belle. 'And tell us all about it.'

And yes: curiosity. After all I'd heard about him, how could I not be curious?

Even so, I probably wouldn't have gone if David hadn't been so indifferent. Probably it was a mask, put on to show Hugh that he wasn't interfering with my freedom. But it hurt a little, none the less. If only he'd said, 'I'd rather you didn't go, Ros.' If only he'd said, 'Stay here with us, Ros; this is where you belong.' That's all I ever wanted: to belong. If only he'd come with me, made it a fortnight's holiday for the two of us. If only, if only.

13

It was raining in Wigmore Street, but the brass name-plate glowed with the light of a sun I hadn't seen since my arrival in London. The building was plain, dignified, anonymous. The street, though in the heart of the city, felt strangely deserted except for the traffic. No tourists seemed to make their way here. Well, there wasn't much for them: just offices, a few shops and, a little way down the street, the Wigmore Hall, its quaint canopy stretching out over the pavement. An odd address for an actors' agent.

Inside, the dark stairs gradually brightened, lit by a skylight, as I climbed to the top floor. Another brass plate, right at the end. The end of the line; all passengers alight. I stifled a nervous laugh. Then I breathed deeply and tried to regain control. Don't be ridiculous. You don't even want to be his client. You're only curious. You have his card; this is a rare opportunity to peer at the phenomenon, the *Wunderkind*, the *Teufelskind*. The devil's child. Will he have horns? Another nervous laugh. Oh for heaven's sake, just go in and see.

The outer office was light and airy, no hint of diabolical flames. A jar of freesias stood on the desk. Behind it sat the secretary, a plump matronly woman with neat grey hair. Someone's granny, and a friendly one at that. She smiled encouragingly. The last whiff of sulphur vanished.

'I have an appointment with Mr Hirsch,' I said. 'Ros Rawlinson.'

'Ah, yes. Do sit down, please.'

I sat in the elegant but comfortable chair indicated. She rang through. Then she turned to me and smiled again. 'Mr Hirsch is on the telephone. He won't be long.'

I tried to imagine the 'atmosphere' which had made the previous secretary flee. Hard to believe. There were prints on the walls: good ones, reproductions of paintings by Chagall, Kandinski, Klee. Nothing particularly ominous. I riffled through the magazines on the low table by the chair. All the usual trade stuff: *Plays & Players*, *Drama*, *Plays International*, *The Stage & Television Today*. Nothing out of the ordinary here either. True, scattered among them were some less expected magazines: *Times Literary Supplement*, *Opera*, *Musical Times*, catalogues from recent art exhibitions. A little unusual but hardly alarming. Altogether a pleasing office, a nice mix of the brisk and the homely.

I picked up a copy of *Drama* and began to flick through it. A door clicked open. I looked up. Hanno Hirsch was outlined in the doorway. Smiling. 'Miss Rawlinson. I'm so pleased you could come.'

I rose from my chair and went to meet him. He shook my hand and ushered me into the inner office. Devil's child? He could hardly be more charming. But then, devils were, weren't they?

His office was even more light and airy than the outer one. Two large windows looked across Wigmore Street and flooded the room with (though reason told me I must be wrong) sunshine. The walls were the colour of fresh cream, the carpet a slightly darker shade of the same. There were prints here, too: on one wall a large Klimt, on another a Rouault glowing like a secular stained glass window. There was a large pale oak desk which had obviously come from an antique shop rather than an office supply catalogue. At one end of the room were two comfortable chairs matching those in the outer office and flanking a low table on which stood an abstract sculpture. Hanno Hirsch indicated one chair, sat down in the other. No officious desk between us. He crossed his legs, laced his fingers together and smiled again.

I looked steadily into his face, memorising, looking for traces of the golden stag. There were none. All I saw was a disturbingly handsome face, gentle but strong. If anything, he reminded me of Astrid, with just the faintest hint of something Slavic in the heavy cheekbones and strong definite nose. On the other hand, the carved vertical lines on his face were distinctly Scandinavian, Max von Sydow. His mouth was firm, too, though not at all stern. But the most remarkable feature was his eyes. The high cheekbones gave them a faintly eastern appearance which made one anticipate black. Instead, they were a warm brown flecked dazzlingly with gold, so much of it that they seemed almost to *be* gold. His thick honey-coloured hair reflected his eyes. He was wearing a honey-coloured cashmere sweater and trousers just a shade or two darker.

But the most striking thing was not any particular feature of Hanno Hirsch or of his office. Rather, it was the deep sense of peace and harmony which seemed to fill the room, touching everything in it, including myself. It was as if I had entered a wholly different world, far removed from Wigmore Street or London or anywhere else. I could feel my muscles relax, the tension fade as I gazed serenely at the man who was in some sense the source of it all. I hadn't experienced such a thing since my first sight of Farleton Hall, that delicate floating palace which had seemed a haven in my fraught world. There was a feeling of benign power, as if all the energy which elsewhere was dissipated by anxiety was here gathered together in all its primeval strength, ready to be turned to good. Devil's child. Were they mad, these rumour-mongers who would say such a thing?

'We will have coffee shortly,' he smiled. 'Coffee will suit you?'

I nodded, entranced, as if he'd offered me the Koh-i-noor diamond.

He was looking now at the sculpture on the table between us. It was white, a three-sided pyramid, on one edge of which was balanced a second piece in the shape of a crescent moon. With one finger he stroked the curve of the moon. 'Do you like it?'

I had no opinions on modern art. All I could sense was that this sculpture was one with the room and its owner.

It, too, radiated tranquillity. I nodded. 'It has a feeling of harmony.'

He smiled, setting the gold flecks of his eyes dancing. 'You see? The sculptor has fooled you, as he does everyone. He is a very clever man. Look now,' he went on, and deftly moved the sculpture to a slightly different position. 'What do you see now?'

I had to look closely before I understood what he meant. Then I saw. One face of what had appeared to be a perfectly even pyramid was in fact broader than the others. The moon, which had seemed to balance on one edge, was in fact slightly to one side, precarious. The moon itself was not a perfect crescent; one side was slightly larger than the other. The whole piece, which had seemed so balanced, was a study in imbalance. And yet it continued to emanate harmony. 'How strange,' I murmured.

He stroked the moon again and at his touch the sculpture seemed transformed into a swan, with the moon its neck and the triangle its body. At another stroke the swan became a tortoise. Was I really seeing this? I blinked. The piece became an abstract sculpture again.

'You have been in London long?'

'Just a few days.'

'You have seen the new *Pétrouchka*?'

I hadn't.

'Another piece of illusion,' said Hanno Hirsch. 'A ballerina pretends to be a puppet who in turn pretends to be a ballerina. These things have great charm, don't you think?'

I agreed, uncertainly.

'They also have great power,' he added.

The room was warm. I wondered if the heat emanated from him, as it had done so disturbingly in my dream and in my dressing-room. But the terror which had accompanied it before had vanished, and with it my fear. What on earth had made me connect this charming man with the ambiguous stag of my dream?

The door opened and the secretary entered with a tray.

The scent of coffee filled the room. Hanno Hirsch pushed aside the sculpture – a piece of enamelled metal once again, its magic gone – and made room for the tray. The secretary set it down and left. Hanno Hirsch poured. The china was pure white and plain. Plain but good, like everything else in the room.

The coffee was delicious. I settled further into my chair, awash with contentment. The conversation flowed: concerts, art exhibitions, books. Not a word about the theatre. Oddly enough, I didn't even notice this conspicuous gap, not at the time. Nor did it occur to me that this was a highly unorthodox interview between two people who had come together to discuss a possible business arrangement. I noticed nothing, only a sense of peace and happiness.

Then Hanno Hirsch glanced at his watch and rose. I realised with a shock that the interview was over. Nothing had been decided, nothing had been said at all. Then another surprise. He ushered me into the outer office, helped me into my raincoat and put on his own. We left the office together.

'You have no plans for lunchtime?' he smiled.

I said I had none.

'Then you will come with me to a concert?'

I agreed, as if it were the most natural thing in the world to end an interview with a concert.

It was still raining. I remembered the sense of sunshine flooding his office. It must have been some form of lighting which I hadn't noticed. His raincoat was another shade of the honey-gold which seemed to clothe his world. My own felt mundane beside it.

We strode up Wigmore Street. Then we turned into Chandos Street and a moment later arrived at a side door of Broadcasting House. Other people were entering the building but the doorman greeted him with special warmth, as if he were a regular.

Inside, we settled into two seats near the front. The little auditorium had an air of fusty comfort. It seemed to suit Hanno Hirsch, who nodded a greeting to several people sitting near us. I thought back on what Belle had said, that Hanno Hirsch rarely went out and then only to plays which would yield clients. She'd also said no one knew him. Everyone here seemed to know him.

'What is the concert?' I asked.

'A young string quartet, making their BBC début. There are two pieces, a Haydn and a Schubert. You like string quartets?'

'I haven't heard many.' One, actually. Jas had taken me to a concert in Cambridge. I'd been bored silly.

'The Haydn is a jewel. The texture is as light and clear as a mountain stream. It might amuse you to try a little trick as you listen. Try, just for a moment, to block out the other three instruments and imagine the music with only the leading violin. You will hear something very interesting.'

The BBC announcer walked down the aisle and on to the platform. He sat down at a little desk at one side and chatted informally to the audience. Then there was a brief silence. A light went on and he spoke into the microphone, introducing the concert. Another pause. The musicians entered from a side door, bowed to the audience, then settled themselves in front of their music stands. Another pause and the music began.

I wasn't bored. The Haydn was a jewel. I tried the trick and was dismayed to hear the delicate texture vanish, leaving only a single banal line of music issuing from the first violin. The tune which had seemed so delightful died, lost every shred of its charm. Indeed, there seemed to be no tune at all. Quickly I restored the other instruments. The music sprang back to life, the first violin glittering once again. It was a disturbing experience and one I didn't repeat with the Schubert.

After the concert we filed out of the auditorium and into the rainy street. Hanno Hirsch smiled down on me. 'You must be starving. You will have some lunch with me?'

We walked again through the rain. Taxis sped past. It didn't seem at all odd that he didn't hail one. He walked the streets of London as David did the paths of his forest, entirely at home in his environment. A taxi would have been as out of place here as in the forest. I was deeply contented.

We turned into a side street and entered a tiny restaurant. There were only four tables, all of them empty – it was well past two o'clock by now. The Greek proprietor and his wife greeted Hanno Hirsch as warmly as the BBC doorman had done. Yes, it was his territory, his forest. We settled ourselves at a table. On it was a bowl of marinated garlic cloves and olives. We nibbled them and drank the warming red wine until our food arrived. The food was simple but excellent. Like Hanno Hirsch's office. Like the Haydn quartet. Everything in his world seemed to have that simple excellence so easily overlooked by a mind not at peace with itself. My mind was at peace. There was nowhere else in the world I would rather be. I couldn't remember ever being as happy as I was at that moment.

Again we talked about everything except the theatre. The concert we'd just heard was also omitted from the conversation. When finally, towards the end of our meal, it made its appearance, I still didn't suspect what was coming.

'And did you try the little trick?' he asked.

'Yes, I did.'

'And what did you hear?'

I described it as best I could.

Hanno Hirsch smiled. 'This is something musicians know but many listeners never discover. The quartet is a unity. You *think* you are hearing a pretty tune on the first violin with just an accompaniment by the others, but it isn't so. Remove the other three instruments and the tune vanishes, the music dies. The leading violin is no more important than the others. Do you agree?'

I agreed.

'I am sometimes called a "starmaker", a rather vulgar variant of the kingmaker. I find the term distasteful. There are no stars, only fine actors who sometimes play leading roles. It is the public, not I, who call them stars. To me they are no better than the humblest walk-on. A great deal of lip service is paid to the idea of the company being a unified whole, but rarely is it put into practice. Everyone hungers to be a star. I have no use for such people.'

His voice was low and soothing, as it had been when talking of inconsequential matters. Slowly I began to understand that this was no inconsequential matter.

'If you wish to be a star,' he continued, 'you must find your own way. If, however, you wish to be a fine actress, then I believe we could have a long and happy association. But there are conditions.'

I sipped my coffee, knowing I should be alert to a hundred red lights of warning flashing in front of me. Knowing but not feeling. I was too filled with a sense of well-being to hear the implications of his words.

'As you know,' he continued, 'the usual practice is for actors to find their own work. The agent then negotiates the contracts, a limited though important function. This is not my practice. If you wish me to be your agent, you must put your entire career into my hands. I will find the work for you. You need do nothing but wait for me to tell you what your next role will be.'

I should have been astonished, but wasn't.

'But if once, even once, you refuse a role I have selected for you, then our association will be at an end.' He smiled pleasantly. 'You have potential, Miss Rawlinson, but you have been spoiled by too much success too early. There is a great deal you must unlearn. I propose that for one year at least, you play nothing but the smallest roles, and only in the commercial theatre. Commercial theatre is hell. The rehearsal period is ridiculously short; there is no time to think through a role or a production and no director will encourage it, or you. Your directors will be tyrants, each in his own way. You will hate every minute of it, but at the end of one year you will be ready to begin properly.'

We rose from the table. He paid the bill, helped me into my raincoat, put on his own.

We were in the street again. It was still raining. 'Say

nothing now,' said Hanno Hirsch. 'Please think carefully about what I have said. Tomorrow morning – not before – please phone me and give me your decision.' He shook my hand and smiled. 'Goodbye, Miss Rawlinson.' And vanished.

'Bloody cheek!' said Hugh at dinner that night. 'Tin-pot Svengali!'

'Potential?' cried Astrid. 'How can he say this thing?'

Neither of them had seen me act. They took on trust the extravagant praise they'd heard at the lodge.

'Of course you'll refuse,' said Hugh. 'Get on the phone to that Jas or whatever his name is. He'll get you something. "Smallest roles" indeed!'

We were in the big through-room which served as both kitchen and dining-room and occupied the whole semi-basement of the house. The house – on Vincent Terrace, just across from the canal – was one of those tall elegant Victorian ones. Through the french windows of the dining area I could see the tangled back garden Astrid hadn't had time to control. Rain poured steadily down over the jumble of neglected shrubs. No sense of invisible sunshine here, though the room was a nice one, full of the warmth of wood and quarry tiles.

'You *will* refuse, won't you?' said Hugh anxiously, noting my silence.

'Of course.'

I smiled across the table at him. Away from David he was a different person: elfin, amusing, full of good-humour. The good-humour was thinner than usual tonight, after my brief account of the day's events. I was touched that he should take my side so fiercely.

'But at least you meet this *Wunderkind*?' said Astrid. 'You tell us now, please, everything of this mysterious man?'

I laughed. 'There's not much to tell.'

And, strangely, there wasn't. All the vivid detail of our encounter had vanished, along with the man, outside the little restaurant. Had I met him at all? Did he even exist?

The whole day seemed unreal. I couldn't be sure of anything. Perhaps this was why no one could give an account of Hanno Hirsch. He didn't exist. Or, if he did, he left no trace. A veil seemed drawn over my mind as I sat at the dining table, trying to say something, anything, about Hanno Hirsch.

'The accent, at least?' Astrid tried. 'He has or has not?'

'I'm not sure.'

'But impossible!' she laughed. 'Me, you hear my accent, yes?'

'Yes.'

'And this man, either he has or has not?'

'I'm afraid I really can't remember.'

'Then he can't have much of one,' said Hugh, logically.

'I suppose so.'

He laughed. 'He obviously didn't make much of an impact – apart from that snotty remark. What else did he say?'

I gave him a rueful smile. 'I'm sorry to be so monotonous, but –'

'– you really can't remember,' Hugh finished. 'Not much of a conversationalist either, eh? Never mind, Ros, it was worth a try. Now you know he's a fraud, you can forget about him and have a proper go. That fellow Jas – I'm sure he can fix you up. He seems to be doing all right for himself. Heaps of contacts by now.'

Hugh seemed so keen I should stay in London and make a serious attempt at establishing a career that I hated to disappoint him, but I still had no intention of staying beyond the fortnight. A break from the tedium of country life, a quick fix of urban excitement, that's all I wanted. Hirsch's damning remarks and insulting proposition only reinforced my intentions.

Even so, I wished I hadn't met him. There was something deeply disturbing about the whole encounter which my rage at his insult didn't dissipate. While in his company I had become utterly passive, lost all volition. That wasn't at all like me. I had a strong will and no inhibitions about using it to get my way. How had I let this man dominate me? And now, absent, there was this weird amnesia. That, too, was unlike me. I had a good memory.

I stayed downstairs long enough to help with the washing up, then headed towards my room. I had a craving to be alone. Also uncharacteristic.

On the ground floor was an elegant drawing-room, Hugh and Astrid's bedroom and bathroom. On the next two floors were more bedrooms and another bathroom. One of the bedrooms was mine. I'd been adamant about staying only a fortnight and so had declined the lovely little self-contained studio flat which occupied the whole of the attic. Astrid had agreed with me. 'It is so sad to be separated up there,' she had said. 'You must live with us, as family.'

But something odd was happening. As I climbed the stairs to my room, Hugh and Astrid seemed to fade, shrink, become vague toy figures somewhere in the house below. At the same time, the veil was lifting over the day's events. By the time I reached my door, I could see Hanno Hirsch almost as clearly as if he were standing there. Every detail, every golden fleck of his eyes. I hesitated. Should I go downstairs and deliver my report?

Like a sleepwalker, I opened the door and entered my room.

The next morning I awoke in a temper, every word of my conversation with Hirsch branded on my mind. The outrage! The insolence! Who was this smooth-talking bastard to pass judgment on my acting, acting which had been praised by some pretty important critics? How could I have sat there and listened so passively? I should have jumped from my chair, delivered an equally damning judgment on his proposal and swept out of the restaurant.

Furious at having left it so long, I dressed quickly and went down to the telephone. Hugh had gone to his office. Astrid was practising for her concert. Fiery chords bulged the door of the drawing-room, adding flame to my intentions. I knew exactly what to say. The secretary would answer the phone. I wouldn't even ask to be put through to Hirsch. I would, in my smoothest, coldest voice, just ask her to pass on a message. 'Please tell Mr Hirsch,' I would say, 'that I've thought over what he said and come to a decision: I find his judgment an outrage and his proposal an insult. I decline it.' I wanted her to know what kind of a person her boss was. I wanted to make it quite clear that just because I was a provincial actress I wasn't going to be pushed around by anyone.

I dialled. The phone rang for a long time. Perhaps she'd gone out to fill the coffeepot for another victim.

I was about to put the receiver down when I heard, 'Hanno Hirsch.'

My innards gave a lurch. So be it. I would speak to him direct.

'Mr Hirsch?' my voice said. 'Ros Rawlinson. I've thought over what you said and come to a decision: I agree to your terms.'

14

Oh, the exquisite irony: even the rehearsal room was the same. I pushed open the church basement door and, sighing, entered. The paint had all but finished its self-destruction in the intervening years, leaving grey concrete walls oozing damp. The puny windows squashed below the tatty ceiling had accumulated a few more years' worth of cobwebs, shutting out the last of the light. The naked bulb had dimmed with dust. I looked balefully at the radiators, still pumping their ice cubes. It was September and I was freezing already.

Only the people were different, not the close-knit band from the ADC but a motley crew of novices and veterans, mostly strangers to each other. We stood about awkwardly, glancing at the man who could only be our director. He was a short, squat bullet of a man. He looked like a prison officer. I shivered, then walked up to him, forcing a smile on to my face.

'I'm Ros Rawlinson,' I said. 'Your parlourmaid.'

Parlourmaid. How could Hirsch do this to me? In the same basement where I'd rehearsed the role of Rosalind, to be reduced now to the tiniest part in *Pygmalion*. Parlourmaid. Six speeches. Diligently I'd underlined them in my script. Six. Each a few words long.

The director scrutinised my face with more interest than a parlourmaid warranted. Hirsch again. He'd set this up. The director would be curious to see Hirsch's latest protégée. 'Good,' he said at last. 'Punctual.'

The last of the cast arrived. We settled into a circle of wobbly chairs.

'Introductions,' barked the director.

Meekly we went the rounds, stating our name and role.

I glanced enviously at the woman playing the housekeeper. At least she had some decent lines. Even the housekeeper was a better role than mine.

Even more enviously I looked at the raven-haired beauty who was to play Eliza Dolittle. She stood out from the others, radiating a sense of calm, oblivious of the dismal surroundings and the little Hitler of a director.

Adolf leaned back in his chair, passed a sardonic smile round the cast and began. 'My *Pygmalion* . . .'

I groaned inwardly. *My*. Not even the knee-jerk solidarity of *our*.

'My *Pygmalion* is to be totally different from everything that has gone before.'

I groaned again. That's what they all said.

'By some idiotic slip of the pen Shaw sub-titled it "A romance in five acts". The five acts is indisputable. As for the romance,' he smiled a superior smile, 'the author was mistaken. Others have played it for laughs.' The smile disappeared. He looked sternly at his circle of schoolchildren. 'We will play it in earnest. Deadly earnest. We will not encourage laughter. We will discourage even the slightest trace of humour.'

Was the man mad? The play was hilarious. No one could subvert those lines.

'I want my audience to leave the theatre in a fury. They have come to see a light sparkling romance. They will leave having seen the truth of the class system exposed in all its horror.'

He was mad. Hanno Hirsch was mad. We were all mad to agree to this absurdity. I looked at the raven-haired beauty. She smiled. Serenely.

After the third rehearsal I arrived home in a fury of my own. I stormed up to my attic flat and flung myself into a chair, shaking more with anger than cold. No way could I continue with this farce. I looked round the flat. Hugh and Astrid's predecessors had turned it into a charming little eyrie. I'd moved into it as soon as I'd accepted Hanno Hirsch's offer and broken the news to David that

I'd be staying on – experimentally – for a little longer. I must have been as mad as the director, to leave David for so long and for so little.

I shut my eyes and tried to conjure up the phone call which had started it all. 'I have chosen for you the role of parlourmaid in *Pygmalion*,' the warm honey-coloured voice had announced. 'One of the most difficult roles I know. If you can play this role convincingly, you can play Lady Macbeth.'

It was difficult all right. Deadly. There was nothing to it. Nothing but six bland announcements of arrivals to Professor Higgins' flat. No one, not even Peggy Ashcroft, could have done anything with it. I suppose a parlourmaid was necessary, but did it have to be *me* wasting *my* time on it? I could be at home, with David, enjoying the beautiful autumn colours of the forest. I could be at York, sinking my teeth into a juicy leading role.

Right. That's it. I sprang from my chair, decision made, and marched down the stairs. Why hadn't I done this before, after the first gruesome rehearsal? A quick call to Hirsch, cancelling our fledgling partnership. Then one to the Führer and presto! – back on the train to Yorkshire.

My hand reached for the phone. It rang.

'Miss Rawlinson? Hanno Hirsch. I'm required to attend a small reception at the Austrian embassy tomorrow night. You would be free to come with me?'

Always the statement formulated as a question. The memory of that magical day I'd first met him washed over me, bathing me in a warm golden light. I could feel my willpower drain away, replaced by his. I could hear my voice saying, 'Why, yes, I'd love to come with you.'

A parlourmaid opened the outer door. A second stood by an inner door. A third announced Hanno Hirsch's name and mine to some official who shook our hands and then turned to greet the next arrivals. Inside the reception room another dozen parlourmaids circulated with trays of wine and canapés. No doubt they all had different titles, but they were parlourmaids all right.

Hanno Hirsch smiled down on me, his golden eyes dancing with amusement. 'You see? Nothing wasted.'

I burst into laughter, the only response to such a delightful trick.

'Observe them well,' he said with mock seriousness. 'You may never again have a chance to observe so many in one place.'

I observed and, strangely, learned. Their grace, their deftness with the trays, their quiet smiles which didn't seem forced, their smooth invisibility. Quality parlourmaids. The Austrian embassy was an important one, and rich. They could afford to hire the best. So could Professor Higgins.

'Yes, a terrible role. I did warn you,' said Hanno Hirsch. 'But also a small one. It will leave you time in which to observe the other actors and the whole process. "A learning experience" I believe is the phrase.'

'The director's mad.'

'Oh yes, quite mad. The production will be a disaster.'

I stared. 'Then why have you put me in it?'

'As I said. A learning experience. If you can survive it with your faith in the theatre intact – not to mention your sense of humour – you will be well on your way to becoming a fine actress.'

My head reeled and it wasn't the wine.

Hanno plucked another glass from a passing tray. The parlourmaid smiled. He turned back to me. 'Never mind. The play will finish in three weeks.'

'The director didn't say it was a fixed run.'

'It isn't. It will fold. Three weeks, four at the most.' He smiled. 'My dear Miss Rawlinson, do you really think I would keep you in such an absurd production longer than that? We have work to do this year. You must play as many roles as possible in that year, and for that we need short runs. I fear the delight with which these mad directors greet my unaccustomed interest in them will be short-lived.' He held his wine glass to his face, gold against gold. '*Prosit!* Now come. You must meet some people.'

I followed, still stunned by what he had told me.

Stunned but amused. Discord was impossible in his presence. That peace and harmony I'd experienced in his office was portable. Each cluster of people we approached brightened as they saw him. He introduced me: 'My client, Ros Rawlinson.' People watched me closely after that. Several apologised, said they hadn't heard my name, could I repeat it? So that was it, the Hirsch technique. By the end of the evening they would all know one more name to watch for in the theatre.

'Am I allowed to ask how you come to be invited to the Austrian embassy?' I said as we moved away from one group towards another.

'Oh, a simple favour I did a few months ago. A cultural exchange. This is a very minor reception, you know. Every so often the embassy gathers together the arts people to repay them for past favours. We are put together because arts people are notoriously unpredictable and can't be trusted to behave themselves at the more important gatherings which politicians attend. Ah, Anna!' He made a half-bow to an elegant elderly woman who turned out to be on the Arts Council. 'You must meet my client, Ros Rawlinson.'

The play folded in three weeks. The few reviews it got were scathing. I wasn't mentioned, of course. I didn't expect to be. Only the raven-haired Eliza – Caroline Gillespie – was singled out for praise, all of it the 'pearl in the dungheap' variety. I tried not to feel too jealous.

After the embassy reception my attitude had changed. I still loathed the production and its director, but I stopped fuming and instead sat back and observed. I even learned to crack a few jokes with my fellow-actors. They were much more fraught than I: their roles mattered more and they knew they were sailing in a doomed ship. I tried to lighten the atmosphere a little, diffusing my tiny portion of the glow which surrounded Hanno Hirsch. So, oddly enough, did Caroline Gillespie.

I didn't even mind too much that the theatre was the Fortune. From star to parlourmaid in the same building.

Nobody came down from Yorkshire for the opening. I think they were embarrassed. My only visitors in the cramped communal dressing-room were Jas, Hugh and Astrid, all of them looking a little sheepish. No Hanno Hirsch, but a single golden-yellow rose with the now-familiar cream-coloured card. On it was written simply, '*Prosit!* H.H.'

'You are ready for another ordeal?' His warm golden voice spoke the word 'ordeal' as if it were 'Christmas present' or 'holiday'.

'Let me guess,' I said wryly. 'Spear carrier in *Coriolanus*.'

'Certainly not. That would be a waste of a good parlourmaid.'

'You're not saying . . .'

'But of course. You have displayed a marked talent for this occupation. The time has come for a promotion.'

'To?'

'The parlourmaid in *Blithe Spirit*.' A fortnight in the Seychelles. A Jaguar. 'A far more substantial role,' he added. 'She has several good lines. I am pleased with your progress. You are pleased with your promotion?'

I knew that as soon as I put down the phone I would not be pleased. I would be furious. I had used the leading role in that play for my York audition. Now I was demoted to its most minor character. But that fury was several minutes away. For the present, enveloped by his good-humour, I could only smile and say, 'Do I get another embassy reception for research?'

Warm laughter rippled from the telephone. 'Ah, no. Your new parlourmaid is a Cockney. For that we must visit the East End.'

The market, Whitechapel Road. Cars crawled stinkily down the middle. On either side, the broad pavements were crammed with stalls, their owners raucously crying their wares. By my side, Hanno Hirsch, his big chest expanding with the delight of it all. A golden giant weaving his way through the merry chaos, pupil in tow. I was trying very hard to be annoyed.

'I'm a classy kind of person,' I protested. 'This role isn't me.'

'Exactly,' said Hanno Hirsch. 'You must extend your abilities, learn to be a Cockney as well as a lady.' He turned and bought two oranges. He tossed one to me and began to peel his own, using his thumbnail as a knife.

I watched, fascinated. Was this another test? I stuck a thumbnail into mine. I would not be beaten.

A few minutes later Hanno Hirsch was neatly eating the segments his artistry had exposed. I was holding the mangled remnants of what had once been a perfectly respectable orange. He shook his head in disappointment. We were passing a bin. Taking my wrist, he held my hand over the bin. I let go. He plucked a clean handkerchief from his pocket and wiped my hands. Then he divided his orange into two equal portions, pedantically counting the segments, and gave half to me.

I was still trying to be annoyed. 'Sometimes,' I said portentously, 'magnanimity is the greatest insult of all.'

'Don't be so huffy. Eat.'

The director was almost human. Even the rehearsal room had improved: a boys' club this time, above ground and just about habitable. A noticeboard announced next week's football teams. Signs said DO and DON'T. Lukewarm water clanked through the radiators. The cubbyhole of a kitchen had an electric kettle that worked. The stage manager had arrived in advance and was brewing tea. She'd even bought a packet of biscuits. We watched worshipfully as she distributed them. Then we settled into the inevitable circle of chairs and waited for our director to speak.

'Let's just have a gentle read-through, shall we? Enjoy it.' We cleared our throats, indulged a last luxurious cough. Then we gripped our scripts, tensing already. Silence. The director looked benignly at the person with the first speech. 'It's all right. In your own time.'

Yes. A boys' club. My first relief turned to disappointment. A weak director. Too good-natured to handle a roomful of unruly egos. After a week of rehearsals the production was a mess.

'It has no shape,' I complained to the telephone. 'He's a real sweetie, but he hasn't got anything to say. No new angle on the play, no angle at all. I'm longing for a sense of direction.'

'A nice man,' the telephone agreed. 'His father wanted him to become a doctor. He should have listened. He would have made an excellent GP. Especially with children.'

'That's it. I feel like a child being coaxed into playing a game at a youth club. Anything to keep the children happy, even bending the rules . . . or not having any at all.'

'You would like to have your dictator back? Perhaps for your third role I might manage –'

'God forbid! But at least he had a sense of direction, even if it was an absurd one.'

'Never mind. It will finish in five or six weeks.'

'Hotline to God?' Or the other. Sometimes I still believed in the devil's pact.

'Just reading the signs. Meanwhile, you will learn how to salvage what you can from a shapeless production. Watch the direction the other actors take. It will surprise you how much coherence they struggle to put in it by themselves. Follow the direction that emerges as best you can. You might wish to try a little shaping of your own.'

'If I can stay awake long enough.'

A trace of steel appeared in the honeyed voice. 'No good actor is ever bored.'

When I put down the phone, I felt like a child chastened by her teacher. Or a woman with a squashed orange in her hand.

The play ran for five and a half weeks. In the end, the actor playing the leading role had virtually taken over the directing. 'Good, good,' the official director had said at every suggestion. Well, it was better than nothing.

No one from Yorkshire turned up for this first night either. I didn't really blame them. Winter was the height of the planting season. Why miss out on any of it for a bit part in an insipid production? Still, I was a little hurt. I'd worked hard on my little role, given it a touch of distinction.

At least someone noticed. The golden-yellow rose was there again. With it a card. 'Well done! H.H.'

'You are rested?' said the telephone.

'Don't use that euphemism,' I told it crankily. I'd just returned from a short reunion with David in Yorkshire. I hadn't wanted to come back at all. I was in no mood for his banter.

'Don't be so touchy,' it replied. 'I have spent more time than usual finding your next part. It required some care.'

'Don't tell me. A Burmese parlourmaid.'

'Certainly not. You have reached the top of that profession. The time has come for something new.'

I waited, wary.

'A ballet dancer,' the telephone announced.

My heart leapt.

'A failed ballet dancer,' it continued.

My heart sank.

'In a new play. This will give you the experience of rehearsing with the author present. The experience is usually unpleasant, but you must have it.'

'Thanks. How long will it run?'

'I'm not sure.'

What? Fallible?

'The play is set in the 1930s – one of those tedious attempts to pull in the nostalgia market. Still, it's not a bad play. And the nostalgia market is a big one.'

'Do I get a chance to dance?' I asked hopefully.

'I'm afraid not. You have a broken leg.'

* * *

To my surprise, there was another 'research' outing. I'd never heard of such a practice. When I tried to question him, he deflected my query so smoothly that only later did I realise. But then, nothing about Hanno Hirsch was ordinary. I was learning to expect the unexpected.

I hoped this one would be to the ballet. Silly me. No one at Sadler's Wells had a broken leg.

The cinema was small, tatty and so far out that we'd had to walk miles after the last tube stop. On the screen, Greta Garbo cavorted her way clumsily through *Grand Hotel*.

'An extraordinary choice to play a failed ballerina, don't you think?' Hanno Hirsch whispered. 'Much too tall and angular. Very like you.'

'Box Office,' I whispered back. '*Not* like me.'

'True. See how awkward she is. No one could believe she had ever had a career in the ballet. And yet . . .'

And yet. Magic. Even in the most unsuitable roles, the Garbo magic was there.

There was magic in the cinema, too. Somewhere in the centre of the auditorium, the tattiness parted to make way for the golden aura which surrounded Hanno Hirsch. No doubt about it: I would rather be in this dump with Hanno Hirsch than at Covent Garden with anyone else. In the short time of our curious business association, I had come to look forward to every meeting, every phone call, with absurd anticipation. I tried not to make comparisons with David, but it was difficult. David had settled into a stubborn determination; everything he said and did was predictable. With Hanno Hirsch, I never knew what would happen next – what role he would choose for me, what curious slant he would have on it, what research expedition he would propose. Each encounter was like a brightly wrapped Christmas present; I didn't know what surprise would be lurking inside. There was a zest to him which I found irresistible.

And infectious. Out on the street again, a bubble of joy rose to the surface and took me with it. I broke away from him and performed the same awkward arabesque Garbo had done in her hotel room. A crack in the pavement intervened. I tripped, even more clumsily than Garbo. He caught me just before I fell and we laughed.

The laughter disguised my confusion. A powerful dose of sexual longing had shot through me at this, our first physical contact. It was absurd, given the layers of winter clothes between us and the foolishness of the circumstances. Absurd but real. When he released me, I could hardly stand.

'I think I've twisted my ankle,' I lied.

He crooked his arm. I took it and together we continued down the street. I pretended to limp a little, to make my lie more plausible.

'My dear Miss Rawlinson,' he said. 'You take your dedication too far. Is it really necessary to cripple yourself in order to play a broken-legged ballerina?'

'My dear Mr Hirsch,' I replied, my head light with an intoxication which bypassed caution, 'is it really necessary to continue addressing each other so formally? My name is Rosalind.'

He laughed. 'And mine is Hanno. Rosalind. Yes, it suits you. Much more than the surname you chose as your pseudonym.'

I lurched, and this time it was for real. How on earth had he known that? Hardly anyone knew it, I'd changed my name so long ago. And if he knew about that lie, did he know about the more immediate one of the twisted ankle? I felt my face flush and was glad for the darkness between streetlights. To divert his attention I asked, 'And yours? Austrian? German? Swiss?'

'I am as English as you are,' he said.

'But your name isn't.'

A light drizzle was beginning to sift down through the dirty city sky. I ignored it, excited by the turn the conversation had taken. I was close to learning something of Hanno Hirsch's origins. I didn't for one moment accept his statement. He might be English now, but everything in his manner and in the slight formality of his speech suggested foreign birth. I wanted to know which country but saw that the direct approach was futile. Instead I said casually, 'What does it mean?'

We were nearing another streetlight. I would soon see his face clearly again. I would watch it closely for signs of concealment.

The streetlight's rays were magnified by the drizzle, turning the area around it into a shimmering circle. As we drew near, Hanno's honey-gold hair brightened to the intensity of the metal. 'My dear Rosalind,' he said, 'you know perfectly well what the word means, as you studied both German and French.'

This time I didn't lurch. I was barely even surprised. If he knew about my change of name, why ever shouldn't he know I'd learned German and French at school? There seemed to be an inevitability about it all. The devil's child, all-knowing.

'I've forgotten a lot,' I said evasively. 'You know how it is with languages learned at school.'

We had reached the streetlight. Hanno stopped under it. The light enveloped his head completely, forming a great golden aureole around it. His hair shone brightly, seeming almost to flicker. A trick of the light, of course; the drizzle was in motion, setting in motion the light itself and everything near it. Hanno smiled down on me. There was nothing uncanny in the smile. 'But of course,' he said. 'There's no reason for you to know every German word, and *Hirsch* is a word one might not encounter in a textbook.'

'Well?' I said, waiting.

'It means "stag".'

15

I brooded a great deal on the coincidence. Hanno the stag, the golden stag of my dream, the stag in the forest. It was coincidence, of course, or so I kept telling myself. I was still convinced I had seen a stag in the forest, but time had weakened my certainty about its colour. The dream, too, I rationalised away. It was natural for my sleeping mind to fix upon so vivid a sight, turn it into a fairy tale in the darkness of the night. As for the resemblance between the stag's face and Hanno's, I wasn't at all sure any more. My glimpse in the dream had been so fleeting, my first sight of Hanno's face in the dressing-room similarly brief.

But none of this rationalised away the power I felt emanating from the man every time I saw him or spoke with him on the phone. The play lasted longer than he predicted, taking me through a Christmas with David at the lodge and out the other side again. Hanno and I had little contact during the run, apart from an occasional phone call. I missed his physical presence, that exotic blend of serenity and excitement he carried with him. In his absence I had to struggle to find my own power to put into my role.

The play was, as Hanno had said, not a bad one. Set in a private clinic surrounded by woodland, it had many of the same qualities as a country house murder mystery. The clinic catered for 'professional' injuries – of athletes, musicians, dancers, all those mad people who push their bodies to extremes, pursuing a narrow professional goal. Deprived of their physical excellence, they met now as equals, broken objects who for the first time had to rely on their minds. It made for tension and a lot of comedy as well.

I had few lines but was on the stage much of the time. It was a challenge, portraying a wounded ballerina in repose. I enjoyed it, and this time I was noticed, albeit by only one critic from a minor newspaper. Still (I thought wryly), my career as a bit part actress was moving ever upward.

The golden-yellow rose was there again, and this time Belle came down for the first night. David and Brendan were behind with the planting, she explained. I accepted her explanation. How could I argue? Balanced against trees, which would stand for hundreds of years, a small part in a play was pretty unimportant.

One consequence of the long run was that I missed Astrid's evening recitals. Just before her marriage she'd won third prize in the Leeds International Piano Competition. Since then she'd been slowly building up a career. The critics were beginning to notice her in a quiet sort of way. The reviews were beginning to coalesce into a picture: Astrid was a 'warm' musician. What she lacked in technical virtuosity she compensated for by the love she displayed towards her composers. She brought out the warmth and depth of their music in a way which endeared her to her audiences. She was quite pleased with her image, as well she might be; technical virtuosity is often easier than the communion with the music which Astrid achieved.

I loved going to her concerts. Partly the music, of course, but also Hugh. Hugh never missed a concert. Well, it was easier for him than for David, being in London. Still, I noticed, and I liked Hugh all the more for it. His adoration of Astrid's talent went a long way towards cancelling out his dislike of David, at least in my mind.

It amused me to stand with him in the foyer before a concert. He was filled with barely suppressed excitement, like a little boy before his birthday party, oozing pride in his wife while at the same time trying to retain a blasé veneer. The tension between the two was comical. He always delivered Astrid to the stage door, and he loved hanging around backstage where people knew he was Astrid's husband.

Once, in a moment of weakness, he confessed how left out he'd sometimes felt at Farleton Hall. His mother and David had shared some interest in the arts. Both had viewed Hugh as rather unimaginative. He'd resented their image of him but, in the perverse way of children, fed it, becoming ever more the philistine interested only in money. Now at last he could share in this exotic world, with his wife an increasingly well-known pianist and his sister-in-law a potentially famous actress. The pride he took in us both was rather touching.

During my stint as the broken-legged ballerina I missed the concerts. Finally, however, she was booked to do a lunchtime concert at the Wigmore Hall. It was her début at this curious venue which was more a club than a concert hall, and I looked forward to it. I'd never been to the Wigmore Hall. Also, there was a reasonable possibility that Hanno would be there. After all, it was practically on his doorstep.

Jas and I arranged to meet Hugh in the foyer – Hugh had a business meeting that morning, would have to dash away at the last moment. It felt strange, walking down Wigmore Street for the first time since I'd gone for interview. The brass plate glowed as before. I had a powerful urge to run up the stairs and ask Hanno to come to the concert. I pictured that great golden face shining with pleasure at my impetuosity, heard the deep laughter of delight. I felt like an iron filing pulled towards its magnet. I resisted, of course. In any case, Jas was with me. I'd intended pointing out Hanno's building to him, but something I still don't understand silenced my words as we passed by.

We arrived at the Wigmore Hall just as a taxi pulled up and Hugh, face beaming, shot out of it.

The foyer was long and narrow and lined with photographs of the musicians appearing that season. Hugh sought out Astrid's and stood by it, reverent. I had to laugh. He looked around eagerly, his bright bird-like eyes willing people to realise that the beautiful talented Astrid they were about to hear was his very own beloved wife. 'You really are impossible!' I laughed.

We made our way through the diminishing crowd. A huge instrument case – a tuba? – was propped against one wall. Some orchestral player nipping in after a rehearsal, I suppose. There was a nice atmosphere, casual but knowledgeable. Scraps of conversation drifted over us. These people knew their music. I hoped Astrid would do well.

Our seats were near the front. Jas and I had told Hugh before that the proper thing for spouses and friends was an unobtrusive seat further back, but Hugh had to be where the action was, smiling at Astrid and urging her to give her best. We'd given up arguing.

I looked around, looking for the golden glow, but there were too many heads in the way. If Hanno was here, it was unlikely I would see him. I settled in to enjoy the concert.

Astrid had a lovely way of coming on to the platform, a mixture of diffidence and conviction. A lovely way of smiling at her audience too, as if they were friends rather than critics who could tear her to shreds with a few strokes of a pen. Her manner invited complicity, said We-are-all-here-together-to-enjoy-this-wonderful-music-yes? Mostly they replied yes.

Hugh was never nervous on her behalf. Jas and I were. We knew she had occasional bouts of nerves, waiting in the wings. We knew how useful a small dose of it could be to get the adrenalin going, but we also knew that too much was a killer. There was a fine balance, and as she played we always willed the balance to be in her favour. Usually it was. Every so often she stumbled over a difficult passage but she recovered well, didn't let it throw her. The audience didn't mind. They were too immersed in the emotional content to fret about the odd mistake.

She was on form that day. The applause was wholehearted, as exuberant as her performance had been. There would be good reviews, more bookings. As we filed out of the hall into the foyer, I was so preoccupied with her achievement that it took me a moment to notice.

There he was, the big honey-coloured head clearly visible above the crowd. Beside him, half-hidden, was another head, darker and smaller. The crowd parted for an instant, then closed up again, but not before I'd seen. It was her all right: Caroline Gillespie.

'I felt jealous, and that's the truth of it,' I confessed at last.

Jas regarded me across the cluttered table. We were lunching together at the National, something we did a lot these days. Jas was rehearsing Joxer Daly in *Juno and the Paycock*. It was, apart from Jas, an all-Irish cast – quite a challenge for my London-born-and-bred friend.

'Sure,' said Jas, with just a touch of the Irish accent lingering from the last rehearsal. 'We all like to think we're the one and only. Part of our giant ego. The same ego, may I remind you, that makes us show off to the audience. Don't knock it. It's our bread and butter.'

'I'm not knocking it. I just feel rather, well, sheepish. Of course he has other clients. I just never thought of them as flesh and blood, I suppose. Phantom clients.'

'Phantom clients for a phantom king. You listen too much to the gossip, my child. I can assure you that Caroline at least is real flesh and blood. But I'm surprised you didn't know she was one of his.'

One of his. I'd felt so proud of being 'one of Hanno's' that I'd never thought the obvious: 'one' implies 'others'. Did he take her on research outings, too? Probably not. She'd been around a while, probably didn't need them.

Certainly she was good – I'd thought so at the time. I'd also noticed that odd sense of calm she had, so like Hanno's, in the midst of those daft rehearsals for that ridiculous *Pygmalion*. I should have realised where she got it from. The Hanno touch, infusing all his clients with that quiet confidence that made directors queue up to give them leading roles.

Jas tapped my hand with one finger. 'Hey, you. Look at me. Are you sure this is just *professional* jealousy?'

'Of course it is.'

'Good. Because the one rumour about our *Teufelskind* that seems to be true is his monkishness. Part of his pact with the devil, they say. Vow of chastity in exchange for genius. Repressed sexuality. All his passion channelled into his work – gives him the edge over the competition.'

I snorted. 'How would *you* know?'

'True,' he smirked. 'I believe in being generous with my passion.'

I laughed. Jas always managed to cheer me up. I liked lunching at the National, too, that sense of being at the heart of things. Not everyone was as keen on the new South Bank complex as I was. All that ribbed concrete and the labyrinthine corridors had already prompted the nickname 'The Lubianka' among some actors. Well, I wouldn't mind doing a stretch in it.

'Well, I wouldn't mind being "one of Hanno Hirsch's",' said Jas. 'How about putting in a good word for me?'

'He has male clients?'

'Of course, dodo. What do you think he is: Svengali? Keeping a harem of pretties for his pleasure? He's a hard-headed, thoroughly professional agent. He just happens to be bloody brilliant. Know what, sunshine? *I'm* jealous of *you*.'

I laughed.

'I'm serious. You stick with him. Bit parts and all. He knows what he's doing. Here's something to knock you down: God asked after you the other day.'

'God being your revered director?' I said in a hushed voice, looking round in case the deity should be passing by our table.

'None other. Said, "Isn't that ballerina girl your chum from Cambridge?" He'd been to your play – they always go if one of Hirsch's people is in it. That's the technique: titillate the directors with distant prospects. Hirsch holds back your talent, lets it accumulate behind the dam while you play bit parts. Then one day, whoosh! – a leading role at last and it all comes flooding out. A star is born. Overnight success. Except it isn't overnight at all. Hirsch has been cunningly preparing the way for years. So repress your jealousy, dear heart, and stand by your man. There's not a better agent in the whole world.'

It wasn't difficult. As soon as I was in Hanno's presence, he wove his golden net about me, made me forget I was just one of many. After my ballerina role there were three more, each interspersed with a brief trip home to David, each with a ritual outing. First came Panope, the ladies' maid in Racine's *Phaedra* (a trip to the British Museum to see the Elgin Marbles followed by lunch in another Greek restaurant where the waitress was, said Hanno, a perfect modern-day Panope). Then came the repulsive Mildred in O'Neill's *The Hairy Ape* (yes, a trip to the zoo).

But when he assigned me the role of nurse to Catherine in *Suddenly Last Summer* I put my foot down. 'Hanno, I am *not* going to a mental hospital.'

'Would I be so crude?'

We went instead to Harrods. 'Catherine is, of course, perfectly sane,' said Hanno. 'It's the people around her who are mad – snobbish Americans trying to force her into denying the truth. They're driven almost insane with the desire to get their hands on her legacy. Greed and fastidiousness. Look around you.'

'I think you're being a little unfair.'

'Am I? Let's tail those two – a mother and daughter, I presume.'

We tailed them, from perfumery to furs to the restaurant, where we settled at a table next to theirs for coffee. Their dialogue was choice. So were their accents. I listened and learned.

A year had passed. My apprenticeship was over. My roles had progressed from tiny to, well, smallish. Towards the end I'd had a mention in several reviews. Hanno again. The critics knew I was one of his, wanted to be first in print with the news – it would look good in later collections of their works. I could see what Hanno was doing. So could the critics and directors, but they all played the game, knowing that if they didn't someone else would, someone eager to display an early appreciation of Hanno's latest fledgling. There was nothing supernatural about it at all. The real mystery was how Hanno had launched himself in the first place, established this awesome reputation seemingly from nowhere. That and his unknown origins. I looked him up in several directories, theatrical and otherwise. No mention. It was as if he didn't exist.

I stayed too long at the last-night party after *Suddenly Last Summer*. I also drank too much, talked too much, got myself into an overexcited state which didn't bode well for sleep.

Sure enough, there I was, seven o'clock in the morning and still awake, turning my chaste attic bed into a battle-ground in search of the one position which would allow sleep. Finally – dazed, sober and cranky as hell – I got up. There was too much adrenalin still pumping through me to pretend any more. I needed action to work it off. A long walk around Islington. Why not?

I crept down the stairs, past Astrid and Hugh's room, feeling absurdly like a child sneaking out of its parents' house. Good hearty snores. The front door latch barely made a sound.

Then, early morning London. Well, early for me. It was rather lovely, despite the dark grey overcast sky. There was less traffic than usual and fewer pedestrians, too. I thought of Hanno. He probably took early morning walks all the time. He had the feel of London imprinted on his feet. We'd walked a lot on our outings. He never apologised for not using a taxi; he took it for granted that people walked. I rather liked that. I rather liked a lot about Hanno Hirsch. I was (I thought with a pang) going to miss him when I went up to Yorkshire the next day. In London there was always the possibility of an unexpected phone call. In Yorkshire there wouldn't even be that. I really ought to give him my Yorkshire number, I said to myself. In case the right role came up suddenly. It would be awful to miss it just because he didn't have my number.

Well, well, what a coincidence: here I was on Wigmore Street. Why not just pop up to his office? I looked at my watch and frowned. Nine o'clock. I didn't know what office hours he kept but in our trade they weren't likely to start this early. I looked up at his windows. I hesitated. I'd never turned up unannounced. Still, other people no doubt did. Jas often stopped in for a chat with his agent. His agent's office was like Charing Cross station at rush hour, Jas said. That's what agents were for: someone to talk to when work was slow or spirits low. And I had a perfectly good reason to see Hanno. I needed to give him my Yorkshire number, I really did.

Anyway, the street door was open (I tried it). True, there were no sounds as I walked past the other offices, up the stairs, along the final corridor to Hanno's office. I paused at the door. Voices, faint. Probably his secretary was in the inner office with him, talking about the day's appointments. Well, I needn't stay long. I knocked on the door and listened hard. Music, too, equally faint and yet sufficient to drown out the voices. Odd. Hanno wasn't the musak type, he took his music seriously. Suddenly all sound ceased. In the silence I heard first my heartbeat and then, like an echo of it, footsteps hurriedly approaching. The door opened.

Hanno gazed down on me, obviously trying to conceal his astonishment. There was a scent of fresh shaving cream and his hair was rumpled. It wasn't like him to be absent-minded, to forget to comb his hair before going out. Then he smiled and I forgot everything except my pleasure at seeing him.

'Rosalind! This is a surprise!'

'I'm sorry to come so early,' I said. 'I'm on my way to Yorkshire. I suddenly remembered you don't have my home number. In case a role comes up,' I finished lamely.

'Of course. Foolish of me not to have asked you before. Do come in.'

I entered the outer office with him.

'I'll just get my address book,' he said, and went into his own office.

It didn't occur to me to wonder why it would be in his office rather than on the secretary's desk, but something in his voice made me stay where I was rather than follow him.

If it hadn't been for the arrangement of the pictures I would never have seen. The huge Klimt in the inner office was at right angles to the windows. From where I stood in the outer office, the glass covering the print acted as a dimmed mirror reflecting the wall opposite, the wall behind the chairs where we'd sat during that strange interview over a year ago. On that wall was another print, a very tall one.

Or had been. Where it should have been, I now saw reflected a half-open door. Beyond it a bed, one nearly as rumpled as the one I'd left two hours ago. Then Hanno's shape obliterated it. My vision swayed and in an eye's blink the bed disappeared, the door disappeared, and I saw reflected once again the tall print with Hanno standing in front of it. I'd heard nothing, not even the click of a door shutting. I blinked again, wondering if I'd imagined it all. I hadn't slept that night, I was a trifle hungover – it would have been easy for my senses to play tricks on me.

Then Hanno entered the outer office. He went straight to his secretary's desk – 'Of course, here it is' – and opened the address book. He took down my number and then smiled. 'You look as if you could do with a coffee. Good party last night?'

I laughed, at ease again. 'Very. And yes, I overdid it.'

He snapped the book shut. 'A better idea: how about breakfast? There's a nice little place just round the corner. You have time before your train?'

The train. Oh God. I'd told him I was on my way to Yorkshire. It had been such a tiny lie; I *would* be going, tomorrow. 'Heaps,' I said. Then noticed my lack of luggage. Could I try Left Luggage? Then I remembered. King's Cross was just a few streets away from Vincent Terrace. Wigmore Street was approximately three miles distant. There was nothing for it but the truth.

'Actually, I'm not leaving till tomorrow. The truth is, I couldn't sleep. I took a walk and, well, ended up here.'

Hanno laughed his big open laugh, cancelling my embarrassment. 'Splendid! And you must be starving! A big breakfast, then!'

As we clattered down the stairs I forgot about my lie and forgot, too, what I'd seen behind the hidden door. All that mattered was being with him again, drinking in his vitality, recharging my own batteries. 'Are you sure this is just *professional* jealousy?' Jas had asked. I'd said it was. I'd hoped it was. Now I wasn't so sure. I craved Hanno's presence.

The café was of the type I now associated with Hanno: small, friendly, inexpensive and good. He had the Londoner's instinct for such places. Clearly he was a regular here. The proprietress greeted him by name and waved him to what was obviously his usual table.

'I'm so pleased you came,' he said when we'd sat down. 'I may need to phone you soon. Negotiations for your next role are going faster than I expected.'

'Am I allowed to know?' Normally he refused; he didn't like to say anything until it was settled. 'After all, I've graduated now, haven't I? If it's a big role I might want to take the script with me to Yorkshire, do some learning there.'

'Oh, it's big,' he smiled. 'In a four-hander. You'll like it.'

'Stop teasing!' I laughed.

Our breakfast arrived, a huge English plateful each. My hangover vanished. I was starving. I ate greedily, prodding Hanno with my questions between mouthfuls. Finally he gave in.

'But you must tell no one,' he said. 'A revival of *Who's Afraid of Virginia Woolf?*'

My eyes nearly popped out of my head. 'Not Martha?' I said, barely daring to hope. It was the role Elizabeth Taylor had made famous in the film version. Possibly the most succulent role in the whole of the modern repertoire. What a role to –

'Not Martha. Caroline Gillespie's already signed up for that.'

The bacon stuck in my throat. I swallowed it with difficulty.

'Honey is a far more difficult role,' he smiled.

'Second fiddle always is.'

The smile vanished. 'Rosalind. You know my views. Remove the second violin from the string quartet and you have an insipid piece not worth listening to.'

I looked down at my empty plate. Two demons were doing battle in my head. One shouted rebellion, urged me to tell him what he could do with his second fiddle. The other, meek, felt like a chided schoolgirl now contrite.

'Rosalind.' The voice summoned me back to the café. He was still unsmiling but the voice had a gentle undertone. 'If you wish to have a different agent, or go your own way, you are free to do so. There is no contract. There is nothing binding you to me.'

Wasn't there?

'But if you wish to continue with me, you know my conditions.'

I nodded.

He relaxed a little. 'All I ask is that you tell me now. I don't wish to waste my time, or the director's, if you don't want the part.'

I looked into his gold-flecked eyes. There was a touch of sadness in them.

Then, somewhat to my surprise, I felt myself smile. 'Of course I want it, Hanno. How could you doubt?'

16

On the train the next day the two demons resumed their battle. Of course it was a good role. I was extremely lucky to be offered it, after only a year in London and a series of bit parts. In any other circumstances I would have jumped at the chance. So why was I so upset?

Caroline, of course. If the leading role had gone to anyone else I wouldn't have minded. I was a good enough actress not to resent my colleagues. The talentless ones weren't worth it – they would fall by the wayside soon enough. As for the good ones, they deserved admiration, and I wasn't slow to give it.

But not to Caroline. She was one of his, and higher up the ladder than me. All the critics who came to the play would do so knowing that both of us were Hanno's clients. They would expect quality, and get it. They would also get a few sparks flying. And Hanno knew, of that I was sure. He was deliberately playing me off against her to make a production that would carve its little niche in theatre history. There was something cold and calculated about it all that made me shudder. Devil's child. Yes, I could almost believe it.

Then the other demon appeared, asking why all the fuss? After all, Caroline had never been disagreeable to me. Far from it. She'd been the most charming colleague imaginable during that ridiculous *Pygmalion*.

Then a series of backyards hung with laundry shot past the windows, sheets flapping in the wind, and I stared blankly at the truth. I saw again the rumpled sheets mirrored in the Klimt's glass, heard the faint voices that had stopped the moment I'd knocked on the door. I had a pretty good idea whose the voices had been and who had been in that bed. My teeth clenched tightly as a surge of sexual longing swept over me, followed quickly by shame.

I was married, and to a husband any woman would envy. If Caroline wished to play that kind of game to get to the top, good luck to her. I didn't need to. I would make it with talent alone. My anger jerked violently from Caroline to Hanno. Of all the cheap, predictable stunts. To have a squalid little hidey hole tucked behind his office for the seduction of clients. My God. Right back to the Hollywood director's couch. I'd thought better of Hanno. Surely a man like that didn't need to bribe his bedmates? Monk indeed. I would tell Jas, tell everyone. All this crappy mystique turning him into a legend. Nothing but a rumpled bed in a sleezy cubbyhole.

I got off the train at York in a righteous rage. There was David, waiting, his handsome face so patently honest I could have wept with gratitude. Instead, I flung myself into his embrace with so much force I almost knocked him over.

It didn't last long. It never did. My homecomings were always a disappointment. Always there was the same happy reunion, the joyful first evening when we all chattered excitedly, filling each other in on the events of our separate lives.

And then, the next morning, the separate lives again. Each time I came home I felt it more acutely. Things were happening fast at The Folly, things I'd had no part in forming. Even the name. It was official now. In a fit of pique, David had taken on the name the locals sneeringly gave us. There it was, a brand new sign plonked on the entrance gates:

THE FOLLY
PRIVATE

Belle wasn't pleased. 'As a joke, all right,' she said the next morning as we baked bread together. 'But David's gone way beyond that. He won't have anything at all to do with the locals any more. I keep telling him, "What's the point of setting an example if you don't let anyone in to see?" Does he listen? Does he hell.' She shut the Aga door on the batch of loaves and turned to me. Her big cheery face was becoming careworn, her exuberant blonde hair sprinkled with grey. My friends were ageing behind my back. 'Ros, could *you* try talking to him? A fresh voice, you know.'

'I'm the last person he'd listen to,' I said. It was true. David regarded me almost as a visitor myself. One of these days I would arrive to find him scowling behind the bars of the gate, pointing pointedly to the sign. Private. No entrance.

A clattering in the cobbled courtyard caught my attention. I looked through the big windows to see Brendan coaxing the latest addition out of the stables. Ysbaddaden. 'How he's grown!' I exclaimed.

'Hasn't he just?'

I went out to watch. David had bought a Shire mare in foal, hoping for a nice little filly he could train from scratch. Instead, he'd got a strapping great colt. Ysbaddaden.

'Uss-what?' I'd asked on the first visit after his birth.

'Uss-path-*ad*-an,' David had pronounced, slowly, as if I were a dimwit. 'King of the giants in Celtic mythology. Father of the giantess, Olwen.'

'And will he father an Olwen?' I teased.

'Some day. Yes. I hope so. We may as well start our own breeding line, since we're landed with a stallion anyway. We thought we'd give them all giants' names.'

We. Always this 'we' that didn't include me any more.

Ysbaddaden had been a big fellow right from birth. He'd doubled in size since I'd last seen him. I watched Brendan training him on a lunge line. Around and around the courtyard the colt pranced, his silky feathered fetlocks shimmering in the autumn sun. 'Walk, you little devil!' Brendan called to him.

Ysbaddaden tossed his gorgeous head, glared at Brendan, then slowed down to a walk. Brendan was a genius with horses. He never pandered to them, never let them get away with anything. But they sensed in him an enormous well of love and loved him in return. So did I. Brendan at least stayed the same, always the big red-haired blue-eyed stage Irishman, except that he was real.

Brendan saw me. 'Rosie, come and fuss him about a bit,' he called. 'He needs to get used to new people.'

New people. Brendan would be horrified to know how deeply the words had cut. I walked up to the colt, took him firmly by the halter and stroked his glossy neck. I didn't like to admit I was rather nervous of horses. Ysbaddaden sensed it and tossed his head impatiently. Brendan joined me. 'Manners, son.' The colt glared at him again and was still. 'A fiery little article already,' said Brendan. 'He needs a firm hand and that's a fact.'

Right now Brendan's hand was seeking the place on the throat the colt most loved to have stroked. The colt closed his eyes in pleasure. I could almost hear him purr.

'He'll be more than eighteen and a half hands by the time he's done with growing,' said Brendan. 'He'll be pushing Chester out of the records.'

'Chester?'

'Buchanan's star Clydesdale in Glasgow. They use him for delivering the Black & White whisky. Sweet as a lamb, though. Unlike some I could mention.' He scowled at the colt. The colt rubbed his head against Brendan's shoulder.

He was beautiful, even I could see that. His coat was darker than many Shires', a strong pewter grey that gleamed with the same inner light as the metal. He would probably lighten a bit in time, Brendan said, and his size would make him popular as a stud. 'We'll put him on a hiring society's books, bring in a bit of extra cash. We won't be able to breed from him ourselves all the time, once he's sired a few mares for us. Not a good idea, incest.'

'Why?'

'I don't really know. There's not a lot of evidence either way. Most likely it's just a hangover from the taboo on human incest. Still, breeders keep off of it, just in case. A lot of time and money tied up in a single horse. This brute'll be worth a treasure by the time we get him trained.'

I went back and sat on a windowsill while Brendan continued the training that would turn Ysbaddaden into a treasure. It was hard to think of him in terms of cash. To me he was just pure beauty. Watching the already heavy grandeur of his springy step, I could see why people fell in love with these horses. They were straight out of myth. The gentle giant, full of graceful strength. Rhiannon would have loved the colt. She would have adjusted to the loss of Farleton Hall, would have thrown herself into The Folly's project with her usual enthusiasm. I still missed Rhiannon. I couldn't fill the empty place she had left. I had tried, heaven knows, but I was the wrong person. My heart simply wasn't in the work the others devoted themselves to. I knew it was good; on every visit I walked in the forest, admired the new things that had been done. But I admired as an outsider gazing in through the window, forever excluded. More and more my world was elsewhere, down on the grubby glittering stages of the West End. I never felt excluded there. How could I? I was 'one of Hanno's', part of an exclusive inner circle. Directors welcomed me. Other actors envied me. I had a future there.

And here? I looked at the scene before me: the magnificent Ysbaddaden, coat gleaming and fetlocks flashing, performing his paces with spirit and dignity; behind him, Belle's garden bright with autumn colour; behind that, the craggy face of the cliff, its surface glittering as the waterfall caught the sun; beyond that, the intense blue sky hanging serenely above the invisible moor. It was beautiful. Every element pleased, all of them together formed a picture so idyllic it screamed out for a camera. I am a camera, I thought, the bland surface on which this beauty is recorded. For whom? For what?

Filled with autumnal sadness, I went inside and studied my script.

'Rosalind? Hanno here.'

A bubble of joy rose in me at the sound of his voice.

'I'm sorry to call you away so soon,' he said. 'The contract's here, ready for you to sign. Bill wants to start rehearsals next Monday. I told him you'd be there.'

'Of course I'll be there.' Hanno had never phoned me at The Folly. Never before had my world entered David's. The corner of the kitchen containing the phone had suddenly become an oasis where I belonged. I looked at David, eating his dinner and watching me with vague curiosity. Brendan and Belle were watching, too. I felt childishly pleased. I could feel myself taking on substance, becoming a whole human being. No longer the onlooker, I was at the centre of my own world, linked to my own reality by 230 miles of telephone cable. 'Of course I'll be there. I've memorised most of the part already.'

Hanno's warm laughter travelled down the miles of wire. 'Rash girl. It might have fallen through.'

He didn't believe that any more than I did. Hanno's negotiations never fell through. I wanted him to go on talking for ever, to keep me real. 'So what's the research for this one?' I tried. The play was about two academics and their wives, already drunk from a party, drinking on through a violent night in which the sham of their lives is exposed. Not a lot of scope for a research outing.

Hanno laughed again. 'This will test my ingenuity.'

'I have faith in you.'

We talked a little longer. When I returned to the table, I tried not to glow too much with pleasure. Everyone was watching me. No one was talking about lunge lines or harness or brashing or felling. Everyone was waiting for me to speak. For once.

'That was Hanno,' I said. 'He's signed me up for a new part. I have to go back to London.'

There were cries of 'So soon?' 'You've only just got here!' Belle asked what the part was.

'Honey, in *Who's Afraid of Virginia Woolf?*'

She stared. 'Already? Are you serious?' She shook her head in wonder. 'You really are moving up fast. So it's all true? What they say about Hanno Hirsch?'

I shrugged with a modesty I didn't feel. 'He knows what he's doing.'

Brendan looked wary. 'And all that about the pact with the devil?'

I laughed. 'Sour grapes, I expect. He's a perfectly ordinary human being.' I didn't believe that, but I never liked talking about Hanno. Belle had often pressed me for information. I'd been as evasive as I could be without offending her. Hanno was private, not the sort of person you gossiped about, even with a close friend. I noticed that once again I'd succumbed to his spell, forgotten my anger as soon as I heard his voice. It was like living on a rollercoaster, my feelings about him swinging so violently that I never knew what I thought.

David was eating quietly, as if the conversation had nothing to do with him. In one sense, it didn't. But in another – 'Hanno thinks it'll be a long run,' I said casually. What I was really saying was: it'll be some time before I come home again. Do you care?

'How does he know?' Belle asked.

'He has a kind of intuition about these things.' Still no reaction from David. 'Will you come and see me?' It was a general question, though I meant it for him.

'Would we miss a thing like that?' Brendan laughed. 'Our own Rosie, hitting the big time at last!'

'Will *you* come?' I asked David directly.

He looked up, a little bemused. 'Of course I'll come. Maybe not the first night – it depends on work. But if it's a long run, there'll be plenty of time.' He smiled. 'I'm really pleased for you, Ros. It's good: doing the work you do best. I know that myself, now. I know how much it matters.'

Other things matter, too, I wanted to say. Does it really not worry you, having a part-time wife? Does it really not worry you that I probably spend more time with my agent than with my husband? Do you care that he's called the devil's child, Svengali? Do you care that I've put myself in his hands? Do you care what happens to me?

Do you care what happens to us?

17

Memo from H.H. to R.R. Plans to infiltrate secret installation progressing well. Rendezvous Friday 21 hours. Disguise imperative. Suggest Mata Hari look. Confirm.

The note was waiting for me when I arrived in Islington. I'd had my own phone installed in the attic flat a few months ago. I reached for it.

'Are you serious?'

'I am always serious,' said Hanno's voice.

'The Mata Hari bit, too?'

'Of course.'

'Secret Agent R.R. confirms ready for duty,' I said.

'Psst,' I said as I walked past the big leonine figure leaning against a lamp post. He detached himself from it and followed a few paces behind. I was wearing my best black silk catsuit and shades. Hoping to blend into the night, you know. I whistled a few bars of *Lili Marlene* as I sauntered casually into the tube station. The voice behind me joined in the chorus. I sucked in my breath and shot him a warning glance. He shut his mouth. Fast. I looked round at the people swarming past: no signs of suspicion, but you never could tell.

The train was crowded. I slid into the last seat available. On one side, a green lamé girl with a giant orange Afro. On the other, a pair of fiery revolutionary's eyes above a Zapata moustache. Looming over me, the honey-blond and beige figure, holding lightly to the strap and reading the adverts. Whistling *Lili Marlene*. I looked straight ahead at the blackness of the tunnel walls.

At Camden we rose en bloc and flowed out of the train,

out of the station, on to the pavement. I paused, pretending to search for something in my handbag, waiting for Beige Gold to give the signal. He jerked his head infinitesimally towards the road. I followed. So did the orange Afro and the moustache. So did half the contents of the train, all of them disguised as people going to a party: black leathers, embroidered peasant blouses, Biba dresses, combat wear. Bearded Jesuses. Kaftans. Jeans. Patchwork quilt skirts. Steel-rimmed glasses. Tank tops. A floppy hat shredded at the edges. Big leather belts carved to death. Two or three women in ordinary party dresses. Two or three men in suits.

I hung back a little, watching the pageant. The honey-coloured figure slowed down, too. The people flowed past us in colourful dribs. We were alone at last.

I couldn't keep up the act any longer. I fixed on Hanno a stern look. 'All right. What's this all about?'

He regarded me mournfully. 'You flunk.'

'I'm not in a spy school. Nor is Albee's play. Well? Are you going to explain? Where *are* we going?'

'To a party, my dear Mata Hari. A party which is your research project. You will spy diligently.'

We strolled down the street and he continued, 'Our host is a senior lecturer in politics at University College. Not the cosy little college of *Who's Afraid of Virginia Woolf?* but it's the best I can do. If you're lucky you'll get an updated version of the party the characters have just left at the beginning of Act One.' He bowed, like a court messenger who's just handed over his dispatch.

I laughed. 'I should have known!'

'You said you had faith.'

'I do. But how on earth do you know a senior lecturer at University College?'

'Ve haf vays.'

Always the same: never a straight answer to a straight question. 'I've been to academic parties before, you know.'

'I know. Eight years ago.'

The precision took my breath away. It was uncanny

enough that he knew so much about me and I so little about him. But he seemed to have my biography at his fingertips, ready for instant consultation. 'And how do you know that?'

'Ve haf vays.' He smiled and changed the subject so simply that I barely noticed. 'The party is just to refresh your memory. Also, the production Bill has in mind is updated, so this should be nearer to the mood he'll aim for.'

It was a long walk. I tried to use it to winkle out more information about the strange contacts he seemed to have which gave him access to embassies and academic parties. I learned nothing.

The street in front of the house was crammed with eccentric vehicles, the house itself brightly lighted and welcoming. It was one of the solid Victorian terraces colonised by university people. Our host, Brian Somethingorother, was younger than I expected – clearly something of a *Wunderkind* himself – and gave the impression of knowing Hanno quite well. I wondered again at the secretive image Hanno had. It was as if he avoided his own kind but, outside the theatrical hothouse, moved freely and with little aura of mystery.

We helped ourselves to wine from the long table in the conservatory. '*Prosit*,' said Hanno. 'To a profitable evening. Listen well. These are interesting times for academia. Cuts are in the air. Backs are being bitten. Ambition is rife but threatened. You have a good ear, Rosalind. In a few hours you can learn what it feels like to be the young wife of a young academic on the way up. Every wife or girlfriend here is a Honey.'

'No Marthas?'

'Perhaps.' He smiled, a great golden searchlight that seemed to illuminate every corner of the conservatory. 'I'll introduce you to a few people to get you launched. After that, you're on your own.'

I smiled back with difficulty. I'd made the mistake of treating an outing like a date, my mentor as . . . well . . .

as a boyfriend. But to him this was just work, however attractively packaged.

'I'll make sure everyone knows you're an actress,' he continued. 'Academics like theatre people – they're non-threatening. The wives – and you must concentrate on the wives tonight – will speak more openly with you than with the other wives.'

'Hanno,' I said quietly, 'do you ever do anything that isn't work?'

He looked at me for what seemed a long time. 'My life is my work,' he said finally.

How alike they were, David and Hanno, despite their different surfaces. Both of them obsessed with work, unwilling or unable to see anything beyond it. I watched Hanno from the tail of my eye all evening while listening to the anxieties of the Honeys. I was remembering the party where I'd first seen David. David had seemed out of place among the brightly dressed and chattering actors – a dark, brooding Hamlet, I'd thought at the time, completely self-sufficient, wrapped up in his own vision. Hanno didn't seem at all out of place among these academics. He had the same mixture of lightness and gravity. Once or twice I caught snatches of conversation and was surprised to find he was talking politics. A crazy notion flitted through my head: was this spy business more than a joke? It seemed improbable, but it was odd how little was known about him. And there'd been that embassy reception, too. What better cover than an actors' agent? It could hardly be less suspicious. No. Hanno was far too brilliant at his work to be doing it part-time.

New arrivals kept coming – after a play, a concert, another party. I didn't pay much attention; I knew none of them. Suddenly, however, while the tenth or so Honey was telling me her life history, another voice sailed above the chatter. A trained voice, and familiar. 'Hello, darling. Sorry I'm so late.' I looked round in time to see Caroline, gorgeous in a red velvet dress, giving our host a theatrical hug.

I wasn't the only one who'd heard. Hanno turned round

sharply. The look of pleasure on his face cut through me. She didn't hug him. She didn't have to. I remembered the rumpled sheets in the hidden room. Also remembered that she was the star of the play I'd been brought here to research.

My humiliation was complete. Quietly I left the room and went to the conservatory. I tried to be reasonable. Hanno had never pretended I was anything other than a client. This evening he'd made it even clearer with his insistence that I was here to work. It also made sense that he should connive to have us both at the same party. He was doing the director's work for him, giving both of us the same background material with which to approach the text. Very sensible. Efficient. And cold.

The door opened behind me. It was Caroline.

'Ros, what a lovely surprise! I've just been talking with Bill tonight. He said you were signed up to do Honey. I'm so pleased! I can't imagine anyone who could do it better!'

Her enthusiasm seemed so genuine I felt ashamed of my antagonism. 'Martha's a wonderful role,' I said. 'I'm sure you'll be marvellous in it.'

'It's going to be a strong production. Bill's put a lot of thought into it.'

'So has Hanno.'

'Hanno?' She seemed surprised. 'He doesn't have much to do with it, does he?'

'He brought us to the same party for research.'

'Research? What an extraordinary idea. I didn't even know he would be here.'

'Then how? I mean . . .'

She laughed. 'Brian's wife is an old friend of mine. We were students together at LAMDA.' She poured herself some wine. 'So what's all this about "research"?'

Did she really know nothing about these research outings? Had Hanno never taken her on them? 'Just that this is an academic party,' I said. 'A chance to observe academics socialising. As in the play. Research,' I ended lamely.

A scrap of delighted laughter from Caroline. 'Good heavens! I hadn't thought of it but you're absolutely right! How amusing. Well then, let's go in and do a little observing.'

I hung back, reluctant to be seen entering a room with Caroline, eclipsed by her greater beauty and fame. 'Hanno brought me here specifically to observe. I assumed he'd asked you to come for the same reason.'

She seemed genuinely puzzled. 'I didn't even know he would be here.'

'Oh, of course. You said. Sorry. I just thought . . . I thought you knew him quite well.'

She laughed. 'Does anyone?' Then she looked at me more closely. 'He *brought* you here? I didn't think he ever took anyone anywhere. I assumed he was a loner.'

I thought back to the two of them in the foyer of the Wigmore Hall. It was just possible that they'd met there by accident. It was also possible that the voice I'd heard coming from the secret room belonged to someone else. After all, I'd barely heard either voice over the background music. And it was difficult to believe that Caroline was lying. Of course she was a formidable actress, but she had no reason to lie.

Then a marvellous thing happened. I felt as if a physical weight had suddenly been removed from my head and at the same time experienced a rush of real affection for Caroline. What on earth had possessed me, to imagine secret meetings between them, to turn against this perfectly decent woman for no reason at all? I smiled at her, and this time it was genuine. 'Never mind. Let's go and observe.'

All the signs were good. The director, Bill, was a joy to work with. He had a strong vision of the play but was sensitive enough to persuade rather than browbeat us into sharing it. We talked it through as thoroughly as we could in the ridiculously short rehearsal period allotted us. I could feel the play taking shape, feel the excitement of the other three actors, too. It was a strong cast, no doubt about it. Whatever Hanno's motives, he'd been right to push Bill into putting Caroline and myself in our roles. Sparks flew all right, but not antagonistic ones. Caroline was one of those strong, quiet actresses who draw others into responding at her level. Just watching her become the vulgar drunken Martha was a revelation. No type-casting here, just first-rate acting. Well, I was hardly type-cast either. I couldn't be further from the simpering idiot who was Honey, but with Caroline drawing me on and Bill's sensitive direction, I could feel myself becoming the character. After that, it was a snowball effect, all of us rolling through rehearsals with increased momentum, harried by the hectic schedule and yet impatient to get on the stage and let rip.

It was altogether an exhilarating time: by day the manic rehearsals, by night an equally manic round of concerts and plays, getting in my quota before our run began. Nearly every night I went out somewhere with Jas (he was also in rehearsal) or Astrid or Hugh, and sometimes all three.

Jas was practically a member of our Islington household by now. Astrid adored him and poor culture-starved Hugh was chuffed to include among his friends 'a member of the National, you know'. They were happy foursomes, those evenings, and none more so than Jas's birthday. I'd bought tickets for a concert at the Wigmore Hall as a birthday treat. It was really a treat for Jas because it was madrigals, and the rest of us didn't particularly like madrigals.

'All this "Hey nonny" nonsense,' Astrid scoffed as we approached the Wigmore Hall, her Swedish practicality making a rare appearance. It combined with her dark, heavy exoticism to produce a picture of a *grande dame*, a queen with court jester in tow: Jas, cavorting beside her and singing.

'Oh mistress mine, be not a swine. Thy dignity offendeth me.'

Astrid was trying hard not to smile. Jas, more than ever the leprechaun, continued his wooing.

'My pretty tune will make thee swoon, if thou relent thy harsh judgment.'

Hugh and I were already creased with laughter, more at the sight of the two of them than at Jas's awful ditty.

'So let thy clown erase thy frown, and teach thine ear these songs to bear.'

There followed a crash course in How To Appreciate Madrigals which was more comic than informative. By the time we reached the Wigmore Hall we were in no fit state to appreciate the music.

I hadn't been thinking of Hanno when I booked the tickets, but naturally I glanced at the people in the foyer. The foyer was long, narrow and crowded, and Hanno was at the far end. I refrained from pointing him out to my companions. I don't think he saw me at all; he seemed intent on reading the publicity leaflets. Interest, of course, but also the pose of a lonely man trying not to look lonely. I felt oddly moved by the sight.

Normally we would have gone for some supper afterwards, but Astrid was anxious to get home. She was off on a tour of provincial music societies the next day and wanted one long last night in her own bed before facing the suitcase life. Also, her nerves were threatening again. We tried to calm her down. 'They won't notice a few wrong notes,' we said. But nerves aren't rational. Worse, they have a nasty way of gaining momentum. One wrong note leads to the expectation of another, and more often than not the prophecy is self-fulfilled. I was worried about her but tried to hide it for fear of making things worse.

So there we were, Jas and I, alone on the pavement outside the Wigmore Hall. Neither of us was hungry but, 'How about a drink?' said Jas. 'There's a pub just down the road.'

It was coincidence, of course, that the pub was directly opposite Hanno's building. Coincidence, too, that the only free table was right by the window, though the wind whistling through a crack in the pane might have explained its vacancy.

'Brrr,' said Jas. 'This calls for a hot toddy.'

The publican thought he was mad. We settled for rum instead.

I never saw Hanno enter the building. I wouldn't have seen anything else either if I hadn't been looking so hard and working out which windows were his just at the moment when the faintest possible outline appeared round the edges. Working late, I might have thought, if I hadn't gone on watching long enough to see two adjacent windows take on the same barely-visible outline. It didn't take long to work out that they could only belong to the hidden room.

I looked at Jas. He hadn't noticed anything. But then, he had no reason to be watching the windows so closely.

I don't know what possessed me, but by the time people started drifting out of the pub, I had made up my mind: I would beard the lion in his den. I would find out the secret of that hidden room. I tried to talk myself out of it. Hanno's private life was none of my business. Worse, if I barged in on it, he would almost certainly turn against me, erase me from his clients' list and his life. But I was feeling strong these days, and stroppy. Also, rum was not my accustomed drink. Whatever, I felt invincible and nosy as hell. I was tired of Hanno's secrecy, of this mystique he'd built up around himself.

'You go on,' I said to Jas. 'I'll get a taxi home.'

It took a while for the taxi to come. Jas lived much further out than I did and in the opposite direction. He would take the tube home. I calculated how long it would take for him to leave Wigmore Street. Then I tapped on the glass.

The driver was surprised. Wigmore Street? But I'd just left there. Yes, I explained; I wanted to go back. I didn't even try to make up an excuse. There was none that would be plausible.

The street was almost deserted. Standing on the pavement, I felt a twinge of doubt. What if Hanno had left by now? I didn't really like being here on my own. I scrutinised the building. It took a while for my eyes to adjust sufficiently to see the faint light at the edges. It had disappeared from the office windows but was still visible from the two next to them. Taking a deep breath, I went across the street and rang the bell.

Insanity, courage, stupidity. Whatever it was that had propelled me into this absurd situation, the moment I heard the bell echo through the building I felt it drain from me. I didn't even know what the bell was for. Was there a night watchman? A concierge? What if no one answered the bell? Well, I could always get another taxi. I rang the bell again, and, after a shorter pause, a third time. Damn it, the lights were on, Hanno must be there, he must come down. I rang a fourth time, and a fifth, the intervals between growing shorter and shorter.

At last, footsteps. I didn't know Hanno well enough to recognise his step. For that matter, I didn't know him well enough to make this outrageous intrusion. I clenched my teeth, cursing the impulse that had brought me here. I'd need a fine bit of acting indeed to get myself out of it.

And then a voice behind the closed door. 'Who's there?'

I closed my eyes in relief. I might not recognise his footsteps, but the voice was unmistakable. 'Ros,' I said.

A pause. 'Rosalind?'

'Yes.'

A clatter of keys, locks, bolts. Then the door opened and Hanno stood before me. He made no effort to disguise his astonishment.

'Rosalind? What on earth are you doing here?'

'That book you wanted to lend me – about academics. *The History Man*. I just happened to be in the area and thought . . .'

'*Now?*'

'I've just been to a concert at the Wigmore Hall. Being so near, I thought . . .'

'The concert ended an hour ago.'

'I've been in the pub.' That was it – the inspiration I'd been praying for. Suddenly I saw how to play it. I smiled a little sheepishly. 'Actually, I was in the pub before the concert, too. To tell you the truth . . .'

He stared at me. Rum has a powerful odour. He must have smelled it, come to the conclusion I wanted. 'Rosalind . . .'

'Well . . . yes . . . a trifle tiddly, perhaps. Am I being too dreadful?' It was Honey speaking. I hoped he wouldn't recognise her.

'And what made you think I'd be here?' His smile was that of a schoolmaster amused by some foolish prank by a pupil.

'I saw your lights.'

The smile vanished. 'You'd better come in.'

If there were any lights in the hall, Hanno didn't choose to use them. We made our way up the stairs slowly, Hanno a dim shape barely outlined by the skylight far above. I was thinking hard, working out the next stage. Coffee. I would ask for a coffee. I ran the scene through my mind. Yes, coffee, that would do it.

He opened the door to the outer office and ushered me in. The door to the inner office was shut. 'You'd better sit down,' he said. 'You look a little shaky.'

I nodded and sat down. 'Actually' – my sheepish grin again – 'I could do with a coffee.'

'I don't doubt.'

And then, oh miracle, it all happened just as I'd hoped. He went behind the secretary's desk and fetched the electric kettle. I was pretty sure that the nearest tap would be in the Gents, and that was on the next floor down. It should give me plenty of time.

The moment the door closed behind him, I rose noiselessly from my chair and tiptoed to the door of the inner office. Please God, let it be open. I turned the knob as quietly as I could. The door opened without a sound. I went in. A single feeble light burned in Hanno's office. I cursed the few moments it took my eyes to adjust. Then I made my way carefully across the room to the long thin print which I knew concealed the door to the hidden room. I'd hoped it would be open, but Hanno was clearly too careful for that. I eased my fingers behind the print and ran them down both sides. A tiny knob interrupted them. I moved it to left and right, pushing gently all the time. How long had Hanno been gone? Finally I felt it give. I pushed a little harder and the whole panel began to swing open. My heart was crashing about so hard I could barely breathe. Only a few seconds more and I would see . . .

The door was open. I stood on the threshhold peering in, feeling like a fairy-tale child who'd stumbled upon a secret hut in the depths of the forest. Wide-eyed, I took in the scene.

It was a perfect little jewel of a room, about the same size as Hanno's office. There was little space for furniture, but the few pieces were beautifully chosen. A divan bed against one corner of the wall opposite the windows was covered by a creamy silk spread. In the other corner a beige leather armchair was pooled in golden light from a yellow-shaded lamp. An open book was face-down on the chair – clearly I'd interrupted his reading. In the centre of the room was a small table and a single chair, both painted ivory with the mouldings picked out in gold. A chest of drawers and a wardrobe – also ivory and gold – stood against the wall nearest me. A beige carpet covered the floor. Most of the wall space was taken up by floor-to-ceiling bookshelves. An archway in the wall opposite me led to a tiny kitchen. A door beside it no doubt led to a bathroom. A bowl of creamy freesias stood in the centre of the little table.

The room was exquisite. Both elegant and homely, it was a little oasis in the dull workaday world of Wigmore Street. I stood there, enchanted, forgetting time and forgetting, too, that I'd hoped only to have a quick look. I'd intended to see what I could and then flit back to the outer office to be waiting, all innocence, for Hanno's return, my curiosity satisfied and Hanno none the wiser. All forgotten as I stared, charmed by the little room.

Until I felt a hand on my shoulder, heard his voice close to my ear: 'Rosalind.'

18

I froze. When finally I turned to look at him, all I could do was hope that some miracle would tell me what to do next, hope there might be a way to salvage something from the ruins.

What I saw astonished me. No anger, no contempt. Just sadness, but a sadness so intense that it cut through me far more harshly than any anger. My God, what *had* I done? Through crass nosiness I'd ruined everything, betrayed the trust we'd felt in each other. I'd cut the heart out of my own life. During those dismal moments when neither of us spoke, I saw my career, just on the verge of blossoming, wither. I didn't want to act any more, not with Hanno gone. Nothing mattered. I wished I was dead.

'I'm sorry,' I whispered.

He nodded – not in forgiveness, I didn't expect that – but in acknowledgment. I didn't know what to do. I wanted to leave, just slip quietly out of the room and out of his life, but he was standing behind me. We were both trapped in a scene that had no obvious ending. My shoulder was burning where his hand still rested on it. Something stirred in me. The burning, and that sad, disappointed look in his face. I'd seen it before. My dream. The golden stag. He'd looked at me like that when David had called me back to him. Then the sparks from his antlers had set me alight and turned the dream into a nightmare. I shivered.

'You're cold?' said Hanno, bringing me back to the present. 'Come and sit by the fire.'

I shivered again, this time from apprehension, but he was already propelling me towards the armchair. I sat down obediently. Hanno crouched in the space between the chair and the bed and turned up the heat on a small electric fire set into the wall. He still had the kettle in his other hand. When he stood up again, he smiled. Incredibly, he smiled.

'Since you're here, you may as well make yourself comfortable.' He walked across to the tiny kitchen and plugged in the kettle. I watched, confused, as he opened a cupboard and took out a coffeepot. I'd completely forgotten about the coffee.

'I don't really need it,' I said dully. 'I'm not drunk.'

'So I gather.' His back was turned to me, I couldn't judge his mood. I felt utterly lost. 'One doesn't need to be drunk to enjoy a coffee,' he continued. 'Perhaps you'd like a brandy to go with it? We must talk, you know. A brandy might be helpful.'

'Yes.' My voice was croaky. I cleared my throat. 'Yes, thank you.'

He took two glasses from a wall cupboard and poured the brandy. The kitchen was neat, clean, orderly, every possible space used to the maximum. The rest of the room was the same. I now noticed how cleverly it had been designed, no space wasted, every comfort catered for on a miniature scale. Even music, two speakers tucked into corners of the bookshelves. The music I'd heard that morning when I'd seen the hidden room reflected in the glass, seen the rumpled bed. I looked at the bed and only now registered that it was a single one.

Hanno was standing before me, handing me a glass of brandy. He took his own to the little table, turned the chair round and sat down facing me. In the silence the water trickled through the coffee filter. '*Prosit*,' he said at last, lifting his glass to me.

'*Prosit*,' I echoed. The brandy felt good.

A single bed, a single chair by the little table, a single armchair. Had this tiny room ever held two people?

The filter stopped dripping. Hanno got up and poured the coffee. He moved a little bedside chest to the side of my chair and put the coffee on it. Then he returned to the table. We sat for some time just watching each other.

The long vertical creases in Hanno's face looked deeper and stronger than ever, his face sombre. Finally he broke the silence.

'How long have you known?' he asked.

'A few weeks,' I answered mechanically. 'That morning I dropped in. I saw the open doorway mirrored in the Klimt.'

He nodded, thoughtful. 'I did wonder.'

We said nothing for a while. I couldn't bear to look at his face. I looked round the room instead. There was something about it that disturbed me, that didn't make sense. It was inappropriately furnished for a seducer's den. What was its purpose? Suddenly I saw. I looked at him in astonishment. 'You *live* here.'

'Of course. What did you think?'

How stupid I'd been. That was why he wasn't listed in the phone book. I'd assumed he was just ex-directory, guarding his privacy. I should have realised the moment I glimpsed the room weeks ago. 'But it's *tiny*,' I said.

He shrugged. 'I don't need much. I have London.'

That little café round the corner where we'd had breakfast, where he'd seemed to be a regular. He always had his breakfast there, it was his kitchen. The Wigmore Hall and Broadcasting House, they were his living-rooms. And the way he strode the streets of London, so much more at home in them than anyone I'd ever known. He *was* at home; they were the corridors of his house. The whole of London was his dwelling.

'So now you know,' he said. 'What do you intend to do?'

'Do?'

'Report me to the authorities?'

'What on earth for?'

'Rosalind, it must have occurred to you: I'm living here illegally.'

'I don't understand.'

'This is an office building. It's against every conceivable regulation to live here. Fire, security, local authority rules.'

'You mean nobody knows?'

'The cleaning lady knows. She discovered early on.' He managed a faint smile. 'I make a small unofficial service payment to her. You understand. And now you. I don't suppose you came here to ask a similar payment?'

My cheeks burned. 'What do you think I am? A blackmailer?'

'I don't know what you are, Rosalind, or why you came here tonight. Perhaps you'll tell me?'

I couldn't tell him about the rumpled sheets, my unreasonable jealousy. Suddenly I remembered the ex-secretary, the one rumoured to have fled because she thought her employer in league with the devil. 'Your last secretary,' I said. 'Did she know something?'

'You know about her?'

'Not much. Only that she left because she was afraid of you.'

Hanno smiled. 'I did my best. She was becoming suspicious. My alarm didn't go off one morning. I woke up late on a morning she happened to arrive early. She knew by the post that I couldn't be here, so when I emerged from my office . . .'

Smelling of fresh shaving cream. Of course, that too. 'So you played the devil's child?'

'It didn't take much. She was rather flighty. Since then I've been more careful.'

'But *why*? *Why* is it so important to live here?'

And now, I was sure, something evasive crept into his manner. 'It suits me.'

'But surely there are residential areas nearby?'

He rose and refilled my coffee cup. 'I was young and short of money when I first came to London. I wanted a good office in a good part of town. There was no money left for a flat. This room was derelict when I rented the office; for just a little more I could have it as a storeroom. The landlord's firm was in financial trouble, they couldn't raise the money to do it up. I moved a camp bed into it. I meant it to be temporary, but I found myself doing it up bit by bit. I was lucky. The firm's always been pretty disorganised; they forgot about the room. It's remained just a storeroom as far as they're concerned. I'm a good tenant. The cleaning lady was the only person who had reason to be curious until now. Rosalind, I need to know: what do you intend to do?'

The voices I thought I'd heard. A record, the spoken bits in an opera perhaps. How stupid I'd been to jump to such conclusions.

'Rosalind, tell me.'

'Why does it matter now? Surely you can afford to rent a proper flat by now?'

'This suits me,' he said shortly.

Again I had a feeling he was being evasive. I surveyed the room again. How could someone who'd lived so long in London accumulate so little?

'I need to know,' he said again.

A sequence of scenes passed sadly through my mind. All those happy times together, wandering through the street market, gleefully eavesdropping on the rich Americans in Harrods, the lunchtime concert, the trip to the zoo. I looked into my brandy, wishing again I could annihilate myself. Or, better still, turn the clock back, pretend this night didn't exist.

His voice seemed to come from a long distance. 'I'm in your hands, Rosalind.' He looked round the lovely room, as if taking leave of it already.

I smiled despite my misery. What words from a Svengali. 'Well, that makes a change,' I said.

'What do you mean?'

'When you first took me on. Your "conditions". That I must do exactly what you told me. That you would shape every detail of my career as long as I obeyed without questioning.'

He opened his hands, palms up, like a magician showing the audience he had nothing to hide. 'Then we have reversed our roles,' he said with a faint smile. '*You* may tell *me* what you wish me to do.'

Something was happening. The atmosphere was beginning to lighten just a fraction. The deep black awfulness of my act was fading. Was there really some hope after all? 'I'm no Svengali,' I said cautiously.

'No? But you want power. All actors do. The power to change lives. You have the power to change mine very considerably.'

The room was becoming luminous, like a clearing in a forest. In the centre appeared the magician, offering me the time-honoured wish. Anything you wish, my child: gold, power, fame, love, eternal life.

'Well?'

Well. What *did* I want? I had no use for wealth, and the power to stir an audience was already within me. Fame would come of its own accord, and I was too young to fret about mortality. Love? I had that, didn't I? David, Belle and Brendan at The Folly; Astrid and Hugh and Jas in London. I looked deeply into Hanno's gold-flecked eyes. I think I honestly believed at that moment that he could grant any wish.

The curtains behind him were shimmering. They were a pale golden yellow, as light and ethereal as everything else in the room. No doubt some kind of blackout curtain lurked behind them, but I'd forgotten about that. The secrecy of the room was no longer the secrecy of an illegally inhabited room but of a hidden fairy-tale kingdom the curious child had stumbled upon. My eyes blurred for a moment, dazzled by the golden backdrop, the gold of his hair, the gold of his eyes. 'One day,' I whispered.

The picture clicked back into focus. My agent, Hanno Hirsch, regarded me across the small space, the beginnings of a puzzled smile on his face.

'One day with you,' I said, a fraction louder now. 'My wish.'

He was scrutinising my face intently.

'You asked what I wanted you to do,' I said. 'That's what I would like: for you to spend one day with me. Doing whatever *you* would most want to do with such a day.' I smiled, trying to pretend it was a perfectly ordinary wish.

'That's what you want of me?' he said at last.

I nodded.
'That's all?'
I nodded.
'Not a contract with the National?' he smiled. 'I could probably manage that by now.'
I shook my head.
'Just one day with me?'
I nodded.
'My dear, inscrutable Rosalind. You shall have it.'

19

It was a beautiful morning, sharp, cold and bright, when we met at the gates of St James's Park. The first hard frost of the year had come and crisped the grass into tiny white spears. It had etched white the edges of the few remaining leaves before sending them floating down to lie on the grass. Their colours, not quite hidden by their new decoration, shone through faintly, turning the park into a rich watercolour of palest green and russet and gold.

We walked through the park, warmer than we might have been. The sun was switched on full strength and doing its best to counteract the frosty air rising from the ground. The two met somewhere near our heads, setting up a delicious turbulence of warm and cold. The park had never been more beautiful. I had never been happier.

Some time had passed. It hadn't been easy finding a day that suited us both. I was bound by rehearsals, Hanno was away on weekends. Finally he managed to alter some appointments and clear a day – a rare day when I wasn't rehearsing – to fulfil his promise. 'I'm your slave for the day,' he'd said on the phone.

'Where are we going?'

'Secret. Mystery Tour.'

'But what do I wear?'

'Good stout shoes.'

My good stout shoes *phlumphed* along the path. Hanno was wearing a camelhair coat which made him look distinguished in a nice quiet way. Above it his honey-gold hair gleamed in the sun. I noticed with surprise a few silvery threads in it, as if the frost had had its way even with him. I was in my late twenties; Hanno, I guessed, in his late thirties, though it was hard to pinpoint an age in that strange face of his with its combination of austerity and warmth. I loved his face and often watched it surreptitiously when his attention was elsewhere.

I'd been nervous of this meeting. Hanno had every reason to despise me, a brash spy barging into his hidden room and then demanding a day of his life for hush money. But there was no trace of resentment on his face as we walked through the park. He seemed as happy to be there as I was.

We reached the pond. He burrowed into his pocket and drew out a rumpled paper bag. Instantly a million ducks and geese whizzed to his feet, squabbling with each other for a ringside seat. I laughed to see him – so big and tall – rising out of the seething mass. He handed some of the bread to me, then popped a piece into the beak of a Canada goose. Uproar. Necks strained, beaks snapped, flippers stamped in outrage. As fast as we could distribute our offerings, more birds appeared.

An old woman arrived with a whole carrier bag full of bread. The bulk of our admirers took one look at her and deserted us without so much as thanks. An old man walked on to the bridge and placed breadcrumbs in the palm of one hand. He held it out. A squadron of sparrows alighted on his hand, queuing all the way up his arm and shoulder. Hanno shook out the last crumbs from his paper bag and admitted defeat. We walked on.

'And this is how your ideal day begins?' I queried, amused.

'Certainly.'

'The gods often have winged messengers,' I said. 'Do they whisper things to you as they gobble? Is there a coded message in their cackle?'

'Do I look like a god?' he returned.

Yes, I wanted to say, but didn't. The god of all free and mysterious things.

We descended into the tube and re-emerged some time later at Old Street. 'Where are we going?' I asked.

'Secret. Mystery Tour.'

I sighed. This was quaint punishment indeed for my

nosiness, my uncovering of his lair. Be thou condemned for ever to wonder. We walked. Old warehouses loomed over the street, thwarting the sun. *Phlumph phlumph* said my Good Stout Shoes.

Sounds were oozing from the cracks around the unpainted door of a warehouse. The door groaned with the weight of the sound. Hanno put it out of its misery and opened it. We entered. The sound flowed around us, unrestrained: a piano thumping out music while a flock of black birds disguised as dancers went *phlumph phlumph* all over a splintery floor. A rehearsal room. I shivered as I gazed at the dancers, their bodies thin and defenceless in black leotards, their legs alone wrapped in warmers. No wonder they were making such a frenzied job of it. To keep warm.

'This is all too familiar,' I said to Hanno.

'No, it isn't. These are dancers. You're only an actress.'

'Hanno!'

He laughed, his laughter a great outpouring of sun rays which seemed instantly to warm the frozen room. 'It pleases me to make you angry,' he said. 'When you're angry, your eyes shoot green sparks, like an elf's welding torch.'

It wasn't often that Hanno complimented me. 'Jas said I should go into films,' I ventured. A BBC contact had questioned Jas about me: would I be interested in a small part in a costume drama? Hanno had refused even to consider it. 'Jas says my "peculiar" eyes are wasted on the stage.'

'That's exactly why you should stay on the stage. Do you want to become known as The Girl With The Peculiar Eyes?'

'I want to become known. Full stop.'

'In time, and through the theatre. Shush now. Watch the dancers.'

'Hanno, will you ever let me do a film?'

'Probably not.'

'But *why*?'

'Isn't that obvious, you goose?'

'No. Tell me.'

'Because,' he gave me an exasperated look, 'you're too beautiful. And before you go all gooey with flattery, let me remind you that beauty is no gift for a serious actress. I had reservations about taking you on.'

'Don't be absurd.'

'Don't be stupid. You'd be type-cast. You'd spend the rest of your life playing Sweet Young Things. You'd never be offered a decent role. Who would cast the glamorous Ros Rawlinson as Mother Courage? In the theatre a good make-up artist can disguise your unfortunate looks. Now be quiet and watch the dancers.'

I clamped my mouth shut. Why could I never be angry with Hanno when I was with him? He insulted me, he made me walk miles, he fed me cheap meals and never took me to the opera. He was a rude old skinflint and I padded after him like an adoring little poodle. Bah! I turned away and watched the dancers, knowing it was useless trying to drum up the indignation I should feel.

The dancers were good. Before long I forgot about Hanno, enthralled by this strange ritual, so like my own rehearsals and yet so different. A tiny old woman about two feet high prowled the edge of the marked-out dance floor, shouting things in a foreign accent and – I thought at first – a foreign language, until I realised it was merely the French terminology of ballet. If I was a poodle, she was a terrier, snapping at the heels of the thin black birds. Why didn't they turn on her, reach out their long necks and bite the shins of their diminutive tyrant? Finally one of them shot back a retort. To my surprise, the terrier roared with laughter. Then the other dancers laughed. Even the repetiteur, huddled over his badly tuned piano wrapped in overcoat and scarf, gave up playing and joined in the joke. A moment later a scowl replaced her grin and the dancing continued.

'Which ballet is this?' I asked Hanno.

He told me.

'Will you take me to see it when it opens?'

'No.'

'Will you let me take you to see it when it opens?'
'No.'
'You really are infuriating.'
'I don't like things when they're finished. I like to see things being created.'
I studied his profile, wishing I could get inside that head of his just once. 'What a strange person you are,' I murmured.
He gave me his Max von Sydow look, stern as hell. 'You told me to give you a day doing the things *I* most wanted to do. I would rather watch a rehearsal than a final performance.'
Stubborn. My God, he was stubborn. Beneath that creamy charm which had so captivated me the first day lurked a mind that went its own way, disregarding all the norms. Like David, I thought with a sudden stab of guilt.
I turned away and watched the dancers.

Phlumph phlumph went my Good Stout Shoes. We were outside again. 'Where are we going?'
'Secret. Mystery Tour.'
We'd stayed long enough to share a coffee break with the dancers. The repetiteur had come over to join us – he seemed to know Hanno fairly well. He was a young man, not long out of music school, trying for the big break and meanwhile patching together a living doing things like this. I thought he'd be resentful, playing a wonky old piano for a bunch of people to rehearse to, but he loved it. 'It's great – watching a thing being created, being a part of it.' Hanno sent an I-told-you-so look in my direction. I avoided it. Just before the rehearsal resumed, the young man went to the piano and played a Scott Joplin rag just for the fun of it.
'My sister-in-law is a pianist,' I said now, to break the monopoly of our footsteps on the soundscape.
'Yes, I know.'
'You seem to know everything,' I sighed. 'Can I never surprise you?'
Hanno laughed. 'Is that how you see me? Omniscient?'

'Yes. You clutch your knowledge to you like a one-man cabal and never let anyone in.'

'And is that why you demanded your day? To see what I would choose? To penetrate my innermost life?'

'Yes,' I said, and suddenly saw it was true. That hadn't been my reason when I'd blurted out my request in the hidden room. Then it had only been the old blind desire for his company. But the more I knew him, the more I knew I didn't know him, and the more I wanted to know. 'But I also know it's useless.'

'Good. Then you can release your enquiring mind for the simple enjoyment of the day. You are enjoying it?'

'Can you doubt?'

We walked in silence for some time. 'My sister-in-law is a *good* pianist,' I added, taking up the thread again.

'Yes. But she suffers from nerves.'

I stopped dead and stared at him. 'How on earth can you know that?'

He smiled sadly. 'Part of my one-man cabal? No, much simpler. I've spent my life among performers. One learns the signs. I'm sorry for your sister-in-law. She *is* good and could become even better, but she may not have the chance.'

I didn't want to think about Astrid. She'd returned from her provincial tour in none too good a state, and her first concert at the Queen Elizabeth Hall was coming up. She was worried, much more than she'd ever been before. 'She'll manage,' I said.

'I hope so.'

We turned and walked through an archway. Inside was a huge rectangular courtyard. There was a familiar whiff about it. 'Where are we?'

'The Whitbread stables – can't you smell?'

'Ah.'

We entered a corridor lined with box stalls. Large inquisitive heads appeared over the top of the dutch doors. Very large. My conscience gave another twinge.

'Shires,' Hanno explained. 'You've seen their hitch?'

I had. The famous team of greys delivering barrels all

over London. How odd. I'd never made the connection with – 'My husband keeps Shires,' I said. It felt better to bring it into the open.

Hanno looked at me in surprise. 'He does? I didn't know that.'

I smiled faintly. 'Not omniscient after all?'

'I never claimed to be. That's your fantasy. What does he use them for?'

'Forestry. He's trying to rescue a derelict forest. He uses the horses for pulling out single logs. They don't damage the surrounding trees like a tractor does.'

He knew I was married, of course, but we'd never talked much about David. It was better to keep quiet about it, Hanno said. Casting directors were a little wary of married women – the split commitment and, above all, the fear of a pregnancy at the wrong end of a run.

'It must be lovely,' he said. 'A beautiful horse like that working in a forest.'

'It is.'

'How can you bear to leave it for London?'

'I bear it just fine.'

A large grey head reached over and nuzzled my hair. I scratched the mare between her ears. She closed her eyes in pleasure, like Ysbaddaden under Brendan's hand.

'She likes you,' said Hanno.

'Horses like anyone who gives them what they want.'

'This is obviously old hat to you. If I'd known, I would have taken you somewhere else.'

'Ah, but this is *your* day. And is this what you would normally do?'

'Not often – I don't have much time. But I like to come into the City occasionally and when I do I try to stop in here.'

I regarded him with curiosity. 'Strange man. I wouldn't have guessed a passion for heavy horses.'

'Not a passion. Admiration. Aesthetics, if you like: they are very beautiful.'

'Is that your secret? A passion for beauty?'

'Perhaps.'

'But you don't like beautiful actresses.'
'I like beautiful acting.'

Our next stop was a small City church, St Margaret's, on which a hand-lettered notice announced a lunchtime recital. It all looked very modest.

'Some of the City churches are used this way,' said Hanno. 'Students from the music schools get some experience of a live audience, people working in the City get a free concert. You've never been to one?'

I shook my head.

'They're charming occasions. Often the parents come, often it's the first public appearance their child has made. Come inside.'

We sat down in a pew and read the little programme we'd been given. A violinist with a Scottish name and a pianist who was her teacher. In the pew behind us several people chattered away excitedly in Scottish accents.

Sure enough, two of the voices belonged to the girl's parents, one to a brother and the rest to friends. Had they really come all the way from Scotland for this small occasion? The parents were fiddling with a little tape recorder, anxious that it wasn't working properly. The brother was trying to help and trying to calm them down at the same time.

Finally the soloist appeared, with fiery red hair and a faceful of freckles. She looked incredibly young and sweet and nervous. She was led down the aisle by her teacher – like a wedding, the bride escorted by proud father. I felt suddenly choked. My father would never have done that, nor any teacher I'd had.

The teacher settled himself at the piano, the student at her music stand. They arranged their music, the girl trying hard not to fidget. In the hush that followed, I heard the click of the tape recorder behind me and a reluctant whirr as it began to record. The teacher and the student exchanged one last smile: his full of encouragement, hers full of trust. There was nothing in it of family bond or of sex but of a deep love in sharing the music they were about to play. I felt close to tears.

The music began. Her playing was a little harsh, uncertain. I held my breath, as I often did when Astrid performed. Soon, however, the girl began to gain confidence, her playing more sweetness and beauty.

The final piece they played was the Schubert A major sonata. The church vanished. I was in the Long Gallery at Farleton Hall, Rhiannon beside me. Listening rapt to another music student in another lifetime. The day my engagement was announced. I closed my eyes in pain. When I opened them, I was back in St Margaret's, hearing the applause. It was surprisingly vigorous, given that it came from perhaps two dozen people huddled together in the little church. Someone – a fellow student, I guessed – came down the aisle with a bouquet for the soloist. She clutched it as if it were the most precious thing in the world.

'I love these concerts,' said Hanno as we left the church. 'They're so full of hope.'

I nodded, still too moved to speak, not trusting my voice. We walked in silence for some time. 'What do you think will happen to her?' I asked at last.

'She'll probably end up as a music teacher in a small town in Scotland. Not entirely discontented, and with some happy moments to remember. Today will be one of them.'

'And me? What does your crystal ball predict for me?'

'You could be one of the finest actresses of your generation,' he said simply.

I caught my breath. Hanno had never spoken like this before. 'How do you know?'

'I *know* nothing. I only read the signs. But if it pleases you to see me as a fortune teller, please allocate me nothing more exotic than a cupful of tea leaves.'

'And where do you find your tea leaves?'

'You haven't guessed? Your background. I looked quite carefully into your past before I made my first approach to you. Are you shocked?'

'A little.'

'I can't afford failures. Many people have talent; few have the drive to use it. Your background suggests you're one of the few. Our Scottish violinist – I'm only guessing – probably has had too comfortable a life. Your life too has had comfort of surroundings but not of the mind. You have a desperate need to be loved. So? Everybody wants to be loved. But not everybody is driven as you are. And the only way you know to achieve that love is through success. You will go far. And now that I have thoroughly infuriated you with my businesslike analysis of your plight, we will eat. In here, please,' he finished, holding open a door.

My face felt like a nuclear reactor about to go critical. How could he move so easily from his obvious warmth towards the violinist to this cold calculation of my prospects? I would never know this man. There was no way into his mind. And yet we were bound together more tightly than the violinist and her teacher. Rage, frustration and fear did battle inside my head. My knowledge of his hidden room was nothing compared to his knowledge of my mind. I felt like a butterfly pinned to a board.

We were in a small, ordinary sandwich shop. I scanned the fillings behind the counter. Not so ordinary. Hanno ordered a salt beef sandwich. Automatically I ordered the same. While the man behind the counter was making up the sandwiches, several more customers arrived. The man called to someone in a back room. A young girl came out to serve but stopped dead when she saw Hanno. 'Mr Hirsch!' she cried. And ducked into the back room again. The customers kept waiting seemed unconcerned. A moment later the girl reappeared with an old woman waddling behind her. The old woman cried, 'Hanno!', waddled out into the room, arms outstretched, and into Hanno's embrace. The people at the little tables looked up once, then returned to their sandwiches. The young girl attended to the new customers while the old woman spoke excitedly to Hanno. He was replying in German, but the woman's dialect was incomprehensible to me. She glanced at me once and said something. Hanno shook his head. She seemed a little saddened, then brightened again and continued her chatter.

Finally our sandwiches were ready. At the same time, the woman seemed to extract a promise from Hanno and then waddled contentedly into the back room again. We sat down to eat. 'I don't suppose you'll explain,' I sighed.

'But of course,' he replied, 'though you might have guessed: we are in a Jewish establishment, and this is the best salt beef sandwich in the whole of London.'

I glared at him. 'You know that's not what I meant.'

He raised an eyebrow. 'Ah. You mean my friend. It surprises you that I have a friend?'

'Frankly, yes. A cold, calculating, bloody-minded monster like you doesn't have friends.'

'Sometimes, Rosalind, I'm very fond of you. Especially when you make your eyes into an elf's welding torch. Eat your sandwich.'

I bit into it furiously. It was delicious. Of course. 'You're Austrian,' I said.

'I am as English as you are, Rosalind.'

'But you were born in Austria.'

'Yes. There. Are you happy? You have discovered my great secret. Now you know everything there is to know about your mysterious agent.'

I knew nothing I hadn't already deduced from his slightly odd syntax and our visit to the Austrian embassy. He was teasing me yet again, and yet again I failed to be as angry as I should have been. 'Ah, Hanno,' I sighed. 'Why are you so mysterious?'

He smiled. 'You are the one who sees the mystery. You read into me what you wish. The truth is very dull: I am an Austrian-born actors' agent working hard to make a career for myself and my clients. Is that so mysterious?'

I sighed again, knowing better than to pry any further.

Phlumph phlumph went my GSS.

'How are you holding up?' Hanno asked, peering down at my shoes.

'Fine,' I lied. 'Where are we going now?'

'Secret. Mystery Tour.'

It materialised at last. The British Museum. We walked up the steps. 'We've been here before,' I reminded him. 'To see the Elgin Marbles.'

'This is different. No more questions.'

We went to the enquiry desk. Hanno gave his name and the name of someone who evidently worked at the BM. The woman phoned through. Then she smiled and directed us towards a nearby gallery. 'Straight ahead, right to the end.'

We walked what seemed a very long distance, all the way down a long straight gallery lined with cases full of books. At the end loomed a huge pair of dark wooden doors. In front of them stood two guards clanking their keys. Hanno gave his name and that of the other man. One of the guards opened the door and watched us proceed down another corridor – much shorter – to a tatty modern reception room where a secretary met us and nodded to the guard to lock the door again. Ahead was another door. I raised an eyebrow but Hanno smiled serenely, unperturbed by the latest mystery he was submitting me to. 'Wait here, please,' said the secretary. And disappeared through a crack in the next door. A moment later she returned, smiling, and ushered us into a room.

We had reached our goal at last: the Medieval Department. It was a large, light and airy room overlooking a side street. The walls were lined with reference books, the centre space crammed with cluttered desks and filing cabinets. A man rose from one of the desks and came to meet us. He was middle-aged and dressed in a quiet grey suit which tried to efface its wearer. He had a mild, kind, intelligent face. I liked him immediately. Hanno introduced us. He shook my hand. There was something courtly in his manner.

'You've come at last,' he said to Hanno. 'We'll go and see it immediately.' He had a brief consultation with one of his colleagues. Then he returned to us, holding a large ring of keys.

Outside the room again we entered an antiquated lift. It groaned its way upward and then stopped with evident relief. We got out and walked down yet another corridor. This one was narrower and clearly not open to the public. There was another locked door, and another. Finally we entered a strange room which seemed to consist of the narrowest corridor of all, lined on both sides with locked cabinets.

'Where are we?' I asked Hanno's friend.

'A storeroom behind one of the displays upstairs,' he explained. 'This wall is a false partition; on the other side is part of the medieval section open to the public.'

'Who would have guessed?'

He smiled and unlocked one of the cabinets. Inside it were strangely shaped and strangely wrapped parcels. There were several strongboxes, too. He removed one of these, unlocked it and drew out an object wrapped in padded material. He exchanged a look with Hanno and unwrapped the object.

I gasped aloud. It was a crown, gold and studded with large lumps of stone in every colour. The shape was simple, just a plain circlet perhaps an inch and a half high. The gold was roughly worked and the stones were all different sizes and shapes. It looked very old, very important and very beautiful. I wanted to look at it for ever. I think the two men must have felt the same. None of us spoke for a long time as we drank in the beauty of the crown, breathed in its emanations of a time long past. I longed to touch it, connect myself up with its mysteries, but I didn't dare. I scarcely dared breathe for fear it would disappear and I would wake up again in the mundane world.

Finally our guide spoke, more to me than to Hanno. 'This is our newest discovery,' he explained. 'It was found in the private collection of a man who died without heir. The documentation with it suggests it may be very old indeed, possibly as early as the eleventh century. The only crown we know that resembles it in any way is the earliest one in the *Schatzkammer* in Munich. Of course the documentation could be false – it's been sent to us with the crown for verification. We'll do our best, but we may never know much about it.'

I glanced at Hanno. His face was rapt. Still gazing at the crown, he said to me in a strange and very quiet voice, 'A *real* mystery for you at last, Rosalind.'

Our guide smiled and said to me, 'Hanno knows no more about it than anyone else, but I knew he would appreciate its beauty. It will be a long time before it's on public display. So far the only thing we can verify is the genuineness of the gold and the stones.' He turned the crown slowly in his hands and named them: 'This is a diamond, and this a ruby. Emerald, sapphire, topaz, amethyst, opal, beryl . . .' The list seemed endless. Goosebumps rose on my arms. I hadn't realised they were precious stones; they had none of the brilliance of cut gems. They gleamed dully from their settings, all full of potential not yet realised.

Of course. That's why Hanno had been summoned. The potential. The thing in the process of being created. The roughness of the gold and jewels was far more powerful than that of the expensive jewellery one could buy in polished and perfected form. The value of these huge stones as raw material for the cutter's blade was enormous, but the crown untouched was beyond price.

Then an extraordinary thing happened. Simultaneously, we looked up, away from the crown, and before I knew what was happening, our guide had lifted the crown and placed it on my head.

I cried out, almost in pain, with the suddenness of the act and with fear at the contact with its magic. The gold seemed to burn into my scalp, the jewels pulsate inside my brain. And then, when I thought I could bear it no longer, something changed. I was lost to time and place, conscious only of an ancient warmth flowing through me. I could feel tears rising to my eyes. Before I could check them, they overflowed, running down my cheeks like warmed gold, as if the crown had melted in its own heat and turned to tears.

'Rosalind, what's wrong?'

The voice came from far away. Then his arms were around me. 'It's all right, Rosalind, don't be frightened.' A handkerchief gently wiped away the tears. The corridor came into focus again. Hanno's face, full of concern and excitement, hovered in front of me. The crown was still there. I could feel its weight but I could bear it now. I turned to our guide, meaning to apologise, but he smiled in that gentle courtly way, as if we were in a medieval castle and he the court magician, a Merlin accustomed to bringing about such transformations.

'The crown is full of power,' he said. 'I've felt it myself.' Then he laughed quietly. 'Who knows? Perhaps it was made by a magician.'

The rest of the day is a little hazy, overshadowed by the awesome experience of the crown. We went to a book-binder's workshop afterwards. I dimly remember an old warehouse by the docks full of rickety staircases and odd little workshops that seemed to have been there for ever. In one of them a Polish friend of Hanno's restored old books. Hanno had come to collect a book his friend had just repaired for him. It was a nineteenth-century edition of *Doktor Faustus*.

'It's not particularly valuable,' said Hanno, 'just a rather attractive edition.'

I tried to read bits of it but the Gothic script defeated me. I watched instead the bookbinder handling a sheet of gold leaf. He didn't breathe as he handled it, let alone speak; the slightest movement would have blown it away. And then, like magic, the gold lettering began to appear on the cover of a book.

Hanno and I sat companionably in a corner of the room while this was happening. A sense of peace pervaded the workshop, peace and timelessness. I could almost believe we were in nineteenth-century Warsaw, or Vienna, or Paris. Like so many immigrants, the old man seemed to carry his previous existence with him, in the way a tortoise carries his shell, both home and encumbrance.

It was dark when we left. We walked in silence along the river. I'd been born and raised in London but had never had strong feelings about the place. Tonight, however, it seemed deeply foreign and very beautiful. The lights reflected in the river glittered like jewels, the dirty water lapping the embankment whispered sweetly. Headlights of cars wove enchanted webs of gold through the cold air. The roar of engines thrummed pleasingly in the distance. It was as if some magus had managed to transform even this city into a place of warmth and beauty and magic.

It was the crown, of course. I knew that, though I still didn't know why.

A Turkish restaurant this time, another of Hanno's cheap but excellent eating places. That no longer surprised me either, his nose for the undiscovered best. I was beginning to understand just how much this was his city. In six months, a year, others would discover this little restaurant. It would be filled with those in the know, it would lose its special qualities. By then Hanno would have moved on to the next, always in search of the potential, the thing in the process of being created.

We'd finished our dinner and were having coffee. 'Do you feel better now?' he asked.

I knew he wasn't referring to the meal. 'I'm fine. I suppose I made a fool of myself,' I added, 'but somehow it doesn't seem to matter.'

'Can you tell me how it felt?'

'Not really. Something like a sense of suddenly being in touch with the ineffable. Sounds ridiculous, put like that.'

'No.' He sipped his coffee and watched me across the table. 'I've underestimated you, Rosalind. I'm sorry.'

I smiled. 'You mean you thought I was a cold, brittle, ambitious little brat who just wanted to be rich and famous?'

'No. But tough. I didn't realise you'd be so sensitive to the crown.'

'Not an everyday occurrence: being crowned in a storeroom of the British Museum,' I said lightly.

'No. You seemed to become someone from another age.'

I could feel goosebumps rise on my arms. 'Who was she, Hanno? Do you have any intuition?'

He shook his head. 'A young queen, I suppose. Probably very beautiful. You were very beautiful, wearing it.' He smiled. 'Those notorious eyes of yours. They really did seem to become an elf's welding torch, bringing out the hidden light of the jewels. As if, for a moment, they *had* been cut and polished.'

'Something was being transmitted.' I took a deep breath and said it. 'Love. An overpowering strength of love. I don't think it came from her, though. Perhaps it was simply the love of the craftsman as he created this beautiful work of art. Thank you for taking me there, Hanno. It meant something, even if I don't know what. In fact, thank you for the whole day. I've been very happy.' The words were rushing to my head now; I knew I should be stopping them but I couldn't. Something had changed that day, our relationship had moved into a more personal realm. 'Hanno, I'm sorry I barged into your room like that. It was unforgivable. And I'm sorry I held you to ransom. I had no right to demand a day of you like this. Though I'm not sorry for the day. I've been very –' Tears were threatening to rush out with my rash words.

He put his hand on mine. 'Strange Rosalind,' he said. 'You could have demanded much more, and didn't.'

20

I didn't see him again until several days later, and then in circumstances so strange that I hesitate to describe them.

The whole episode began with Astrid's Queen Elizabeth Hall début. I'd been worried about her ever since her return from the provincial tour, and as the concert approached I was more worried still. I'd never seen her this nervous before. I tried to pretend it wasn't all that bad; she'd pulled herself together before, she would do so again. But I wasn't convinced. I was glad the play was still in rehearsal, leaving my nights free. I wanted to be with her if – I cut the thought short. Hugh was well-meaning but ineffectual. 'Buck up, old girl.' That sort of thing.

We arrived in good time. We went with her backstage and stayed long enough to make sure she was in reasonably good spirits. Then we went into the foyer. The QE Hall was a wonderful place if you were in the right mood, but tonight I felt only the oppressiveness of all that heavy grey concrete.

The auditorium, too, felt like a big grey concrete cave, vaguely threatening. I thought about the cosy club-like atmosphere of the Wigmore Hall and wished we were there instead. Certain theatres had a reputation for being difficult to play. I wondered if the QE Hall was a musicianly equivalent.

Concerts never start on time. Neither do plays. I was used to it. Still, it seemed to be taking longer than usual between the last arrivals and the start of the concert. Probably my imagination, I told myself. But the time stretched on. And on, and on. The audience could feel it, too; they were becoming restive. They were ready and nothing was happening. They'd quietened down of their own accord. Now they were over-ready and beginning to murmur. It wasn't my imagination, that much was clear. Astrid, be strong. I willed my own strength to enter into her.

Then the man walked out on to the platform and I knew it was all over. I barely heard what he said: regret . . . unforeseen circumstances . . . indisposed . . . I closed my eyes and cursed the gods of music. How could they do this to her? Then I shot out of my seat and headed for the door leading backstage. I was dimly aware of Hugh scurrying to catch up, of the audience beginning to leave. I didn't care about any of them.

'I'm her sister-in-law,' I snapped at an official who tried to bar my way. I pushed past him and went straight to the room where we'd left her.

She was sitting at a tiny table with her back to the room. Her arms were folded on the table and her head rested on them. Her face was hidden. She wasn't crying – there was no motion whatsoever in her body. I think that frightened me more than anything. People were standing about, not knowing what to do. I tried to smile at them, anxious not to antagonise them as I'd antagonised the obstructive official. We needed them on our side if Astrid was ever to get out of this. Then I pulled up a chair beside hers.

'Astrid,' I whispered. 'It's only me – Ros.' I put my hand gently on her shoulder.

Hugh had caught up at last. He was hovering behind us, pleading with his wife, 'Buck up, old girl. Try.' I waved him away with a fierce warning look. I didn't know what to do with Astrid but I did know that Hugh would be even worse. One of the people in the room took him in hand. I looked back at Astrid. Still no reaction.

'Astrid,' I said.

There was a slight movement. Her voice, so faint I barely heard it, whispered, 'I'm sorry.'

It would be useless to try and reassure her, soothe her with meaningless words. 'I'm sorry, too,' I whispered. 'It must hurt like hell. I don't know how to make it stop hurting.'

'. . . sorry.' Fainter than ever.

Then the tremors started. First a slight quivering of her smooth dark hair. Then, like an evil spirit travelling sleekly down her spine, the tremors spread, finally taking hold of her entire body. I put my arm round her shoulders and rested my head against hers. 'Not tonight, but later, we'll try to find a way out of this,' I said. I think she nodded, but it was hard to tell. The trembling had taken possession of her completely.

It was one of the worst nights of my life. What it was like for Astrid doesn't bear thinking about. Somehow we managed to get her home and put her to bed. I heaped the blankets on, though I knew that the shaking had nothing to do with chill, or fever, or anything else answerable to bodily tending. Hugh was useless. 'If only she'd *try*,' he wailed. Astrid wanted to be alone. I understood that but Hugh felt personally affronted. He couldn't accept that what was happening was out of anyone's control. He demanded a doctor. Astrid refused. I agreed with her, but I did give her a good strong sleeping pill.

The next morning I phoned Jas. If anyone knew what to do, it would be Jas. By then he was thoroughly established and had a multitude of useful contacts. I explained what had happened. After a shocked silence there was an anguished stream of invective against the gods that told me more than anything else how deeply fond of Astrid he had become.

And then, the straw I'd been groping for: he gave me the name of a clinic specialising in nervous disorders. It was much used by actors – for acute stage fright – and musicians. Violinists, Jas told me, often suffered tremors. There must be something the clinic could do.

I phoned immediately and made the earliest appointment I could.

That night was the first preview of *Who's Afraid of Virginia Woolf?*. Astrid declined to come – she would jinx it, she said. I knew she wouldn't, but I respected her feelings. 'Maybe when the run is going a long time and good and safe, then I can risk it?' she smiled mournfully.

The following morning Astrid and I went to the clinic. She'd been diffident about asking me to come with her. The breakdown had destroyed more than her ability to play; it had damaged every aspect of her self-confidence. '*Of course* I'll come with you.'

The clinic was small, modern and friendly. Everything that could be done to put people at their ease had been done: nice furniture, potted plants, big windows letting in the sunshine. Astrid was fairly calm and even a little bit hopeful. She was unexpectedly naive in some ways; she had faith that 'the professionals' would put things right.

We had arrived just a few minutes early and were the only people in the waiting-room. I think that helped, too. So when the outside door opened I frowned slightly, irrationally resenting the intruder. But my annoyance turned to delight when I saw who it was.

'Hanno!' I cried. Then I saw there was someone with him, a very pretty young woman with blonde curly hair. She looked sharply at me with a mixture of disapproval and alarm.

And Hanno?

He glanced at me once, as he and his companion made their way to two chairs opposite. He smiled in a vaguely pleasant manner, as if I were a stranger whose presence needed only this slight acknowledgment. Then he turned his attention to the young woman.

I had no time to think about what this extraordinary behaviour could mean:

'Mrs Farleton?' the nurse said, coming up to us from an inner office. We both acknowledged the name and then laughed. Astrid wanted me to come with her to see the doctor. The nurse made no objection.

When we left the clinic, Hanno and his young woman were gone.

Over the next few days I brooded endlessly on the chilling little scene, trying to make sense of it and trying to maintain a shred of self-respect. Why had he cut me dead like that? And why was he at the clinic anyway? The most obvious answer was that the woman was a client suffering from stage fright; it wouldn't be out of character for Hanno to take a frightened young actress there himself. But that didn't explain why he'd ignored me. Surely Hanno could be civil to one client in the presence of another? It just didn't make sense.

But the more I thought about it, the less I thought her an actress. We're a distinctive breed, we can recognise each other a mile away. We might as well have A for Actress branded on our foreheads; there's no hope of disguising ourselves from each other. No, she wasn't an actress, I was pretty sure of that.

At this point my brooding became darker. I tried to think she was simply a friend of his, but it didn't work. Hanno didn't have friends like that. His friends were old women in sandwich shops, medievalists at the British Museum, Polish bookbinders. I could see no context for a friendship between Hanno and this pretty but bland young woman.

When I could pretend no longer, I faced reality. She was his girlfriend, or perhaps just *a* girlfriend, one of many. What on earth had made me think he had no private life, that his world revolved entirely around his clients? Vanity, of course, the same vanity that had made me so shamefully jealous of Caroline. The crazy irrational desire to be The One And Only. I didn't even bother to wonder why he should cut me dead in the presence of a girlfriend. My need for further explanations disappeared. The beautiful day we'd spent together had lost its specialness. A precious little corner of my life had vanished.

I threw myself into my work as compensation. After the previews came the first night. David came down for it, nudged no doubt by Brendan and Belle, who sent fervent good wishes and the promise that they would come themselves in a few days. Now that there were horses at The Folly, someone had to be there all the time to look after them.

I was relieved to see David. He seemed so fresh and real after the fraught events of the past week. Even his hands, with the lovely scent of resin which no amount of scrubbing could ever erase. It was a happy reunion, though a short one. The atmosphere in our Islington house was so oppressive – Astrid's collapse, Hugh's lack of understanding – that David soon fled north again. I couldn't blame him. I wished I could flee somewhere, too.

The one bright spot in this whole period was the play. It was a smash hit. Hanno had predicted a success, but I doubt if even he had known how big. I suppose a lot of people had seen the film and came out of curiosity to see how Caroline would compare with Elizabeth Taylor. Frankly, rather well. We gave an evening of such intensity that the audiences went away reeling. We played to full houses most nights. Our reviews were sensational, and with such a small cast, all four of us had detailed praise.

'If I believe even half of this,' I said, showing one of the cuttings to Jas, 'my head will swell to the size of a pumpkin.'

Jas read the cutting and handed it back with a show of scorn. 'Lies, lies, every word of it. You really were terrible, Rosie – I've seen better performances at school plays.'

I slapped his cheek and he laughed.

And then, several weeks into the run, something wonderful happened. There has to be a first time for all of us, and we all remember it vividly, no matter how often it happens later. For me, it was a grotty café on Tottenham Court Road where I'd stopped for a quick coffee. The tables were close together – not my kind of place at all – and the couple at the next one looked up as I squeezed into my seat. Looked up, then looked at each other, and then at me again. There was a whispered consultation. Finally the girl leaned over and said shyly, 'Excuse me, but are you Ros Rawlinson?' I said I was. She beamed. 'We saw you last night at the Duchess. You were absolutely wonderful!'

And there I was, signing my very first autograph. I felt

like a fraud, as if I were impersonating a famous actress.

I hesitated some time before telling Astrid, fearing to hurt her. I was horribly aware of the contrast: at the moment that my career was truly taking off, hers was coming to an end.

The trip to the clinic had been a failure. She'd been given beta-blockers, a drug that acts powerfully on the nervous system to prevent tremors. Orchestral players use them a lot, but Astrid was one of those innocents who slice an aspirin in half about once every three years. The sleeping pill I'd given her on the night of her collapse was the most powerful drug she'd ever had. She regarded the beta-blockers with deep distrust.

'Try it just this once,' I pleaded. 'If you don't, you'll spend the rest of your life gnawed by doubt. Who knows? Once might be enough; it might break the pattern.'

It was a risk and she knew it. If the drug didn't work and a second concert aborted, the effect would be devastating. But she knew, too, that she would never forgive herself if she didn't try, would always wonder if perhaps it might have worked.

Fortunately, her next engagement was a fairly low-key one – a music society in a distant suburb. I felt awful that I couldn't go with her but I was performing every night except Sunday and Hugh had a business trip out of town. It was sheer good luck that Jas was between plays. He went with Astrid and probably did a better job of calming her than I could have done.

Well, it worked, more or less. She got through the concert, but she wasn't pleased with her performance. 'Something was missing,' she said. Jas had thought her wonderful but admitted he was no expert. Nonetheless, she was sufficiently encouraged to try it a second time, and a third. The result was the same: all right, but . . .

The end finally came at the Conway Hall. It was a Sunday night concert, so we were all able to go together. I too was no expert, but I did wonder if the voltage was a little lower than usual, the effusion of warmth a little muted. During the interval I eavesdropped. There were murmurings of doubt. The Conway Hall audiences aren't known for their malice. I had to take it seriously.

And then, the review: a small one and utterly damning. It was the last concert Astrid ever gave. Hugh was furious – as much with Astrid as with the critic. 'Can't you try a little harder?' he said. They had a row. After it, Astrid came to my attic in tears. It was no use, she said. For an orchestral player, perhaps, but the solo world was a ruthless one: every flaw showed. And even in an orchestra it wouldn't work for ever. One pill this time, two pills the next, then three, until the player became so fuddled that eventually he got the sack. Better to go now, with at least a little bit of dignity intact, before the one bad review multiplied . . .

Astrid's career was over.

21

The run went on and on. We transferred to a bigger theatre and still we filled most of the seats most nights. Our contracts were re-negotiated – Hanno was as shrewd with contracts as he was in placing his clients in the right productions. Several more people recognised me in the streets or in shops – nothing like as many as recognise film or television actors, of course, but enough to make me realise that I was on my way to the top.

It was an exciting time, but frustrating, too. The play began to go dead on us. Too much familiarity. We got together to talk it through again, tried out new approaches, shook new life back into it. I was beginning to feel like a seasoned performer. The daily routine was now so familiar that it gave a welcome sense of stability to my life.

Then, just as the run threatened to turn into its own kind of nine-to-five, Hanno hauled me out of it. The play would continue, but without me; he would volunteer another of his clients to replace me. This I learned not from a phone call but from a quick note torn off a memo pad: *Suggest you do Hilde Wangel in Master Builder.* There followed details of producer, director, cast and so forth, ending with: *Let me know immediately if you agree.*

I was stunned. It was a magnificent part in a magnificent play, one of Ibsen's finest. Further, Hilde and her eponymous architect were indisputably the stars. I had truly arrived. I should have been ecstatic, but my joy was marred by the coldness of the note.

Hanno had sent the usual yellow rose and card at the opening of *Virginia Woolf*, but it was no longer enough. What had happened in the short time between that glorious day together in London and the chilling encounter at the clinic? I reviewed that day over and over in my mind, looking for some small thing I might have said or done to offend him. Nothing. We *had* been happy, in a foolish, innocent way. Perhaps something had happened in his own life to change his attitude towards me? If so, there was nothing I could do unless he brought up the subject himself. If only he had phoned, just once during that run, everything would have happened differently.

His note was still in my hand. I didn't trust my voice enough to phone him. Instead, I wrote a note of my own: *Yes. R.R.*

There was a gap between my withdrawal from *Virginia Woolf* and the first rehearsals for *Master Builder*. I would use it, as I'd always used such gaps, for a trip back to Yorkshire. I needed the break more than ever. Keeping my role fresh over such a long run had been exhausting. Added to that was the increasingly fraught atmosphere between Astrid and Hugh and my own disappointment over Hanno. Altogether I was fed up with London, eager for the simple life of The Folly and David's solid presence.

But first, a quick detour to Stratford. Jas had finally made it to the RSC and was playing his first role there: Cassius in *Julius Caesar*. I'd missed the first night because of *Woolf*; now was my chance to make up for it.

So I was feeling in holiday spirits when I entered Paddington station that Friday, clutching my suitcase. My thoughts were already far from the city. I barely noticed the people around me until suddenly I saw a heart-wrenchingly familiar figure just two ahead of me in the ticket queue. Hanno. He seemed to be alone. I peered round the man in front of me and saw just a small weekend bag. Obviously not a holiday. Then Hanno was at the ticket window and I heard the words, 'Chipping Moreton.'

I turned my head away as he left the window. I was wearing a foolish floppy-brimmed hat I'd bought in one of those antique clothes shops. It completely hid my telltale strawberry hair. I was pretty sure he couldn't have recognised me. When I dared, I let one eye peer out from under the rim to watch the direction he took. There was nothing in his manner to suggest he'd seen me.

God knows what possessed me. I truly think that when I arrived at the window I intended to buy a ticket to Stratford. But my mouth opened and the words 'Chipping Moreton' came out of it.

'Single or return?'

'Uh, single.'

Too late. There I was, holding a ticket to a place I had no intention of going to. I was shaking now, utterly confused. I'd lost my place in the queue. Should I go back to the end, explain that I'd made a mistake and get my Stratford ticket after all?

Then Hanno's honey-gold figure swerved round a cluster of people and disappeared. Without thinking, I dashed forward, weaving my way through the thick holiday crowds. I glimpsed him up ahead again and hurried. There were so many people I would be well hidden even if he should think to glance behind, though I couldn't think why he would. There was nothing furtive in his manner. I remembered that our day together in London had been postponed a bit because he was 'away at weekends'. I hadn't thought to wonder where he went.

We were on the platform now. I had to hope I looked inconspicuous. Not much chance. I was taller and thinner than most women and had the loose-limbed movement characteristic of all actresses. Eyes were drawn to types like me regardless of what we wore: in this case, a dark green sweater, matching trousers and hat and the Good Stout Shoes. I kept myself well hidden behind the other passengers, peering out just in time to see him board the train.

I got into the carriage behind his and sat down. My heart was crashing about so violently I could hardly breathe. I was near to panic, trapped in a train going somewhere I didn't want to go to, and all because of some idiotic mistake at the ticket window. I tried to calm myself. There would be a conductor. I would explain my mistake, ask him the best way of getting to Stratford from the next stop.

But as the train started up, I knew I wouldn't. I knew exactly what I would do. I would get off at Chipping Moreton and follow Hanno like some disgusting little sneak, like I had done the night I'd uncovered his Wigmore Street lair. Some part of my brain was connected to his so strongly that I *had* to follow him. There was no reason, no explanation. I was an automaton.

Tears of frustration were threatening. It was me, not Astrid, who should have gone to the nerve clinic. My mind was unbalanced. I was a puppet controlled by his strings. I was Trilby hypnotised by her Svengali. As the train rumbled along, I thought bitterly of all the rumours about Hanno Hirsch. They were true, in some deeper way that was far more potent than black magic.

The journey seemed to last for ever. I fell into a dull trance, no longer fighting my compulsion. I would do what I would do, and that was that. I barely noticed all the stops or heard the names called out. I didn't have to listen. Those golden threads would draw me after him when the time came.

'Chipping Moreton,' said the mechanical voice.

I rose from my seat and moved dumbly towards the door. I held back just long enough to let other people go before me so that Hanno would have a head start. Then I alighted from the train.

His figure, in the ubiquitous cream-coloured sweater and trousers that seemed to be his uniform, was visible some way ahead. I left my suitcase at the station and followed discreetly, using doorways and people for concealment.

Before long we were on a country road. My heart began to thump as it had on the train when I'd realised I was trapped. I was trapped again, this time in the openness of the countryside. There were no people to hide behind now, only an occasional tree and hedges and bends in the road. Once or twice my cover ran out. If he'd glanced behind then he would have seen me. How on earth had I got myself into this awful situation? I was an actress trained to exhibit myself, not a spy schooled to conceal. Of all people to trail after Hanno Hirsch, I was the worst candidate.

The hedgerows grew lusher and I breathed a little more easily. It was easier to hide now, and with my dark green clothes, any glimpse through a hedge would reveal nothing. Then a new thought. Hanno was a strong walker. How long was this particular string, how long my journey to this unknown destination? Somehow, I would have to get myself back again. There were limits to my leg power.

I stopped behind a nice thick piece of hedge. I could, of course, go back now. It was the obvious thing to do. Hanno had no idea I was there, of that I was sure. All I need do was turn round and walk back the way I'd come, cure myself of this madness. Just one wrench of my will and I could do it.

But I couldn't. Meekly I followed my Pied Piper, oblivious to the lovely summer day. The hedgerows were undoubtedly crammed with flowers I didn't see. The air was probably thick with the flight of birds. I saw and heard nothing, not even his footsteps far ahead. My head was empty of everything except the single imperative to conceal myself and follow, like a starving man intent on the single task of cracking open a coconut.

There were crossroads and turnings everywhere. Each time Hanno chose the smallest and most obscure. The road grew narrower and rougher. Finally it diminished to a gravelled road the width of one car.

Then he vanished. I'd held back at a bend, and when I cautiously moved forward again, the road was empty. I stopped, wary. Perhaps he'd sensed my presence after all and drawn back into the hedge to wait. He would emerge from the hedge with a knowing smile on his face. The hunter hunted. I hesitated. I could still go back, though by now I wasn't at all sure which turnings to take. I thought of Arachne, then Hansel and Gretel. At least Hansel had had the nous to scatter a breadcrumb path, even if the birds ate it up. St James's Park, feeding the birds. A spasm of nostalgia wrenched my innards. So happy. What did it matter now?

Hardly caring if I were discovered, I started walking again.

A motorist would have missed the turning entirely. A tall hedge, about eight feet high, had been allowed to spread its upper branches in an arch over the entrance. The metal gate beneath was barely wide enough for a car and was painted a dark green that blended into the foliage. Beyond it a faint track – no more than two tyre marks – was also green, mossed by infrequent use and by the dripping trees on either side. It went into the wood and then curved, cutting off any further view.

I looked around. There were no more turnings in sight. I went up to the gate. It was padlocked. This had to be where he'd gone, calmly locking the gate after him, locking me out. I leaned against it, feeling more foolish than ever. All this way for nothing. Served me right.

Yet again the obvious thing was to turn round and find my way back to Chipping Moreton. Yet again I couldn't. I walked on, trying to peer through the tall hedge. There was a ditch between it and the road, and without going right up to the hedge there was no way I could see through it. The futility of my crazy quest was complete.

Then the hedge turned at right angles to the road. I jumped the ditch and followed it. I was now in someone's field and would have difficulty explaining my presence if an irate farmer came along, but I didn't care. There was no ditch here – I could just about see through to the wood inside. That's all there was: a lovely patch of woodland. And still I followed the hedge, not knowing what else to do. At one point a surprisingly substantial stream emerged from it to be channelled into a big culvert. I walked over the culvert.

A little further along, the hedge again turned right angles and again I turned with it. The back of the woodland was thinner. Golden shafts of sunlight slanted through the greenery and lit up the woodland floor. Here and there I glimpsed a little clearing.

Then, somewhere in the middle of that back length of hedge, the trees thinned further still and I saw the house. It was some distance away and partly hidden by the trees, but I could see the distinctive golden stone of the Cotswolds and the simple shape of a farmhouse. Farmhouse? Gingerbread house. This hidden wood with its hidden house was utterly separate from the world outside. No ordinary people lived within. Certainly the high hedge spoke of an extreme desire for privacy, a boundary between the real world and the fairy-tale world inside. I was filled with longing, once more a child with my nose pressed up against the window of the pastry shop, once again excluded.

The sun was strong. It scattered its gold among the wildflowers beneath the trees, shone in gnat-filled rays against the trunks of the trees. But up ahead it gathered itself together in one mighty beam to pour itself over the house. The house seemed truly to be made of gold; it gleamed as brightly as if the little Polish bookbinder had covered it with gold leaf. A trick of the light, of course – the position of the sun and the house and myself. But it was difficult to dispel the illusion of a gilded cottage set magically in the middle of its miniature forest.

I was so entranced that I almost forgot about Hanno. Suddenly there was a motion and the door of the house opened. From it stepped two figures, also burnished gold. Then they were gone, hidden by a clump of shrubs near the house. I watched for some time, wondering if they would reappear, but they didn't. Suddenly I was nervous again.

I walked on, still following the hedge, hoping it would eventually bring me out on to the road. It turned again, and a little further on was another big culvert taking control of the stream which obviously ran through the whole wood. I stopped once more, caught by the sound of voices, but it was only the stream, chuntering along its boulder-strewn bed and setting up a sound like the singing of small invisible creatures. Lovely music. There were ferns growing alongside the stream. Its mossy banks looked so inviting I longed to lie down on them and listen to the stream, but it was on the other side of the hedge, as firmly barred to me as if within a fortress.

Then I froze. There *were* voices. This time I was sure. A moment later two people stepped out from among the trees on to the mossy bank. A slim arm pointed at the stream. It was the curly-haired woman from the clinic, and beside her was Hanno.

22

I stood there for a long time, fused to the hedge, green against green. My stillness and the colour of my clothes guaranteed my concealment, but that wasn't why I stood there so long like a green statue shoved up against the leaves. It was shock. I don't even remember seeing the couple leave, nor do I remember prying myself away from the hedge and making my way back to town. I have no idea how I found the way or how I discovered that Chipping Moreton was a mere twenty miles from Stratford. I must have bought a ticket and got on a train but I don't remember that either.

I'm ashamed to say I barely took in the play, though I must have reacted satisfactorily to it and to Jas's performance, for he seemed happy enough when we went out for dinner afterwards.

Only on the train to Yorkshire the next day did my mind begin to thaw, and then it was like floodwaters suddenly released by the collapse of a dam.

I had loved Hanno. Now that it was over I realised this simple truth that anyone else would have recognised months ago. My mind flowed dumbly back, looking for the moment, but there had been no love-at-first-sight, no flash of illumination. It had built up so slowly that I hadn't even noticed until it was gone. Perhaps someone else would have detected the early signs if Hanno and I had ever been together with friends. But our strange little excursions had been isolated from the rest of my life. We'd been hermetically sealed from knowing observers, with no chance of a gentle warning from a friend.

It seemed crazy that one could love so strongly without knowing it, but it had happened. That was the real mystery. The other mysteries, those surrounding Hanno himself, were no mysteries at all. The hidden room in Wigmore Street was now explained. It was just a *pied à terre* that cost him almost nothing. His real home was the golden cottage in the woods. That was why he was so frugal, too, and why he was so disturbed when I discovered the secret room. A house in such expensive countryside, with its own protective acres of woodland, would cost the earth. Nearly everything he earned must go into it. And the weekends he was never in London. Of course: he was at home.

With his wife. Well, there it was. There was no point in pretending any more. Possibly she was his mistress or girlfriend instead, but it hardly mattered. She was the reason for his sparse social life. London was just the place where he worked to earn the money to go home to her. Perhaps he went home some evenings, too. No wonder he didn't want a proper flat. The single room was quite sufficient.

And there was more. These were painful thoughts, but I had to think them. I now realised that the love that had been hidden from me had very possibly been visible to him. Several times I'd felt him attracted to me – above all, during our day in London – only to feel him draw back again. My face flushed with shame. He must have seen me as a temptress, and perhaps he had been tempted, but always he had resisted and gently pushed me to arms' length again. I could have no complaint against him. He had behaved – and here an old-fashioned term came to mind – he had behaved 'honourably' at all times. He had never led me on. It was me who had led him on, most outrageously when I demanded from him one day as the price of my silence.

At this point my shame became complete. He could so easily have called my bluff. He must have known I would never reveal his hidden room. Instead, he had bowed to my childish demand and given me a day he could otherwise have spent with his wife. And the awful thing was that now that I knew the truth, I loved him all the more.

His quiet restraint, his dignity, even his faithfulness to his wife. He was worth loving. No doubt many of his female clients fell in love with him. No doubt he turned them aside with the same gentle courtesy.

It was me who was the villain of the piece. I had failed to read the signs and had barged into his life with no encouragement from him. Worse still, I had a husband of my own, and one who deserved better of me. I suppose it was David who'd prevented me from making an even greater fool of myself. I was less modern than I liked to think. I took marriage seriously enough to see it as a bar against casual affairs. If I'd been free, very likely I would have thrown myself even more shamelessly at Hanno.

At this I felt a rush of gratitude towards David. He had unwittingly prevented me from even greater rashness. As the train moved north, the image of David grew stronger in my mind, along with another old-fashioned word. I had betrayed David. Not in body, and not even in mind, as I'd been unaware of my betrayal until now. But on some deeper level still, I'd been unfaithful to him with Hanno.

I didn't deserve either of them.

It was a new and chastened woman who stepped off the train at York.

I was well into rehearsals when the morning sickness struck, and then it took me some time to suspect what it was. Finally, however, I had to acknowledge that food poisoning couldn't be singling me out so persistently. Yes, I was naive, despite the sleek professional image I seemed to transmit to others.

I told no one, not even Astrid, until the doctor confirmed my suspicion. Then, one long rainy night in my attic, I held a conference with myself. What to do. I was very calm. I had to be. This first stirring in my body would have consequences for a lot of people. I had to consider them all.

It shames me even now to admit that my first consideration was for the play and for all the people working on it. That in itself should have told me all I needed to know.

We were too far into rehearsals for me to back out; there wasn't time to find a replacement before opening night. Already tickets were selling well. There was a sense of alertness in the air, at least in that strange, rarified air of the theatre, perfumed with sweat and hope. The reason for all the excitement was the casting of the two main characters: Hilde and Solness, the fanatic young visionary and the hypnotic old architect. Our Solness, Julian Steen, was probably the most august actor of his generation, a living legend. To cast opposite him an actress who'd shot into the public eye only months ago set the jungle telegraph buzzing. It was deliberate, of course, a calculated risk, and it had worked. To pull out now and let my understudy take over would destroy the production. The public didn't want her. They wanted me. No, there was no question of cancelling my contract. That much at least was straightforward.

Beyond that, however, the choices were far murkier, and they weren't mine to make alone. I would have to talk to David. I tried to imagine his reaction and couldn't. That, too, should have told me something: how little I knew my own husband, how far we had drifted apart. But how could I know him when I barely knew myself? I tried to imagine life both with and without the child, tried to startle myself into a reaction which would tell me how I felt. It didn't work. Either way the picture refused to come clear. I simply didn't know what I wanted.

David was planning to come down for the opening. I think he did this more from a sense of duty than pleasure – the magic of the theatre had never really touched him, though he'd done nothing to stand in the way of my career. When I phoned and asked if he would extend his stay in London for a day or two longer, he seemed surprised and I think rather pleased. We'd been happier together in Yorkshire during my last trip than for many years, probably because I'd banished all thoughts of Hanno from my mind and made more of an effort to appreciate David. Clearly David had noticed. Yes, there was hope.

The day after the opening, David and I went for a long walk in Kew. There, under a magnificent old beech tree, I told him. By the time he left again for Yorkshire, we had made our decision.

The play was a triumph, an even greater success than *Virginia Woolf*. The reviews were ecstatic. Even the most hardened old critics dropped their defences and admitted that we were doing something special. There were cards and telegrams every night and flowers, too, often from strangers. I was signing my autograph more and more, and learning to do it graciously, hiding the insecure little girl who still couldn't believe this was real.

I loved every bit of it, but most of all I loved working with Julian. Just being on stage with him night after night was electrifying. I was used to very high quality actors indeed, but Julian was in a class of his own. He had that rare ability to become the character so thoroughly that he fooled even those of us who knew the tricks of the trade. It was his performance, demanding to be matched, that drew the rest of us almost effortlessly on to that higher plane that he inhabited all the time. He *was* Solness, I *was* Hilde, and while we played our breathless deadly game together, nothing else existed.

Backstage, his role dropped away with equal ease and he became a charming old man, almost like a father to me. I worshipped him like any disciple would, but as far as he was concerned, we were equals. In time the crippling awe I felt towards him diminished and I found myself regarding him as a friend. I soon discovered he was a shrewd and observant friend.

'There's more to it, isn't there, Ros? More in it for you than a great role in a great play,' he said one night. Then he raised that famous quizzical eyebrow and vanished in a throng of admirers.

He was right, of course, though he didn't know the reason I hurled myself into my performance with such violence. I felt as crazed as Hilde. I knew this would be my last role for a very long time. I had to make the most of it, had to store up the delicious sensations to live off in the future when I was far removed from it all. It was a wild kind of mourning, and a celebration, too. And if there was a touch of hysteria to my performance, so much the better. Certainly the audiences thought so.

And so the nights went on, each one ticked off on the mental calendar that brought nearer the day I would have to face Hanno. I wasn't looking forward to that day.

I made an appointment to see him. Very formal, very proper. We hadn't seen each other since our day out in London and I wasn't sure how to handle it. What I did know was that our relationship now had to be as business-like as possible.

A rather famous actor was leaving as I arrived – another of Hanno's clients. That helped. It reminded me that Hanno dealt daily with male as well as female actors, that he was indeed a professional agent and not a Svengali.

Hanno's desk was spread with papers – a particularly awkward contract, he explained. That helped, too.

We settled into the comfortable chairs by the little table with its sculpture. Behind us was the concealed door to his *pied à terre*. Nothing in his manner or mine showed that either of us knew about it.

The secretary brought in coffee. Everything was as it had been on that first day I'd come to see him, a nervous new recruit not knowing what to expect. Now it was Hanno who didn't know what to expect. He must have been puzzled, but his face betrayed no curiosity. It was, as always, full of geniality and courtesy.

'I have something to tell you, Hanno, and I'm afraid it won't please you at all.'

Hanno poured the coffee.

'I wanted to tell you before anyone else. Anyone else in the theatre, I mean.'

'Milk? Sugar? No, of course not. I remember.'

'I'm pregnant, Hanno.'

His hand was perfectly steady as he handed me my coffee.

'It's not due for some time. I can carry on about two months longer. After that, I think it'll begin to show. I'll have to leave the play.'

'Two months. Yes. It's kind of you to tell me so far in advance, Rosalind. Thank you.'

'I thought, if you knew, there might be someone else you would have in mind.'

He smiled. 'I'm not the casting director.'

I smiled in return. 'No, but you often like to . . .'

'Twist the casting director's arm a fraction? Yes.' He sipped his coffee. 'I have no one else in mind, but I'll give it some thought. Though I don't think anyone else could play that role as well as you.'

Strange how much a compliment can hurt. He'd constructed my career so carefully, with this – the role of Hilde – as the keystone. And now I'd let him down. 'I'm sorry, Hanno. I feel I've let you down.'

'Nonsense. The production will be nicely established by the time you leave. I might have taken you out of it by then anyway. To move on to the next.'

'Yes. Well. I don't know when that . . . I mean, I don't know what any of this means for my career. If I still have a career.' If you'll still be here if and when I return. If you'll still bother with me.

'Most actresses marry and have children. If that meant the end of their careers, there would be no actresses left,' he smiled.

'No. I suppose not.'

'Though it's difficult to see how you could commute between Yorkshire and London.'

'Yes. I haven't really thought it all through yet. But I do want to come back. I couldn't give up acting, not for ever.'

'No. It would be difficult. Someone of your quality.'

I bowed my head under his praise.

'Well,' he said, his voice a little brisker, 'in that case, make your announcement as soon as possible – tonight, in fact. The director first, of course. To give them time.

If you handle it well, they'll remember. It will help if . . . when you decide to come back.'

'Yes.'

There was a little silence. Then, 'You're pleased, Rosalind?'

'What? Oh. Yes. Of course. I mean, I don't have to . . . I mean, no one has to have a baby.'

'No.' There was another silence, longer this time. Then, as I watched, something strange happened. His face became old and filled with sadness. 'Sooner or later they all want children,' he said, so quietly it was almost as if he were talking to himself.

He'd never lost himself so entirely in my presence. 'Not all,' I said cautiously. There flashed into my mind another woman, the pretty little blonde of the golden cottage. And with it came a moment of illumination. Children. There had been no signs of children inside that fairy circle. It had been summer, a time when children would be at home. No sound, no childish clutter. Could it really be that simple? Yes, I thought it could. The seclusion of their life together. Hanno's utter devotion to his work. His reluctance to reveal anything about his private life. Hanno and his wife were unable to have children.

I looked up at him, afraid to see that sadness on his face now that I knew what it meant. But he had recovered completely and was smiling at me.

'Your husband is pleased, too?'

I wished he wasn't doing this to himself. 'Yes,' I said. 'More than I expected, actually.'

'Oh?'

'I didn't think he was the type. I mean, he hates the whole heritage business. Passing the estate on from generation to generation. He detested his father. And he sold the family home – no thought of passing it on to his children. So I didn't really think he would be all that keen.' Why couldn't I just shut up?

'But he is.'

'It's not the name or the estate or the prestige of the family. I think it's the trees. They take a long time to grow. David wants someone to be there – to care for the trees, the land – when, you know, we're all dead.'

'You must think very highly of your David,' he said quietly. 'It's a fine heritage to pass on. A forest. A *real* heritage.'

'Yes, I suppose it is.'

Then he smiled, and the Hanno I knew – urbane, courteous, in control of every situation – was back. 'Well, what can I say, Rosalind? I wish you all the very best for the future: you, your husband, your child . . . and the trees.'

I felt a sudden rush of love for him, a new kind of love this time. But all I could say was, 'Thank you, Hanno.'

23

When I next saw Hanno, I was divorced. I don't want to dwell on the years between. Some things hurt too much even now. And some things are too private. It's enough to say that in due course Matthew David Farleton was born. It was an easy birth, as if Matti, even while in the womb, felt diffident about his arrival. Not a child to make a fuss or demand attention. But then, he didn't need to. He was a charming little creature, right from the beginning. There was a touch of solemnity about him, even at his merriest, that appealed deeply to everyone who knew him. And the one thing I can say is that despite his inauspicious beginning, he was a wanted child and much loved by all of us at The Folly.

David was overjoyed, as well he might be. Matti was very much his child: the same dark hair and dark, serious eyes, the same combination of sturdiness and grace. If David had tried to imagine his ideal heir, it would have been Matti. From me he had only a certain delicacy of feature: a fine nose and exquisite little hands which would some day be more expressive than his father's great resin-stained paws.

Belle and Brendan had been unable to have children of their own. It wasn't something they brooded on – they accepted it cheerfully enough and got on with the business of living. But when Matti arrived, they were as ecstatic as David and myself, and I realised what marvellous parents they would have been. They had to restrain themselves from taking over the child completely.

I didn't begrudge, not at all. I was grateful for the wholeheartedness of their love. It eased my own conscience. I could never quite banish the trace of guilt from knowing that Matti had had to be a choice. The pull of the theatre had been strong, as strong as the desire for Matti. So finely balanced it had been that Matti might well not have come into existence at all. But as soon as he arrived I threw myself into motherhood as passionately as I'd thrown myself into my work. Half-measures were alien to me. I fully intended to be as good a mother as I had been an actress.

It might have worked, too, if it hadn't been for the school. The Folly had moved on from just using heavy horses in our own forest to breeding them as well. Other private foresters were beginning to realise the advantages of horse over tractor, and the National Trust, with its emphasis on conservation, was interested, too. Unfortunately, there seemed to be no one who knew how to train or use such horses, and there was nowhere for them to learn.

'Why not here?' said Brendan one night.

That was the beginning. For weeks the house was filled with argument. David was, predictably, opposed, as he always was at any prospect of outsiders invading his realm. Brendan and Belle were for. The 'students' wouldn't be outsiders, they would share our ideals. It was the chance we'd been waiting for: to teach other people what we'd learned – not only about horses but also about the use of the countryside in general. It was the perfect opportunity to spread the green revolution beyond our own ghetto.

Our? Their. No one asked my opinion. Yet again I was on the outside. The three of them had become such a tightly knit group that even now, when I'd been home for so long, no one thought to include me in their plans. I tried to be generous. Why should they consult me? After all, I'd never taken much interest in the running of the place before. It was my own fault, cutting myself off from my home all these years.

None the less, my resentment grew. Whatever happened at The Folly would affect me as much as anyone else, and the one thing I knew for sure was that I emphatically did not want a school. I pictured all my lovingly restored rooms invaded by a bunch of spotty-faced youths, the tranquillity of our evenings smashed by yobs pounding up and down the stairs, trannies bellowing pop music, television blaring out football matches. Matti being hauled about by macho brats filled with lumberjack fantasies, picking up their foul language and even fouler ways. A school. My God, how low could we sink? For the first time ever, I was almost glad that Rhiannon was dead. At least she didn't have to witness the final desecration.

We had rescued her portrait from Farleton Hall and hung it on the landing of the main staircase. It was as close to a central position as the higgledy-piggledy house provided, and from it she gazed down on everything that happened at The Folly. Soon she would be gazing down on a hoard of marauders, helplessly watching them wreck the last remnants of her life's work. She'd trusted me to salvage the best bits of the Farleton heritage, and over and over again I had failed. I'd failed to prevent the sale of the Hall and I'd failed in my attempt to bring either it or The Folly to life, to fill them with happiness and laughter again. Instead, The Folly was to be filled with crass adolescents who got their kicks playing with chainsaws.

One day, while bringing Matti downstairs, I stopped in front of the portrait. I held him up so that his little face was level with hers. 'See, Matti? That was your grandmother. Rhiannon. Isn't she beautiful? She would have loved you very much. She would have –' I stopped, suddenly choked with grief and rage. She would have seen Matti as new hope, as a symbol that her life hadn't been wasted after all. And she would have trusted me to do everything I could to rescue what little remained of her grandson's inheritance.

That was it. From then on it was no longer a matter of my wishes but of my son's future, and I opposed the school with passion. David had begun to waver. I thought he would welcome my support. I thought he was merely being worn down by the persistence of the others and would be grateful to me for shifting the balance.

He was not. Almost immediately, he changed sides and

joined Brendan and Belle. There it was: the three of them against me.

It was the ultimate humiliation, and I couldn't help but take it personally. Even now I wonder if he would have stood out against the school if I hadn't spoken up. I was bewildered, and very hurt. We had seemed to be getting on so well together, and with Matti's arrival I was beginning to feel we were a family at last.

All gone. In a matter of minutes, the debate ended. The Folly was to become a school.

I was stunned. Soon the hurt turned to anger. There were rows. David and I had never rowed before, except when he sold Farleton Hall. All our tensions and disagreements had remained below the surface. What resolutions there were had been deceptive. Now it all came out in violent arguments, night after night. I moved from our room and established myself and Matti in the Tudor Room where we had played Romeo and Juliet so long ago. Finally I issued the ultimatum. David would have to choose. The school or us.

Dangerous things, ultimatums. Those who issue them usually lose. I lost.

I don't want to talk about the divorce. There's no point. I now see the inevitability of the whole thing. For years we'd been drifting apart – less from antagonism than indifference. I'd tried to take an interest in David's world and failed. David had barely even tried to enter into mine.

That our two worlds had also been physically apart for so long was probably the most crucial factor. I'd persuaded myself that because I lived in David's brother's house I was still a part of the family, hadn't really moved away at all. I couldn't have been more wrong. When Hugh and Astrid and Jas and I had been together, we'd rarely talked about David. When I'd been with David and Brendan and Belle, we'd rarely talked about the Islington household and even less about Hanno. For years I'd been living two separate lives, trying to be two separate people with two separate sets of friends in places which were 230 miles apart. And for years the London actress had been growing stronger and stronger while the Yorkshire squire's wife had faded.

If it hadn't been the school, it probably would have been something else. When David wasn't resenting my lack of involvement he was resenting my interference. I resented his resentment and his inconsistency. He couldn't have it both ways, I said; if he wanted me to be involved, I must be involved in the decision-making too. The pot calling the kettle black, he retorted; I'd been having it both ways for years, swanning off to London when it suited me and returning to Yorkshire only for holidays and to produce a child I was now trying to turn against him.

That was when I hit the roof. It was Matti and his heritage I was trying to protect.

Protect against his own father?

Yes.

He was hurt and enraged by turns, but at least some good came of it; when at last the settlement was drawn up, he couldn't object to the one clause I demanded: that Matti have priority over any future children David might have by a second wife.

David agreed with savage certainty. There would be no second wife, he said grimly. One had been quite enough.

It was, of course, custody that tore us apart. I refused to leave Matti in a crazy household isolated from normal life and filled with disreputable 'students'. David refused to leave him with an actress who would be out at work nearly every day and every night. Nannies were no substitute, he said. Nannies came and went; Matti would have no stability in his life.

And then, the most unexpected *deus ex machina*. Astrid sailed in, seemingly from a cloud though in reality from her own strife-torn home. Her marriage with Hugh had been disintegrating steadily from the night of her breakdown at the Queen Elizabeth Hall. We now discovered that what Hugh had loved about Astrid was her talent, and not even that for its own sake but for the prestige it conferred on him. From the moment she faded from public view, his love faded also. Now he was divorcing her, in the most cold-blooded manner imaginable. As there were no children, he was successfully fighting alimony, giving her instead the Islington house. This she would fill with music students. The rent would bring in some income and the rest she would make up with music lessons at home.

That was the key. Astrid would always be at home. To David's amazement and mine, she offered to become Matti's legal guardian.

It was absurd, of course, and yet another humiliation for me. To live in the same house as my son, who was the ward of my landlady? And yet, and yet . . .

In the end, we agreed. I suppose David was sufficiently satisfied at my humiliation, while I was simply relieved to get Matti away from The Folly. And the truth is, one could hardly imagine a better mother-substitute than Astrid. Her spontaneous warmth surrounded him with love. Further, David and I both trusted her. She was the ideal link between us. I would still see Matti when I wasn't working, and Astrid would bring him to The Folly to see his father during school holidays. From the wreckage of two marriages, some good might still be salvaged.

The lawyers thought we were mad, but finally they agreed that there was no other solution.

As soon as the divorce was final, Matti and I set off for London.

24

I made no appointment this time. I didn't mean to surprise him into new revelations or discover more hidden rooms. I simply happened to be in the area. What could be simpler than to pop up and make an appointment in person? I wouldn't see him, of course. It was lunchtime, he would be out. Probably the secretary would be out, too. Well, a trek up the stairs wouldn't kill me.

The secretary was in, the same one as before – clearly Hanno had done nothing to scare her away yet. She smiled and greeted me as if she'd seen me only yesterday. As if I belonged. The familiarity of it all was overwhelming. Perhaps I did still belong? Perhaps there was still a chance to return to my old life?

When I tried to make an appointment, she said, 'Why don't I just ring through? He's with someone now, but I'm sure he'd like to see you if you don't mind waiting a few minutes.'

Thirty seconds later, a famous producer left and Hanno was framed in the doorway.

'Rosalind!'

The warmth in his voice, the joy on his face – so powerful that even the secretary seemed startled. He strode across the room and I even think he would have embraced me if she hadn't been there. Instead, he took my hands in his while sunbeams poured down over us from the rainy skylight.

'Hello, Hanno. I'm back.'

'So I see!' he laughed. 'And just in time for lunch!'

'Oh, I didn't mean –'

'But *I* mean. Unless you have other plans?'

'No, none, but –'

'Good!' He gave a few instructions to his secretary, and together we went towards the door. The phone rang. 'I'm out!' called Hanno, and hustled me from the room. As soon as he'd shut the door he took my hands in his again and gave me a long, searching look. 'I was afraid you would never come back. It's been a long time.'

'Yes.'

'And what does this mean?'

I looked away and shrugged. The divorce was too fresh. I didn't want to talk about it, though I knew I would have to.

Perhaps he guessed. 'We'll have lunch first,' he said, 'and then talk. But please, tell me one thing only: are you *really* back?'

I understood and nodded.

We ran through the rain. The little Greek restaurant was unchanged, and the table by the window. We ordered our food. When the wine arrived, Hanno raised his glass to mine. 'To the future?'

As we ate, he filled me in on what had been happening in the theatre during my absence. Some of it I knew from Jas, but Hanno always seemed to have sources of his own, information available nowhere else. I was keenly aware of the unasked questions, but only when we'd finished eating and moved on to our coffee did they begin.

'The child?' he asked quietly.

'A boy. Matthew David Farleton.'

'He is well?'

I nodded. It seemed a strange question. Most children are well and if Matti hadn't been, I wouldn't be here, talking with Hanno.

'And you are pleased?'

'He's a lovely child. I hope you'll meet him some day. We're both . . . living in Islington . . . the same house as before. Matti and me, I mean. With Astrid.'

Hanno gazed out of the window, where nothing was happening. Then he turned back to me. 'Rosalind, I don't wish to pry, but . . .'

'Divorced.'

There was another silence. 'If you feel like talking about it, I'm listening,' he said quietly. 'But of course you may not.'

And, suddenly, I did. That quiet reserve, so comforting. Of all people, he was the least voyeuristic . . . and the most understanding. For the first time since the divorce, I did want to talk.

And so I talked. I knew that some of it sounded bad, my opposition to the school snobbish. Perhaps it was in part. But there was more to it, a whole history of David's destruction: of his heritage, his own past, his relationship with me and with everyone outside the closed circle that was now The Folly. I couldn't let Matti grow up as a freak, excluded from the rest of the world. I think Hanno understood. Certainly he passed no judgments. It wasn't the first time I'd noticed his reluctance to judge others.

'And so Matti will be an only child?' he asked when I had finished.

Was he only thinking of future contracts broken by future pregnancies? 'Yes,' I said. 'I certainly don't intend to marry again. And I'll never make another child act as a bandage over a wounded marriage. That's what shames me most of all – that I did that to Matti. I never gave a thought to *his* life, *his* future. It's a rotten thing to do to a child.'

'No one's motives for having a child are above reproach, Rosalind. If everyone thought only of the children, few would be born.'

It was a devastating statement but delivered with a sadness that softened the harsh words. His face had taken on that age-old appearance I'd seen during our last interview, when I'd announced my pregnancy. We'd been talking about children then, too. It occurred to me that somewhere in that golden cottage among the trees there was a child after all, some small, sad creature also damaged by unthinking parents. That strange visit to the nerve clinic – could there be a connection? But he was tactful enough not to pry into my private life. I had no intention of prying into his.

'And so,' he said at last, 'you are ready to work again?'
'Yes.' My voice was much too emphatic, even bitter.
He looked up from his coffee in surprise. He put the cup down. 'Rosalind, please don't let this harden you.' Then, as if realising he had overstepped a boundary, he smiled apologetically. 'I'm sorry. It's not my business to tell you what to do and how to feel. But I care about you, Rosalind. Bitterness is alien to you.' For once he seemed to be having difficulty finding the right words. 'When I mock you and say that your eyes are like an elf's welding torch, it's not entirely in jest. There *is* something elfin about you. You belong to sunlit glades and laughter. You're a bringer of joy, Rosalind; that's what the gods intended for you. Ignore me if you wish – you have every right. But please, listen to the gods.'
No one had ever spoken to me like this. It was the most beautiful thing anyone had ever said, far more meaningful than the most ecstatic reviews. And coming so soon after the ugly divorce. I felt close to tears. A bringer of joy. Could there be any purpose in life finer than that?
'And now,' he said cheerfully, 'down to business. You return at an opportune time. The RSC is about to begin casting for the next season.'
'Hanno!'
He fended off my excitement. 'You have pestered me long enough to turn you into a poorly paid state employee mouthing The Great Man's words. Very well, I submit. But,' he shushed me with a wave of his hand, 'this is an area over which I have less influence than you may think. No one has seen fit even to tell me which plays are to be performed. We must bide our time just a little longer. Meanwhile, I must ask you a crass question, namely, how are you for money?'
'Fine.'
'Are you telling me the truth? Remember, this *is* my business.'
'Yes, honest.' I put my hand on my heart. 'The maintenance for Matti goes to Astrid, of course, but I have some money of my own.'

'Good. But before you enter the dungeons of the RSC, you would do well to rake in a few more shekels to add to your hoard. This is a precarious trade, as you well know. Even if the RSC takes you into its motley band, there will be a goodly chunk of time between casting and the first rehearsals – possibly some months. I suggest that you use them well. Now, the one guaranteed producer of shekels is Alan Ayckbourn. I happen to know that his latest offering is about to transfer from Scarborough minus its leading lady . . . who has chosen an inopportune moment to become pregnant . . .' A sly look here.

I had to laugh. Hanno, my wry old friend, was back.

'It should take only a small twist of an arm or two to put you into it,' he continued. 'Producers of comedy are always after my clients. I resist often enough to whet their appetites, so that when finally I give in, with a great show of reluctance, my bargaining position is considerable. If I do succeed this time, it will be with a fixed-run contract designed to take you up to the RSC season, and it will be for a great deal of money. There. I have broken two of my rules for you today: I have discussed a future role before knowing whether I can secure it, and I have revealed to you the deplorable secret of my success.'

I laughed. 'You fraud! You've revealed nothing! Don't think you can fool me!'

'Perhaps not. But I *can* make you laugh.'

And then I saw what he had done. No, I wouldn't become hard or embittered, not now.

'If you get that nice fat Ayckbourn role,' he continued, 'you will have to work like hell. You will come cold into a fully-fledged production. You will have to fit in with it and catch up fast. And this, you tough little elf, is why I have confined you for so long to the West End. Too many actors go into the subsidised theatre too soon. They grow fat and complacent with the lovely long rehearsal periods and the even longer discussions on esoteric matters of text and interpretation. This undoubtedly produces great art, but it also produces actors who wilt under the roughness of commerce. You have become a seasoned old pro,

Rosalind. I expect you to do me proud. There. I have revealed another secret. I am just a lazy old agent who does nothing. It is my clients who make my reputation for me.'

'I'm shocked. All right, since you've broken so many rules already, please break another. Tell me what you would like me to do at the RSC. Ideally.'

'Would I be so presumptuous?'

'Yes.'

'If I were a magician whose wand would conjure up the perfect season? Very well. I would choose three plays, three roles, all of them light and youthful.'

'Ophelia?'

'Ophelia,' he said drily, 'is hardly light. And it's a thankless role, impossible to play well. In any case, you have done two heavies in a row: Albee and Ibsen. Comedy is notoriously difficult, you must master that first. You are like a race horse belting along the track with no thought of conserving your energy for the final sprint. Think. All those foolish opera singers who tackle Wagner too early and ruin their lovely voices for Mozart. All those string quartets who plunge into late Beethoven and lose the light touch needed for Haydn. Shakespeare is undoubtedly the master, but his language is too rich for young stomachs. It dulls the palate for more delicate flavours. Consumed too young, it produces those appalling Shakespearian voices. If you did a Cleopatra now, or, God forbid, a Lady Macbeth, you would never again do justice to Noël Coward.'

'Who cares?'

'I do – and don't be such a snob. There are few good roles for women in Shakespeare. Don't wear them out before your time. Mercifully, you're too young for some of them. But also too old already for a Juliet.'

'Ouch.'

'That hurt? Good. You're in your thirties already, Rosalind. Make merry with the light youthful roles while you may – you have little time left.'

'Thanks. All right, what's it to be?'

'Alas, not my choice. But I would love to see what you could do with Miranda. And Rosalind. You were far too young when you did Rosalind for that foolish ADC production.'

'*Foolish?*' I could feel the hackles rise. *As You Like It* was my talisman, my good luck charm, one of the few shreds of my past on which I could look back with unadulterated pleasure. We had been *good*, damn it.

'Oh, it had some merits,' he conceded.

'Quite a few, evidently. You sent your card to my dressing-room. Or have you forgotten?'

'I forget nothing.' His smile was maddeningly urbane. 'Nor do I forget that you declined to respond. May I ask what you did with it?'

'Tore it up.'

'You what?' He looked disconcerted, and a little annoyed.

'Tore it up. I'd never heard of you. I thought you were a dirty old man propositioning the chorus.'

He roared with laughter. 'Dear Rosalind – you have made my day. You see? You had spirit even then, you impertinent chit.'

And I laughed, too. Like lovers, taking amusement at recalling their first clumsy approaches. I shook the image away. 'Hanno, there's something that always puzzled me. You sent that card on the opening night. Why did you come to that play in the first place?'

'Cambridge, of course.'

'You saw it at Cambridge? But how did you know it would be worth your while going there to see it?'

'My spies sent word that a delectable young thing was making a mess of the role but had some potential.'

'You rat!'

'And they were right. None the less, I decided to wait, to give you time to mature a little more. But when the production transferred to the Fortune – you see? I forget nothing – I feared that some other agent would snap you up and ruin you. And so I moved in. Confident, of course, that my card would do the trick.'

'I hope you were furious when I didn't respond.'

'It was, I admit, a blow to my ego.'

'Good.'

'Cruel Rosalind.'

'And York? Did you have spies there, too?'

'Sheer chance. I happened to be travelling through. I bought the local paper and saw your name heading the review of that Barrie play. This time, however, I was more cautious. It had been some years since I had seen you; you might have been ruined by then. I waited until after the play was over. Then I presented my card in person.'

And I had burned in the heat of that strange vision, the golden stag made manifest in the tiny dressing-room. It all came back with shocking clarity. The nightmare, the stag's face and then Hanno's, so alike. That tantalising but terrifying golden radiance. For one mad moment I wanted to tell him. I wasn't convinced it was chance that had brought him to York. Something had linked us together long ago and made inevitable the succession of events leading to this rainy day in the little Greek restaurant. Suddenly my mind flew back to the golden cottage in the Cotswolds, and I knew with absolute certainty that somewhere in the woods that surrounded and protected it was a clearing identical to the one in which David and I had made love and I had conjured up the vision of the golden stag. I shivered.

'Rosalind, are you all right?'

His voice snapped me back to the present. I looked at him across the table. No hint of the golden stag. No trace of mystery. Hanno was right. It was something in myself, not him, that made me long for him to be a magician who would whisk me away from an insecure world and transport me to the magic land where everything was possible. He was, as he'd tried to tell me so often, simply a hard-working agent . . . and friend.

That was more than enough.

25

Hanno had done more for me that day than any magician could. He had shaken me out of the bitterness that was the aftermath of my divorce. He had dispelled my guilt and self-pity and kicked me back into reality. Most of all, he had given me the greatest gift of my life. He had called me a bringer of joy.

In the time that followed, I tried to live up to those words, using every free moment to bring joy to Matti. I did it in the only way I knew: by giving him what Hanno had given me. Together, Matti and I sailed the streets of London like the mythical explorers of the past, delving into all the secret corners unseen by the too-busy and too-familiar. The countryside was David's; I could give him nothing of that. But I could open up for him the enchantments of the city.

They were happy days. Everywhere we went I felt Hanno's presence glowing beside me. Hanno, my invisible guide. Sometimes we had visible companions, too. Jas came along whenever he could, and Astrid. Occasionally one of her 'lodgers', the music students who now filled her rooms, also came. Matti was a sunny child who brought out the best in everyone. Their goodwill in turn delighted him, and so began the lovely upward spiral of affection – given and received – which was his own gift.

There was no doubt in my mind that our decision to appoint Astrid his guardian was, however bizarre, the right one. I'd always had great respect for her. Now, watching her pick up the fragments of her shattered life, this respect grew even greater. Not once did she bewail her ruined career or her husband's defection. Other people destroyed. Astrid built. All the passion that had gone into her playing she now channelled into her teaching. Her students adored her, as did her lodgers. The house was a happier one now than it had been while Hugh was there.

Hugh was heavily involved in property development, especially in the docklands. He established himself in a luxury flat along the river and reverted with suspicious ease to a bachelor life. He even made one or two advances towards me. It was entirely in character. I was the rising star, a suitable candidate for his ego. And it would give him special pleasure to capture the woman his brother had failed to keep.

I loathed him.

On one of our expeditions, Matti and I found ourselves by the old warehouse where Hanno had taken me to see the ballet rehearsal. Timidly, I entered the building. It was a different ballet but the same pianist. He even remembered me. I questioned him about his job and told him about Astrid. He didn't know of any openings just now, but he would keep his ear to the ground. Actually, he continued, he was picking up more performance work these days. If his luck held, his own job might come vacant in a few months . . . I gave him our phone number.

Yes, we weren't doing too badly, Astrid and I agreed. Life without men wasn't such a disaster. In fact, it was rather agreeable. Once or twice the sound of a student practising the Schubert sonata wafted up to my attic, bringing with it memories of Farleton Hall, David, the past. It hurt, but not for long.

As for Matti, clearly he was thriving. His tiny life was filled with new people and places and events. I pictured his life at The Folly. Even without the dreaded school, I would have been unable to give him more than a desultory social life in Kirkby Langham. The humiliation of not having custody had all but vanished. And when I resumed work, absenting myself from the house more and more, I had to admit that Astrid made a far more stable centre of his life than David or I ever could. *If everyone thought only of the children, few would be born*, Hanno had said.

I think he was right. But now that the deed was done, I could at least put Matti before my own pride and accept the supremacy of Astrid in his life.

Hanno had no difficulty getting me into the Ayckbourn play, and I soon acknowledged the wisdom of his choice. There had been enough heaviness in my life; it was a relief to throw myself into a comedy.

The play was, as Hanno predicted, a great success. I couldn't take much of the credit; it would have succeeded regardless of the cast. For the first time in my life I saw people queuing for tickets. Further, we were playing at the Theatre Royal, Drury Lane. Just across the street was the tiny Fortune Theatre where Jas and I had had our first taste of the West End. I remembered the night we'd gone to the opera and afterwards stood in front of the Fortune, watching the theatre-goers disperse. I remembered, too, his fantasies of our future fame.

Well, he'd been right. Jas was now very famous indeed. It's even possible that the scene he'd conjured up – a pair of television viewers suddenly remembering seeing us in front of the Fortune that night – had come true. After a highly successful season with the RSC he'd done some work with the BBC and the new Channel Four and then returned to the West End in a position to command fat fees. He could hardly go anywhere without flocks of people asking for his autograph. Now he was back with the RSC.

As for me, the lack of a television appearance meant I was much less well-known to the public, but my reputation in the theatre was none the less sufficient to interest the RSC. After some preliminary discussions which were the most terrifying of my life, I was offered a contract.

Hanno wasn't being only modest when he said his influence with the RSC was limited. The RSC had firm ideas of their own, and while they respected Hanno's opinions, there were other factors at work. One of these was Jas. It was sheer good luck that they'd decided to do *As You Like It* this season, and Jas used every means fair and foul to capitalise on it. They'd already cast him as

Orlando and were about to approach my friendly rival, Caroline, to play Rosalind, when Jas began his campaign. Of course Caro was a darling, said Jas. Super actress. Actually, he'd always pictured her as Celia – didn't they think she'd make a terrific Celia? As for Rosalind, well, as it happened, his old friend Ros Rawlinson was about to make a spectacular comeback at Drury Lane. Fixed contract, fabulous fee. Matter of fact, he'd been talking with Ros just the other day. Reminiscing about the good old days with the ADC, that amazing *As You Like It* they'd done together. Didn't remember? Gosh, everyone else did. Transferred to the Fortune – a real coup. Terrific reviews. Yes, that's right – Rosalind. She'd been a smashing Rosalind even back then. And now, of course, with all that experience . . . Yes, Hanno Hirsch, she's one of his . . .

And so they discussed, argued, interviewed, negotiated . . . and made their decision.

'We've come a long way, old girl,' said Jas as we drove through the countryside.

'About a thousand miles, it feels like. Jas, where *are* we going?'

'Why, to Stratford, of course!' He began singing: 'We're off to see the wizard . . .'

'You know what I mean.'

'Secret.'

I sighed, fated, it seemed, to the company of men with secrets. Hanno's mystery tour of London, Jas's meanderings through the English countryside. The 'secret' in this case was our digs. The RSC owned a number of properties around Stratford to rent to its actors for the season, but some people – those who'd been around a while – found places of their own. Last year Jas and his then Friend had found just such a place – a jewel, and dirt cheap, too More than that he wouldn't say, jealously guarding his find. When the Friend decamped to London, Jas offered to share it with me.

I accepted eagerly. I was frightened enough of my first

season with the RSC without the hassle of strange digs. To have a ready-made nest was both convenient and comforting. To share it with my dear old friend was beyond my wildest hopes. The future was indeed looking good.

Now, however, I was beginning to wonder. We were nowhere near Stratford. We were nowhere near anywhere.

'This place doesn't exist,' I said flatly.

'Oh ye of little faith.'

But it was nice being in the countryside again. The land, though hardly as spectacular as that around The Folly, was agreeable. Human scale. Gentle rolling hills, fields full of horses (this was hunting country), patches of woodland, all of it just beginning to take on the first faint haze of spring green. I suppose we're all divided, split between a longing for the land and the desire for city excitement. We want space, but at the same time we want company. Some try to solve it with a cottage in the country or a *pied à terre* in town. I thought of Hanno, with his split life, then of David, so firmly rooted in his land that even a trip to Kirkby put him in a bad mood.

'Not quite Langhamdale,' said Jas, as if reading my thoughts. 'But rather jolly, don't you think?'

'Land doesn't have a sense of humour,' I said.

'Neither do you. What a po-faced old misery you are. Missing Matti?'

'Of course I am.' This was the first time I'd been truly away from Matti, and I didn't like it one bit.

'And David?'

'Not much.'

'Not a bad old stick, Sir White Rose,' Jas went on. 'I rather liked him. But he should have known better – trying to take you from us.'

'He didn't. It was me who left.'

'Then *you* should have known better, dear heart. You were born for the theatre. Even the great H.H. saw that, way back in Cambridge days. How is he, by the way?'

'Fine.'

'Tsk tsk. Still as close as ever?'

'There's not a lot to say. He's just a very good agent. You know that already.'

'Funny how no one talks about him – no one in the inner circle, that is. Tight-lipped bunch of disciples he has. What's the trick?'

I laughed. 'The trick is that it amuses us to see people like you invent fantasies about him.'

'Humph.' Silence. 'I still think it's a cabal. Or a coven. You all go up to Hampstead Heath every full moon and have orgies.'

'Of course.'

'Take me along?'

'Nope.'

'Spoilsport.' Silence. 'Well, Rosie, if ever you're daft enough to remarry, stick to the trade. Plenty of nice actors about. And directors. And agents. How about old H.H.?'

'He's –' Just in time I stopped myself from saying he was married. '– not my type,' I amended. But he was. Ever since the divorce I'd had a hard time squashing my own kind of fantasy, with Hanno at the centre. Over and over I reminded myself of the pretty little blonde, but even that was growing thin as a barrier against my day-dreams. After all, she might be his sister. Or the wife of a friend. That house might not even be his. He might simply have been visiting that weekend I'd spied on the enchanted circle. I even managed to persuade myself that Hanno had been less reserved towards me since my return. It was possible that the holding back I'd sensed in him stemmed from my marriage rather than his.

I shook away the crazy thoughts. One of the benefits of being at Stratford would be the distance it put between myself and Hanno. In London I was getting into the habit of hoping for a phone call, a note. We had in fact got together a few times during the Ayckbourn run. Hanno, conscientious as ever, wished to fill me in on the Stratford scene.

'You take a lot of trouble over me,' I'd said to him once.

If I'd hoped for a declaration of special interest, I'd

been disappointed. 'You missed out on drama school,' he'd explained. 'The things I tell you are things drama students pick up there.'

'Hence the research outings?' I'd already learned that none of his other clients were treated to these.

He nodded and then added, 'And it's amusing. I enjoy thinking up appropriate connections.'

For *As You Like It* we'd gone to Kew, taking Matti with us. The connection had been, Hanno admitted, a slight one – even Kew's wildest reaches could hardly compare to the savage Forest of Arden – and we'd spent most of the time simply discussing the text. I was surprised at how knowledgeable he was. Clearly the theatre was far more to him than a matter of actors.

'And where does Matti fit in?' I'd teased.

'We'll cast him as a squirrel.'

I saw a snapshot never taken: Hanno with Matti on his shoulders, standing against the trunk of a big Wellingtonia. The big blond magician juxtaposed with the little dark elf, sunshine zeroing in through the leafless trees to illuminate the picture with a golden glow. And then another picture: David and I at Kew. A beech tree that time, when I'd announced my pregnancy and we'd discussed whether or not Matti should be born. The result of that decision then perching on Hanno's shoulders, the two of them bathed in a golden glow.

The glow faded and I returned to the present. We'd just passed – too late for me to see – a sign announcing the name of the little town we were entering. Not a very inspiring town. I said so to Jas.

'Exactly,' he smirked. 'That's why no one's found it. No one bothers to look for digs here.'

'What? This is it? The secret place?'

Smirk, smirk. 'Just wait.'

I watched the drab streets go by. Here and there a garden sprouted one of those pink flowering cherries I loathed, their blossom clashing with their bronzed leaves. There were forsythias, too, clashing with both. They were just coming into flower. They would be in flower for much of our stay.

'Yuk,' I said.

'Oh ye of little faith.'

We passed by the railway station, equally uninspiring, like so many small town stations, with neither the grandeur of the London stations nor the prettiness of the rural ones. It looked like every small town station I'd never seen. In fact, I could almost believe I *had* seen it before. In fact . . . I jerked my head back, but too late – it had disappeared from view.

It was on the far edge of the town. Already we were driving along a road with buildings thinning away fast. Buildings that were also slightly familiar. More than slightly. Then they were gone, trees taking their place along the country road. Trees I had hidden behind. And the hedge, only just beginning to green up.

The road went on. Oh yes, I knew it all right, knew it with the intimacy of the slow-speed walker who has ample time to see all.

It was Chipping Moreton, and we were driving right towards Hanno's hidden cottage.

26

Jas's cottage was indeed a jewel. Originally a two-up-and-two-down labourer's cottage, it had been modernised just enough for comfort but not enough to spoil it. No copper canopy over the fireplace, no electric candles on the walls, no coloured bathroom suite with fishy tiles. The kitchen cupboards had been built in plain pine by a local joiner. The house was white-painted throughout, allowing the lovely views through the windows to form the decoration.

The house was tucked away among the maze of narrow roads which threaded the countryside. There was a small cottage garden run wild in front and a rough orchard at the back running down to the river. Birds were going mad in the trees. The evocative scent of damp earth and growth infused the air. It was utterly charming.

'Apologise?' said Jas.

'Apologise. It's gorgeous.'

He gave me the back bedroom. I unpacked, then tried out the cushioned window seat and contemplated the view. It cried out for a Constable, with its patchwork of fields and woods and lanes, the hedges acting as stitchwork to hold the view together. Most of the trees were in copses or lining the rivers and streams. About a mile away, however, was a larger and squarish wood which seemed to have been determined by the boundaries of a former field. Even at this distance I could discern a slight gap which indicated a clearing in the middle. I was pretty sure it was Hanno's wood. What a strange quirk of fate had brought me here.

The heavenly scent of food was wafting up from the

kitchen. Jas's latest passion: gourmet cooking. Quickly I rose and went downstairs to join him.

There was no time to think about the nearness of Hanno's house. The next morning we drove into Stratford for our first rehearsal. Jas's cottage was twenty miles from Stratford – no doubt another reason it had evaded other actors. I wondered briefly if Hanno had bought his own retreat with that in mind: near enough to attend plays, far enough away to keep his location secret. Assuming that he did own it and did wish to be secretive.

Then we were driving over the bridge. There it was, the stretch of river with the big ugly building along its banks flying the RSC flag.

'Isn't it gorgeous?' Jas breathed. 'Still gives me a thrill. If I'm tottering the boards at ninety I'll still feel like a kid that doesn't believe his luck. Can you believe it, Rosie? We *belong* here. Inside that mess of ugly buildings some of the greatest minds in the world are beavering away to breathe life into the old man's words. *And we're a part of it.*'

Goosebumps rose on my arms. No actor in the world can be immune to the magic of Stratford. It's where we all want to be. Mecca. We may grumble sometimes, chafe under the weight of all the bureaucracy. We may defect from time to time – to the National, to the big money of the West End or Broadway. But we always come back.

We parked the car and entered the Conference Hall which was our rehearsal room. 'Here we are, sunshine,' said Jas. 'Home for the next seven weeks.'

It was a beautiful room: high, light and airy. Huge circular skylights beamed down on us and at one end Gothic doors opened out on to garden and river. 'See.' Jas pointed to another building on the river. 'Over there: the Dirty Duck.'

The room was full of relics from previous productions: thrones, swords and sceptres, an old wind machine, props which had been handled by the greats. There was a big table under one of the skylights. Around it people were gathering. The director, the assistant director, the deputy stage manager, actors. A few I knew already, including Caroline, our Celia. Jas introduced me to the others. The atmosphere was tense but happy, like the first day of school for those pupils who know they're at the top. But no matter how august some of the names or large the bank balances, there was a sense of being in it together. The famous company spirit. How right Hanno had been to keep me away from it so long. It was unutterably seductive. Seven gorgeous weeks in this lovely room rehearsing one of the greatest plays ever written with the best talents in the world. I was reeling already. I remembered all those dismal church halls and warehouses with their iced radiators, the cranky directors and overworked actors all rushing headlong into something, anything, which would get the show on the road on time. No wonder so many were botched. Here there was no excuse. The conditions were ideal. If we couldn't come up with a magnificent production, it would be our fault entirely, there would be no one to blame but ourselves.

The first days were mainly given over to cuts. Shakespeare's plays are rarely performed in full – they're too long and often badly shaped. The modern audience, used to modern pacing, won't stand for it. I expected battles, each actor resisting cuts to his own part, but even here there was a surprising amount of cooperation. The company spirit. If we didn't agree on this, we would be off to a bad start.

At the same time we read through the text and discussed interpretation. Our *As You Like It* was to be a black comedy, a biting satire on love and marriage, with more emphasis on the sardonic Touchstone and melancholy Jaques than Orlando and Rosalind. I didn't mind that either. The text had plenty of scope for it and I had acted long enough now to know there was no such thing as a definitive production.

Then we left the safety of the table and ventured out on to the space marked out by a proscenium arch: our 'stage' for the rest of rehearsals. We'd already seen the set designs. Now we had to impose them on to the blank space we were working in. It was surprisingly easy. Everything seemed so much easier here, with a smooth mechanism in place to free our minds of anything not necessary for the work we had to do.

Did I forget Hanno during all this? No. I'd given up even trying to banish him from my mind. He was with me always, my mentor. Not bossy, no how-would-Hanno-want-me-to-do-this, nothing to interfere with my own thinking. Just a gentle presence forever demanding my best.

He seemed closer than ever the night Jas and I went to see *Hamlet*. The season had already begun for some of the company. There were performances most nights and matinées, too – always different so that the busy tourist could take in two different plays in one day. Beside me an elderly couple had been chattering away in German with such animation that the woman's programme had slipped from her lap. As she began to lean down to look for it, a spasm of pain crossed her face – probably arthritis. I swooped down and, after a brief search, retrieved the programme for her. She thanked me in English and with a warm smile which illuminated her whole face. Only when she looked away did I see, in retrospect, her eyes. They were flecked with gold. A lot of gold. Hanno's eyes.

From then on I could barely concentrate on the play. At every opportunity I stole a glance at the woman. It wasn't just the eyes. The whole face bore a remarkable resemblance to Hanno's. Once again my mind raced to conclusions. It couldn't be coincidence, not with Hanno's house so near and Hanno himself so prominent a figure in the theatre world. Surely this was a relative of his? It was difficult to imagine him having relatives, but there must have been some – at the very least a father and mother. It was even possible that this *was* Hanno's mother.

The curtain went down on Act One. Should I simply ask her? There was nothing preventing me. It would sound reasonable enough: excuse me, but I couldn't help noticing a sort of family resemblance between you and my agent, Hanno Hirsch. If my hunch was right, she would probably be delighted – what a coincidence, meeting one of her son's clients like this. Then I remembered the hidden room, my furtive spying at the golden cottage. No, never again. Whatever his private life, it was his. I had no right to pry.

Hanno's presence seemed nearer still when the first weekend came. Very likely he was there now, tucked inside the little wood only a mile beyond my window.

And then it was Sunday, my first day off. Jas was driving over to visit some friends who were with the Bristol Old Vic – would I come along? Smashing people, would love to meet me. Of course I should go. Of course I would go. I opened my mouth to say yes . . . and heard my voice utter some idiotic excuse. Too lovely a day to spend in a car. Would really like to explore the area a little, get my bearings. I knew I was lying, even to myself. The truth was that I couldn't leave, not with Hanno so near. The same invisible threads which had drawn me along that country road years ago now wound themselves around me, binding me to Hanno's wood.

All the more reason to avoid it. I would set off in a different direction, follow the course of the river. It was the obvious walk to take, and clearly I wasn't the only one who thought so – a footpath ran alongside it.

From the moment I stepped outside the back door I felt at peace. This was a gentler form of nature than I'd known at The Folly. The tall grass of the orchard was littered with daffodils nodding in the slight breeze. The verges of the path were crammed with primroses and cowslips. The river was lined on both sides with willows, some of them trailing their lower branches in the water. Their leaves were half out, fresh with new life. Elsewhere growth was more advanced. Stately horse chestnuts already hinted at that dark heavy look, while the whippy branches of a few larches were shockingly bright, a stunning contrast for the sharp outlines of the blackbirds. One of them, swaying somewhat on the wobbly top, was piercing the air with his syncopated rhythms. Beside me the river answered placidly. Spring had never felt more spring-like, as if I were emerging from a winter that had lasted for years.

I honestly didn't know about the bend in the river. Its route was so masked by trees and its curving so gradual that it had turned a right angle before I noticed it had turned at all. Nor did I remember the nondescript bridge which took the road over it a little later. Only when I climbed up the bank to cross the road did I see, just a little further along, the unmistakable high hedge with the trees inside it rising tall against the clear blue sky. Hanno's wood.

My first reaction was fear and a desire for concealment. Then annoyance. Why shouldn't I be here? It was a clearly defined footpath. I had as much right as anyone else to use it.

I crossed the road and returned to the riverbank. The path was now running parallel to one side of Hanno's wood, a field's-width away. Straight ahead I could see a small hill, also wooded, around which the river curved away again in the opposite direction. I hurried towards it, anxious to be out of sight of Hanno's wood. The hedge which surrounded it was thick with the bright green of newly leafed hawthorn; no one inside it could see through. I was perfectly safe from discovery. None the less, I quickened my step. Already the land on my other side was beginning to rise. It was thickly covered with birches, their leaves just beginning to emerge in a pale olive-green through which the barer branches made a delicate tracery. Beneath them were some hazels, also beginning their growth. The path and the river were curving beside it, hugging the contours. Not much longer and I would be out of sight.

Then I saw them. Two people, just ahead of me, dawdling along the path with their backs to me. A brief stab of fear quickly subsided. No blond heads these, but grey, and beneath them the bent bodies of an elderly couple.

They must have heard me, for they turned and paused on the path, no doubt waiting so that I, the faster walker, could pass them and leave them to amble along at their own pace. But my heart sank, for already I recognised the woman: the one whose programme I had retrieved just a few nights before. Could I pass unnoticed? I doubted it. Unless her sight was very poor indeed, she was sure to recognise me. Not for the first time in my life did I wish myself plain, the anonymous face forgotten in a crowd. And I could hardly pretend not to remember her, not with those amazing golden eyes. Taking a deep breath, I switched into performance gear.

'Hello again!' I smiled. 'What a lovely morning for a walk!'

'It is so,' she replied in her heavily accented English. 'And you holiday now, to see the plays?' Her smile was dazzling, a touch of youth in the withered face.

'Sort of.' Would she recognise me two months from now when she went, as she almost certainly would, to see *As You Like It*?

'So good, to come early,' she nodded. 'Before crowds, and with the earth so fresh.'

I agreed and would have passed pleasantly on if she hadn't turned to her husband and began, 'Here is the kind lady who –'

She stopped, her attention suddenly diverted, as mine had been, by a scuffling on the hill beside us. We all turned simultaneously to see Hanno descending towards us at speed.

What thoughts raced through his mind in those few seconds I can't imagine. It must have been a shock, this first coming together of the public and private lives he had so rigorously kept apart until now. He must have been desperate to find a way of minimising the damage. Only one thing was certain: that it would be useless for either of us to pretend we were strangers.

'Rosalind!' The pleasure in his voice was almost convincing.

'Hanno!' The surprise in mine was, I hoped, a better performance.

We began to speak simultaneously, then laughed.

'But you know each other?' exclaimed the old woman.

'Most certainly we do,' said Hanno smoothly. He had nearly recovered. He must already have calculated that I would notice the resemblance. Any attempt to disguise his relationship with the couple would be as futile as to disguise our own. 'Mother, Father, this is Ros Rawlinson – one of my most promising clients. Rosalind, my parents.'

'Good heavens!' I exclaimed. 'I had no idea! I'm so pleased to meet you.' We shook hands. 'Are you on holiday here?' I asked.

'But no,' said the old man. 'We live here. We have a little walk this morning before coffee, yes?'

That was it. Coffee. From the moment he uttered the word, we were locked into a civility which none of us could avoid.

'But, *gnädige Fräulein*, you must come to take coffee with us!' he said gallantly.

His wife turned to him and, while maintaining a friendly smile for my benefit, began to say quietly in German, 'But the –'

'Rosalind speaks German very well,' Hanno said quickly. It was meant as a warning but disguised as a gift. 'And so you *certainly* must come and have coffee with us. My parents will be so pleased to meet someone who speaks their own language.'

It was a bold move – to dispel any suspicion from my mind before it could form. No one seeing us on the path would have guessed that anything was amiss. I might not have guessed myself, if I hadn't followed Hanno that time and seen the padlocked gate, if I hadn't connected up his mother's words with the notion of something to hide.

So when Hanno said, 'I'll just go on ahead and put the coffee on,' I knew it wasn't just the coffee that needed his attention.

'We are too slow for Hanno,' his father laughed. He looked at the greenery his son was clutching.

'Sweet cicily,' Hanno explained. He handed it to his father and then strode off down the path ahead of us. We turned and followed at a slower pace.

Hanno's father held out the sweet cicily to me. 'You know this plant?' He crushed some leaves and wafted them under my nose. A lovely scent of aniseed rose from them.

We talked about the sweet cicily and other plants of the neighbourhood. We talked about the countryside in general, and about the town, Chipping Moreton. We talked about everything except ourselves and the one person who linked us, Hanno. Were they curious about this woman who knew their son in his London setting? I was certainly curious about them. But we were all waiting for Hanno to rejoin us and give us our cues. What was it that he'd gone on ahead to conceal, as I was sure he had? Surely he had no reason to whisk the pretty blonde out of sight? Wife, sister, friend of the family – surely there was nothing untoward about her presence there?

When we arrived at the discreet entrance, Hanno was there already. The gates were open and he was standing – as if merely in welcome – in a position that concealed the padlock. As I walked up the mossy drive with his parents, I heard the soft clank of the gates closing again. I looked just in time to see him turn the key in the padlock. Our eyes met.

He caught up with us. 'We've had some trouble with prowlers recently,' he explained.

Recently. The gate had been padlocked several years ago.

'And this,' he said, with a sweep of his arm, 'is our tiny estate.'

It was lovely. On either side of the faint green drive stood trees of every imaginable species. Some of the obvious ones I recognised from The Folly: oak and ash, birch, beech, maple, rowan, all the traditional trees of the English countryside. Others Hanno had to point out. It was a side of Hanno I'd never suspected.

'You really do know about trees,' I said admiringly.

'But of course!' exclaimed his mother. 'Hanno plants himself all of them.'

'Is that true?' I asked.

'Nearly. It was just a field with a house in the middle when we bought it. There were only a few trees. The rest I planted.' He smiled. 'So now you know my secret. During the week I pretend to be the complete urbanite but at weekends I turn into the peasant I am at heart. Jekyll and Hyde. You will keep my secret, won't you, Rosalind? It would ruin the exotic image you tell me I have, if the theatre world pictured me grubbing about in the soil playing Johnny Appleseed.'

He had said his piece with disarming self-deprecation, but I wasn't fooled. There was some other reason for keeping his country household a secret. He was using his urban image as an excuse to keep me quiet.

We were nearing the end of the drive. From the road there was no evidence of a house inside the wood. Now I saw why. A large island of trees had been planted where the drive ended, completely masking the house. The track branched around the island and came out on to a gravelled area in front of the house.

'Oh, Hanno, it's beautiful!'

The golden cottage was certainly gold – the warm honey-coloured stone of the Cotswolds. But cottage it was not. It was, in fact, a small Elizabethan manor house, and one of the most perfect I'd ever seen, with mullioned windows and quaint chimney pots and a wonderful two-storey porch. The walls were hugged by climbing roses, a few of them just making their first tentative venture into leaf. A narrow border on each side of the porch was crammed with hyacinths, fritillaries, vincas, sweet violets, daffodils and a few early tulips. Between them the clumps of snowdrop foliage looked like green hedgehogs.

We entered the house. A wide stone-flagged passageway ran straight through to the back door opposite, the door through which Hanno and the young woman had emerged. There was no sign of her now, in the passageway or in the sitting-room. This was at the back of the house, overlooking a large lawned garden and the woodland beyond. It was reasonable enough for me to approach the windows and admire the view, but I was looking for the woman. No trace of her. The sitting-room had plenty of feminine touches, but Hanno's mother was the obvious source.

As we drank our coffee we talked about London, Stratford, the theatre. There was a total absence of anything personal. I could have found a gracious way of questioning them about their origins, their move to the Cotswolds, their family. I'm not sure what stopped me – perhaps the indefinable sense of sadness that seemed to tinge the elderly couple and call for restraint. I tried to put it down to the high cheekbones, just like Hanno's, producing that hint of Slavic melancholy. Or the distinctive vertical lines on their faces, again like Hanno's, which suggested an inwardness given to brooding. Hanno's parents had, like so many old couples, grown to look like each other. Even their once big-boned frames had shrunk to a similar size and shape. They were handsome people still, and must have been quite dashing in their prime.

I explained my presence in the neighbourhood. They were startled to hear of Jas's cottage; Stratford people didn't normally have digs so far out. No, they didn't know the cottage, didn't know much about the town. They led a very sheltered life, they apologised. They had grown accustomed to the peace and quiet of their little enclave. (Who did the shopping? Who dealt with emergency repairs? How often was that gate unlocked?)

The coffee was drunk, the cakes were eaten. Automatically I rose to take my leave. Must you go so soon? Yes, I must. Well then, perhaps another day. Hanno would provide a guided tour of the woodland he had planted. I didn't question why this couldn't be done now. Though never once relaxing their hospitality, they were, I was sure, anxious for me to leave.

Hanno walked with me to the gates and unlocked them. He smiled. 'I suppose it must seem a little paranoid, but it makes my parents feel safer.' He hesitated. Then, 'Rosalind, I would be grateful if you didn't mention this to anyone. You see, my parents are really very timid – much more so than you might imagine. They're getting rather old now, and it does strange things to the mind, living alone and unprotected. Few people passing by would even think there was a house here. It's better that way.'

Millions of old people lived in houses protected by nothing more than a token garden gate.

Perhaps he had read my mind. 'There are no neighbours here to call on for help. The best protection is for no one to know they're here at all.' He smiled again. 'I know I can trust you, Rosalind.'

It was, despite the smile and the apologetic manner, an order. I had no choice but to obey it.

27

In the time that followed I tried not to think too much about the Hirsches and the strange secluded life they led, but it was difficult. Luckily I had other things to occupy my mind: the novelty of Stratford and the intensity of our rehearsals. If I'd thought that the long rehearsal period would be leisurely, I was wrong. It was as strenuous as the hectic few weeks of the West End. Nor was it confined to the hours spent in the Conference Hall. We spent many evenings over meals at the Dirty Duck, thrashing out even more details of interpretation. The Duck, alias the Black Swan, was an extension of the RSC, a restaurant-cum-pub run by people who knew the theatre well. Sometimes an older member of staff would sit down with us and recall some golden age, tell us anecdotes about the greats who had preceded us.

And then there were the voice calls, individual sessions with the voice coach. This was a revelation. I'd never been taught anything about projection except the vague instruction to 'Try and project a little more, dear'. No one had said how. No one had explained the weird mechanism which could be coaxed into cooperation. I'd been straining my voice to make it fill the bigger theatres. Now I was learning to do it with ease. Altogether the RSC was proving to be a complete education, filling in everything I had missed by not going to drama school. It was even better, really, for now I was older and more capable of understanding.

None of which meant that I forgot Hanno. Far from it. As each weekend approached, I was filled with the sense of his imminent nearness. Also with the hope that he would invite me back to see his wood. I didn't expect it, though. I was sure that he was hoping I'd forget all about it. No doubt he would have a sheaf of excuses at hand to explain why he'd never got in touch.

The whole spring and summer might have passed without another meeting if Jas hadn't been, despite appearances, an old-fashioned knight. One evening we were driving back from Stratford when we saw a car parked on the verge and a woman struggling to change a wheel. Jas to the rescue. He pulled up behind, got out of his car and went over to do his knightly duty.

I got out, too, just pleased to be in the soft scented air and also to show that Jas's intentions were entirely honourable. After all, it was dusk, and she appeared to be alone. She raised her head as we approached . . . and I looked straight into the face of Hanno's pretty blonde.

She recognised me, I was sure of it. Even after all these years her face showed the same fleeting panic I'd seen at the clinic. It lasted only a second. Jas put up his hands in the time-honoured gesture of surrender. She smiled. He offered his assistance.

'I should say no, I am liberated, I do my mechanics. But oh, such a business!'

I should have known. The same heavily accented English.

She stepped aside gratefully. She'd already done half the job. Jas finished it in no time and we were on our way again.

'A tourist up for the season?' said Jas. 'Can't be a lot of Germans living in the Cotswolds.'

I didn't tell him that she was almost certainly Austrian and a relative of Hanno Hirsch. I had kept my promise to Hanno and said nothing of his family.

Jas sniffed. 'Didn't even recognise me.'

'Aw, poor Jas. Maybe she doesn't have a telly. Cheer up. She'll probably come to the play and shriek out, "But yes, that is the kind man who my wheel changes!" Bring the curtain down.'

The next night Hanno phoned. 'Rosalind, are you alone?'

'Yes – Jas is out with a friend.' It was Saturday night and I was enjoying my solitude.

'Could you come and see me tomorrow?'

'Of course. Is this the long-promised tour of your estate?'

A brief silence. 'I'm sorry about that. I'll explain everything when you get here. Can you manage some excuse? Say you'd like a walk on your own?'

'I can. But I hate lying to Jas. He's my oldest friend, you know.'

'Yes, I do know, and I'm sorry. If it were only my business I wouldn't ask this of you.' Another pause. 'You haven't told him about the other Sunday?'

'Of course not. Though I still don't understand all the secrecy.'

'I'll explain everything tomorrow.'

Not much chance of sleep after that. Years of accumulated curiosity gathered into a single knot like a swarm of bees buzzing over my head. When I did manage to doze, strange images flitted in and out of my sleep. For the first time in years the golden stag returned, and this time his face was unmistakably that of Hanno Hirsch.

The next morning I walked the river path to the bridge and then came up on to the road. The verges were bright with dandelions drinking in the sun. It was a lovely day but I was too preoccupied to notice much.

Hanno was waiting for me at the gates. With him was the woman. My first reaction was relief. She had haunted my thoughts for years, along with all the other unsolved mysteries of Hanno's life. Now she was out in the open.

Hanno introduced us. Then he said, 'Christa is a nurse and a therapist.'

The clinic.

She must have read my mind. 'It was a shock, that you say "Hello, Hanno" at the clinic. I pretend not to notice, and then you and the friend are called and so I think perhaps there is no problem. I say nothing to Hanno about this because I think all is forgotten. But then, on the road this week, I see you recognise, and so I tell Hanno. Better you not know, but,' she shrugged sadly, 'too late.'

We began to walk up the drive. The sun must have been pouring down over us but its warmth was lost on me. I felt as cold as death. I hadn't realised just how much I depended on Hanno to be the calm, still centre of my world, just as David had been so long ago. The infallibility I invented for him was a part of it. Now, for the first time, I had to acknowledge that he was, after all, human. No devil's child, no magician, but a human being who must have some awful illness I'd never suspected. The trees were crashing down on me, I barely saw where we were going, I heard nothing.

'Rosalind?'

His voice summoned me from a long distance.

'You were miles away.' Incredibly, he was smiling. 'We're taking you to meet him now. It will be rather disturbing. I hope you're ready.'

Meet whom?

We had arrived at the front door. We entered the wide passageway, then the sitting-room. Hanno's parents were there, standing by the windows. As we entered they came towards us. I was indeed disturbed. They had aged a great deal since our first meeting, and their faces, though welcoming, were grave.

'We are so pleased that you come,' said Mrs Hirsch.

Light was flooding in through the windows, dazzling my senses. I suppose it was that, and the sleepless night before, that produced the hallucination: instead of two old people, there seemed to be a crowd in the room, suddenly parting, like the Red Sea, to reveal a single person sitting on the window seat.

It was Hanno.

I don't know how long I stood there, rooted to the floor. My ears were buzzing and the only lucid thought I had was, 'Yes, I am insane. This is what it's like to be insane.' Other than that, my mind closed down completely.

Then Hanno was standing beside me. And yet, he was still sitting on the window seat. I blinked, trying to dispel the double vision. There was a soft touch on my elbow. Hanno's hand. Then we were both of us walking across the room towards the window seat. Hanno rose from it. I looked from one to the other, not even trying to make sense of it.

'Rosalind,' said the Hanno beside me, 'I'd like you to meet my brother, Joachim.' He spoke in German. 'Joachim, this is my friend, Rosalind.'

The other Hanno smiled shyly and put out his hand. In a daze, I took it.

'It was Joachim you saw at the clinic,' the first Hanno was saying. 'Poor Rosalind. I wish I'd known. You must have been terribly confused.'

Have been? I was confused now. 'I don't understand.' My voice sounded like that of a robot.

'Joachim and I are twins,' Hanno said. 'Identical twins, though in fact it's not that difficult to tell us apart. But at the clinic there wasn't time to notice. If only you'd told me, Rosalind. I would have explained. Though we always hoped there'd never be a need to explain.'

Now Mrs Hirsch was beside me. 'Come and sit down, please. Christa will make some coffee.'

She, too, was speaking in German. I sat down. Then we were all sitting, in a conversational little group, as if this were a perfectly normal social occasion. The other Hanno, the one called Joachim, had returned to his window seat. He smiled across the room at me. I smiled back, uncertainly. Very slowly I was beginning to realise that this was indeed another person, but the resemblance was so extreme that my senses were still confused. Joachim. Brother. Twin.

'Would you mind very much,' Mrs Hirsch was saying, 'speaking in German? Joachim understands no English. He understands little German either, but he is happier when we speak German. We are very fortunate to have Christa. Without her, nothing would be possible.' She smiled at the nurse.

Nurse. Therapist. She wore no uniform and seemed in every way a part of the family.

Christa left to make the coffee.

'Joachim has a nervous disease,' said Hanno. He spoke in a matter-of-fact way, as if we were discussing some item in the newspaper. 'It didn't show itself until he was about seven. Then the disintegration began. Since then he's barely developed at all, at least in certain ways – mentally, including language. He understands very little of what we say, even in German, but we prefer to speak openly in front of him.'

'We try,' said Mrs Hirsch, 'to provide a normal atmosphere.' She smiled sadly.

The sadness, the melancholy. My mind was clearing. I almost wished it wasn't. For several appalling minutes I'd thought it was Hanno's life that was blighted. The relief of discovering that it wasn't had been short-lived. His twin brother. I was remembering all the things I'd heard about twins, about the strange telepathy that so often existed between them. Hanno, with his brilliant mind, and Joachim, with, I had to suppose, the mind of a seven-year-old child. I closed my eyes, suddenly weighed down with the sorrow that surrounded me. 'I'm so sorry,' I murmured. I hated myself. What feeble words for a lifetime lived like this.

'We're sorry, too,' said Hanno, 'to burden you with this. It would have been better if you'd never known.'

How could he be so solicitous of my feelings? I saw myself suddenly as a silly little butterfly who'd been flitting about Hanno's life, filled with my own longings, never imagining that beneath his calm exterior there existed this other life hidden away among the trees. 'The hedge,' I said. 'The gate.'

Mr Hirsch spoke for the first time. 'Children can be very cruel. When I was a student, there was a boy like Joachim in the flat below. A teenager with the mind of a child. The children of the neighbourhood were merciless. Often he would come home covered with bruises.' He paused. 'I never thought I would have such a child myself.'

Christa arrived with the coffee. Her simple cheerfulness

was incongruous with the story I was hearing. After pouring, she sat down among us.

Mrs Hirsch took up the story. 'When we came to England with the children, we discovered that the English were no better. Hanno was very good to Joachim; he protected him as much as he could. But even so, we had to move many times. Each time, new children would gather like little demons, waiting to torment Joachim. It was even more difficult in England, as Joachim knew nothing of the language.'

'And then,' said Mr Hirsch, 'Hanno began to earn some money. We had saved as much as we could, and together we managed to find enough to buy this house and the land around it. By this time we realised that the only way to protect Joachim was secrecy. There are no children living nearby, and we hope that those in the town and the village will simply never find out. So you see,' he smiled, 'what may appear to you to be a prison is a protective shell.'

'We had very little choice,' said Mrs Hirsch. 'Because of the language, there was no possibility of putting Joachim into an institution. And in any case . . .'

'His life is better here with us,' said Mr Hirsch. 'We understand him. And Christa knows what to do in the bad times.'

'Every so often there's news of a new drug or a new treatment,' said Christa. 'Then we go to the clinic. Always hoping. But the truth is, there's very little that can be done for Joachim other than provide a reasonably comfortable life.'

'And for that,' said Mrs Hirsch, 'we need secrecy. It may appear very melodramatic – the mad son in the attic. But the hedge keeps people out, and it also keeps Joachim in. Nobody knows he's here. As far as the locals are concerned, we are just two old people being looked after by a kind relative,' she smiled at Christa, 'and with a son who comes to visit on weekends.'

Hanno laughed. 'It may astonish you, but it never occurred to us that Stratford would be a problem. We've lived fairly openly. People know that a Mr and Mrs Hirsch live here and that their son is called Hanno. But the name means nothing outside theatrical circles, and such circles seemed a very long way away.'

'Until that Sunday,' I said ruefully, in my clumsy German. 'What a shock it must have been for you when I came blundering onto the scene.'

'It was,' he admitted. 'We never thought anyone from Stratford would look for digs this far out. Let alone you.'

I was beginning to adapt at last. There was something reassuring about the conversation and the matter-of-fact way they spoke. These people had had a long time to adjust to their situation. To them, it was a form of normality. Their own attitude was beginning to penetrate to me. Several times I had looked across at Joachim. Each time he had smiled disarmingly, like a child. However tragic his situation, there was nothing tragic about his manner. I realised then what a good job these people had done, to create for him a setting in which he could thrive to the best of his abilities.

'I think you must know,' I said quietly, 'that your secret is safe with me.'

Hanno nodded. 'Thank you. Though I still wish it hadn't been necessary. It's a burden, keeping someone else's secret.'

How much more of a burden it must have been for these people. I thought of my crass spying – on the hidden room in Wigmore Street, on the golden cottage glimpsed through the hedge.

Once again the coffee was drunk, the cakes were eaten, only this time there was no sense that it was time for me to leave.

'And now,' said Hanno, rising from his chair, 'it's time for that tour of the estate. You don't mind if Joachim comes with us?'

'Of course not.'

'And after that, we would be very pleased if you could stay for lunch,' said Mrs Hirsch. 'We do it properly, you know – roast beef and Yorkshire pudding.'

And now, stepping outside into the sunshine, I felt its

warmth at last. We were standing outside the back door, the same door through which I'd seen Hanno (or was it Joachim?) emerge on the day I had spied. Hanno must never know about that. The crudeness of my curiosity. The quiet dignity of the inhabitants.

Hanno was watching me. 'You're taking it well.'

I was touched by his concern. 'And what about you? And your parents?' I said quietly.

He shrugged. 'We've had many years to adjust. There are problems, yes, and there will be more problems in the future. But inside our little enclave we live quite peaceably.'

There was a lawn fringed with flowering shrubs. Immediately beyond it the woodland began. As we started down a path, Hanno said, 'We weren't entirely truthful the first time you came here. I didn't plant all these trees myself; Joachim and I planted them together. Isn't that so?' he said to his brother. 'You and I planted all these trees together.'

Joachim nodded happily.

Seeing the two brothers together, I wondered how I could have mistaken Joachim for Hanno. The resemblance was strong, yes, but so were the differences. There was something soft and unformed about Joachim, as if, despite his size, he'd failed to take on the clear, sharp outline of an adult. And he was rather clumsy. While Hanno bore his size with grace, Joachim moved in the uncoordinated manner of a child. But most striking of all was the absence of sadness in his face. He, the centre of this family tragedy, seemed unaware of his plight.

'Joachim knows his trees far better than I do,' Hanno went on. 'He knows each one individually. He also knows exactly the right place to suit each tree. Sometimes we disagree about where to put a tree, and whenever I've overruled him, the tree has done badly.'

He was still speaking German, partly to me and partly to Joachim. I don't know how much Joachim understood, but he nodded happily.

'Joachim must have got his way here,' I said. To one

side of the path was a stand of birches freshly in leaf. Beneath their light graceful canopy, the grass was crowded with anemones and wild violets. On the other side was a clump of willows. A swathe of celandines cut through them, forming a bright golden pathway of its own.

'There's probably an underground stream there,' said Hanno. 'These are the things Joachim seems to know intuitively. He was determined to plant willows there, and he was right.'

As we walked further into the little wood, I began to see the skill that had gone into planning it. The path took advantage of every slight contour of the land. Here it skirted a tiny hill planted thickly with rhododendrons to disguise the route and provide a surprise around the corner: a carpet of early bluebells basking in the sun filtered through a hazel copse. A little further on was a giant beech tree ('One of the few we didn't plant.') delicately hazed by the first scattering of acid green leaves. Further still several oaks were just beginning to unfurl their bronzy leaves. There were conifers, too, singly and in clusters. Their dark shapes were reassuring, a touch of the immutable; without them, I felt sure that the whole effervescent mass of trees springing into leaf would lift right off the ground and float away into the sky.

I had never seen a more beautiful woodland, not even at The Folly. There, the realities of commercial forestry had spread a sense of the earthbound over the land. It was lovely, yes, but I was always aware that they were trees planted to be cut down. Here it seemed as if the trees would live for ever, quietly forgotten by the chainsaw. 'I see why you were so interested in David's work,' I said.

He smiled. 'We began our plantings simply as something Joachim and I could do together. But trees are addictive. They sink their roots in your mind. This was an empty field when we bought it. There were a few old trees but nothing had been allowed to regenerate. Now it's nearly filled. Soon there'll be nothing for us to do. It seemed such an immense space – ten acres. We thought it would take a lifetime.'

We had arrived at a stream. I recognised it as the one which, at either end, was channelled into the culverts I had walked over. In fact, it seemed to me that I recognised the exact spot. This is where Christa and Hanno – yes, it must have been Hanno – had stepped out on to the bank while I watched. She had pointed to some part of the stream and said something which my dazed mind had failed to hear.

And now it was Hanno who was pointing. 'Joachim nearly drowned here a few years ago. He slipped while trying to cross the stream and hit his head on a rock. Christa found him just in time. He has no sense of danger, you see.'

Of course. Like a child. And into the Garden of Eden the serpent glided. It was so easy to forget, surrounded by such beauty, that it was all created for the fearless child who would never grow up. He would have to be tended carefully every day of his life. What would happen when Hanno was no longer there to look after him? I pictured Joachim, a wizened old man with the mind of a child, forced at last into a world where no one loved him. How much more often Hanno must have pictured this very thing. In that moment of revelation, I understood the quiet but authoritative steadiness which characterised Hanno. And I looked at Hanno as he stood beside the stream, talking to his brother. Hanno, my agent, my friend, the centre of my childish fantasies. I remembered another moment of revelation: on the train up to Yorkshire after seeing him at this very stream with Christa, when I realised that I loved him.

Suddenly I felt a new kind of love sweep over me, softer and yet stronger. I wanted to take onto myself the burden, relieve him of the strain of keeping himself strong for his family. But would someone who had spent his life closed inside this family responsibility let me in? And was I being honest? I had spent my own life longing for someone strong and protective – first David, and now Hanno. I could so easily, with all my own insecurities, become just another burden.

A hand settled on my shoulder, soft and a little clumsy. I looked up into Joachim's face. On it was a smile with just a touch of a child's mischievousness. With his other hand he was pointing to a circle of clear blue sky enclosed in a leafy frame above us. The circle was empty, the wood silent. A second later a curlew soared across it, its wings golden in the sun, and the silence parted to let through its rich melodious call.

28

Sunday lunch in an English country house. The classic meal, beautifully cooked, lustily eaten. A big table in a dining-room flooded with sunshine. Outside the open windows ten acres' worth of birds were chattering away. Inside, a roomful of people also chattered. What could be more normal? Except that the conversation – ranging from rehearsals to rabbits in the garden to the nervous system – was entirely in German.

Joachim, they told me, was unable to speak. The disease attacked only certain kinds of nerve endings, including those necessary for speech. Some other motor nerves were also affected, which explained his ungainly walk. And yet his hands were as coordinated as those of any adult, and his hearing was acute. He was a strange mixture of child and adult, clumsiness and grace. Please, would I take another potato?

They almost wished, they said, that I had stumbled upon their secret sooner. It was a relief to be able to speak to someone outside the family. None the less, they apologised again and again for burdening me with their troubles. It was no burden, I assured them, and yes, I would love another carrot.

We talked of Hanno's life in London, though not about the hidden room in Wigmore Street. When Hanno referred to his 'flat', I realised that he'd allowed his parents to think he lived more luxuriously than he did. No doubt he wished to spare them the embarrassing truth: that everything he earned went into the house in the Cotswolds.

They were astonished to hear of Hanno's reputation, the almost mythical status he had in the theatrical world.

But yes, they knew he was successful – they sometimes saw his clients on the television. Why had they not seen me on the television? When would I appear on the television? When the time is right, said Hanno, and not before. I made a face. We all laughed.

They were proud of Joachim, too, and the skill he lavished on his trees. The garden was also Joachim's. The disease hadn't damaged his sense of aesthetics. He understood the mysteries of colour and form far better than the rest of them did. There was no doubt that without the disease he would have developed a brilliant mind, just like his brother. And here they shrugged, accepting the cruelty of fate. It was no use complaining, they said, and really, they were fortunate in so many ways.

I was becoming terribly fond of these people. Mr Hirsch spoke little, but when he did it was with an old-world courtesy peppered with '*gnädige Fräulein*'. He was a true Viennese gentleman, and irresistible. Mrs Hirsch was more animated, with a charm which again I felt was uniquely Viennese. It was easy to imagine them in their natural setting: the cafés of Vienna, the opera, the elegant city streets. Easy, too, to see the source of Hanno's own charm. I remembered our day in London, his knack of finding the unusual and interesting, the way he walked the streets as if they were the corridors of his house. These were urban people, and yet they had the grace to turn their secluded exile into an art form.

And Christa? No, she laughed, not Viennese; just a country girl from Styria. She had trained in Vienna and specialised in nervous disorders. But she had been happy to leave the city and work with her single patient in such beautiful surroundings. No, her life was good, she had no complaints. Usually she had the weekends off – when Hanno took over. But she was always happy to come back to the house in the wood.

After lunch we returned to the sitting-room for coffee, all except Joachim. Clearly the novelty of having a visitor was wearing off. I didn't feel offended. I was rapidly adjusting to his ways.

And then, from a room nearby, came the sound of a Chopin nocturne. Surely it couldn't be . . . ?

Oh yes, they nodded; it was Joachim. He played quite well – couldn't read music, of course, or anything else. But he listened to the radio and stored the tunes in his head. Tunes but not words; the disease was very selective. Yes, quite possibly he would have become a musician, if . . . And they shrugged again and smiled

At the first sign of fatigue in his parents, Hanno rose and asked if I would like another walk around the grounds. His parents usually had a nap after dinner. Christa would fill the dishwasher and then spend the afternoon reading. As for Joachim, once he started he would play the piano for hours. He often played himself to sleep. Christa would find him slumped over the keys, smiling happily to himself in his dreams.

As we left the room it seemed to me that Hanno's parents had lost much of their haggard appearance. There was a sense of peace in the room.

'You're good for them,' said Hanno when we'd stepped outside.

'That's a lovely thing to say.'

He smiled. 'I always suspected there was more to you than a pretty face and talent.'

'Lovelier still. Take care: a few more words and my head will swell.'

'We always hoped no one would discover us here. But if it had to happen, I'm glad it was you.'

I put my hands to my head. 'I warned you.'

He laughed. Then he removed my hands and, making a circle of his own, placed them on my head like a crown. A shiver went through me as I remembered the crown at the British Museum. 'Come and see more of the wood,' he said. 'There's much more of it than you would suspect. Joachim has booby-trapped it with paths, all of them leading to special little places he's created. There's one in particular you didn't see this morning.'

Once more we plunged into the maze of paths that Joachim had designed. I thought about The Folly. So many parallels. Two beautiful woodlands with a house hidden in the middle. Two mazes – one the wood itself, the other the house. Two groups of people banded together in a common cause, keeping the outside world at bay. I felt sorry for David. He had no need to guard his secrecy so fiercely. Hanno did. I knew the cruelty of children, understood the need to protect Joachim.

None the less, 'It seems so sad,' I said, 'that nobody else sees what you've done here – not just the wood, but the world you've created for Joachim.'

We'd been walking in single file down a path. Hanno stopped and turned to face me. 'You must keep silent, Rosalind. We're trusting you.'

'I know, and I won't say anything. But seeing your parents open up today . . . it must be hard on them, never having anyone to visit.'

'But you've visited. And I hope you'll come again. It would make my parents very happy.'

'Of course I will, if you're sure. But there's nothing special about me. You know actors – we're a good-hearted bunch of butterflies. Jas would love it here, and I'm sure your parents would adore him.'

'Very probably. But actors talk. Sooner or later it would get back to the town. My poor Rosalind – it's a hard thing, keeping a secret like this. No one knows it more than I do. I've spent a lifetime being two people.'

'Well,' I said lightly, 'now you can be one person; with me at least. Since I know both of you now.'

A glimmer of the London Hanno returned. 'I'm not sure that's a good thing, you sly little elf. You'll take advantage of me now that you know I'm not the diabolical Svengali you thought I was. Enough talk. Straight ahead – we're nearly there.'

He took my hand and led me through a narrow green tunnel. The trees were so close together and so low that we had to squeeze through them like potholers through a subterranean passageway, or swimmers beneath a vast green ocean. 'Is there a gingerbread house at the end, with a witch waiting to put us in her oven?'

'Shush. The wood is full of her familiars. Here we are.'

We stopped at the edge of a clearing. My heart thudded. No witch could be as frightening as what I saw. It was the same clearing, right down to the last detail, the same one in which I'd seen the golden stag all those years ago. I felt my hand go cold in Hanno's. His own seemed to burn in contrast. The same ring of birches, their delicate little leaves catching the high-up sun. Now, as then, the sun glanced off the leaves and turned them to gold, while the breeze, setting them in motion, seemed to make of them a shower of sparks like the ones that had shot like arrows from the antlers of the golden stag. And just over there was the place where he had been, or would appear, that vision of fear and longing which David had laughed away but which I knew was real. I shut my eyes, not wanting to see.

'Rosalind, what's wrong? You're like ice.'

I was shivering uncontrollably, despite the heat from Hanno's hand. 'I've been here before,' I whispered.

He gripped my hand harder. 'Look at me, Rosalind. Tell me what's wrong.'

But I wouldn't look. I knew what I would see if I did: the head of the golden stag with its face the image of Hanno's. I could feel myself going limp with despair. I had wanted to be strong for Hanno. Instead, I was collapsing into a useless child at the memory of a nightmare. Slowly, and with what seemed like superhuman effort, I opened my eyes and looked at Hanno.

He was Hanno, not the golden stag. The long vertical creases of his face seemed deeper than ever, carved by his own private nightmare. The fear was receding now, and I felt an absurd impulse to raise my hand and with my fingers trace the lines of his face, memorise them with my fingertips. I smiled uncertainly. 'I'm sorry. It was just a sense of *déjà vu*.'

'It must have been a frightening one.'

'It was.'

'Would you like to tell me about it?'

Would I dare? My feelings towards Hanno had always

been so confused: fear, love, trust, anger, and now the new respect, knowing what he'd done for his family. He'd always felt both close and distant, and I'd hurtled between the two sometimes within the space of a few seconds. My vision of the golden stag was intensely private. I'd told it to David and he'd laughed, indifferent to the power it had for me. If I told it to Hanno and he, too, laughed . . .

I looked down. Beneath the delicate canopy, the ground was covered with wild bedstraw. Then, when David and I had used it as our bed, it had been past its flowering. Now it hadn't begun. Reason told me it couldn't be the same clearing, and yet . . .

'You'll think it ridiculous,' I said.

'Try me.'

He led me into the centre of the clearing. We sat down. Above us birds were twittering. They had been silent then, the only sound the muffled flutter of wings as their flight festooned the trees.

Hanno was watching me. 'I'm waiting.'

He had been waiting for me in the other clearing, too, his eyes mournful and cold, beckoning me to leave David and follow him into the forest. 'In David's forest,' I began slowly, 'there's a clearing just like this.' I stopped. Please don't say the obvious, I prayed. A ring of birch trees, a carpet of bedstraw – there could be a dozen clearings like it all over England.

'Go on,' he prompted.

'A long time ago, David and I found the clearing. It was late summer, I think. We were young, not yet married. We made love on the carpet of bedstraw. And then we fell asleep.' High overhead a plane droned, too distant to see. I watched its vapour trail chalk the blue circle of sky enclosed by the trees. 'When I woke up, I saw a stag step into the clearing.' I looked at Hanno. He was still Hanno. 'A beautiful creature. Too beautiful to be flesh and blood. In fact . . .' I hesitated, but it was too late now. 'In fact, he wasn't. He was gold. From the tips of his antlers down to the lovely little hooves. Gold. Not a reflection of the sun. Really gold, I'm sure of it.'

'And then?'

'He disappeared. As visions do. As mythical creatures do. Later – a month, perhaps two – he came back in a dream. Exactly the same, except that this time his antlers were shooting sparks and he was beckoning me to come with him. I began to move towards him, but David called me back. And that was when it turned into a nightmare. Because suddenly a terrible heat was radiating from his body. I began to go to him again, and as I approached, my own body caught fire. I was literally burning to death. But the thing that made it even more terrifying was that the stag had taken on a human face. And the face,' I turned to Hanno, 'was yours.'

We sat very still for a long time, so still that a chaffinch, fooled into thinking we were statues, hopped into the clearing and began to peck at the ground. Once or twice he glanced at us, as if suspecting. His eye was black and shiny.

'When was this?' Hanno asked at last.

'Years ago. The summer after my first year at Cambridge.'

'We hadn't met. How could you know it was my face?'

'That's what's so uncanny. I didn't. Until you came into my dressing-room at York. I recognised you immediately. From the dream.'

Hanno let out a long breath. 'No wonder you looked so terrified.'

'Did I? I don't remember anything – except your face and the stag's and the sense of a great heat emanating from both of you.'

'Poor Rosalind. I wish I'd known. And yet you came to see me in London.'

'The stag was frightening, but compelling, too.'

The chaffinch had dashed to the edge of the clearing from which he now glared at us. We'd broken the contract, turned into humans after all.

'I'm beginning to see,' said Hanno. 'Why you felt there was something superhuman about me. Why you tried to turn me into myth.'

'And the rumours about you,' I added. '*Wunderkind*, devil's child.'

'That's the kind of thing people always say when someone keeps his private life private.'

'Yes. But,' I turned to him, pleading for his understanding, 'there's more to it, I know there is. There's too much to be coincidence: your face and the stag's, the two clearings, even your name – "stag". I tried to laugh it away myself, but I still feel . . .' I trailed off, not sure what I did feel. An idea was beginning to form, but I didn't know how to put it to him. 'Hanno, please don't laugh at me, but I can't help wondering – is there any possibility that one day that summer you came into this clearing and an image of me flitted through your mind? I know it sounds vain – why should you think of me? And yet . . .'

'And yet . . .' he repeated slowly. At least he wasn't laughing.

'I mean, you'd seen me in the play at Cambridge. Is it possible, however briefly?'

The bird, impatient, had returned to the clearing, determined not to be thwarted by the inconsiderate humans who'd usurped his territory. He was pecking vigorously now. The sense of normality he created steadied me for Hanno's next words.

'It's more than possible, Rosalind. It's certain. I remember it. I'd been very struck by your performance. And then, one weekend, I came into this clearing with Joachim and we sat here, just as you and I are sitting here. Not saying much, just thinking our separate thoughts. The clearing made me think of the Forest of Arden, the play . . . and you.'

I held my breath while my heart crashed about, almost out of control. *I hadn't been imagining it.* There *was* a connection between us, going back all those years. The invisible threads that bound me to Hanno, leading me back to him always – they weren't just the fevered invention of a lovesick mind.

'There's something else I haven't told you, something I've never talked about with anyone,' he was saying. 'The magic powers people like to imagine I have – there's some truth in it. But it's not the devil. It's not even me. It's Joachim.'

'Joachim!'

My outburst was too much for the chaffinch. He fled in terror.

'Don't forget,' said Hanno, 'we're twins. It's not surprising that there's something special between us. After all, we began life as one person. Joachim's disease doesn't alter that. And one thing I know for certain: it was Joachim who was intended to be the brilliant one, not me. The intuition he has for plants and colour and music – it would have developed into something far greater.' He turned to me. 'He would have been a genius, Rosalind. And I don't use the term lightly.'

He had spoken quietly, but there was pain beneath the words. Who could ever know whether or not he was right? But now I saw what lay behind that pervasive sadness. It was more than compassion for Joachim. It was guilt, however unreasonable. One egg which had divided unfairly, the cells of the disease choosing to follow Joachim and leave Hanno free.

'And you think Joachim communicates something of this to you?' I asked.

'I don't think it. I know it. I've felt it so many times, and always, when I listen, he's right.'

'And so this intuition you have – about which actors are likely to amount to something –'

'It's Joachim's. I sit in a darkened theatre watching a play like anyone else, judging, evaluating, watching for the signs of real talent. And then, suddenly, it happens. It's not spectacular, no mystical voices guiding me, just a sense of heightened awareness, but a powerful one. Suddenly I'm seeing and hearing so much more than before. And then it's utterly clear to me – the entire future development of the actor. It's so clear, so obvious, that I'm baffled when I sometimes read reviews and realise that others haven't seen the same thing. I'm amazed at their stupidity. But of course they're no more stupid than I would be without Joachim.'

We sat in silence for some time. I felt utterly confused. Who was the golden stag? Hanno? Or Joachim? And what had happened in the clearing on that day so many years ago?

'I'm glad I told you all this,' he said finally. 'For years I've felt weighed down by your awe. I've felt like a fraud, knowing that none of it is really mine. But I couldn't tell you that without telling you everything. And then today, seeing your admiration for what I've done here, I could see myself through your eyes: the loving son, the caring brother. But it's not like that. All I'm doing is giving back a small part of what Joachim gives to me. Can you understand that, Rosalind? How else could I respond? So please don't praise me. Don't turn me into a myth. See me as I am.'

'Everything's changed, Hanno. You must realise that, too.'

'Yes.'

I looked up at the glittering gold of the birch leaves. 'I've been here before,' I said quietly. 'One summer, years ago. I followed you here from Paddington station.' The clearing was suddenly very quiet. In the stillness I heard my words. The one thing I had meant never to tell him. 'I followed you all the way here, and through the hedge I saw you talking with Christa. Then I went home. I never meant to tell you. I knew it would sound like spying. But it wasn't that. Something just drew me along. I had to follow.'

And now the strange force of those gold-flecked eyes was on me. 'And do you know what it was?' he asked.

'I didn't then. But I do now.'

I looked down at the fresh young foliage of the bedstraw. A scattering of lady's smock rose above it. I reached out with the unthinking gesture of a child to pick it, then stopped. Above, a chaffinch suddenly burst into a rich cascade of trills. Then Hanno placed his hands on either side of my head, turned my face to his and kissed me.

29

I gave my order and watched the girl behind the counter write it beside my name. A coincidence, of course, that this should be the first day she remembered my name. And then again, perhaps not. It was a day of firsts, this first day since Hanno and I had become lovers.

The canteen was crowded. Above the heads, one arm waved frantically. I moved towards it and traced it to Jas. He was sitting with Caroline, both of them defending the place they'd saved for me.

'You were miles away,' said Caroline. 'Jas practically dislocated his arm.'

I sat down. Or rather, I floated into the chair. Everything was insubstantial today.

'Look at her,' said Jas. 'See? I told you – she's in love. I recognise the symptoms.'

'You would,' Caroline scoffed.

'She sneaks out to meet him under a haystack. Isn't that right, Rosie?'

'That's right,' I said.

Caroline turned the full power of her scorn on him. 'There is no hay in May,' she pronounced grandly.

'Is.'

'You city git.'

'All right then, a turnip field. So who's the lucky swain, Rosie?'

'Secret.'

'That's *my* trick,' he protested.

'Not any more.'

The girl called my name. I went over to collect my food, leaving behind a haze of mystification. Better to keep near the truth, I'd decided. It was the best smokescreen of all.

'Seriously, Ros,' said Caroline when I'd returned. 'What got into you today?'

'Even the old man had goosebumps,' said Jas. 'And he doesn't impress easily. Give the punters half that on first night and there'll be queues all the way to London. Come on: tell.'

I wished I could. 'Something just clicked,' I said instead, which was true enough. Nor was this the only incident. Something had happened during my voice call, too. The coach had been working on my weakest point: how to whisper convincingly and yet be heard at the back of the stalls. Suddenly I'd done it, without even knowing. 'Terrific!' she'd called from the far end of the room. 'You're there!'

Jas was muttering to Caroline. He glared at me. 'Anabolic steroids.'

I raised my hands in surrender.

The drug of love, more powerful than any steroid, continued to work its magic. A fundamental change had taken place in that clearing. In one afternoon, a confused knot made up of all the fears and anxieties I'd hauled with me from childhood had been undone. The sense of release was overwhelming, and the most wonderful thing of all was that it had happened to both of us. At the same moment that Hanno banished my nightmare, I freed him from his own myth and allowed him to become human. The two people who rose from the bedstraw that afternoon were two new people, quite other than the ones who had entered the clearing. The lines carved by sadness were still on his face, but as remnants, relics of a closed past which had now opened up to let me in. The chasm between his London life and the life he led with his family was bridged, and for the first time he felt himself to be whole. That I should be able to be such a power for good was a revelation, as much a gift to me as to my lover. It helped to lift the weight of my past failures from me.

That I had failed – as wife and mother – I had to accept. But now I could see how inevitable it was. Whatever gifts

I had were simply not domestic. I had followed that route blindly, because women did. Jas had been right. I should have listened to him and accepted that I belonged to the theatre. I had fought against my natural destination and damaged not only myself but David and Matti. That the wounds weren't greater was entirely due to Astrid and Brendan and Belle.

It was hardly surprising, then, that the power Hanno had given me was now channelled into the theatre. A new Rosalind – both Shakespeare's and mine – walked on to the stage of our rehearsal room. The old man (as Jas disrespectfully called our director) wasn't the only one with goosebumps. The performance stunned me, too. I even dared hope that this was the beginning of what Hanno and I had always longed for: that I would indeed climb from the ranks of the good to become great.

As the weeks went by in a cloud of happiness, it seemed that my hope might be justified. That first breakthrough hadn't been a fluke. Day after day my rehearsal performances grew in depth; Sunday after Sunday Hanno and I returned to the wood. New leaves unfurled above our heads, new flowers sprang up beneath our feet, and the bedstraw of our clearing finally sent out its tiny white flowers and perfumed our couch with its magic. The connection between the two was crystal clear. Just as I had healed the split between Hanno's private and public life, Hanno had healed the same split in mine and made me whole. The Rosalind who loved and the Rosalind who worked were the same person, each infusing the other with new strength.

Whispers began to be heard around the RSC, though not about Hanno; however much Jas might grumble and threaten to expose my secret lover, we had too much respect for each other's privacy for that kind of thing. No, the whispers were about the transformation taking place in the Conference Hall.

The whispers reached all the way to London, and when opening night finally arrived, there was a buzz of excitement in the auditorium. The critics were out in force, primed already with the rumour that something was going to happen.

It did.

The most stunning Rosalind I've seen in forty years of theatre-going, said one critic.

If it were possible to speak of a definitive Rosalind, this would be it, said another.

A Rosalind infused with magic.

Set to become the finest Shakespearian actress of her generation.

A phenomenon.

The newspapers lay scattered around me. None of them mattered. For the hundredth time, I leaned over the golden-yellow roses and breathed in their fragrance. For the hundredth time at least, I read the simple card which had accompanied them, the one message that mattered: *For a great actress. H.H.*

The season ran its course. Winter arrived. The RSC moved to its London home at the Barbican. The play re-opened to a new storm of excitement. The newspapers were filled with ever-more-enthusiastic words of praise. My dressing-room was filled with flowers and messages. Famous directors came backstage to meet me. The fan mail grew.

And where was Hanno during all this? Where was my demon lover, my Svengali, the magician who had wrought this miracle?

In his office in Wigmore Street, quietly getting on with business-as-usual. That the business was now augmented by directors and producers begging my professional favours was 'hardly surprising, my love. These things snowball. Flavour of the month. Enjoy it while it lasts.'

'You rotten old thing,' I murmured into his chest. Then I hugged him tighter.

We were in his office. I had made an appointment, as I always did – not because I feared to stumble upon some unexpected secret but because I respected his business. But as soon as the secretary had rung through and Hanno had ushered me into his office, I had flung my arms around him, starved, as always, of his physical presence.

'Seriously, Rosalind.' He kissed my hair. 'Don't be too hurt when it fades, as it will. And don't be worried either. The people who matter will still be there, quietly negotiating with me long after the public fuss dies down. This is the real thing, my love. Well done.'

The telephone rang. He released me with a last quick kiss and answered it. 'Hanno Hirsch.' Pause. 'No, I'm sorry, she has another year to go on the RSC contract. Give me a ring in six months.'

I had tiptoed behind his chair. 'Hey, you,' I said when he put the receiver down. 'I've come to proposition you.' I put my hands on his shoulders.

He twisted his head round to peer up at me. 'Literally?'

'Yup. What would you say to becoming my toy boy?'

'You shock me, Ms Rawlinson.'

'Good. Well?'

He grasped one of my hands and kissed the palm. 'I'd say that your maths are deplorable. I'm far too ancient to be anyone's toy boy.'

I rubbed my face in his hair, where there were indeed some silvery threads. 'Okay. Can I become your mistress instead?'

He swivelled his chair round and pulled me on to his lap. 'Sweet Rosie O'Crazy, you're my mistress now. Or I'm your greying toy boy. As you like it.'

I laughed. 'Be serious. Now that I'm disgustingly rich and famous I discover that the fairy godmother deleted one item from her package. Shall I tell you what it is? Shall I tell you my heart's desire?'

'Tell.'

'I want to make an omelette for you.'

My lover's laughter rang out, all but shaking the windows of his office.

'I mean it, you hard-hearted Hanno,' I said sternly. 'More than anything in the world, I would like you to come home after a hard day negotiating my contracts and sit down by the fireplace while your adoring mistress presents you with an omelette, a jug of wine . . .'

'. . . and thee. Sweet Rosalind,' he said softly, 'do you know where you'd be when I came home from the office? In your dressing-room at the Barbican, listening to the calls over the Tannoy. The fireplace would be cold.' He took my head in his hands and smiled sadly. 'We are not domestic animals, you and I.'

I avoided his golden eyes. 'Well then, scrambled eggs. For breakfast. Oh, Hanno, I would so love us to wake up together in the morning like two ordinary human beings. Is it so much to ask?'

'The *Teufelskind* and The Phenomenon brushing their teeth together?'

'Hanno, I'm serious. I love you far too much for these brief encounters. And I think you love me, too.'

'You know I do.'

'Well . . .' I said, kissing one eyebrow, 'it so happens that a rather lovely little house has come up for sale just a few streets away from Astrid's.' I kissed the other eyebrow. 'If I just happened to buy it, might you just happen to move in with me?'

The eyebrows drew together in a frown. 'I think that's called Being A Kept Man.'

I kissed the eyebrows apart again. 'And is that why you've avoided becoming involved with women all these years? Knowing you had to spend everything on your family? Fear of becoming a kept man?'

'You overestimate the temptation. A fine actress and a fine woman are two different things. I never expected them to come together.'

'Well then, make the most of your amazing good for tune: come with me and be my love.'

'You *are* tempting,' he laughed. 'And I'm tempted.'

'Go on: be a devil's child.'

'Wicked Rosalind.'

'Not as wicked as you think. I'm not after a wedding ring, Hanno. That I can promise you. I've learned my lesson there. No ties that bind. Just the two of us, free to live and love together. I'm not a schemer trying to ensnare you – I respect you far too much for that.'

'I know that, too,' he said, suddenly serious. 'You're an honourable lady, Ms R. If you'll accept such a frumpy old compliment.'

'I will.' I kissed his nose.

'And as your honourable agent and therefore unofficial financial adviser, I'm obliged to tell you that you should buy it regardless.'

'Of?'

'Whether my toothbrush moves in with you.'

'And will it?'

'It might. Tentatively.' He put his arms round me. 'Be patient with me, Rosalind. I'm a hardened old bachelor, not accustomed to passing the marmalade.'

'Then we'll have separate jars. I can bear it.'

'But can you bear my solitary ways? You've had practice living with someone. I've been alone all my life.'

'I'll teach you,' I said. 'And I'll break you in gently.'

'Sweet Rosalind,' he murmured into my hair.

It was a wrench, leaving Astrid, and an even greater wrench leaving Matti. But the truth was that I barely saw either of them any more. We did manage to have breakfast together, but when Matti returned from his playgroup, I was gone, not returning myself until long after Matti was asleep. I remembered Hanno's words: *If everyone thought only of the children, few would be born.* I knew now that he'd been thinking of Joachim, but it applied equally to Matti. The fact that I hadn't intended being a breakfast-only mother was beside the point. I should have thought through his life more seriously, realised that sooner or later I would return to the theatre where I belonged. I knew, too, that Matti would scarcely notice one less face at the breakfast table, surrounded as he was by so many people who adored him. Part of me was grateful that I had so little impact on his life. Another part mourned. I don't think I could have left at all if the house hadn't been so near Astrid's. I knew that after seeing Hanno off I would be able to take Matti to play-group or school.

The day that Hanno and I entered our house for the first time was a revelation. We were beginning this *together*. Before, I had moved into a place and a lifestyle already set up by someone else: Farleton Hall, The Folly, Astrid's house, even the digs Jas had found for us in Chipping Moreton. This was our house and our life, to make of them whatever we wished. The fact that the money which bought it was mine made no difference to me, nor, I think, to Hanno. After all, my talent alone wouldn't have earned it without his shrewd management of my career.

Hand in hand we walked through the modest rooms as if they were salons of a Venetian palazzo. No one would have recognised us – the darling of the RSC, the world-famous star-maker. I was in my mid-thirties, Hanno ten years older, and yet we were the youngest of young lovers mutually dazzled by our good fortune.

'Look – there's the fireplace where you'll sit while I cook your omelette.'

'This omelette is taking on mythical status. Will it have a secret ingredient to turn your frog into a prince?'

'He's always been a prince. Will you bring that nice cream leather armchair from your lair to put by the fireplace?'

'Of course.'

I threw my arms around him. 'Oh, Hanno, I feel drunk on love.'

He held me close. 'We've been too sober too long.'

We went through the kitchen and out into the garden. It was high-walled and private. A winter wind was rattling the branches of the trees and shrubs, scooping dead leaves up in little russet whirlpools to fling them down somewhere else. At one end was an arbor laced with the bare branches of climbing roses. We sat down side by side on the little bench within.

'Here's where you'll come on summer mornings to learn your lines,' said Hanno. 'You'll forget the time and look up in surprise when Hanno the houseboy comes up the path bringing your coffee.'

And so we played our games. The bedroom overlooked the garden. 'Let's keep it simple,' I said. 'No frills or gilt to distract us. We'll decorate our room with our love.'

'A carpet of bedstraw will do me fine.'

And so began our life together. I won't pretend it was all bedstraw and roses and mythical omelettes, but Hanno had at least warned me. Years of living alone and guarding the secret of Joachim had made him intensely private. Sometimes he moved about the house as if I weren't there. Then he would come out of his trance with shock and bewilderment in his golden eyes and stare, puzzled, at the stranger who shared his life. They were frightening moments and made me wonder if I knew him at all. There were forces in him that I didn't understand, depths I still seemed unable to penetrate.

Time, I told myself. All in good time. He had lived so long alone, I couldn't expect the transformation that had begun in the clearing to be completed in a few easy months. He needed time and I needed patience. That I had and in abundance. Love had given it to me. So had Hanno, in making me build up my career step by little step rather than catapulting me towards instant fame as any other agent would have done. I had waited patiently for my career. I would wait with equal patience for Hanno.

None the less, I was a little hurt by his reticence about his past. I had told him everything about my own, just as I had told David in the first days of our engagement. David, another private person, had responded by opening up to me completely. Hanno didn't. All I knew about him was that he and Joachim had been born in Vienna but had come to England with their parents while they were still children. He had always considered himself Viennese, though, and had returned to the city as soon as he could. It was there, and in Berlin, that he had quickly gained a reputation as a *Wunderkind*. He had begun acting and directing on the radical fringe and had soon attracted the attention of monied backers. Within a few years he was one of the most sought-after figures in continental theatre, always at the cutting edge, always startling the public with his innovations. He was noted, too, for his diversity, equally at home in opera, ballet and theatre.

Then, abruptly, he had returned to England and become an agent. It didn't make sense. Why should someone who'd been at the centre of the action suddenly retire into the background, contenting himself with constructing other people's careers rather than his own? Whenever I asked, he shrugged and said merely, 'It was time for a change.'

There had to be more to it; something had precipitated the change. It occurred to me that the something was a woman. An unhappy love affair? A married woman? A tragic death? Any of these could, with a man as intense as Hanno, cause him to leave and start a new life elsewhere. But whenever I tried to probe, I could feel him closing a door on me. Finally I stopped trying.

As time passed, Hanno seemed to adjust to our shared life. The moments when he awoke from a trance and stared at the stranger who was me diminished. My desire to probe into his past also diminished. We were happy as we were; there was no need, really, to delve into areas that were perhaps best left alone. We were developing our own shared past, in the little house in Islington.

We were also sharing my son, even though he continued to live with Astrid. Hanno's affection for Matti was one of the things I loved most about him, and Matti reciprocated wholeheartedly. More than once I wished that Matti could meet Joachim, too. They both had a touch of magic about them: the child and the child-at-heart. I could imagine the rapport between them so strongly that it was almost as if they knew each other already.

None the less, I kept quiet. Joachim's past encounters with children had been so disastrous that ten acres of woodland and a hedge had had to be built around him to protect him. For me to invade it with Matti would be an impertinence.

In the end, it was Hanno who suggested it, and to my surprise his parents agreed. It was a happy weekend. I'm not sure it would have worked with any other child, but Matti was both sensitive and pragmatic. All we had to do was explain that a disease had robbed Joachim of his power of speech.

'That's all right,' said Matti. 'I can do the talking for him.'

He did, chattering away to Joachim as they walked among the trees. Hanno and I walked behind, amused by the sight of Matti, the noisy little midget, entertaining Joachim, the silent gentle giant. It wasn't one-sided, though. Joachim's gestures, however clumsy, were as eloquent as any speech. The poignance was overwhelming.

'Joachim has so much to give,' I said softly.

'And so few people to give it to. We can't change the world, Rosalind. Don't try.'

Our own world continued to be a small one. Only a few close friends even knew we were living together. Astrid, of course, and Jas. Jas's reaction to the news was more dramatic than anything he'd ever done on stage. His jaw dropped, his lanky body froze in amazement, his beady black eyes stared first at me, then at Hanno, then back at me.

'Damn it all, Rosie, you might have told me!' Then his eyebrows shot up in sudden enlightenment. 'The haystack!' he cried. 'So *that's* the peasant swain!'

Jas became Hanno's client. Normally Hanno chose his clients early, long before fame overtook them. But he recognised the chemistry between Jas and myself and wanted to exploit it.

'He must play Ferdinand to your Miranda,' he said. 'Before you're both too old.'

Our *Tempest* was a sensation.

Hanno tried to arrange my work to give me breathers, but even so I was often rehearsing one play by day and performing another by night. I didn't mind. I had infinite energy these days. Love does that to people, gives them almost supernatural strength. I was in love with Hanno and in love with my work, doubly blessed and more, because my work and my lover were so much a part of each other.

The next few years flew past in a glorious whirl. I played the best roles in the best plays – though Hanno still kept me away from the giants. There would be time enough and more for Lady Macbeth, Gertrude, the strong older women created by Ibsen and Chekhov.

Finally, and after much twisting of his arm, Hanno allowed me to make a film. It was British, and good, but that made no difference to Hanno.

'You'll regret it,' said Hanno.

I did.

30

Christmas in New York. Alone. I sat by the telephone in my rented studio apartment overlooking Central Park. Outside a load of sleet was coming down. It had been coming down ever since my arrival in the city. Even snow would have been bearable, would have given a Merry-Christmas look to the scene.

This was, incredibly, my first trip to the States. Hate at first sight. The sleet didn't help, but even blue and balmy California would have turned me off. Every cell of my body shrieked, 'I don't want to be here.'

The film had produced my first really bad reviews. Hanno had been good about it, refraining from I-told-you-so. We agreed it had been a worthwhile experiment but that I wasn't cut out for the film world. I'd been miserable the whole time. I couldn't adapt to the bittiness of the schedule, the shooting of scenes out of order, the tiresome waiting around while nothing happened, the lack of continuity and passion. Above all, I couldn't adjust to the lack of an audience. It wasn't my ego that craved it; it was my desire to create. On the stage I had been part of an artistic whole being created night after night, always slightly different and always with the audience helping us to create it. In the studio, nothing was being created except a mountain of film footage which someone else would scissors-and-paste into his own vision.

None the less, the film was a popular success, and even more so in America. Everyone was amazed. The American film market was notoriously difficult to break into. Many of my colleagues had been trying for years, and I had done it with just one film. It was the eyes, of course, my peculiar faceted green eyes. Jas had always said they would be hypnotic on the big screen and it seemed he was right. The millions of people they hypnotised in the cinemas had never seen me on stage, didn't realise it was a so-so performance. They fell in love with my eyes, just as they'd fallen in love with Marlene Dietrich's legs, Raquel Welch's boobs and Yul Brynner's pate. They wanted more. Hanno refused. As far as we were concerned, it was an experiment that had failed and should be quietly forgotten.

We thought that was the end of it, but the next thing we knew, a West End play I was in suddenly transferred to the States. Hanno told them it would have to go without me.

But: no Ros Rawlinson, no deal.

The rest of the cast were desperate. For some of them this was their big chance to get into the American scene. I could have pulled out, there was nothing in my contract to cover such a transfer, but it would have created a lot of ill-will and resentment. I had no choice. I went.

The provincial tour was exhausting, as tours always are. The play was fairly well received but there was a general air of disappointment. The reason was obvious: nobody could see my eyes. At that distance they were two anonymous dots in my face. We arrived in New York already demoralised only to go through the whole thing writ large. There were murmurings of discontent among the cast. The murmurings grew louder. One day they exploded in a nasty scene. It was all *my* fault, they said. Me and my damned eyes. If I'd let someone else take over my part none of this would be happening.

I was stunned. As soon as I glued my jaw back into place, I reminded them that I'd wanted to drop out, that it was only to please them that I'd agreed to the whole awful trek. If they wanted me to leave, fine. I would fly back to London the minute they found a replacement for me.

It was out of the question, of course, and they knew it. There were apologies, even a few tears. But the damage was done. The tight knit group we'd been in London had fallen apart. If only the critics would pan it we could all leave, but no – the play limped along regardless, with reasonable reviews, reasonable audiences and a backstage atmosphere which was almost unbearable. It was the worst experience of my whole career.

And now it was Christmas, with the sleet slamming into the windows and grating on my mind like chalk on a blackboard. The Christmas break was tiny. Only one member of the cast had bothered to brave the double jet lag for the dubious pleasure of a day with her family. The rest had ingratiated themselves with Americans or got together for a restaurant Christmas.

I'd been too depressed to make any plans at all. Christmas is a brutal time, Families Only. What was my family? A pair of parents with whom I'd long ago lost touch; a son who belonged more to Astrid and David than to me; and a lover who was bound to his own family by the ties of tragedy. Merry Christmas.

The one thing I'd been looking forward to all day was phoning Hanno. Now I wished I hadn't. What he told me chilled me far more than the sleet or the frosty atmosphere among the cast.

Christa had gone for a long and much-deserved break with her family in Austria, leaving Hanno and his parents to cope with Joachim alone. This wasn't unusual. Christa needed her holidays and no one begrudged her. Normally they managed well enough on their own during these periods. But this time everything had gone wrong. On the previous afternoon, Joachim had found a small gap in the hedge and had somehow managed to wriggle through it. He had never done this before, never shown any sign of wanting to see the outside world. It had taken the family a while to realise what had happened.

By the time they discovered Joachim, he'd already been discovered by a gang of boys playing by the riverbank. Worst of all, it was Hanno who found him. The boys had taken one look at Hanno and Joachim together and turned bug-eyed with amazement. Hanno had salvaged the situation as best he could, but the damage was done. Now the family was holed up, trying to work out what to say if the boys reported that there were *two* Hanno Hirsches living at Joachim's Wood. To top it off, Joachim had enjoyed his outing. Now he was restless. He had tried several times to slip away, no doubt hoping to find another hole in the hedge.

Merry Christmas indeed. As soon as I put down the receiver I turned up the central heating and sat for an hour or more, a block of ice in my tropical sublet. Hanno had delivered his report in his usual calm and measured language but nothing could soften the impact of the words. A new housing estate had sprung up on a bare field not far from Joachim's Wood and the gang of boys, bored in their isolation, already had some notoriety. Having discovered Joachim, would they give him up so easily? The whole fragile structure of Joachim's Wood was threatened.

I emerged from the gloom of my reverie to see the gloom of darkness which had descended on Central Park. I shut the curtains and paced the room. What time was it in England? Even that disorientated me. There was nothing solid to hold on to, not even the ticking of clocks three thousand miles apart.

There was no clock ticking in my rented room but I could hear the old grandfather clock that had ticked through countless meals in the kitchen at The Folly.

The Folly. Oh my God. I'd forgotten to phone Matti.

I lunged for the phone as if a few seconds would make all the difference. It took ages to get through but it was worth it. Instantly the room was filled with the warm presence of Belle.

'Ros, how lovely to hear your voice! Yes, everything's fine! Well, nearly everything. Hugh's here – the girlfriend chucked him out on Christmas Eve and he turned up in the middle of a blizzard without so much as a phone call. He's being his usual obnoxious self. Sozzled, of course. Other than that, we've had a lovely day. How about you?'

'Fairly awful – sorry to be such a Scrooge. The play's falling apart and the public won't let us give it a decent burial. So we're cranking it out night after night and praying for the boos to begin. Right now I'd give anything short of my Equity card to be at The Folly – Hugh notwithstanding.'

'Oh well, Hugh's Hugh, we're used to his little ways. But I'm sorry you're having such a bitch of a time. When does the run end?'

'We're signed on till Easter but we're hoping it'll die before that. Anyway, never mind my moans. How's Matti?'

'Hysterical with joy. We've got a couple of house guests and he's flirting like crazy with the pair of them. Really turning on the charm. Captive audience, you know.'

'I know. But who are these house guests?'

'Ros, I can't talk any longer – Matti's right here and he's practically wrenching my arm off trying to get at the phone. You'll have to ask him yourself.'

Two seconds later he was burbling my ear off across three thousand miles.

'. . . and so she raced up the moor in this horrendous blizzard and all by herself she found the sheep and rescued them and then she almost fell down the waterfall and did something to her ankle and so Daddy had to go and rescue her and then she –'

'Who she?'

'Charlotte, Mummy – I told you. Anyway, and then Brendan rescued the sheep again and the dog and the cat and the hens and Effie and so we all went out in the troika today with Ymir in the snow and I held them all by myself when Daddy had to shovel the snow at the gates and afterwards I had the reins and drove them myself – there was Sif and Olwen too and we . . .'

I listened contentedly to my son's voice talking the telephone wires into a white heat. The play was a disaster, Joachim's Wood was in upheaval, Hugh was a bastard, but for those fifteen minutes or so that Matti's voice poured into my ear none of it mattered. I didn't even mind too much that he didn't say a word about the presents I'd sent. Matti was happy. All was well with the world.

There must have been some transition but I didn't hear it. The next thing I knew, Matti was saying, '*Everybody's* here. We miss you. When are *you* coming, Mummy?'

My heart sank. Over the years Astrid and I had explained to him what my work was like, why I was so seldom around to see him. I thought he had understood. Now, in a few thoughtless sentences, he had unravelled the whole fabric and exposed me for what I was: the absentee mother, longed for and never there. I tried to stitch it back together again: it was late at night, he didn't know what he was saying, he was hyped up by having a larger-than-usual audience at The Folly.

'I'm coming home at Easter, Matti – maybe even before. It's not long to wait.'

There was an explosion of delight at the other end and another dose of burblings. Suddenly I realised. He'd misunderstood. He thought I was coming to The Folly at Easter. That shook me. He'd always considered Astrid's house his main home. What had happened to make him suddenly zero in on The Folly like that? When finally he ran out of steam, I asked to speak to his father.

'David, what's going on up there?'

'What do you mean, "What's going on?" Christmas is going on.' His voice was irritable. No doubt Hugh had been aggravating him.

'Matti's talking about The Folly as if he were planning to live there for ever.'

There was a long silence. Then, 'It's late. Matti's tired. He doesn't know what he's saying.'

'David, if you're thinking of going back on our agreement, think again. That's a legal document, you know. Astrid's his legal guardian.'

'Ros, I'm not a child. I know what the law says.'

I tried to tell myself I was being unduly suspicious. If David had simply denied that Matti was moving to The Folly, I might have let the matter drop. But for some years I had worried about what would happen as Matti grew older. I knew David would want to have him there more and more, to share his enthusiasm, to teach him to take over the forest.

It would have to happen some time, but not (I was determined) while Matti was still at school. I refused to let him grow up in isolation with a man who so fiercely shut out the world beyond The Folly's gates.

'Then why is he talking as if he were staying there?' I persisted.

'Ask him,' he said shortly.

'I'm asking you. Matti's incoherent, he's exhausted – you've kept him up too late.'

'And whose fault is that? We were waiting for you to phone.'

The barb hit home. None the less, I removed it and went on doggedly, 'He's incoherent – all he can do is babble about some woman rescuing a bunch of sheep in a blizzard. Who is this Charlotte anyway?'

There was another long silence. 'Just a neighbour. She bought Cappelrigg Farm after John Jowett was killed.'

'What's a woman doing with Cappelrigg Farm?'

'Farming it, what do you think?'

Suddenly my mind whizzed back and I heard again the words which should have shrieked out at me first time round. *Just a neighbour.* If David was surly with the outside world in general, he was surliest of all with his neighbours. In all the time I'd known him he'd had nothing whatsoever to do with anyone living up in Keldreth.

'So what's "just a neighbour" doing as a house guest at The Folly?'

'For God's sake, Ros, she sprained her ankle! I could hardly send her home like that in a blizzard!'

Oh yes he could. I felt a new kind of chill creeping over me and knew that however high I turned up the central heating, this one wouldn't disappear. 'How old is this Charlotte?'

'How the hell should I know? I didn't ask for her curriculum vitae.'

'You must have some idea,' I said. I knew I was making a fool of myself but it was too late to stop.

'Thirty maybe. If you're so nosy, talk to her yourself. I didn't think you were interested in anything up here.'

I removed the second barb. 'I'm interested in anything that affects my son. I told him I was coming "home" at Easter and he thought I meant The Folly.'

'That's his problem.'

'Well, it's mine, too – now. He expects me to go to The Folly at Easter. I can hardly get out of it now, not without making myself look like a total shit.'

'Suit yourself.'

'Thanks. I really appreciate the warm welcome. What's got into you, David? I didn't realise you hated me so much.'

'I don't "hate" you. I've got my own life to live, that's all. You're not a part of it. Come if you like. I'm sure Belle and Brendan would be delighted. Astrid and Matti, too. As long as you don't interfere with our work you can do as you please.'

A few weeks later Hugh turned up in my New York dressing-room. I could tell at once that he had something up his sleeve. His tall willowy frame was all a-flutter, like a tree being agitated by an unaccustomed wind.

I wasn't as displeased to see him as I would normally be. My dressing-room was a bleak place these days. No friends to drop in, just the occasional Slightly Famous oozing insincere praise. At least Hugh was, well, familiar.

'So how's our brilliant superstar?' he asked as we settled into the ostentatious restaurant he'd chosen for our late-night dinner. Hugh had made a killing out of the late 1980s property boom and was now extremely rich.

'Bored. Dying to get home. How about you? Still chucking people out of their cosy slums to put up office blocks?'

'Past history, my dear. I've moved on. Now I'm chucking out peasants to build estates on their cornfields.'

'In London?'

'London's "out" these days. Fresh air. We all want

executive houses in Arcadia, don't we? Our own little taste of rural bliss.'

'I thought the green belt was all used up.'

'Too suburban. People want the real thing these days.'

'And where's that?'

'Why, the Cotswolds, of course.'

The waiter arrived with our wine. I watched impatiently as he and Hugh went through the tedious ritual of testing in case Jesus had turned it back into water. My mind had flown instinctively to one very small and very special part of the Cotswolds. Joachim's Wood. Hugh couldn't possibly have found out, it had to be coincidence. But the irritating way in which he seemed to be leading up to some revelation made me nervous.

'A pretty long commute,' I commented as soon as the waiter left.

'Your success,' he toasted. 'Computers. No one has to set foot in London any more. The Cotswolds have always been a honeypot for London weekenders. Now it's expanding. I've got my eye on a couple of nice little patches ripe for development. Lush woodland with good access. Perfect for a discreet sprinkling of luxury houses, each with its own bit of woodland for privacy and pastoral pretensions.'

'I don't suppose that's how you'll advertise them,' I said drily. Then, keeping my voice casual, I added, 'Whereabouts are they?'

He named them. Neither was anywhere near Joachim's Wood. I breathed again.

'What about planning controls? I thought trees were "in" these days.'

'There are ways and means,' he said.

'I'll bet there are.'

'Actually, I'm thinking of taking over one of the plots myself, turning myself into a bit of a squire.'

'*You*?'

'Why not? There comes a time. Back to the soil which nourished us. Even the most outrageous man-about-town has a scrap of it lurking in his concrete soul.'

I snorted.

Hugh seemed offended. 'Nothing on the scale of our beloved David, of course. I wouldn't presume. But a nice big house, swimming pool, spacious grounds, a few acres of trees to play around with. How does it sound?'

'Totally out of character.'

'Is it?'

Again, the portentous weight to seemingly ordinary words. 'Hugh, what are you playing at?'

'Ah. Well. I had a bit of an epiphany at Christmas.'

'You had more than that. Belle says you were sozzled.'

'Save me from the puritans. Actually, that's what set the grey cells in motion. For the first time since you left there was a spark of life in the dreary old pile, to wit, a charming lady neighbour and her London chum. Quite made me re-think the whole rural idyll.'

I steadied my hand as best I could and set my glass down while my mind added the new piece to the jigsaw. Charlotte. The lady farmer, in her thirties, now 'charming'.

'Made me re-think a few other things, too,' he went on.

'This neighbour – what's she like?' I asked casually.

'Charlotte? Smasher to look at and bright, too.'

'What's she doing running a hill farm?'

'What indeed? Tells me she used to work in the City. Then one day she and her friend – Effie's an interior designer – stopped at a pub in Kirkby where the farm was being auctioned and she bought it on impulse. Can't see our David ever doing anything on impulse, can you? That's what made me think. You know, Ros, you and I married the wrong people. David should have –'

'I don't suppose she'll stick it very long,' I said. 'This Charlotte.'

'On the contrary. She's dug herself in. It's not as crazy as it sounds,' he added. 'Her dad was a gentleman farmer from Sussex; she helped him out quite a bit. She knows what she's doing, more or less. Says she wants to get back to her roots. See? Everyone's doing it, why shouldn't I? This place in the Cotswolds –'

'I'm surprised David let her in. She must be the first visitor The Folly's had since, well, since Jas, I suppose.'

'I wouldn't be surprised if there's something going on. She's his type. Earnest.'

'I thought you said she was charming. And impulsive.'

'That too. But beneath it all she's got that same dogged determination as David. Give her a few years and the rest will fade away and she'll be a plodder. Just like David. Just like Astrid. You know, Ros, you and I married the wrong people.'

I switched into automatic pilot as Hugh droned on. He had supplied quite a few of the missing pieces, and while the jigsaw was still far from complete, a strong picture was emerging. An attractive young woman, intelligent, impulsive and charming but steady and determined. Above all, passionate about the countryside. And David had let her stay at The Folly for most of a fortnight. Sprained ankles didn't take that long to heal. With sickening clarity an image of the future rose above Hugh's babble: Charlotte, slow but sure, worming her way into David's heart; David and Charlotte marrying; David and Charlotte (slow but sure) winkling Matti away from me.

How naive I'd been. I'd blithely assumed that neither David nor I would ever remarry, and on that assumption I'd placed my future. On that assumption I'd agreed to Astrid becoming Matti's legal guardian, to give him the stability and continuity which neither David nor I could provide.

And now David was about to provide it. I saw how the courts would view Charlotte. The perfect stepmother. David and Charlotte the perfect parents, a nice tidy nuclear family ready-made by adding Matti. I saw too how the courts would view me. I'd given Matti away, that's how they'd see it. I hadn't even tried to get custody. I must have been pretty indifferent to sign him away like that. That such a view was utterly false, that I'd done it for Matti's sake and to avoid the destructive wrangling of a full-blown fight, no one would see. They would take him away from me and there was nothing I could do about it.

'Well, how about it?' a voice said.

I closed my eyes in a convulsion of pain. A hand closed over mine. I opened my eyes and saw David's brother. What was Hugh doing here, and all these other people? For one crazy moment I thought I was in court. Then I saw the restaurant, remembered how I'd come to be there.

'Are you all right?' said Hugh.

I looked down at his hand, still on mine. There was something reptilian about it that made me shudder. Hugh withdrew it but not his gaze.

'You look as pale as the ghost of Christmas past,' he said uncertainly.

'I'm sorry.' I tried to smile. 'I'm just tired. A lousy run, too many late nights.'

He smiled ruefully. 'And here I am giving you another one. I should have picked my time better. How about it? Shall I make an appointment? Choose your time: when would you like to be proposed to? Or do you have an answer now?'

'What?'

Hugh laughed and put on an excruciatingly bad American accent. 'Ros Rawlinson, you sure do know how to make a guy feel wanted. You didn't hear a word I said, did you?'

'I'm sorry.'

'I've been telling you about my epiphany. This Christmas. When I suddenly saw that you and I had married the wrong people. David should have married Astrid – they're both plodders. Whereas you and I were made for each other. We've got good red blood in our veins, not sap. Well, how about it? It's not too late. Second marriages are all the rage. Exchange one brother for another. A nice little country estate near Stratford for the season, a flat in town for the winter.'

I stared. What on earth was he talking about?

'I'm asking you to marry me, Ros. You know I adore you. Always have, always will. I may not be the squire of an ancient estate in Yorkshire. But I've got a heap of money instead and every penny of it just waiting to be lavished on you. I could give you a good time, Ros. How about it? Could you bear to be Mrs Farleton again?'

31

We never meant to become engaged, Hanno and I. We didn't need to. No piece of paper could hold us together or keep us apart. And after Hugh's unwelcome proposal, nothing could have been further from my mind than marriage.

It happened by accident. Or fate. Call it what you will. I returned from New York a physical and mental wreck. Hanno and I had kept in close contact throughout our long and miserable separation and he knew the score. We'd agreed it was time I had a break and he'd taken care not to commit me to any work for a while.

I returned at Easter. I suppose spring was springing and mother nature performing her annual miracle but I didn't see it. All I saw was Hanno, glowing against the tawdry plastic and concrete. Hanno radiating love and concern, searching the crowds for the worn-out snip of a girl who was me. Hanno's face lighting up in a million watts, the vertical creases pushed aside to make room for the huge smile of welcome. Hanno's arms flung out like windsails nearly decapitating a pair of grey businessmen.

I dropped everything and flew to him with the single-mindedness of a missile and in a final blinding flash I was in his arms and his arms were crushing me and with the few scraps of breath I had left I was crying, 'Hanno Hanno Hanno!'

We clung to each other all evening too, curled up together on the sofa in front of the fire. He was concerned about my state of mind and all the things that were worrying me. I had told him about Hugh. I'd also told him my fear that David and Charlotte would take Matti away. He didn't insult me with soothing words. He understood. We agreed that I must find out more, and the best way to do that was to go to The Folly. I'd promised Matti anyway – he was there with Astrid already.

Neither of us looked forward to another separation so soon after my return. Hanno didn't try to disguise how miserable he'd been in my absence. The long months had been hell for him, too. 'I'm going to shoot your agent,' he murmured into my hair later that night. 'Sending you away for so long. Who does he think he is, anyway?'

'A tyrant. He exploits me.'

'Demand compensation.'

'I may just take you up on that.' I rolled over, propped myself up on one elbow and gazed into my lover's face. It was looking more worn than usual. Age, partly – he was now in his early fifties. But also care. Joachim's Christmas Eve flit had been repeated several times. Hanno had been summoned to smooth things over. Not to mention patch the holes in the hedge. The gang of boys was rumoured to be growing in number and nastiness. We were both under strain and showing it. 'You know what I would really love?' I said softly. 'A day in London. With you. Just like the wonderful day you gave me all those centuries ago. I fell in love with you that day, though I was too stupid to know it at the time.'

The lines on my lover's face seemed to vanish and just for a moment I saw him as he'd been that day, both of us young and vigorous and full of the future. He took me in his arms. 'You shall have your day,' he said, and kissed me.

We didn't go to any of the same places. You can't go back – even I know that much. Instead, my lover unrolled a new map of delights to make our own on that blissful early April day filled with the zest of daffodils and of Hanno's presence. It was spring all right – how could I have missed it? The parks of London were awash with colour and with the heady scent of green and growing things. Even in the pit at Covent Garden, where he'd talked a friend into letting us perch for a dress rehearsal, the smell of sweat and effort was mingled with the promise of spring.

Hanno didn't even know about the jeweller's shop; it wasn't part of our itinerary. It just happened to place a convenient canopy over us when a sudden shower burst from a cloud and obliged us to seek shelter. We stood beneath it, arms entwined, softly singing the silly old song in praise of April showers. We must have made a daft picture, especially the rain-spotted sunglasses I now wore to escape recognition, but we didn't care. That's the nice thing about London: you can make a fool of yourself in peace. Nobody minds, nobody withers you with a behave-yourself glare.

I don't know what it was that made us both turn round simultaneously and peer through the jeweller's window. At the same moment, the cloud vanished and a ray of light shot between us and lodged on a single item, or so it seemed to us. We gasped – again simultaneously – at what the sun's spotlight revealed.

It was the crown, the exquisite medieval crown of roughly beaten gold and uncut stones which Hanno's friend had placed on my head on that other day of magic. The same crown, except that some new magic had condensed it into a ring. We didn't say a word, struck speechless not only by the coincidence (this of all days!) but by the sheer beauty of the tiny thing.

We didn't speak either as we entered the shop together, or when Hanno placed the ring on my fourth finger. Only then did I utter a small cry of disappointment. The ring was too big. It was out of the question to brutalise it by making it smaller. The continuous band was complete; to cut a piece out would destroy it.

Then I shrugged and even managed to smile. After all, I didn't own the British Museum's crown either. One didn't have to own a thing of beauty to make it one's own. It was sufficient simply to look, to drink in the loveliness and imprint it on one's memory. It was enough to have seen the ring and be reminded of all the awesome things the crown had spoken of: the love of the long-dead craftsman who had made it; the promise of unfulfilled and unfulfillable perfection contained in those uncut jewels; the challenge emanating from it as if to say, 'Only in your imagination can I be made perfect, and your imagination is more perfect than any jewel can ever be.' The strange sense I'd had then and had again now that this heartbreaking circlet was a symbol of what I must try to do in my own work, night after night to strive for the ultimate which could never be achieved and was more precious for its elusiveness. I turned my hand over to see every detail while I could and to fill myself with its purpose. Then I raised my other hand to remove the ring and give it back.

Suddenly Hanno's hand was on mine. He removed the ring and placed it on my middle finger instead.

It fitted.

'I know it's the "wrong" finger,' he said. 'But some things are more important than convention.'

As we left the shop, I glanced back and saw the jeweller's beaming face, and it seemed to me that it was the same face I'd seen at the British Museum. But I must have been mistaken.

'Hanno, we don't need to be engaged. I don't need proof of your love.'

We were standing on Waterloo Bridge, still entwined as we had been by the jeweller's shop, only now one hand bore the ring.

'I know that,' he smiled. 'If you were the sort of woman who needs proof, you wouldn't be the woman I want to marry.'

I laughed. 'What a perverse old thing you are!'

He raised one eyebrow. 'Is that your answer?'

A barge was passing beneath us, bringing with it a whiff of the sea, its wake spread out like a cloak behind it, the sun picking out the ever-changing little ridges like lines of a woodcut. I looked at the lines of my lover's face, also like a woodcut. I disentangled myself from him and cupped his face in my hands. The ring pressed into his cheek and gleamed dully, the topaz seeming to reflect the gold flecks of Hanno's eyes. His hair, gold and silver, blew a little in the breeze and tickled my hand. 'Do you need an answer?' I said.

And then I kissed him. Right in the middle of Waterloo Bridge.

We were packing. Our bedroom, which we had promised to decorate with love, was in chaos. I was dizzy with excitement and fear, too agitated to think about which bits of clothes I would need. It was Friday night. We were driving to the Cotswolds together. The next day I would drive up to Yorkshire on my own. Both trips were fraught.

I sat down on the bed, brooding yet again. 'I just have this awful feeling.'

Hanno stopped between the wardrobe and the bed, holding a shirt on its hanger. He smiled. 'It's called hunger. We'll stop somewhere on the way – the others will have eaten long before we arrive. They're not expecting to put on a celebratory dinner.'

'Exactly. I wish you'd told them. I wish it were all over.'

He put the shirt down and came and sat beside me. He put his arms round me. 'Sweet Rosalind. We've been through this before. It would be demeaning if I went alone. We *are* together.'

I leaned my head against his. 'I just have this feeling that they're going to object.'

'My lovely foolish girl. You know they adore you.'

'As a friend, yes. An occasional visitor. Not as –'

'And as Joachim's friend,' he said softly. 'Don't forget that. You're the only person they've trusted with the knowledge. That matters, you know. That you understand what he's like and accept him. That they can talk to you freely about him.'

'All right, as a confidante, too. But a daughter-in-law?' Hanno's parents had never enquired too closely into his London life. I turned to him, anxious for him to understand. 'Hanno, they never expected you to marry. They've had you to themselves for more than fifty years. It'll be a shock to them.'

'A lovely shock,' he smiled. 'And all the lovelier for being delayed so long.'

Then he stood up briskly and began folding the shirt. He always did these things for himself. He'd done them so long that it would be ludicrous for me to play the solicitous fiancée. Everything had been as it was for so long. How could he expect his parents to welcome an intrusion into the carefully formed pattern of their difficult lives?

'In any case,' he said, 'they have no say in the matter. There's nothing on God's earth that will make me give you up, Rosalind. Not now. *Nothing*. Do you understand?'

There was something hard in his voice which made me look up in sudden apprehension. And just for a moment I saw the hard gleaming nuggets that were the eyes of the golden stag.

Hanno's profile was outlined dimly against the dark countryside whizzing past. It was a strong profile. Everything about Hanno was strong, though touched with a gentleness which was another kind of strength. So many people depended on him. His parents, Joachim, Christa. All the clients who put their careers – which is to say, their lives – into his care. And now me, still on edge after the months in New York, eaten up by fear of rejection, fear of loss.

Hanno had offered to come to Yorkshire with me. I'd been tempted, knowing that his own strength would bolster my own. But it was all so vague, my anxiety that David and Charlotte might marry and take Matti away. It seemed better to make a quiet visit on my own. I would probably learn more that way.

His profile blurred briefly as he glanced at me. 'You do realise that we'll be a respectable married couple, too. If worse came to worse, we could make a reasonable showing in a new custody case – given that you're his mother.'

I smiled, comforted already. 'You're reading my mind again. Sometimes I wonder if you are a *Teufelskind*.'

'Your mind is rather transparent these days.'

'You're very fond of Matti, aren't you?'

'Very. He's got a touch of the elf about him. Like his mother.'

'Not many men would want to take on another man's child.'

'I don't see him that way. He's simply Matti. Himself.'

'Are you absolutely sure you don't want us to try for a son of your own?'

'Quite sure,' he said quickly.

Too quickly, really. It was another of the puzzles I would probably never solve: why a man so patently fond of Matti was totally against having a child of his own. It was the one thing that had worried me about our engagement: however much I might love a child by Hanno, I was in no better a position to be a mother now than I had been with Matti. I had learned my lesson good and proper: I was not the material of motherhood, I was an actress. I would do far more good and no harm at all by continuing to do the thing I could do well, and that was to create on stage a mirror in which the audience could see that part of themselves normally hidden. A small enough contribution, perhaps, but the one offering I had to give.

'I still think Matti is better off with Astrid,' I said. 'Nothing's changed. The Folly is still cut off from the world Matti needs to know, and I'm still not around to look after him without having a nanny, and that's what David objected to.'

'Perhaps. I just want you to know that I'll help you in every way possible.'

I leaned over, despite objections from my seat belt, and kissed Hanno's cheek. 'Thank you.'

It was dark by the time we approached Joachim's Wood. The moon, nearing its fullness, was obliterated by a thick mat of cloud which was leaking drizzle over everything. To my right I dimly discerned a piece of even blacker blackness which I recognised only by familiarity as the smooth wooded hill where I'd first met Hanno's parents. The dark lightened into that sunny day. I'd rounded a curve in the path which followed the river and there, suddenly, were the two old people. A minute later Hanno had scrambled down from the hill to join us.

'What were you doing up there?' I asked now.

The lights of the dashboard illuminated his smile. 'I'm not that much of a mind-reader. Context, please.'

I supplied the context.

'Picking some sweet cicily,' he explained. 'The first leaves of the year.'

'But wasn't there some growing by the path? Why go up the hill to pick it?'

'What a shrewd little detective you are. Yes, there was another reason. Some children had started playing around in a clearing at the top – I'd seen a bonfire once or twice. I went to have a look. I was afraid Joachim would see the bonfire and become curious. Or the children would cross the river and snoop around the hedge.' The smile flashed again briefly. 'Like someone else I know.'

'Ah. And the sweet cicily was just an excuse.'

'I didn't want my parents becoming anxious. I told Christa, of course, but we've both tried to protect them from too much thinking. It wasn't a problem when we bought the place. There was only a small village then, across the field on the other side of the hill. Hardly any children at all – one of those dying villages. And the bonfire was a false alarm – nothing ever came of it. But now, of course, there's the housing estate where the field used to be. The rest you know.'

We had arrived at the gates. I took the key from Hanno and, when he'd driven through, carefully locked the gates again. Absentmindedly, I slipped the key into a pocket and got back into the car, my mind preoccupied with Joachim. The uncertainties over his future, now more precarious than ever, made my own broodings over Matti shrink in importance. At least Matti was a normal, healthy child. Did it matter so very much who had custody, as long as he was happy?

Hanno's parents weren't happy. I hadn't seen them for some time and was startled by how much they'd aged again. Two wizened old people greeted us that evening with a sadness which no warmth of welcome could disguise. Even Christa looked subdued.

'Has Joachim been out again?' Hanno asked.

Christa nodded. 'I put him to bed early tonight – with the drugs. The drugs are needed more and more. Still, we manage.' She smiled with the practice of many years.

We were in the sitting-room. Already I was dreading the announcement we would make that evening. Everything was wrong. The juxtaposition of joy and despair was too extreme. I couldn't help thinking of my first engagement, the wedding plans snapped off by Rhiannon's sudden death. There was no question of death here – Joachim was extremely healthy and his parents strong despite their cares. But the atmosphere was too heavy to bear the lightness of an engagement. Despite their affection for me, I felt like a frivolous intruder trailing with me irrelevant concerns about Matti and marriage.

'What happened this time?' Hanno asked.

We were speaking German, as we always did at Joachim's Wood. That, too, made me feel peripheral. My German had improved but was still clumsy in comparison.

'The gang of boys have become fixated on Joachim,' Christa explained. 'They came up to the hedge today and called for him.'

'But they don't know his name,' said Hanno.

'I'm afraid they do. My fault. The first night they had a bonfire – they've started that, too – I went searching for him, calling his name.'

I pictured Christa stumbling across the fields at night, looking for her oversized charge. How long could this go on?

'Is there any talk yet?'

'I don't think so,' she said. 'I go into Chipping Moreton more often now, to listen. But I have no plausible reason to go to the village, so I don't know if anything is said there.'

'But have any adults seen him yet?'

'No, I'm pretty sure they haven't.'

'So with luck the boys' parents will think "Joachim" is a fantasy friend.'

'With luck. The other worry is all these stories of "Satanic abuse". Regardless of whether there's any truth in them, they make people nervous and suspicious.'

'Someone might start listening to the boys and wonder if "Joachim" is real,' said Hanno.

'Exactly. It wouldn't take long then to discover who he is.'

And nobody would believe that he was harmless. I could see it all now. Even if the gang did nothing to Joachim, swarms of adults would descend on him, locking him up in some soulless institution to protect their children. The children were far more dangerous to Joachim – he with his strange lack of fear – than he was to them, but nobody would see it that way. Devil's child. It would be Joachim, not Hanno, branded by that name. There was indeed a kind of magic to Joachim, and people would sense it. But they would assume it was the wrong kind of magic. The almost mystical feel for soil and plants that he had, the wonderful intuition which Hanno felt flowing through Joachim into him, Joachim's rapport with the music which entered his hands when he was at the piano, the innate goodness which had been preserved in Joachim – none of it would matter. To the public, he would be a mental defective, a monster threatening their children.

I closed my eyes with the pain of it. When I opened them, I saw the same pain mirrored in the eyes of Joachim's parents. They had said nothing throughout the discussion. They'd sat side by side on the sofa, passive in their despair, two old husks emptied of any joy, any capacity for joy.

After that, the conversation tailed off. It was difficult to talk of light and pleasant things. And it was impossible to introduce the subject of our engagement, not now. Perhaps in the morning. Though it was hard to see what difference a new morning would make.

Finally Christa went out to make a bedtime cup of tea for us all. I felt desperately tired. I'd barely slept at all for several nights – jet lag, worry about Matti, the long depression over the New York run. And now Joachim's future. There didn't seem much prospect of sleep tonight either, for any of us.

Then, 'Mother. Father. Rosalind and I have something to tell you.'

My eyelids, which had been sinking with the weight of too many sleepless nights, shot up. I jerked my head towards Hanno, desperate to catch his attention, to warn him off.

Too late.

'I hope you'll be as pleased as we are. I hope it will give you something to feel happy about.'

'Hanno, not now,' I murmured.

He turned his gold-flecked eyes on me, those eyes so like his parents'. 'There'll never be a "right" time, Rosalind,' he said mildly. 'You must see that.' Then he looked back at his parents and said, 'Rosalind and I are engaged to be married.'

What happened next was so shocking that even now I can hardly bear to remember it. I don't know what I expected. Confusion, perhaps. Certainly surprise. A mixture of pleasure and anxiety and even a tinge of regret, which would have been disappointing but bearable. It saddened me that circumstances would almost inevitably prevent an effusion of joy to match mine and Hanno's. No, I didn't expect joy, but I certainly didn't expect what did happen either.

As if a powerful current had suddenly been switched on to surge through the sofa and through her own body, Mrs Hirsch shot to her feet and cried, '*No!*' Her eyes were wild and her face was distorted into a horrible grimace and she stood there, as strong as one of the Furies, shrieking, '*No! No! You can't do this! No! This is monstrous, monstrous! How could you even think of such a thing? No! No! NO!*'

32

As I sped north, Mrs Hirsch's face, twisted into a grotesque mask, flashed on to my windscreen with every passing car. Each headlight was imprinted with the image. It hurtled towards me, over and over, looming ever larger until it filled the windscreen and then vanished to make way for another.

It was raining hard now, the windscreen wipers working furiously. If only they would fling away the picture once and for all. But no; here she came again, again emanating revulsion from the headlights that were her gold-flecked eyes. I wanted to close my own eyes to shut it out, but some small scrap of me labelled self-preservation kept me going through the night.

My last minutes at Joachim's Wood kept up a continual replay. She had loomed over me, a small woman made huge by frenzy, her hands raised in child-fists as if she would beat me out of existence. Then, abruptly, she had collapsed. In the confusion that followed I slipped away unnoticed. I took time only to remove the ring and place it on the table by the door. Then I left the house.

I was very calm, so much so that even then I recognised the unnatural calm of delayed shock. Calmly I removed Hanno's suitcase from the car. Calmly I got in and negotiated the island of trees that screened the house. Only then did a slight disturbance intrude into my methodical movements: Hanno, bursting from the house and calling, 'Rosalind! Rosalind!'

I ignored him and carefully rounded the island. A flash of light in the rear-view mirror showed Hanno running straight through the circle of trees in an attempt to catch up. I pressed my foot harder on the accelerator.

'Rosalind! Rosalind! Come back, damn you! Stop!'

In no time at all I'd come to a gravel-spewing stop in front of the gates. I got out quickly and with nimble fingers plucked the key from my pocket. I undid the padlock, opened the gates wide and drove through. He was running up the drive as fast as he could, but not fast enough. I leapt from the car again, placed the key where it would be clearly visible beneath the opened gates and returned to the car. I even had time to think how thoughtful I was, leaving behind the key so that he could lock the gates once more, lock behind them the terrible world which was Joachim's Wood. Then I was speeding away from the nightmare which had become real. My last sight of Hanno was a pale interruption to the darkness of the road behind me, paler, smaller, and then gone.

I didn't think about anything at all as I drove through the night. There was nothing to think about. The rejection which I had feared had happened. It was no concern of mine why. It was all over now, the foolish fairy-tale dream of a second chance, smashed into oblivion by that twisted face. My life had been snapped in two. The past was dead and with it a large chunk of myself. Dimly – calmly, even – I wished the whole of me had gone with it. I had no desire to live, but live I would, because, somehow, one did. What the new life would consist of I had no idea and no desire to imagine. It was a robot driving that car. I was a machine draped in flesh to disguise the workings of whatever mechanism had been set in motion to keep me going.

I don't know what time I arrived at The Folly but it must have been the small hours of Saturday morning. It was still dark, still raining. At least these gates weren't locked. David's glaring eyes were better than any padlock, shutting people out of his self-contained world.

I parked the car and went round to the courtyard. A spare key was kept on a small hook hidden beneath the ivy. My fingers fumbled among the leaves and a tiny spurt of fear surfaced – the first emotion I'd felt since . . . well, since. It vanished on contact with the cold comforting metal.

I let myself in quietly. I wasn't expected until the afternoon, there was no virtue in arousing the whole household. I crept through the maze of corridors, remembering even to avoid those floorboards which creaked. Not a sound, from me or from anyone else. The house might have been deserted. To some extent it was; the 'students' were still away on their Easter break. On the few occasions I'd returned to The Folly, I'd always managed to avoid the students. I'd tried to avoid David, too, slipping up north to see Brendan and Belle while David was off somewhere on forestry business. This would be the first time I would see him in years. Strangely, the thought didn't worry me as it would have done in the past. Well, I didn't have a past, did I? Not any more.

I reached the top of the south-east tower and opened the door to the room which had been kept as 'mine' ever since I'd left The Folly. I switched on the light and felt an infinitesimal lifting of spirits.

It was the Tudor Room, my favourite of all the ones I'd so lovingly restored in those early days at The Folly. I'd made a good job of it. The wide oak floorboards gleamed dully in the artificial light. On them were several lovely old rugs. The room was on two levels, the downstairs furnished as a little sitting-room. A circular staircase rose to a sleeping balcony. David and I had played Romeo and Juliet here, the day I'd ended the long resentful mourning of Farleton Hall. I'd leaned over and called my Romeo to me and he had sped up the stairs to his Juliet. The bed then had been old and dusty and bare. Now it was made up invitingly with a sweet-smelling duvet patterned in Tudor roses. Dear Belle, always methodical. She'd readied the room well in advance. A bowl of narcissi stood on one table, poised to open their petals and release their scent on my arrival.

I opened my suitcase and withdrew my nightgown. It was fragrant with lavender, warm and comforting as I let it fall into place over my body. These things that hadn't mattered before mattered a great deal now. Small comforts. Small considerations.

I climbed to the balcony, got into bed and switched off the light. The darkness surged in through the windows, the moon still covered by its leaky cloud. I was glad for the darkness. I didn't want to see the moon. I knew whose face would be imprinted on it.

Did I sleep? Perhaps. Perhaps not. If so, not for long. Soon it was dawn. The grey light of an overcast day came through the windows at the same moment I heard the first distant sounds of the awakening house. I'd forgotten how early they got up at The Folly. Their lives were shaped around the daylight needed for work in the forest.

I crawled out of bed, feeling as grey as the day, and made my way down to the washbasin I'd disguised as a tall Tudor chest. I looked into the mirror above it, expecting it to reflect the haggard old woman I felt myself to be. It seemed to me that I'd aged several decades through the night, and I was almost indignant to see the fresh young face which stared back at me. Of course. The face of an actress, never reflecting itself. Nothing but a surface on which to carve each successive character I played. I was nearly forty, but my face, geared to playing younger roles, had remained absurdly youthful. I looked back at it with disgust. Then I washed, dressed and went downstairs.

I didn't plan a dramatic entrance; I'd just forgotten that no one knew I was there. When I opened the door into the kitchen, five faces turned and stared at the ghost they thought I was. The tableau would have been comical if I'd been in the mood.

'Surprise,' I said feebly.

Matti was the first to break the picture. 'Mummy!' he yelled, scrambling from his chair and rushing to me. I swept him up in a big hug, forgetting he was almost too heavy to lift now. His dark little face, so close to mine, had never looked more elfin. He grinned as if this were a trick I'd devised for his benefit. I wished it had been. I wished a lot of things in that moment, most of all that my life had been wholly different with just Matti and David and me living a normal life, whatever that might be.

But the moment passed when I set Matti down and forced myself to meet David's dark forbidding face. One brief pang and then I felt nothing. His smile of welcome was strained, obviously put on for the sake of appearances. We had taken care not to play ourselves off against each other in the dreary battle for Matti's love. That it had worked was clear from our son's openness. It never even occurred to Matti that David might be annoyed to see mother and son so lovingly together.

Then everything disappeared in the tumultuous welcome from Belle and Brendan and Astrid.

'I'm sorry to be such a nuisance,' I murmured to Belle as she hugged me. I invented some excuse to explain my premature arrival.

'How *can* you even *think* such a thing!' she laughed. 'It's lovely to see you, Ros – the earlier the better! But why didn't you wake us up? Thank *God* I'd got the room ready! D'you know, I nearly left it till this morning. Do you think there was something psychic that made me do it last night instead?'

'You and your psychic!' I laughed.

Another kind of psychic, another person, as fair as David was dark.

I pushed the image away. I had no past except the distant past which had contained these people gathered together now in the big happy kitchen. I had been happy, too, in this kitchen, at least some of the time. As I sat down to breakfast, that past struggled to come back and meet me. It couldn't make it all the way to the inside where my feelings had frozen up through the night, but it settled loosely round me like a warm familiar cloak. Well, that was something.

Matti and I spent the morning together, Matti playing the mini-squire and showing me round his domain. His pride – not of ownership but of knowledge – was intense. It chastened me to realise how completely he'd forgotten those earliest years when he and David and I had lived there together.

We had to visit each horse in turn for a formal good-morning. 'And this is Olwen,' he said, flinging open the door and entering the spacious box stall.

A spasm of fear nipped my heart as the massive horse stepped towards the tiny boy. Her hooves were the size of dinner plates – she could squash him without knowing he was there. But she did know. With surprising grace she swung her huge head down to receive his clumsy caress.

'Olwen is Daddy's favourite,' he confided.

I looked at the horse with new interest. She was certainly beautiful, her coat a gleaming pale grey, her silky featherings creamy against her sturdy lower legs. 'Any particular reason?' I asked.

'Just she's special.'

I stepped a little closer and touched the mare's smooth cheek. Her eyes, dark and intelligent, gazed at me with unnerving steadiness, as if judging me.

I said nothing to Matti about Charlotte, waiting to see if he would mention her. That he didn't was slightly reassuring. Clearly he didn't know her all that well. He probably hadn't seen her since Christmas. Out of sight, out of mind. Perhaps.

Nobody spoke of her at lunch either. She was their nearest neighbour, they must have had contact with her since Christmas. That nobody said a thing about her was no longer reassuring. It was beginning to seem a little ominous.

After lunch I took a deep breath and asked David if I could come with him for the afternoon. His acquiescence was chillingly neutral.

The day was pretty chilly, too, despite the thin spring sun which had parted the clouds to filter through the canopy. I shivered in my Arran sweater as I walked along behind him. He was planting some trees, he said. It was past the planting season for most things, but oaks were late into growth and could tolerate a later planting. His voice was devoid of emotion. Well, so was mine.

'The forest is looking good,' I said.

'It's a nice time of year. Trees just beginning to break into growth.'

The trunks of the beech trees were silvered by the sun. Their russet leaves, left over from the autumn, took on a richer colour. The green of the conifers seemed more intense too, in the absence of any new leaves from the deciduous trees. The forest was both subdued and vibrant. Yes, a nice time of year.

We reached the clearing. Briefly – very briefly – the memory of another clearing intruded, but I pushed it away before it could take hold. I was getting good at pushing away such images. A few more days and I would truly be a woman without a past, without emotions. Just like David. Did he have any feelings at all? It seemed unlikely. I watched him set down the burlap bundle of tiny trees. Any feelings he might have were clearly reserved for the trees. I set down the spade and watering can he'd asked me to carry. The spade was gleaming, meticulously cared for like everything at The Folly.

The clearing was quite large, with a grassy knoll at one end. I tested it for damp and sat down. Above, birds twittered their spring songs while David began his work. He pushed the spade into the ground on all sides and lifted a square of turf. After setting it to one side, he began to dig a little pit. The earth, piling up on the other side of the pit, seemed soft and friable. He looked up, as if noticing for the first time that I was there. 'Would you mind filling the can, please? There's a syke just over there.'

So polite. I filled the can, returned to my knoll and watched him plant the first tree. And the second. And the third.

By late afternoon the planting was nearly finished and I was numb with cold and suppressed pain. Every attempt at conversation had failed. There had been no opening in which I might raise the subject of Charlotte. David was perfectly civil but nothing more. Only once had he smiled, in response to something I'd said. The big dark heavy face had lightened and I'd remembered that once, long long ago, I had loved this man. Loved him very much indeed. I couldn't remember what it felt like. 'Love' had shrunk to four letters strung together in a dictionary.

He had begun the planting at the edges of the clearing and worked his way towards the knoll. Now he knelt at the rim of a pit, testing it for depth. I sprang to my feet, anticipating the end of the day's planting, and stood on the knoll. It looked for all the world like a stage. All the world's a stage. The words tweaked a memory.

And then, without thinking, I was declaiming the words. Not Jaques' famous speech but one of the Duke's:

> 'Hath not old custom made this life more sweet
> Than that of painted pomp? Are not these woods
> More free from peril than the envious court?
> Here feel we but the penalty of Adam,
> The seasons' difference.'

I hadn't chosen the words. They'd merely come to me with long familiarity. *As You Like It*. My talismanic play. The Barbican, and before that, Stratford. Further back, the lovely little Fortune Theatre where Jas and I had taken such delight in our London début. And further back still, the ADC at Cambridge. Where I'd met David after that exhilarating first night. I hadn't chosen them, no, but suddenly I heard how appropriate they were to this setting, and for a brief moment, past and present came together into a peaceful unity and I heard myself laugh with pleasure as I moved down from the knoll towards my audience of one.

Suddenly a noise rang out, like the snapping of a dead branch. My head and David's jerked round. There was a moment of eerie stillness. Then a woman stepped into the clearing.

Charlotte. It had to be Charlotte. I looked with dismay at the small heart-shaped face, the delicate features, the anachronistic crown of thick black plaits wound round her head. The mucky old sweater and jeans did nothing to disguise her slim and youthful shape. Hugh was right. She was beautiful. And young – a good ten years younger than me. I could feel my resentment rising. For one tiny moment I had been happy, had forgotten everything except those lovely Shakespearian cadences. And here she was, blundering into my fragile peace. What was she doing here? Had they arranged to meet? No, otherwise David wouldn't have allowed me to accompany him. A thousand acres and she had to choose this clearing.

'I'm looking for a sheep,' she blurted.

I pulled myself together. If ever I had need to use my acting skills, it was now. I laughed with feigned delight. 'Little Bo Peep has lost her sheep! David, you never told me that you stocked *your* Forest of Arden with shepherdesses!' How brittle I sounded. Even my acting was going wrong.

David ignored me. He scrambled to his feet and went up to her.

'I'm sorry,' she said to him. 'There's a gap in the wall over there – a ewe's got through, she'll have a single lamb with her. Have you seen them?'

I scrutinised her face. Was she acting, too?

'Ros, go and get Brendan, tell him there's some patch-walling,' said David.

'Oh, it's not urgent,' she said. 'Tom's put up a piece of corrugated. He's holding on in the lambing field till I get back. I have to go now. I'm sorry I disturbed you.' She turned to go.

I suddenly realised that this was the moment I'd been hoping for without knowing it: a chance to see David and Charlotte together. 'Wait,' I called to her. My voice sounded a little too anxious. 'Please wait,' I added more softly. Then I walked across the clearing and stood before her. 'You must be Charlotte. Everyone says such marvellous things about you at The Folly.' No one had said a word. 'I've been dying to meet you, but David insists you're in the thick of lambing and can't come over.' It sounded plausible enough. Then I put out my hand. 'Well, I'm delighted to meet you. I'm Ros Rawlinson.'

As she very well knew. I don't suppose they'd spoken

to her about me any more than they'd spoken to me of her, but I could see the awed recognition in her eyes. Her eyes were dark blue, almost violet, and very beautiful. In a curiously touching gesture, she wiped her hand on her jeans and gave it to me with a shy smile. 'I'm pleased to meet you, too. I've seen you on stage, of course . . .' Her voice trailed off in embarrassment.

I could see through her eyes the picture I presented: Ros Rawlinson, superstar. The darling of the RSC. Rich, famous, successful. Adored by the public, envied by every aspiring actress. The glitzy cosmopolitan now gracing the humble clearing in which we stood. A spasm of self-disgust threatened. Poor Charlotte. How little she guessed how much I envied her. Her life was still intact. She had a future.

Suddenly, another sound, a thrashing in the undergrowth. A moment later a sheep shot into view. Before I knew what was happening, Charlotte herself shot between David and me and in a spectacular rugby tackle flung herself on the sheep. I didn't know whether to laugh or grind my teeth in envy. The action was so impulsive, so natural – the instantaneous response of a farmer determined to catch her sheep. It was she who belonged in the world, not me.

She stood up, triumphantly grasping the sheep by one horn. A sheepdog had appeared from nowhere to perform a little dance of satisfaction around the mother, and now there was a lamb, too. As it whizzed past, I grabbed it and held it up to my face. It stared back in panic. I could feel its tiny heart nearly bursting the fragile rib cage beneath my hands, but I didn't dare let it go in case it ran away. In this world where everything was natural except me, I clung to the lamb as my own small contribution. I smiled reassuringly at it, then looked at David.

He was smiling too, but not at me. My heart lurched as frantically as the lamb's when I saw the tenderness of the smile he directed at Charlotte.

I don't think she saw it. She was staring down at the pit David had been about to fill. Then she leaned down, still grasping the sheep, and plunged her other hand in the pile of soil by its side. My heart was thumping harder. Something was happening, though I didn't know what.

Then David left me and went over to stand beside her. The symbolism could hardly have been clearer.

She looked up at him. 'Do you know, I've never planted a tree. All those years on my parents' farm and I never planted a tree.' Her voice was slightly tremulous.

David was watching her intently, as if I'd vanished from the scene, as if the two of them were alone in the clearing. 'Would you like to plant this one?' he said at last. 'I'll hold the ewe.' Without waiting for her answer, he took the ewe's horn in his own hand.

'I don't know how,' said Charlotte.

'It's all ready. I'll tell you.'

The clearing seemed unnaturally quiet. The ewe was silent under David's hands. The dog was silent. Even the lamb had stopped its bleating. The birds held their breath. The slight breeze dropped to utter stillness. And then, very quietly, David began to speak.

The effect was extraordinary, as if everything before had been a recitative leading up to the duet at the heart of the opera. And it was a love duet, there was no doubt about that. David's voice had lost its chilled politeness. It was rich and warm and resonant with love. I had heard that voice so often myself, in the distant past, when it had been me he had loved.

My heart stopped thudding, almost stopped altogether, as if it were trying to die. I wished it would. I wished another sheep would lumber into the clearing. I wished a bomb would drop and annihilate us all, anything to stop the aria which was filling the clearing with the quietly impassioned notes of love. That the words were instructions on how to plant the tree couldn't disguise the message beneath them, at least not from me. As for her, it was impossible to tell. I studied her face, the face – perhaps – of Matti's future stepmother.

At last the interminable moment was over, the tree planted. She stood up and gazed at the sturdy twig. The two of them, side by side, quietly pondering their handiwork. There was something in their faces like the peaceful pride of parents looking down at their child. Which, in a way, I suppose it was. They had started this tree into growth, the two of them. That neither of them would live to see its maturity didn't seem to matter to them. Their expression was rapt, almost mystic.

Suddenly she looked up at him and smiled. And I knew.

33

Neither of us said anything about the incident as we walked home, nor did we speak of it at dinner that evening.

Soon after Astrid went upstairs, I followed her and knocked on her door. There was a pause, and a tiny rustle of paper, before she opened it.

'Astrid, I need to talk to you. Please.'

Astrid's room was another of my favourites, a dignified evocation of the Queen Anne period. It suited her. The best piece was a lovely old desk by the big sash windows. It was only there for atmosphere, of course; no one would write to Astrid during her stays here, they would phone. So I was a little surprised to see a single letter on the desk, neatly folded in its envelope.

I sat down on one side of the Adam fireplace with Astrid across from me. 'It's David and Charlotte,' I said. 'How long has this been going on? Please, I'm not being nosy; I do need to know.'

Her lovely face, usually so placid, stared at me with something like wonder. 'You know this?'

'I don't *know* anything, but I saw them together in the forest today and . . .' And what? It was difficult to explain. Two neighbours had planted a tree together. So what?

'And David says nothing of this at dinner?' Astrid mused.

'Nobody says anything about anything in this place,' I observed drily. 'But I'm sure there's something going on. But why is David so secretive about it? He's perfectly free, he can have as many girlfriends as he pleases. That's what puzzles me – the secrecy.'

'I think,' Astrid smiled, 'the secret is from David. That he knows nothing himself. But please, tell me what you see today. Perhaps you know more now than me?'

I described the incident in the clearing. Astrid listened patiently as I explained why it had seemed so significant. She seemed to understand. People often underestimated Astrid, thought her fractured English meant fractured understanding. They were wrong. Of all of us, she was perhaps the most intuitive.

When I finished she sat quietly, her hands folded in her lap, thinking. Then, 'Yes. This is all true, what I suspect so long. But "going on" is wrong. Nothing goes on because David is a fool. I think he loves Charlotte for many months, since meeting in September, but he doesn't let himself think it.'

'And Charlotte?' I asked.

'This I know less, but maybe. Ach!' she exclaimed suddenly. 'These people are so stupid! They love and they refuse to say so even to themselves. They need the heads knocking together, yes? Now I know to go to David and say, "Look, you stupid man. You love Charlotte. Go to her and say so and be done with it!"'

I laughed despite myself, picturing the queenly Astrid bearing down on David with her decree. Then the laughter stopped. What she was describing was what I feared most. This wasn't a story in which I could be a casual observer.

Astrid continued. 'Until you tell me this thing in the clearing, the only evidence I have – see? – I talk like detectives – is a letter from September.' She gestured towards the desk. 'It reveals so little, but something, and so I bring it to Yorkshire to wave in his face and make him *talk*.'

I caught my breath. 'What sort of letter?'

'Oh, something and nothing. To send some money for a school trip for Matti. But also he writes of meeting Charlotte. You know this story?'

I shook my head.

'One early morning in September she walks through the

forest and finds Olwen in a field. Something crazy possesses her, and like sleepwalking she gets on the horse with no bridle and they gallop across the field full of fog. At the end of the field, David, furious but also – though he says nothing – impressed with this impetuous girl. In the letter he says little but even then I read between the lines. And now, what you say tells me this is right.'

Olwen. David's favourite horse. 'Could I see the letter?'

Astrid hesitated. 'Is this right? I feel, letters are private?'

'Yes,' I said quietly. 'But this is one that affects me, too.'

And now there was a long silence while Astrid contemplated me. There was compassion in her face. My humiliation had begun. 'Yes,' she said at last. 'And I forget: there is pain. Even though you leave David and so are free, still it hurts that he loves again.'

And it was true, though I'd tried to deny it to myself. 'Vanity, I suppose,' I said lightly. 'I'll get over it. But it's more than that. There's Matti. Astrid, I have to tell you: I'm afraid. If David and Charlotte marry, they may well want Matti to move up here for good.'

Astrid was clearly dumbfounded. 'But I never think of that! Matti is happy where he is, yes? And he sees you in London and David here and so everything works good!'

'Astrid, tell me what you think of her – Charlotte. Would she do such a thing? Do you like her? What sort of a person *is* she?'

It took her a while to compose herself after her outburst. It was easy to forget that she, too, had a vested interest, that she loved Matti as much as David and I did. She was, after all, more of a parent to him than either of us was.

'I think,' she said slowly, 'that Charlotte is a very good person. I like her very much.'

I listened carefully, knowing that Astrid's opinion meant something. Knowing, too, that she could be trusted. I heard her first words with a mixture of relief and dismay. Part of me wanted Charlotte to be a monster. Another part desperately needed her to be human, and kind.

'And kind,' said Astrid. 'Charlotte feels for other people, too kind to do something that hurts Matti as much as you and me. No, I am sure. This is not something she would do – take him away.'

'Does Matti like her?'

Astrid smiled. 'Yes. But Matti likes everyone.'

'And David? *Is* she the right person for him?'

'Oh, yes. They are much alike. Stubborn. Good with hard work. And the vision, the forest – this she shares with David.'

And I didn't. The forest, which was David's life, was for me just a pleasant place to walk on my rare trips from London.

I stood up. I didn't want to hear any more. These were bitter things I was having to digest. There was only one more thing I needed to know. 'Astrid, please could I see the letter?'

She hesitated a while longer but finally she handed it over.

It was a bit of a wrench, seeing that familiar handwriting. It was even more of a wrench reading the letter. Most of it was dull enough – David always was a dolt with words. But right near the end there was a simple statement: he had met their new neighbour, she seemed surprisingly nice. And then the bombshell. Another simple sentence but one which utterly contradicted the offhandedness of the first: 'I wish I'd met someone like her twenty years ago.'

The words ripped through me. Twenty years ago. In the most casual way imaginable he had annihilated the remains of my past, the part of it he and I had shared. That he probably didn't understand the violence of his statement was no comfort to me. How could Astrid have had any doubts, after reading this letter? And how could David be so stupid, after writing it?

'You're right,' I said, composing my features as I handed the letter back. 'David is a fool.'

I'm still not sure what made me do it, what made me rise from my sleepless bed that night and walk through the rain to that sodden lambing field.

My mind was as churned up as the bed. There was no possibility of sleep. The scene in the forest, the talk with Astrid, the hurtful letter – all of it rattled through my head in disjointed lumps. It was my fault. I had so thoroughly repressed all thoughts and feelings about what had happened before my flight to Yorkshire that my mind had overcompensated and fixed on the day's events with abnormal intensity. Part of me even knew it and tried to tell the other part, 'Calm down. What will be will be. There's nothing you can do to change it. Anyway, why the fuss? What does it matter if David marries again? Astrid's right: they probably won't meddle with Matti, that much at least will stay the same.' But I couldn't feel convinced.

Finally, around midnight, I sat up in bed. All the muddle had come together in a single even more muddled idea: somehow, there was unfinished business. I had to see Charlotte myself. Alone. Just once. And then I would know what to do.

It was as easy to slip out of the sleeping house as it had been to slip into it the night before. Then, too, it had been raining, the windscreen wipers, the headlights, the face –

A row of pegs in the old gun room. On them a row of yellow oilskins. Beneath them a row of wellies. On a table near the door, several torches.

I sailed out into the rainy night. You are insane, I told myself. So what? my self said back. What good has sanity ever done you? Don't be hard on her, someone said. Her? Who? Charlotte? Rosalind? That face in the headlights –

The forest was black as pitch, a pitchy hell full of trees looming over me with terrible faces in their headlights –

The path was muddy. Long skidmarks marked my progress. The torch picked out the rotting leaves of last autumn squashed into the mud, their faces –

Oh, Hanno, someone moaned. Who? said someone else. I hate you, Charlotte Venables. Hate you hate you hate you. I want to annihilate your simpering face, I want you dead, I want myself dead.

The stile was slippery with rain, slimy bits of moss clung to my hand as I clambered over it. And then . . .

Surprise! A stage! A big one, too. Set for the drama of birth and death. Act One, scene one: a lambing field. Black night painted on the backcloth. Centrestage, a Land-Rover. On it, a single strong lamp zeroed in on a sheep lying on the grass. The sheep is bleating. Baa. Enter downstage right, the villain: Ros Rawlinson. Holding herself erect in her dripping oilskin, she makes her way across the field, malice in her heart, towards the unsuspecting heroine. Heroine: Charlotte Venables. Sturdy yeowoman sitting tailor-fashion in the back of her Land-Rover. The back is open. From the little nest she has made for herself out of old blankets, she watches the sheep.

Sheep: 'Baa.'

Ros Rawlinson: 'May I come in?'

Charlotte Venables: 'Of course.'

She scrunched to one side, hindered somewhat by the wheelcase. I climbed in and settled myself into a Buddha position like hers. Together we looked out into the night.

'Not much fun for you,' I said, waving a hand towards the sodden field and the sodden sheep.

'No.' Pause. 'Would you like some coffee?'

'Mmm, lovely.'

She reached behind and fetched a giant thermos. She filled the cup that was its cover and handed it to me.

'What about you?' I asked.

'I've just had some.'

Ever so polite, Charlotte and I. You could almost hear the teacups rattle in their saucers except that it was coffee and only one plastic cup. 'That sheep looks miserable,' I said. Well, there isn't exactly a lot of small talk available in a midnight lambing field.

'She is,' said mine hostess. 'She's supposed to be lambing, but she's having second thoughts. Trying to put off the dread moment.'

'I don't blame her. Couldn't this be done indoors?' And couldn't you ask what the hell I'm doing here?

'It can, but there's too much risk of infection spreading,' said the little shepherdess.

Damn you. Do you really think I squelched my way here to get a lesson on hill farming? Actress to playwright: how much more of this before we get to the action? Playwright to actress: up to you.

Okay. Without changing my tone one iota, I dropped my own little bombshell. 'That was a brilliant piece of upstaging.'

Pause. 'Sorry?'

Damn you damn you damn you. Have you got a mind at all in that pretty little head? 'This afternoon. In the forest. First that amazing display of acrobatics to catch the sheep, then planting the tree.'

At last! I could almost hear the little cogs crank into motion as she realised this wasn't just a polite calling-in-on-the-neighbours. 'I'm not sure I know what you're talking about. It wasn't intentional.'

Wasn't it? I drained the coffee cup and handed it back to her.

And then . . . panic. The script vanished and, like a sleepwalker, I awoke and saw where I was. What on earth was I doing here? What madness had put me in this grotesque situation? The cogs in my own brain were whirling like mad, trying to find a way to explain my insane visitation.

'I suppose you know why I came?' I said, stalling for time and hoping she would give me a cue.

'More or less. Your speech made it pretty clear.'

Speech? What speech? What the hell was she talking about? Then I remembered. The clearing. *As You Like It*. The Duke's words, which she had obviously overheard before crashing in on us. I reviewed the words quickly: Hath not old custom made this life more sweet than that of painted pomp? Are not these woods more free from peril than the envious court? Irrelevantly, a picture of the Royal Court Theatre flashed through my mind.

Good God. Of course! Suddenly I saw – she had misinterpreted the speech! Or rather, she thought I'd chosen it for its bearing on my own life. And David's. She thought I'd used it to announce my intention of leaving the 'painted pomp' of the stage . . . and returning to David's forest! A plan began to form.

'I never wanted to divorce David, you know,' I said carefully.

'Your personal life is none of my business.'

Liar. You're terrified that I've come back to reclaim David. 'It was a matter of logistics, that's all,' I added, keeping my voice neutral. 'David up here, me in London or touring or whatever. No marriage could take that kind of strain.' Too right. I thought of the last tour. A succession of images flew past: New York, sleet, phone, dressing-room, Hugh. The ghastly scene in the restaurant when he'd proposed –

Then it came to me, the bright idea I'd been praying for. Yes. Of course. *Test her*. See how she reacts to jealousy. Fool her into revealing her feelings. Taking a deep breath, I plunged into the heart of my role. 'But lately I've been wondering if some kind of a compromise would be possible. Then it came to me. It was so obvious I wondered why I hadn't thought of it before. There are heaps of nice estates in the Cotswolds, and it's just about near enough for David and Matti and me to live there with a *pied à terre* in London.'

I waited for her reply. Fury? Hysterics? Tears? Given how little anyone talked at The Folly, she probably wouldn't know much about David's past. She would see me as a formidable rival, even now.

But her voice was calm. 'What on earth would David do in the Cotswolds?'

'The same thing he does here. Plant trees. Train horses.

If Farleton Estate isn't worth enough to exchange for something there, I could probably make up the difference. It wouldn't have occurred to me if Hugh hadn't come to New York,' I added.

'What does Hugh have to do with it?'

'Property. He's a property developer. He talked a lot about some properties he has his eye on in the Cotswolds, and suddenly everything clicked into place.'

'David would never go to the Cotswolds.'

There was no emotion in her voice, nothing to betray a love for David. Was she extremely cunning? Or had I misread the scene in the clearing? Perhaps she didn't love him after all. 'I know that. Now,' I said, emphasising the last word. 'I didn't know, then, that there was anything keeping him up here. He'd always been so blasé about the "Farleton heritage", I was sure it wouldn't make any difference to him where he planted his trees. If he planted them near enough to London, we could get together again.'

Still no reaction.

'I didn't know then that there was something else keeping him here,' I added.

I watched her as closely as I could in the dark. Not a flicker. Was there nothing I could say that would shake her out of that bland Buddha pose? 'I didn't realise that he loved you,' I tried.

I thought I detected a slight jerk of her head, but it was so difficult to see anything.

'David loves everything and everyone on his estate,' she said at last. 'That's why the land responds so well to him. That's also why he wouldn't move to the Cotswolds, or anywhere else. It's only his ancestors and the whole business of "heritage" he despises. The land itself is different. He'd never leave that. If he's refused your offer, I'm sorry, but it's nothing to do with me.'

It was the longest speech she'd made and still it told me nothing. I would need to try something even stronger. 'That's not what Astrid says,' I stated.

'Astrid?'

'We're quite close, Astrid and me. She is looking after

my son. We keep in pretty close contact. She wasn't exactly forthcoming, but I finally convinced her that I needed to know what was going on. So she told me.'

At last she turned towards me. But if I'd hoped for a revelation, I was mistaken. 'Ros, I can assure you that nothing whatsoever is going on between David and me.'

I shrugged. 'That's David's problem Mine is that he's so obsessed with you that he'd never leave while you're here.'

'Ros, I'm sorry you're having problems, but I can tell you one thing: David isn't the slightest bit in love with me. Believe me, I'd know if he were. You must have misunderstood Astrid. Her English is pretty idiosyncratic.'

'David's English is fine. Astrid showed me a letter he'd written her last autumn, not long after he met you. David's English makes it perfectly clear.'

'This is ridiculous.'

'Is it? David and Astrid are pretty close, too. Who better to confide in than Astrid, safely in London for most of the year? He's got far too much pride to tell Brendan or Belle, knowing he'd have to suffer their well-meant sympathy every day.'

'He's got far too much pride to tell Astrid either – if there were anything to tell. It's totally out of character.'

'Exactly. He must have been in agony when he wrote that letter. Very likely he regretted it as soon as he sent it.'

'I don't believe a word of this.'

'Charlotte, I've *read* the letter. And when I saw the two of you together today, I knew it was true.'

Something was happening. We'd changed direction and hurtled on to a new plane so fast I felt dizzy. Without even noticing it we'd slipped into first-name terms and into a conversation both intimate and deadly earnest. What was I doing here? What was I trying to find out? What did I hope to accomplish?

Charlotte spoke again, her voice heavy with weariness. 'Well, if he was interested in me then, he isn't now, that I can promise you.'

Weariness . . . and sadness. Yes. My first intuition had been right. She did love him, and in the same obstinate and silent and despairing way that he loved her.

Her voice heavier than ever, she broke the silence again. 'What do you want of me?'

What indeed? I couldn't confess to her that I'd rushed out into the night with no thought in my head except the vague confused notion that there was unfinished business between us. There *was* unfinished business, but it had nothing to do with me. It was between David and Charlotte. I was only the intruder, the muddle-headed first wife descended on her to salt the wound which was of her own making, hers and David's. Despite my own anger and pride and frustration, I felt the first twinge of pity for this woman. But still I had to probe the wound, make one final attempt to force her into the light. 'It must have occurred to you that it wasn't easy for me to come and see you,' I said carefully.

She turned to me. I still couldn't see her, but I could feel a change had taken place in her mind. 'Why *did* you come?' she asked.

I would have to be very careful indeed from now on. She wasn't stupid. One false word and she would see through my act. I would have to play well my role as the first wife returned to claim her family back. Not a role I relished, but the only one that might tell me my own future with Matti. 'To ask your help,' I said quietly.

'What do you mean?'

We had arrived at last. 'If you were to make it clear to David that you're not interested in him, I think he might . . . change his mind. Be willing to leave.' Now. Say it, Charlotte. Turn to me with that proud little head of yours and say it. Show me your indignation and your love and I might even decide to help you, though it wouldn't be easy, for me or for you.

Then, 'It wouldn't make any difference,' she said.

A spurt of anger flashed through me. Damn you, woman, do you have any feelings at all other than pride? 'Then you refuse?' I said coldly.

'It wouldn't make any difference,' she said, impatient this time. 'It's much simpler than that. *David will not leave his land*. If you want him back, you'll have to come back here. I'm sure David would be delighted.'

I clamped my teeth together in barely suppressed rage. I had made a fool of myself and for no purpose at all. To her I was the successful rival and pride had made her strong in loss. There was no way now that she would come into the open.

The sheep was stirring. She bleated and looked at the Land-Rover. In a single neat and graceful move, Charlotte unwound her limbs and sprang out of the Land-Rover.

I followed her. Did she really think David wanted me back? If so, the depth of misunderstanding between them was profound. No wonder she was so careful to hide her own love. 'What makes you think so? Has he said anything to you?'

It was a ridiculous thought. In the next moment she negated it herself. 'Of course not. You should know by now: nobody at The Folly ever talks about their private lives.'

Too true. 'Then why are you so sure?' I persisted.

She stopped en route to the sheep and turned to me. It was raining harder than ever, thick columns of it illuminated in the light trained on the sheep. Charlotte was standing in that light, her face hard in the harsh beam. 'For someone who used to be married to him, you really don't know him very well,' she said. 'Have you ever thought what it feels like to have planted hundreds of thousands of trees? Do you really think he could leave them, just swap them for another bunch planted by someone else?'

I don't know which of us I hated more at that moment: Charlotte for her cold obstinacy or myself for having been fool enough to meddle. 'For love?' I taunted.

Her face was glowing with a perverse superiority. 'There's more than one kind of love,' she said. Then she turned abruptly and rushed off to her sheep.

34

I sat by the little table, a virgin sheet of paper in front of me, a pen in my hand, nothing in my head. I'd pushed the bowl of narcissi to the back of the table to make room. They were fully open now, clouds of scent rising from them and soothing my aching head. It had been so long since I'd slept. I was used to scanty sleep – the hyped-up state after the curtain fell made sleep long in the coming – but this was different. Then there was exhilaration. Now there was only pain.

I felt trapped. I had rashly gone into the lambing field and started a conversation that had led nowhere. The unfinished business was more unfinished than ever. I needed to end it – if possible in a way which would salvage something from that ghastly scene and ensure some sort of a future with Matti. I had no future anywhere else.

Two faces. Charlotte hard and proud and superior in the harsh light from the Land-Rover. Charlotte soft and loving after planting the little oak. It was clear enough now that she loved David, and equally clear that she would never say so either to David or to me. Astrid was right. They needed to have their heads knocked together.

I smiled despite my anger and frustration. One tiny shred of me which hadn't hardened felt a reluctant admiration for Charlotte Venables. She had parried my questions beautifully. She had kept her secret safe, at least on the surface.

My hand began writing without consulting my brain:

Dear Charlotte,
All right, you win.

I stared at the words, picturing her expression as she read them. Would she understand the reference? Or would she think I was conceding victory over David? I couldn't let her think that. Vigorously now, my hand continued:

There's just one thing I want to say. You didn't fool me. You may have fooled the others and even David, but not me.

Good. It acknowledged her victory in the battle of wits but exposed her failure to conceal her love for David. But did she really love him? I saw again that hard face. Might she be just a very clever golddigger? David didn't have much money but the estate was worth a great deal. There was also the prestige of being the squire's wife – quite a coup for a farmer's daughter. She could well be playing an elaborate game to ensnare David. Her resentment at my intrusion could be just a fear of exposure, of her plan failing.

I tore up the page and started again:

Dear Charlotte,
All right, you win. There are just two things I want to say. The first is to let you know that you didn't fool me. You may have fooled the others and even David, but not me. Within minutes of your dramatic entrance in that clearing I had a pretty good idea of how things stood – both ways.

Much better. Nice and ambiguous. If she was a gold-digger, she would get the message. If she did love David, she would get another message. I went on quickly:

The second is to let you know that the estate is tied up – that was part of the divorce settlement. When David dies, the whole lot goes to Matti, and there's nothing anyone can do about it. You won't get a look in, nor will any kids you and David have. If that doesn't bother you, fine. It would sure as hell bother me, and it may explain why David's been so slow: in financial terms, he's got nothing to offer.

Better still. No golddigger would look twice at David after that, and to ingratiate herself with Matti would be useless: the most she could hope to become was a small-time dowager. She had too much pride for that.

And now my own pride faltered. I had to say something about Matti, but however I moved the words about in my head, they came out as a plea. I remembered her other face, the one soft with love after planting the tree. If she could feel that way about a tree, surely she would understand my feelings for my child? I had to risk it.

One last thing. Please don't turn Matti against me. Astrid's been marvellous, and even David has refrained. If there's anything I regret about my life, it's what I did to Matti. It's a rotten lousy trick – bringing a kid into the world to solve his parents' problems. I wouldn't blame him one bit if he hated both of us. The only reason he doesn't is Astrid. Astrid's the only person I know who understands what totally unselfish love is. Hugh was an ass to divorce her. I told him so when he came to see me in New York. He was not amused. So please don't turn Matti against me. You may not believe this, but in my own way I love him very much. Leave me something for my old age, please.

There. It was done. I had handed my future to her. I had put myself at her mercy. It grated – my God, did it grate – but I had to do it.

I read the letter over and over. What now? I had to leave The Folly tomorrow. I couldn't stay in the same house as David after this, and I couldn't risk meeting Charlotte again. I would post the letter on my way to London.

I pictured its reception in her little farmhouse. What would she make of it? I had made clear that I'd seen the truth: that she loved David and that he loved her. Would she still set that stubborn little jaw of hers and deny it, for weeks, for months? For ever? Astrid would confront David with his own letter, but would he take any notice of that either?

I stood up in sudden disgust. A plague on both their houses. Why should I care what happened to either of them, when they didn't care themselves?

And then, even more suddenly, I did care. The image I hadn't wanted to see swam across my sleepy vision. David and Charlotte together. Happy. Astrid was right about that, too. They were a perfect match. If only something could break through their stubbornness and make them acknowledge the obvious.

And then an extraordinary thing happened. My anger and my hatred vanished, melted away in a surge which made my legs so weak I had to sit down. David, he whom I had loved so much, if unwisely, had a second chance. This time he could be loved much *and* wisely. How could I be such a bitch to begrudge him? I, too, had had a second chance, and had come so close, so close . . .

Suddenly the other face, the one I'd been denying for so long, began to glow against the screen of my mind. In letting go of my defensive anger against Charlotte, I had relinquished all my other defences, too. I sat there, helpless now, as the golden warmth of his smile shone through at me. Oh, Hanno. Hanno. Hanno.

I folded my arms on the table, let my head sink to them and wept.

Morning. A tiny furtive sound below. I woke up and with one half-open eye peered through the railings of the sleeping balcony.

Matti, sitting at the little table. In front of him a huge mug of tea. Over it his small hands, trying to keep the warmth in.

I pried open my other eye. The duvet rustled.

Matti looked up. 'Mummy is a lazy old cow.'
'Matti is a rude little boy.'
'It's half past eleven.'
'What are you – some kind of talking Teasmaid?'
'If you say "please" I'll bring it up to you.'
'Please. Bet you can't get it up here without spilling.'
'Bet I can.'
I watched his slow careful progress up the stairs. Dear God, what a beautiful child. How had we created such a wonder out of that tormented marriage?
He arrived with the tea intact. Solemnly he handed it to me.
'Thank you.'
He nodded and, relieved of his burden, sat down on the bed with a *phlumph*. The tea sloshed over the sides. I sighed.
'Belle says are you coming down for lunch?'
'Of course. Even lazy old cows need to eat. Where's your father?'
'Planting trees.'
'Why aren't you with him?'
'I was. Now I'm with you, being the talking Teasmaid.' He smirked.
I took a few gulps of the hot tea and felt almost human. 'Is he coming back for lunch?'
'Dunno.'
I took a few more gulps. 'Matti, will you do something for me? Will you go back to your father and persuade him to come home for lunch? I want to give him something, but don't say that or he won't come. Just use all your wicked little charms to get him to come home. Will you do that for me?'
The smirk split open into a grin. Flattery does wonders with children, whatever the textbooks say.

Lunch. All six of us sitting around the big old table in the kitchen – Matti's charms had done the trick. David was across from me, Matti by my side. Matti was watching me. He knew something was up and he wasn't very good at disguising it. Within minutes I could tell that everyone knew something was up, everyone except David, ponderously eating his bread and cheese and talking with Brendan about some piece of harness that needed repairing before the students returned next week.

When lunch was over, I asked David if I could have a word with him in the library.

'Can't it wait till this evening?'

'There's plenty of daylight these days. You can spare me a few minutes.'

We left the kitchen together. After today, I would never see this kitchen again. We entered the library, with its dark oak bookshelves and comfortable old leather chairs and the light streaming greyly through the tall windows. I would never see the library again either. This was my final farewell to The Folly, though David didn't know it. Nobody knew it except me.

We didn't sit down. There was no need.

'David, I want to ask two favours of you. If you say yes, I'll never ask you for anything else again. I'll leave your life altogether. You'll never have to see me again.'

He frowned, suspicious, as always, of anything to do with me. I couldn't blame him. I'd brought little enough happiness to his life.

'Will you agree?'

'It depends what they are.'

'First, will you promise me that you'll never try to change our agreement about Matti? That you'll let him live with Astrid until he finishes school? After that, if he goes to university – and he probably will – it'll be up to him where he lives.'

'I've never tried to change it before. Why should I now?'

Because your whole life is going to change before this day is over, I could have said, but didn't. 'Will you just promise me that? If you do, I know you'll keep your word. I trust you.' That was certainly true. Whatever his faults, he had a strong sense of honour. He rarely promised anything, but when he did, he never went back on his word.

'All right,' he said slowly. 'I promise.'

And that was that. So simple. It was all over, the months of agonising. Already I could feel my head lighten with relief. I still had something, something. 'Thank you. My second request is that you deliver this letter to Charlotte Venables –'

His head shot up and his face darkened with suspicion.

'– deliver it to her in person and stay while she reads it.'

'What's Charlotte to do with you?'

Quite a lot, I could have said, but didn't. 'David, just this once, please will you trust me? I trust you. Couldn't you do me a little simple justice and trust me, too?'

Silence.

'I mean you no harm, David. I give you my word. If you hand over this letter and stay while she reads it, you won't regret it.'

Silence.

'If you refuse,' I added, 'I'll simply post it.'

That he did register. His frown deepened.

'You can't prevent me from posting it. But it would be much better *for you* if you delivered it in person.' I smiled. 'After all, I'm trusting you not to tear it up or read it yourself. Can't you trust me?'

'Why don't you deliver it yourself?' he said at last.

'Because,' I said softly, 'I'm leaving this house in a few minutes and I'm never coming back. I want to do one good thing before I go, and this is it.'

The heavy features relaxed a little and he almost smiled. With relief at the thought of my departure? Or did some tiny disused memory of the good times we had shared – and there had been some – come back to remind him that I wasn't quite so bad as he thought?

I grasped the hope of the latter. 'David, I wish we could be friends. But if that's not possible, can we at least not be enemies? I'd like to leave this house feeling a little bit like a human being. If you'll take this letter, I can do that. Will you? Please?'

Still visibly reluctant, he took the letter.

'And you'll promise to deliver it and stay while she reads it?'

A long pause. Then, 'I promise.'

I wished I could put my arms around that big dark body of his just one last time, for a little bit of comfort, a proper farewell. Perhaps the time would come when such things might be possible, an unimaginable time of reconciliation. Perhaps, but not yet.

'Thank you,' I said instead.

The Tudor Room, my room for the last time. I would miss it. I hadn't come often to The Folly since the divorce, but I saw now how much those visits had meant. They'd been a small link with the past. After today, even that would be gone. The whole of my past was leaving me today. The years with Hanno had already gone. Now the years with David would vanish, too. I would be adrift in the present and would have to make some sort of future for myself out of nothing.

It didn't take long to pack the few things I'd brought. I sat down at the table to think. It seemed centuries ago that I'd written the letter at that same table. I'd added one more line: *You can let David read this if you wish. It's up to you.* Then I'd signed my name.

Would she let him read it? In the letter was a stark acknowledgment of their mutual love. Why they'd hidden this from each other and even perhaps from themselves I couldn't imagine, but if they read it together, it would be out in the open at last. Charlotte would need courage to show him the letter. I hoped she had it. In detaching myself from my past, I'd detached myself from all the hurt and jealousy I'd felt towards Charlotte. If she was the right person for David, if she could give him a second chance, then I wished her well.

I stood up briskly. Next problem: how to explain a departure as sudden as my arrival had been. I wished I could just slip away, but that wouldn't be fair. I would have to say goodbye to Belle and Matti at least, come up with some excuse for leaving earlier than planned. Despite my years on the stage, I wasn't a very good liar. Acting isn't a lie, it's just a different kind of truth.

I tried to remember where everyone was. David and Brendan were in the forest with Matti. I didn't know where Astrid was, but Belle would almost certainly be in the kitchen. I needed to have the kitchen to myself for just a few minutes. Then I could pretend I'd had an urgent phone call, something to summon me away. Yes, that was it. I would skulk around a bit, wait for Belle to go out into the garden. Then I could –

'ROS.'

The voice was loud but distant: Belle, calling out through the vast house. I opened the door and yelled back:

'YES?'

'TELEPHONE.'

I nearly giggled with the shock of it. What a *deus ex machina*! Whoever it was, all I had to do was compose my lines to give the impression that this was the urgent summons.

Only when I began the long run through the house did I wonder who it actually was. I was notoriously close about my private life, hardly anyone in the trade knew anything about The Folly. The only person who knew I was here was –

'Rosalind. If you hang up on me I'm going to take the first train to Yorkshire and come to The Folly in person, and I'm going to make such an ugly scene there that you'll regret not listening to me. Do you understand?'

There was no soft golden glow in his voice now. It was hard and urgent, like the eyes of the golden stag.

'Do you understand, Rosalind?'

Behind me, Belle bustled about the kitchen. 'Yes,' I said.

'Good. I want you to come home at once. Make any excuse you like. Tell them you've got to see someone at the RSC first thing tomorrow morning. Tell them you've just been offered Lady Macbeth. It's more or less true. They won't know the talks aren't until next month.'

'Why?'

'*Why*? Because we have to talk, isn't it obvious?'
'What about?'
'God damn you, Rosalind, don't talk like a stupid child! I tried to stop you. You wouldn't listen. Now I'm going to make you listen. If you won't come here, I'll come up there, and you won't like it.'
'Where are you?'
'Home. *Our* home, Rosalind. Remember?'
'That's not my –' I stopped. I'd meant to say it wasn't my home any more, but Belle was there, somewhere behind me. I would have to choose my words with care.
'Is there someone else in the room?' he asked.
'Yes.'
'Don't waste any more time on the phone. Get here as fast as you can. If you're not here by six o'clock, I'm coming north.'

35

At five minutes to six I pulled up in front of the house. *Our* house, Hanno had said, but it wasn't, not any more. We would have to sell it. Hanno would probably re-assemble his lair in Wigmore Street. I would find a flat, something new and impersonal, a box to park myself in when I wasn't at the theatre.

I'd done a lot of thinking as I drove south. My small act of generosity towards David and Charlotte had done me as much good as I hoped it would do them. I felt clean again. I was still human, still capable of rising above my petty feelings. Driving along, I had taken a dispassionate view of what was left from the wreckage.

No Hanno. No Folly. But there were two things left. I knew now that David and Charlotte would leave Matti with Astrid. I would still be able to see him. That was a lot.

And then there was the theatre. That was a lot, too. I would have to find another agent, of course. That would create a buzz of consternation. None of his clients had ever left him. But theatre people knew we were living together; I would present it as a simple break-up of an affair. The fuss would die down eventually. Perhaps I wouldn't bother with another agent. Anyone else would be a disappointment after Hanno. I could plan my own career, teach myself how to negotiate my own contracts. I would make mistakes and lose some money but I could afford to. Yes, that would be best. To be entirely on my own. In the clean cool air I would now inhabit.

It was still some way from dusk but there were lights on in the house. A distant clock struck the hour. I got out of the car.

I wasn't looking forward to this meeting but I supposed it was necessary. There would be practicalities to discuss, just as in the break-up of a marriage. I hoped we would be civilised. My act of love towards David and Charlotte – and it was that, however terse the wording of the letter – had given me back some dignity. I hoped Hanno would let me keep it. I needed that to stay in this high cool realm.

I walked up to the front door. It was possible that Hanno would try to persuade me to stay with him. I hoped not. I could never live with him again, not with that demonic face of his mother forever between us. Nor could I expect him to abandon his family. They needed him for Joachim's sake.

The door opened and there was Hanno. My innards gave such a colossal wrench that I could hardly remain upright. I still loved him, probably would love him till the day I died. That, too, I had taken into account. It would be useless to deny it. I would love him silently, with dignity, and at a great distance.

'Thank you for coming,' he said simply.

I nodded, remembering our first meeting at his office. The same courteous formality which made him so different. I loved it. I loved a lot of things about Hanno.

I walked through into the hall and set my suitcase down. 'Where would you like to talk?'

'The kitchen, please. Have you eaten?'

'Yes.' I had stopped at one of those huge soulless complexes along the motorway and had a plastic sandwich. I'd felt at home there. It was about halfway between Yorkshire and London and I'd thought yes, this is where I belong. One of the soulless, adrift, en route.

We went through into the kitchen. It was a nice room, with french windows out into the garden at the back. It was just big enough to take a smallish pine table in the middle. We'd spent a lot of time in this room, Hanno and I, cooking our simple meals together and wandering out into the garden with our coffee. I'd always tried to have a little jar of flowers on the table – in winter just a few twigs with nice coloured bark and a bit of juniper from the garden.

There were no flowers now, but there was something else in the centre of the table, illuminated by the soft glow of the wicker lampshade above. The ring.

'Would you like something to drink?' he asked. 'There's white wine in the fridge. I'm having tea – I'm driving back to Joachim's Wood tonight. I hope you'll come with me.'

'You know that's impossible.'

'Please don't say anything until we've talked.' He put the kettle on and then stood by the fridge. 'Wine?'

'Yes, please.'

I sat down at the table, carefully avoiding the ring. I didn't want to see it but it was difficult to avoid, right there in the centre of the table in the centre of the room.

Hanno poured out a glass of wine and handed it to me. I took a sip and watched him make his tea. He never drank English tea, always China tea in elegant cups. A leftover from his days in Germany and Austria, he said, though he'd said little else about those days. And more remembering: the night I'd lurched into his lair and he'd made coffee for us in the hidden room. Yes, a born bachelor, at home with these little tasks.

Finally he sat down with his tea. The rich smoky scent of Lapsang rose on the grey swirls of steam reaching for the wicker lampshade. 'First,' he said, 'I want to apologise. Though it's a weak word, isn't it? After what you've gone through. And it's all my fault.'

'It was the wrong moment after all,' I said mildly. 'For once your intuition failed you. Not that there would have been a right moment.'

'Not that,' he said. 'What was wrong was that I didn't tell you the truth long ago. I hoped to avoid it. I was afraid you would leave me if you knew who and what I am.'

'*Teufelskind*?' I said lightly.

There was nothing light in his reply. 'Yes. More or less.'

I stared into his golden eyes. I expected them to have altered beyond recognition after that bizarre announcement. At the very least I expected the hard gleaming eyes of the golden stag. But there was only sadness. 'What do you mean?'

'You must have wondered whether there was something . . . wrong . . . with our family. To have produced Joachim. Something genetic.'

'Yes. I did suspect there might be something.'

'So perhaps you understand why I lived as I did. Why I never married. Though it's true, too, that I was never tempted until I met you. Until I met you, it didn't matter very much. Then everything changed. And you were young then. You already had one child. I was afraid you would want another, with me, if – And of course that was out of the question.'

'"If people thought only about the children, few would be born."'

He nodded.

'You could have told me.'

'Not without telling you about Joachim.'

'I see that. But afterwards, after I met him and heard the story . . .'

'I haven't told you everything even now. That's what I have to decide tonight.'

'I see.'

'No. You don't see. You have no idea. And it may turn out to be best to keep it that way.'

'Are you testing me, Hanno?'

'I have no right to test you. I had no right to fall in love with you either.'

There was a long silence. Despite the circumstances, it felt almost companionable. We'd been together so long, Hanno and I, first professionally and then as lovers, that it was difficult to break the habit of simply loving to be with him. Difficult, too, not to smile and say, 'And did you love me at first sight?'

His smile, too, felt inevitable as he said, 'Would I be so crude? I'd seen a great many pretty faces before yours, and talent, too. No, I used the wrong words. I didn't "fall in love" with you. I grew into loving you. As the human being behind the face and talent began to grow. I watched you with wonder, Rosalind. From a bleak childhood and an unhappy marriage, something beautiful was emerging. Will you allow me to use an old-fashioned word and tell you that I came to love your soul? *Geist*. Spirit. Essence. What you will.'

I bowed my head under the weight of his respect. So much I was losing. If only it had been a trivial affair, bodies only, the dazzle of good-looking façades. 'You loved your creation,' I tried. 'You created me, like Svengali created his Trilby.'

'I created nothing. I only guided your career.'

I looked up again, into a face soft with love. Don't make it so difficult, Hanno. I had wanted us to be civilised. Now I wished for a sharp vulgar end to it all. I couldn't bear this much longer.

'But you were married,' he went on. 'And then, after the divorce, you were still young. You would marry again, I thought, and have children. I didn't dare hope. But as time passed and you didn't remarry, I did begin to hope. Part of me wanted you to start a new life for yourself; another part hoped that the time would come when we . . .' He smiled. 'Each year that brought you nearer to middle-age brought you nearer to me. The years you cursed, I blessed.'

'You gave no sign of it.'

'I didn't want to prejudice your future. I wanted you to be free. If someone else had come along who could make you happy, I would have had to accept it.'

The generosity of my lover. In comparison with his patient waiting, my own small act towards David and Charlotte shrank to the meagre offering it was. Oh, Hanno.

'And then it happened as I'd hoped,' he said. 'At first I was wary of living with you, always fearing the desire for a child. But the years continued to pass.'

And then I came back from New York. The child-bearing years, at least the safe ones, were over. And he had given me the second magic day in London, and the ring had appeared, as if by its own magic. I looked at it now, giving out its steady message of potential waiting to be fulfilled. Too late.

'And then, as you said, my intuition failed, in the most stupid way imaginable,' he said. 'I had counted those years of yours so fervently that they were engraved on my mind. I completely forgot that they weren't engraved on my parents' minds. Without even thinking, I took for granted that they knew there was no danger of a child. And you look so young. I had forgotten that, too. If I had told them myself, as you wanted me to do, I could have told them, too, that there would be no child. That terrible scene would never have happened. They would have welcomed you with such joy. Instead . . .' He raised his hands in a gesture of helplessness. 'All that pain you suffered, and all of it avoidable, if only I had *thought*.' His face twisted in a grimace of self-disgust. 'So often you've called me "infallible". Well. Am I infallible now?'

I said nothing. I couldn't speak, couldn't think. This wasn't at all what I'd anticipated. I'd suspected the heredity factor, yes, but in the pain and humiliation after that hideous scene with his parents it had never occurred to me to make the connection. It wasn't only Hanno who had failed to think. My own mind had frozen up with shock, refused entry to any thoughts connected with what had happened at Joachim's Wood.

'So you see why the word "apology" is so inadequate, why I trip over my words in so clumsy a manner. Trying to find the ones that can express . . . that can erase, though nothing can. Trying to tell you that I understand your pain, why you drove away so fast and wouldn't listen even though I cursed you for not stopping and listening. I've felt your pain in my own body and mind these two days and hated myself for being the cause. Trying to find a way to ask you to forgive me.'

'Hanno –'

'To find some way of telling you I love you so much, Rosalind.'

'Hanno –'

'To beg you not to throw away what we had, what we could still have –'

And for the second time in two days, I wept. And then Hanno's arms were around me – clumsy, like his words, because the chair was in the way – and he was saying, 'Don't keep me out, Rosalind, this is us together, please let us be together,' and my own arms were around him, clumsy too, and my voice was saying, 'Yes, yes, yes,' because there was nothing else to say. All the misery of those two days was dissolving. We had been frozen inside a huge river, two small foolish creatures who had wandered into the water at the wrong moment and been trapped in the ice as it formed around us. Now, like a Russian spring, the ice was breaking up with thunderous explosions, the water surging forward in a great rush, carrying us with it.

And then, the quiet peace of the flowing river, summer, as if it had never happened. We clung to each other for a long time, Hanno and I, not daring to release each other for fear the ice might creep back and take possession again. So fragile it all felt, and at the same time so strong. This was how we were meant to be. How had it been delayed for so long? During that time which seemed both brief and endless, our whole life together until this moment seemed to slip away, an unreal prelude that had been waiting for this.

'Oh, Hanno,' I whispered. 'How foolish we've been. Not only you. I should have spoken out, asked you about your past, your family. I respected your privacy too much. If I'd loved better, I would have understood that I had to break through the barriers.'

'I should have trusted you more. I was afraid you would go away if you knew everything. I settled for a love based on not knowing because I was afraid to risk more, and I dragged you along with me through that half-life. And the terrible thing is that I'm still afraid.'

'But why? Isn't it obvious now? I *will* go back with you now, tonight, to Joachim's Wood. We'll face your parents together. I'm frightened, of course, but this time it'll be all right. We'll talk, all of us together, and everything will be all right. Won't it, Hanno?'

Something strange was happening, far more frightening even than the memory of Mrs Hirsch's horrified face. Hanno was retreating again. I could feel his muscles tense, see his face clouding over.

'Hanno, it will be all right, won't it?'

He moved away from me. Immediately I felt the loss of warmth, as if the ice were creeping back.

'Hanno?'

He sat down opposite me again. He was avoiding my eyes. He was watching the ring in the centre of the table with a strange expression on his face.

'Hanno?'

Finally he looked up at me. 'I'm still afraid, Rosalind.'

'But why?'

'I haven't told you everything. Part of me wants to retreat again into the half-truths. To pick up this ring and put it on your finger and pretend that everything will be all right. But it won't. Something will happen again – in a year, five, ten. And then it'll be too late.'

'These are riddles, Hanno. I don't understand.'

'No. There's no way you could. You only guessed a part of the truth, and it's the smaller part. I have to decide whether to tell you the rest.'

'Isn't this something we should decide together?'

He said nothing for a long time. Then, 'Yes. I think it is. *Do* you want to know, Rosalind? Knowing that once I've told you everything, you might turn away from me with disgust? Do you want to risk this?'

My mind was racing. I was a coward, too. What we had, after tonight, seemed so much. Surely it was sufficient? I thought of Bluebeard's castle. Judith had wanted to know, too. The Duke had warned her but she hadn't listened. One by one she'd made him open the secret doors. And, behind the last one, her own destruction. I shivered, trying to think what could ever make me feel disgust towards Hanno. Had he murdered? Was that why he'd fled Vienna at the height of his fame? Only something that strong could explain his fear. But murderers had wives, parents, friends. There might be – what were they called? – extenuating circumstances. It might be possible, yes, just possible . . .

'Think carefully, Rosalind.'

I was thinking. If I failed him now, I would always wonder what was behind that last door, and the wondering would be its own destruction. Yes, I had to know.

I nodded, not trusting my voice.

'You want to know?'

'Yes,' I whispered.

Again he fell silent. Would he withhold it himself? It was, after all, *our* decision, not mine alone.

Then, 'If I tell you this thing, I have to ask you never to reveal it to anyone else.'

The priest at the confessional. Listening to the murderer's account.

'And I have to ask you to promise before I tell you any more. I know that's unfair to you, but it's necessary.'

The priest, forbidden to go to the police with his knowledge.

'Nobody knows this except my parents.'

I looked up hopefully. If his parents knew . . . And they certainly hadn't rejected him. Surely I could love him as steadily as his parents could.

'Are you willing to promise me this, Rosalind?'

'Yes.'

We looked into each other's eyes for a long time, as if feeding off each other to gain sustenance for what was to come. Then he began.

'Once upon a time,' he said, more to himself than to me. 'That's how it should begin. Like all stories dealing with unreal worlds. Though the place where this one begins is real enough: Vienna. But already the unreality creeps in, because this was Vienna during the First World War, an unreal time. Near the end of that war, two children were born, twins. Their father, a soldier, was dead, although their mother didn't know that. She was near death herself.

There was a severe food shortage at that time, and the famous influenza which killed more people after the war than the war itself killed had already begun its work. The mother, probably weakened already by hunger and childbirth, died soon after the children were born.

'Nature has its own kind of brutality. The children born in those tragic circumstances – and they were no less tragic for being common – the children were strong and healthy, everything their parents could have hoped for if there had been parents left to hope. The surviving relatives felt more ambiguous. Most had children of their own and little enough to feed them on. Two more mouths were hardly welcome. None the less, people do their best in these circumstances. The children went to relatives and the relatives looked after them as best they could.

'The story now moves from one war to another. Or rather, to the Anschluss which was for the Austrians the beginning of the Second World War. And another soldier, this time a young conscript in the German army. You will have read many accounts of the day, wave after wave of soldiers, an endless sea of soldiers, marching triumphantly through the city while the citizens, or many of them, waved and cheered and welcomed their ally the invader.

'Well, in those tumultuous crowds there was a girl who didn't welcome the invader. She had been brought up as a socialist in a socialist household and was herself a socialist through and through. This was common enough – Vienna had a long and successful history as a socialist city. But in the early thirties, all this changed. The socialists went underground and with them the young girl. As soon as she was old enough, she became a part of a socialist cell and did what little anyone could do to keep alive the idea of an alternative to the Nazis.

'Possibly the girl saw the soldier in that sea of seemingly identical faces surging through her city, but if so, only as the briefest of glimpses. They didn't meet until some time later, in a café, when the soldier was off duty. A more unlikely pair would be difficult to imagine: the fiery little socialist and the Nazi soldier. Except that the young man was far from being a Nazi. He was a student and a poet, and insofar as he had any political views, he was mildly contemptuous of the Nazis for the simple reason that they had no aesthetic sensibilities at all.

'It was less dangerous than you might think to express these views, providing it was done with care and moderation. And so it was that the young girl began to realise that the young man was quite different than he had at first seemed. This was just as well, as she had fallen hopelessly in love with him more or less at first sight, and he with her.

'You asked if I loved you at first sight. No. Absolutely not. And again no. If I've learned one thing in life it's the folly of unthinking love. Not that any amount of wisdom can prevent it, but at least caution can temper the first madness.

'Not so with these two. They were young and inexperienced; there was nothing that could withhold the passion which consumed them, and it was merely good fortune that these seemingly disparate people had minds capable of a longer relationship.

'It was the only good fortune they had. After much bureaucratic difficulty and delay, they married. It amused them both that they bore the same surname, and there were jokes among friends of the sort when in England a Smith marries a Smith.

'Well, soon the joking stopped. The war began in earnest, and at the same time the young wife discovered that she was pregnant. It was a difficult pregnancy and not helped by the circumstances of the war. As time passed, one of the reasons for her poor state became apparent: she was told that she was probably carrying twins. Soon after that, a second problem began to emerge. The young woman belonged to an extremely rare blood type, so rare that for some years she had been registered to give blood at regular and frequent intervals, as frequent as was safe.

'As the pregnancy progressed it became clear that she was likely to lose much blood and require perhaps more than one transfusion. As you may imagine, these were not the best of times to require quantities of such a rare blood type. And so it seemed like a miracle when the young man disclosed that he was also of this rare blood type.

'Did they ever do more than marvel at this extraordinary coincidence? Did they reflect on a second coincidence, one which had amused them in their whirlwind courtship: the similarity of their eyes, their unusual gold-flecked eyes? Did they think about that third coincidence, the fact that they bore the same surname, albeit the very common one of Hirsch?'

36

Until now Hanno had narrated his story in the same calm voice that had always made me feel so confident in his presence. Only as he neared the end did a tremor begin to appear. His hands, which had held the tea cup so casually, now tightened round the fragile china.

And did I see where the story was leading? Did I begin to make the same connections which the young lovers might or might not have made at that time? I'm not sure. All I knew was that both the high cool place I had inhabited while driving south, and the new warmth of our reconciliation, were leaving me. I was moving into a third sphere which I didn't understand, a frightening limbo in which I could do nothing but wait.

'The twins which she was bearing were, of course, Joachim and myself,' Hanno continued. 'It was an extremely difficult birth, as expected, and, as expected, transfusions were needed. It was some months before she recovered, and by that time her husband had left Vienna, transferred along with the rest of his unit.

'There's little to say about the war years except that they were hard, and made harder still by the absence of the children's father. The years after the war were hard, too, but at least the family was reunited. I won't pretend to remember much of these times. Despite what you say about my phenomenal memory, it's no better than anyone else's in remembering early childhood. Perhaps, too, I blotted it out. All I remember was feeling extraordinarily close to my brother, as is so often the case with identical twins.

'It's possible, then, that I was the first to sense that something was wrong with Joachim. We had a clear line of direct communication – then as now – which needed no words. Very probably I felt this line begin to give off signals which I didn't understand. But I would have been too young to express this to anyone else, only to Joachim. In any case, no early warning would have helped. The fault was genetic and would quietly work itself out until the end. No intervention then or now could prevent this.

'When the fault began to be apparent, our parents sought medical advice, and after much confusion and contradictory opinion, they discovered that Joachim had an extremely rare disease of the nervous system. As rare as the blood group so strangely shared by his parents.

'It's easy now, in telling the story, to see the connections which they should themselves have seen. But the reason for their prolonged ignorance, if this was the case, is not so difficult to understand either. In those days, the late 1930s and throughout the war, people were cautious in what they chose to disclose about themselves. An Austrian socialist and a German soldier would be more cautious still. When they realised that their politics were not incompatible after all, they must have felt considerable relief and a desire not to probe further.

'Do you see the parallel, Rosalind? For years you and I lived together in careful ignorance. The blame is mine more than yours. You spoke honestly about your past. I failed to reciprocate. I had good reasons, of course – just as my parents did, though the reasons were different. But with us, as with them, the unsaid things did their secret work of destruction.

'Even when Joachim's condition was revealed, his parents failed to ask of themselves and each other things which might have helped them to understand. I find it difficult to be censorious. Apart from everything else, their daily lives were now so shattered that there was little time or energy left for the necessary talking. Joachim deteriorated rapidly. Even worse, the neighbourhood children were beginning to sense his strangeness and torment him. This you've already heard about from my parents. I did what I could to protect my brother. The bond of communication and love between us was the one thing left untouched by the disease and is as strong today as it was on the day of our birth. But I was only one and the neighbourhood children were many. Our parents began to move, more and more frequently, but always the children appeared, like packs of wild dogs. We became refugees in our own city.

'I wish I could describe to you a clear and simple day when our parents finally opened up the Pandora's Box of their past, but this never happened. It was a slow and clumsy process. And so, in telling you the story of their lives, I lie by turning it into the connected story it never was. None the less, I can't bear to talk about this much longer, Rosalind, and so forgive me if I rush to the end.

'You probably suspect the truth already. The story is simple enough. My mother – Joachim's mother – was one of the twin children of that woman who died so soon after their birth during the First World War. Because of the difficulties of the time, the twins were separated, each taken into the care of different relatives. At first the two families were in touch with each other. Then, for reasons nobody knows, this communication ceased. The relatives who had taken charge of the other twin, the boy, moved to Germany. He was brought up as a German. In due course, he was conscripted into the German army and returned to his native city on the day of the Anschluss. That boy was my father. His wife was his sister, his *twin* sister. And out of this incestuous love they themselves bore twins. The rest you know.'

It had become nearly dark outside while Hanno narrated his story. The french windows were rich midnight blue oblongs neatly dissected into white-framed segments. Out there in the near-dark a last late blackbird kept up his song in our garden, no doubt celebrating the victory of his perseverance against his rivals. The kitchen light laid a silvery path through the blue and illuminated a clump of daffodils near the door.

I observed these things because I was afraid to observe

what mattered. Finally I turned my bewildered gaze on Hanno. The light from the wicker lampshade was soft. It softened the vertical lines of his face. It glanced off the golden flecks in his eyes. His eyes and Joachim's, so alike, and the eyes of their parents, too. How could it be otherwise? They were a closed circle, the four of them. There was no input from anywhere else and never would be. A closed circle, the end of the line.

Then I saw what I had most feared to see: the fear in Hanno's eyes. He was motionless and to an outside observer would have appeared quite calm, but moving restlessly beneath that calm was the fear that shouldn't be there.

'Hanno.' I reached across the table and put my hand on his. There were so many things I could have said, above all that none of this would make any difference to us. But even that thought, so important to our future, seemed insignificant in the light of what I'd just heard.

The divine abomination. Zeus and Hera. Siegmund and Sieglinde, twins conceived by the god and themselves bearing the hero Siegfried. Isis and Osiris, brother and sister and parents of the god Horus. The royal incest marriages of the ancient Egyptians that made them gods. Cursed and blessed. Above all, outside. Set apart by awe or horror from the normal dealings of the human world. What could I say to Hanno to let him know that I understood both the awe and the horror that had set his own family apart for two generations?

I held his hand a little tighter. 'Hanno, thank you for telling me. I wish you'd told me long ago, but I understand why you didn't.'

Such feeble words. And yet, they were a start. He had been looking down at the table. Now he raised his eyes and I thought I glimpsed the smallest glimmer of something beyond the fear and despair.

And then, in a belated rush, all the things which had puzzled and disturbed me for so long began to fall into place. The reason for Joachim's Wood. It wasn't only the fear for his safety. It was the symbol of a separateness already there from birth. They *had* to live outside the normal. And the strength of the bond between Hanno and Joachim, which had always seemed even more powerful and mysterious than that between ordinary twins. Twins of twins, the power magnified.

And above all, I now understood the aura which seemed to surround Hanno himself. *Wunderkind*, they called him, and *Teufelskind*. Child of wonder, child of the devil. Both god and demon. It was hardly surprising that he was in touch with a reality beyond normal reality and closed to everyone else. That uncanny intuition which he either denied altogether or attributed to Joachim. It was his own, had been from birth. He would always see what others couldn't see.

'How did you come to know all this?' I asked. A foolish question to ask of someone who seemed to know everything by instinct, and yet he was also human, something it was easy to forget in the first shock of his revelations.

'Does it matter?' he said wearily.

The change of tone alarmed me. 'Of course it matters. You said before, this is us together. Don't keep me out. I need to know everything now. Don't you see? It's the only chance we have.'

And now he looked at me for a long time, as if seeking a clue to my state of mind. Horror? Disgust? A desire to flee the truth and return to normal life? I don't think he saw any of that, for it wasn't there. All I felt was an almost unbearable sense of sadness for everything that he and Joachim and their parents had had to bear. And then, to my surprise, I saw his expression change. The weariness disappeared and in its place was a sadness that mirrored my own. I had seen that before, but never so strong, and now I remembered where: the first time I'd dreamed of the golden stag. That extraordinary moment which had haunted me ever since, when he had ceased to be a figure of terror and instead become suffused with that unbearable sadness. He had beckoned to me then, and I had tried to follow, but David had prevented me. I thought I understood that sadness now. What I hadn't known then was how ancient it was, relic of long-past millennia, of myth. He had indeed been a mythic creature, the golden stag. I couldn't have foreseen then that he would also become real.

'Hanno, please tell me everything.'

'There's not much more to tell.'

I managed to smile a little. 'Then it won't take long, will it? And then we can leave for Joachim's Wood.' I stood up with a briskness I didn't feel. 'Meanwhile, I'm making you some more tea. We still live in the real world, Hanno. There's room for banal things like tea, even in our lives.'

I think this shocked him more than a burst of melodrama would have done. He stared up at me as I passed on my way to the sink. 'You're coming with me tonight? After . . . all this?'

'Of course I'm coming with you. Only this time we have to talk. Decide how best to break the news to your parents. Do they know you're telling me?'

'No. They would be horrified if they knew.'

I filled the kettle. The mundane sound of the water rushing in was soothing. I was beginning to wake up from what now seemed a very long sleep. I was also beginning to see that there was a place for me in all this. It was something I had always craved but never found: a sense of belonging, of serving some purpose in the world. The theatre had gone a long way to satisfy it, but not quite far enough. In that awful motorway café I had felt in limbo, cut off from both The Folly and Hanno. No longer. Hanno needed me, and so did his family, though they didn't know it yet. The tiny act of kindness towards David and Charlotte hadn't been a fluke. It was the beginning of something entirely new.

'I can understand that,' I said. 'They've been sealed off from everyone else for so long – your parents. They'll be terrified to let me in. But it's the right thing to do, isn't it? It's time.'

I emptied the dead leaves from the pot, scalded it and spooned in the fresh tea. As the water hit the brittle new leaves, the lovely smoky scent rose. Small comforts, more precious than ever.

I poured out the first cup for him, then sat down opposite again. 'Now, tell me. What happened after your parents discovered the truth?'

And then the miracle. The first small tentative smile. 'You make it all sound so straightforward. "And then . . . and then . . . and then."'

I smiled in return. 'This thing happened, Hanno. It's as real as anything else. It needs to come out into the daylight. Daylight is banal, but it has its uses. Please.'

Another long look. Then he resumed his story.

'They left Vienna as soon as they could and came to London. The resemblance which they'd failed to see for so long now seemed so blindingly obvious that they feared everyone else would see it. They didn't know anyone in London. It was the sort of place where they could be anonymous.

'They lived as secluded a life as they could, afraid that someone would notice the resemblance. It wasn't really necessary. After all, you've seen them together many times and never suspected. People can't suspect what has never entered their way of thinking. And no one expects to encounter what my parents were.

'My parents didn't realise that. As soon as they began to think a neighbour might suspect, or the local children began to bully Joachim, they moved on again. I was their only link with the outside world. They depended on me. As I grew up, I think they also hoped that somehow I would find a way out for them. I didn't know the truth, of course. It wasn't something they would ever have told me. But I felt the weight of their dependence and it made me grow up faster than many children. I did well at school and – this may surprise you – was extremely extrovert. My parents' lives were so turned in on themselves that I turned outward for relief. It was soon obvious that I had a talent for acting. I trained, and as soon as I could I took up my first job – in Vienna.

'Why I went to Vienna is still not clear, even to me. Partly because there was more scope there for a multilingual actor. But it was more than that. I felt powerfully drawn to the city. My childhood memories were fairly hazy and my parents rarely spoke of their time there, and yet I felt a sort of belonging connected with Vienna. And also – although this is difficult to explain – a sense of unfinished business. I can't be more precise than that.

'The work I did in Vienna and Berlin you know about already. All you need to know now is how I came to learn the truth. It was purely by accident. I was working with the author on a play which involved the discovery of hidden secrets about a character's past. For it we needed to know what sort of documentation about individual people had survived destruction by bombs and by the Nazis. To find out, I used my own parents' cases. It was just a convenient device to help my research, no more. I had no suspicions, and no idea of the horror I would inadvertently uncover.

'Well, you know what I uncovered. After that, it was impossible for me to stay in Vienna any longer. I returned to London immediately and retreated into my own hidden world, becoming an agent working behind the scenes well away from the public eye.

'For a long time I said nothing to my parents about what I had discovered. I didn't feel I had the right. I also felt ashamed, like a sneak thief, though I had never meant to pry into their lives, only using them as an example to facilitate my work. But of course my parents are themselves twins and have the same uncanny knowledge of each other's minds, and of the minds of their children. Very likely they began to suspect, soon after my return to London, that I had discovered something. But as they never discussed their situation even with each other, it took time for any of this to come into the open.

'When it did, my parents were devastated all over again. It was a terrible thing to witness. The only way I could make amends was to do everything I could to make their lives and Joachim's easier. I put to use the gift – or curse – which I seemed to have for seeing into the heart of things, put this to use in my work. I quickly gained a reputation which in time earned me enough money to buy Joachim's Wood. It didn't solve all their problems. It never could. But it was something. It was all I could do.

'Sometimes, Rosalind, I've wished I could hate my parents, and sometimes I have hated them, but never for long. Always I come back to the crucial point: that these two people did what they did in innocence. There is a terrible irony in our own lives, don't you think? That your parents, who were free to love and marry and produce children, did so in a way which was monstrous, rejecting their own creation. While my parents, who in a deep and ancient way are indeed monsters, unnatural creatures, produced their children in love and have always treated them with love. Your innocent parents are guilty. My guilty parents are innocent.

'Well. There's little point in saying more. I have no right to ask anything of you. None the less, I have to, because this, too, is unfinished business. I have to tell you that I love you very much and always will. That the miracle I've dreamed of these two days and nights is that despite everything you would allow me to put that strange and clumsy and ill-fitting ring back on your finger in the manner in which we first intended. That I wish you to have the ring regardless, because it's yours in a way that goes beyond anything I can offer you, but that I hope, or wish, or dream, that you might let it become again a double symbol: of yourself and the work you still have to do in your world, and of our love for each other.

'But I also have to tell you that very few women would wish to . . . enter into my world, which is a world of broken taboo and ancient curse and magic of a terrible kind. Very few women indeed, and with good reason. And so if you wish to . . . end our relationship . . . I'll say and do nothing to dissuade you. There will be no recriminations and expressions of . . . regret or disappointment, whatever I might feel. I'll do everything I can to make it . . . as easy as possible for both of us to . . . sever this link between us.

'It's a terrible decision you have to make, Rosalind, and

I wish I could spare you. But things have happened as they've happened and now we have no choices beyond those two. You'll want time to think, I'm sure, and this is right. Perhaps it's for the best that I must return to Joachim's Wood tonight. It'll give you time to think – time away from me and the pressure I may be putting on you, however much I try not to. You may wish to stay here or, if the associations are too disturbing, you may wish to go to Astrid's house and have a clearer atmosphere in which to . . . make your decision. Whatever you feel is best. Please say –'

'Hanno,' I said, and there was no tremor in my voice. I felt clear and strong and, perhaps for the first time in my life, truly whole. 'There's no decision to make. Surely you know that, after all these years.' I smiled and reached out my hand to him and to the ring which gleamed dully in the centre of the table. 'Please. It's for you to do. It's not my ring, Hanno. It's ours.'

37

It was dark by the time we set off for Joachim's Wood, though still early enough to ensure that we would arrive before anyone had gone to bed. That was all I was thinking about now: how we could break the news a second time and in a way which, instead of re-opening an old wound, would bring about some kind of liberation from the self-enclosed world that Hanno's parents inhabited.

It wouldn't be easy. They had lived so long with their secret that it had developed a power even greater than the thing which had provoked it. They would be horrified to discover that I knew. There would be more rejection, even worse than before, only this time I wouldn't run out into the night like a spoiled brat who's been slapped in the face. We needed time, and patience, but in the end it might be possible to open up these lives and defuse some of the strength of the ancient curse.

But was it such a curse? Those years of suppression had allowed the negative side to become so powerful that the other side had faded and almost disappeared, surviving only in Hanno's professional intuition and Joachim's skill with plants. It was, after all, a strange kind of blessing as well, this exceptional sensitivity, this ability to see into the heart of things. It was this that we – Hanno and I – would have to struggle to bring back into the light. Hanno alone couldn't do it for his parents; he was one of them. But I, an outsider, might.

'I wonder if you'll ever stop surprising me,' said Hanno when I'd told him what I was thinking.

'The real tragedy is that your parents have dwelled so much on the negative that they've let the positive disappear,' I said. 'They've also lost perspective. Their situation isn't so very far removed from "normal life", whatever that might be. It's not uncommon for brothers and sisters to be attracted towards each other, sometimes quite strongly. Normally they know who they are and so the taboo prevents anything happening. In a way, these are tragedies, too: brothers and sisters who might have been happier with each other than either of them would be with a different partner.'

'You're still surprising me. Your calmness.'

'That's because you're a part of your family, you've lived with it too long. I can stand outside a little. And my own family was so, well, non-existent, really, that I feel a little less involved with the whole idea of family. It's easier for me to think things through without all the emotive baggage that comes of being a part of a family.'

'You have Matti.'

'True.'

I could see now how selfish my own recent battle for Matti had been. I had begrudged him a possible step-mother, and one who might in fact enrich his life. I thought again of the letter I had written and of the horrible interrogation I had inflicted on Charlotte during that confused midnight visit to the lambing field. What a bitch I'd been. At least I'd salvaged something by writing the letter, though I now wished I'd been kinder in wording it. My generosity had been grudging even while I wrote the letter. Now it was wholehearted. I could finally hope that David and Charlotte would marry, for her sake as much as for David's. Perhaps the time would come when Charlotte and I could meet again, away from the fraught circumstances of her present and mine.

It was raining – again or still, I'd lost track. The events of the last two days had been lived out against the banal backdrop of that dreary kind of rain which I imagine exists nowhere except in England. I watched, almost hypnotised, the monotonous dance of the windscreen wipers. There were headlights in abundance: the Sunday night exodus of country cottagers from the Cotswolds. But the headlights no longer held the face of Mrs Hirsch.

Sunday. 'What happens tomorrow?' I asked.

'I've put a message on my answerphone asking my secretary to cancel all appointments.'

'That's not like you.'

'Strange times, strange measures. There was nothing urgent.'

'Do your parents know we're – you're – coming?'

'I phoned this afternoon while you were driving down. They're not expecting you, of course. I didn't think you'd be with me. I hoped, yes, but I didn't dare hope too much.' He turned briefly to me. In the lights of an oncoming car his face shone with happiness, in contrast to the dreary surroundings. 'It still seems a miracle. I still can't believe you're here, Rosalind. I'm afraid of waking up and finding it was all a dream.'

'Oh ye of little faith,' I smiled.

He smiled in return. 'I've always had faith in you. It's myself I doubt.'

All those people who held him in awe. What would they think if they knew the insecurity and anguish he had kept hidden so long? Well, they never would know, not from me at least. I was bound to silence. I would soon be a part of this strange circle dedicated to the care of Joachim.

A car overtook, going much too fast and barely regaining its lane in time. It rattled me. I had driven north and back again with selfish speed myself, not caring. Now life mattered so much.

I glanced at Hanno – and was shocked to see his face gone ashen in the dim lights of the dashboard.

'Hanno?'

He shook his head. 'Not that. Something else.'

Something strange was happening. I hoped it was just the aftermath of our long evening in the kitchen and the strain of speaking out for the first time. But as I watched, a change seemed to come over his face, actually altering the physiognomy. Not a lot, but enough to turn him into another person, familiar and yet not. I shivered as I realised who it was. Joachim.

'Joachim,' he said. 'Something's wrong with Joachim.'

Of course something was wrong with Joachim. We all knew that. Then I realised. 'Something different?'

He seemed to have forgotten I was there. He accelerated.

And then we were the car that was going too fast, overtaking everyone else. He wasn't reckless like the other, but even so I felt my own foot press down on the floor, pretending to be a brake. 'Hanno?' The muscles under the skin of his face were moving oddly and I think involuntarily, as if acting out some drama of which even he was unaware. 'Hanno, tell me what it is.'

A slight spasm brought him back to me. 'It's happened before,' he said, his voice now unnaturally calm. 'Sometimes it means nothing, just a strong thought going through his mind.'

It was something I'd never considered in depth, all these mental messages passing through to Hanno. I had stupidly seen it as Joachim providing the intuition Hanno used in his work. Now I saw that many of those messages were to do with Joachim himself. What a bewildering world Hanno's mind must be.

Suddenly he flinched as if struck, and his left hand rose to his head – another involuntary gesture, I felt sure. A memory flashed through my mind: the day the crown had been placed on my head in the British Museum. I had flinched, too.

'It's different this time,' he said. 'It does mean something.' Little beads of sweat had appeared on his forehead. They glittered briefly in a new set of headlights. There seemed to be more and more headlights, but I suppose it was just the speed. We were in a film with a mad projectionist speeding up the machine.

I wasn't sure I should speak, distract his attention, but I had to know. 'What's happening, Hanno?' I heard with some surprise a hint of panic in my voice.

'At Christmas. It was like this. When Joachim slipped through the hedge. I didn't know then. What it meant.'

It came out in little bits with long pauses between fragments.

The projectionist became increasingly manic, our film whizzed along and carried us like two puppets jerking through a world of jagged light. I was thoroughly frightened by now. I offered to drive but Hanno didn't hear me. I had never seen him like this. He seemed to have no will of his own. It was no use talking to him any more. He was oblivious of me. He had zeroed in on the connection with Joachim, it was Joachim he was hearing, not me. Was it one way or was he, too, somehow sending messages?

I could only deduce that Joachim had probably left his enchanted circle again. But where he was and what he was doing were probably unknown even to Hanno. Quite possibly it was nothing serious. He might just be wandering round the darkened fields, a little lost and worried because of that, transmitting his sense of disturbance to his brother. The village children couldn't always be there, always waiting for Joachim.

The journey seemed to last for ever, though at the speed Hanno was driving we must have travelled those familiar miles in record time. Even when we turned off the main road and began the tortuous journey along the twisty little lanes he didn't slow down. I suddenly saw the scene from outside: we were in one of those funny old cops and robbers chases, except that one car was missing, the remaining one slewing round the curves as if still pursued or pursuing. A nervous giggle, caught just in time, showed how much my nerves were frayed.

The darkness pressed in hard now that we had left the traffic behind. It felt almost personal, a formless enemy just beyond the windows. I knew I was being paranoid but something about the almost supernatural link between the two brothers aroused other primordial fears. This landscape, gentle and humanised by day, had sunk into its ancient role as forbidden world, sending its human inhabitants scuttling for the safety of their lamp-lit dwellings. We shouldn't be out with only the flimsy metal of the car to separate us from the night. And Joachim didn't even have that. I shivered, expecting any moment to see primitive beacon fires on the scattered hilltops, feeble attempts to banish the threat of the night.

And then, there it was. I blinked, thinking I'd imagined it, but it was still there, a jagged little splash of orange somewhere up ahead and to our right. Involuntarily I looked around for others, but there was nothing but darkness beyond, the whole of the nightscape uniformly black except for the single juddering scrap of light.

I peered hard through the window. It was difficult to see anything clearly; the window was a tangled river of rain and windscreen wipers and Hanno was driving so fast that nothing would stay in focus. But it was a fire, that much I could see. I thought of Joachim's Wood, the trees, but we hadn't reached it yet. This was something else. It was fairly high up and partly obliterated by a mass of bare branches.

'Hanno, look – there. The fire on that hill.'

He only glanced, as if slightly annoyed at my distraction. Then, without warning, he slammed on the brakes so hard that my seat belt dug into my body. A second later he was out of the car.

It all happened so fast that I sat in the car for some seconds, fixated on the fact that we were parked in the middle of a very narrow lane by a curve. Any car coming along would crash into us. Then I, too, was out of the car in blind obedience to something I didn't comprehend.

The rain was pelting down. Within seconds I was soaked. I barely noticed. Hanno was running down the road. Instinctively I ran after him. Then I blinked and he was gone. I fought down the spurt of panic and kept running. Just before the bridge a path turned off to follow the river. As I reached it, I looked to the right and saw Hanno, still running, barely visible in the darkness and blur of the rain. I turned and ran after him. It was the same path I'd walked that day I'd encountered Hanno's parents, with the wooded hill to the right and the river to the left. Then it had been a lovely spring day, full of light and the scent of growing things. Now the hill loomed black beside me and the only smells were of mud and rain and fire. The fire was invisible now, somewhere on the top of the hill, but the sky above it was stained a muddy copper.

A stitch in my side slowed me down. My breath was rasping, I was slithering all over the soggy path.

Then, 'Joachim!'

My first thought was amazement that Hanno had enough breath to yell so loud. Then all thinking was obliterated in the rush of pieces falling into place.

Of course. The clearing on the hilltop where he had found the remains of a bonfire all those years ago. That's where Joachim was. Joachim who had no fear, no understanding of things that could do him harm: water, fire. People. The neighbourhood boys.

I heard a groan and realised it had come from me.

Hanno disappeared again, but this time I knew where. When I reached the place, I turned off into the wood to follow him. There was a narrow path, badly overgrown, seldom used, twisting its way to the top of the hill. I couldn't see Hanno at all now, but I could hear him, like a big lumbering beast breaking the brittle branches that barred his way. I lumbered after him, smaller and slower and without the faintest idea of what I should do but knowing that somehow I had to be there with Hanno.

The smell of the smoke was stronger now, almost obliterating the nostalgic aniseed scent of the sweet cicily we were crushing underfoot. The path wasn't steep but it was long. After only a few minutes I felt I'd been there for ever, couldn't remember a time when I'd been doing anything other than struggling up through the darkened tangled wood, like one of those nightmares where you run and run and never move an inch. Perhaps it was a dream and I would wake up.

I couldn't hear Hanno any more. He hadn't called Joachim again and now I couldn't even hear him crashing through the underbrush. The sound of the fire had crept down the hill, increasing in volume with every step. It was roaring now, a primitive bass with the paler sounds dancing above it of flames crackling and water hissing. How on earth had they got a fire going in this rain?

They. Joachim couldn't possibly have lit this fire by himself. It would have needed paraffin. The children who had tormented Joachim all his life had to be there. I saw them as a single band, spawned in Vienna, always the same, only changing their shape as they moved through Vienna, London and the Cotswolds. I tried to be calm. Joachim was a man now, and big. Surely the children wouldn't, couldn't, hurt him?

And then, without warning, the path ended and I was on the top, my eyes blinded by the glare of the fire. It was still fragmented by the ring of trees which continued some way across the hilltop before reaching the clearing, but the light was so bright that it seemed only a few yards away. The centre of the fire was blotted out by a shape: Hanno, some way in front of me, his body a dark form vividly outlined in fire. I stifled a scream, the man of fire evoking some primeval memory passed down through thousands of years. Reason was deserting me, overcome by the irrationality of darkness and fire. The veneer of civilisation was being stripped away to leave nothing but the naked impulses of my own primitive ancestors. There were only two times here: the present and the ancient. Everything between had vanished.

In my shock I had stopped running. Now I saw that Hanno, too, was standing still. If I'd been thinking, I would have wondered why he had stopped, why gone silent, after his frantic rush up the hill. Above all, why he wasn't seeking out Joachim, who was surely here. But thought had stopped and like a sleepwalker I moved towards him, drew up beside him and stood still.

The clearing was full of children, about fifteen of them, fifteen hefty adolescent boys all dressed in black. Only their faces and hands stood out from the darkness, their hands lifting beer cans to their faces in slow motion. Other than that, they were perfectly still, a static black ring around the fire. But it wasn't the stillness of peace. The clearing was crackling with tension as palpable as the crackle and roar of the fire.

Then the tension broke. In unison, as if in obedience to some unheard signal, they flung away their beer cans, lifted their drunken faces to the sky and shattered the silence with the sound of hunting horns. It was an uncannily accurate imitation, clearly well practised, which made it all the more disturbing. Messages of fear raced up my spine. The scene was both farcical and chilling. I had to believe that during the day these were decent kids like any others, going to school and living with their families. But I couldn't believe it. Some gruesome alchemy had taken the basic material and transformed it, not into gold but into a pack of drunken huntsmen from a more primitive past. I had no doubt that if a fox had walked into the clearing, they would have turned on it like a pack of dogs, deaf to anything but their animal instinct to kill.

And then, almost as if my thoughts were being transmitted, the hunting horns were joined by the eerie sound of dogs howling, and I saw a dozen or more black shapes rising to their feet, pointing their snouts at the sky and emitting the unearthly sound. I had to believe, too, that these were family pets, like their owners living a normal life by day. But in the ghastly light of the clearing they, too, had become something more primitive and frightening. There was something almost formalised about the whole scene, the boys and their dogs acting out a ritual that had gripped them with such power that it was no longer acting.

For the first time since we'd left the car I looked at Hanno, almost afraid that he, too, might have been transformed. I suppose it was that fear which made the relief that flooded over me so sweet. He at least remained the same, the only difference being the look of fascinated revulsion on his face. I reached for his hand. Warm and human. I couldn't guess his thoughts, but he clearly had some left for me, for he closed his hand round mine with comforting familiarity. I wanted to speak, ask him the meaning of all this, but the reality of the everyday had disappeared, leaving us stranded and bewildered and wordless.

Suddenly his hand tightened. I looked at the clearing. The boys had begun moving around the fire in a jerky little dance, screeching with raucous laughter. The dogs were in motion too, swarming around their feet, but at least they'd stopped howling. They were yapping instead. The boys had worked themselves into a frenzy and it was infecting the dogs. One of them – a big ugly brute – snapped at the leg of a boy. He kicked it so hard that it tumbled over several times before picking itself up again and yelping all the harder.

The dance stopped as abruptly as it had started. The noise of the boys and the dogs stopped, too. Into the silence leapt the roar of the fire. It couldn't have lasted long, that moment of suspense while we waited, Hanno and I, hypnotised.

Then it happened, the thing I'd been unconsciously dreading for twenty years or more. Into the clearing, accompanied by two more boys, stepped the golden stag.

He was larger than I remembered him, heavier and stronger, but he moved like a creature whose natural habitat was the forest, accustomed to making his way through the underbrush. On his head was a set of antlers that seemed to symbolise his woodland world, like the winter-bare branches of trees. They were gilded in the firelight, and as he turned his head sparks seemed to shoot out in all directions. And his face. Yes, that too was the same, the half-human half-animal face that had appeared in my nightmare, both threatening and poignant. He was too far away for me to see his eyes, but I didn't have to. I knew the expression in them already: the deep sadness, thousands of years old, of a human being inexplicably trapped in a body that wasn't his own. I knew their colour, too. Not the cold hard nuggets of my nightmare but something gentler and more elusive: the gold-flecked eyes of Joachim.

I had been wrong, all those years. It wasn't Hanno who

was the golden stag, as I'd thought that night when he'd come to my dressing-room at York. I should have sensed it then, and should have understood it clearly the moment I first saw his brother. It was Joachim, not Hanno, who, both cursed and blessed by his heritage, inhabited such a strange mythic world, the no-man's-land between man and beast. It was Joachim who had been touched not by a magician's wand but by blood and transformed into something that had no place in the human world.

Then Hanno released my hand and walked into the clearing and the veil through which I'd been watching Joachim vanished. No longer the golden stag, he was a bewildered man on whose head these callous boys had tied a set of old antlers. Far from gilded, they were tatty, with one of the tips broken off and jagged. It was that more than anything else that aroused my outrage. The lack of dignity in those antlers.

As Hanno strode into the clearing, another veil dropped away and the demons became children again, just a mob of mindless brats saturated with beer. How on earth had these boys had the power to produce such fear in me only a few minutes before? What's more, it was now they who were clearly afraid. They looked from Hanno to Joachim and back again, over and over, the whites of their eyes flashing superstitious apprehension. I had forgotten that some of these boys had probably never seen Joachim and Hanno together, didn't realise that what they were seeing was simply a set of twins. To them it must have seemed as if their horrid little rites had conjured up a ghostly duplicate.

In any case, they had lost control and Hanno had taken it. He stood in the clearing, larger and more powerful in the deceptive light of the fire. Though many of the boys were as tall, they all seemed to shrink in comparison with the giant who now towered above them. I couldn't see his face but knew his teeth were clenched in fury as he said, with a loathing he made no effort to disguise, 'Get out.'

The boys cringed and the dogs at their feet cringed but nobody moved away.

He took another step further into the clearing and bellowed, 'Did you hear me? *Get out of here!*'

Still no movement.

Then I knew what I had to do. I stepped into the clearing myself and walked towards Joachim. 'Joachim, come with us,' I said in German, making my voice as matter-of-fact as possible. 'We're going home.'

At last the spell was broken. The boys stirred slightly. Joachim moved away from the two who had led him into the clearing and came towards me. I held out my hand, relieved to see the bewilderment leave his face and a smile begin to appear. It was a beautiful smile, full of trust and the assurance that he was loved well by those few people who made up his world. Then his hand closed over mine and I was sure that everything would be all right.

Hanno didn't have to tell me what to do; I knew. I must quietly lead Joachim down the hill towards home, leaving Hanno to deal with the boys, to act as a shield in case the boys, deprived of their sport, should suddenly turn ugly again and rebel against the man who had spoiled their game. I didn't like leaving Hanno – there were more than fifteen of them, big strong adolescents with more muscle than brain – but I knew we had no choice.

At the edge of the clearing Joachim turned to look at Hanno, his face anxious again.

'We're going home,' I said to him. 'Hanno will come later.'

He nodded and we started down the hill. The path was so narrow that there wasn't room for two abreast, but I didn't dare let go of his hand. I went ahead, one hand clearing away the overhanging branches, the other clutching Joachim behind me. It was clumsy progress, but with every step I felt a little safer. I could hear Hanno giving orders to the boys to extinguish the fire. The fire was dying anyway and now I heard the sound of earth being kicked on to it. What he was really doing, I supposed, was trying to restore a sense of normality. The boys had worked themselves into a drunken frenzy which could make them dangerous. The banal act of putting out the fire would probably return them to the everyday world.

Suddenly Joachim's hand jerked out of mine. I stopped, instantly frightened, then realised it was only the horrid antlers catching in some branches. I disentangled them and then fumbled with the strings the boys had used to tie them on. I didn't like losing the time, but they would just snag on more branches. In any case, they were so degrading that I couldn't bear to leave them in place any longer. I flung them into the underbrush with disgust and took his hand again.

We hadn't progressed much further before the first sounds of disturbance reached us from above. At first just a low snarling sound, as of a dog about to attack. A glance behind told me the fire was now out. The rain was easing off, too, and without its hiss and the roar of the fire, every sound was magnified. Then there was a second growl, louder.

A moment later the night air was ripped apart. The dogs broke into hysterical yapping. Beneath them was a deeper sound, eerie, as if a huge pack of hunting dogs had suddenly been let loose on a victim and were baying for its blood. I felt confused, disorientated. There weren't any hunting dogs up there, only a bunch of mongrels and their owners. Then I realised. The creatures baying weren't dogs at all. They were the boys. Something – perhaps just that first snarling dog – had jerked them back into their fantasy world.

'Hanno!' I cried.

'Keep going!' he called back in German. 'Just hang on to Joachim and keep going! I'm coming down by another path to distract them!'

I didn't know what to do. Part of me acknowledged that he was right, another part wanted to rush back and be with him. I tried to convince myself that he wasn't really in any danger, that these were after all just a bunch of boys and dogs and not the hellish creatures their awful baying made them appear to be.

I looked back. Behind Joachim I could just see a scrap

of sky through the trees, fitfully illuminated by a moon swathed in cloud. And then something odd. It was as if the sky began to roll itself up from the bottom, filling what had been dark grey with black. I strained my ears in the foolish hope that they would help interpret what was happening, but all I heard was the baying of dogs. The dark increased as I watched and with it the noise.

And then the dark and the noise fused and I understood what was happening. The blackness *was* the boys and the dogs, a mass of them spilling out of the clearing and on to the path, darkening the sky with their bulk and rending it with their howls. I froze. A second later I had gripped Joachim's hand hard and we were running as fast as we could down the path and away from the thing pursuing us. I was insane with fear, the age-old fear of the stricken animal pursued by a nameless horror. I could feel my fear transmitted through Joachim's hand. We were no more human than the creatures behind us. We were –

And then I saw the meaning of the whole nightmare. The hunt. These boys had from the very first sensed the differentness of Joachim and had deliberately set out to turn him into their quarry. He was indeed the stag, but not the golden stag of my vision. He was the helpless solitary animal elected to be killed for sport. For months these terrible children had been preparing him for this night, just a few of them at first, but over time initiating others into their growing band. It was all to culminate tonight in this gruesome imitation of an adult stag hunt. And Hanno and I had come along and spoiled their fun.

The dark mass was moving closer with every second. Inspired by thwarted blood-lust, they were hurtling down the path oblivious of their safety. There was no way we could move fast enough to escape. The beginning of a helpless sob rose in my throat. Then I saw another darkness to my left, a small swelling of the path. I stopped so fast that Joachim nearly knocked me over. I pulled him quickly into the darkness and held his hand hard, holding my breath at the same time. My hope was that they, looking downward into the wood, were unable to see the small dark mass that was us, wouldn't notice that we had disappeared.

It worked. We'd been there only a few seconds when the sounds crescendoed to a pitch that hurt my ears and the path filled with a tumultuous motion as they rushed down past our hiding place. I listened to the cacophony recede. When it seemed far enough away, we emerged, quietly, and quietly continued to descend the path.

We were walking now. There was no point in running. Better to save our strength for when we reached the bottom. Then we would be exposed on the riverside path, then we might need to run like hell. For now, we picked our way carefully, quietly, down the path. I could hear Hanno making his presence known in an effort to lure the boys away from us, but I couldn't tell if it was working. The noise of the boys and the dogs was so diffused by the trees that it was impossible to know where they were.

We must have been quite near the bottom when it happened. The trees on either side of the path suddenly erupted into a black mass of noise.

'Run!' I yelled to Joachim.

And we ran. But it was too late. They were all around us, and within seconds they were on us, over us, a single huge mass knocking us to the ground and trampling over our bodies. Jagged patterns of black and grey flashed through my head. Then nothing but smooth soothing darkness.

I don't think I was unconscious for more than a few seconds. When I came to, I could see the last of them dispersing, vanishing from the path to be swallowed up by the trees. A moment of sheer relief: they had left, miraculously left us alone. Then shock.

Joachim was gone.

'Joachim!' I yelled, forgetting that he wouldn't, couldn't, answer. He hadn't uttered a single word since earliest childhood.

'Joachim!' I screamed regardless. Just an answering yell

from him, not a word but a noise, that's all I would need to direct me towards him.

No sound except the demented baying of the hunters. It was everywhere now, the woods ringing with the noise, bouncing off the trees and echoing down the hillside, turning the night into a nightmare. Through it cut the single note of sanity: Hanno, taunting the boys to find him.

I picked myself up. Every muscle groaned in protest. I could still feel one of the heaviest bootprints on my spine.

'Joachim! Hanno!'

I looked around wildly, not knowing where to go. I had to find Joachim, that much I knew, but where? The hill was a solid mass of noise, no sense of direction was possible.

'Hanno! They've taken Joachim! I don't know where he is!'

'Stay by the river!' Hanno yelled back in German. 'Keep out of the wood! And keep quiet!'

A greyer patch of night showed I was near the bottom of the hill. I made my way towards it, every footstep a small agony. When I reached the path I gazed across the river at the unimaginable peace of Joachim's Wood just one field's-width away. They must know he was missing. Would they send someone to search? Christa at least?

'Joachim is here!' I bellowed across the water, disregarding Hanno's words. I had to try something, anything. 'Joachim is on the hill! Send help!'

I had been heard all right, but by the wrong people. I wheeled round just in time to see the edge of the wood bulge and then detach itself. A moment later a swarm of boys had flung me down again. There were fewer this time. I flailed my arms and legs, hitting out as hard as I could. Teeth sank into my arm, above it an insane drunken face. I felt the blood rush to the surface and with the other arm I lashed out at the head. It swore and jerked away. I felt no more mercy for these boys than they felt for us. I struggled to my feet and kicked out at them, swearing back at them loudly. Clearly this wasn't what they wanted from their game. They wanted a passive gentle victim they could terrorise, not this virago who'd suddenly turned on them. They wanted Joachim. With a single lurch they left me and disappeared again into the wood.

I stormed after them, utterly fearless now, my fear consumed by rage and disgust. I'd learned one thing: Hanno and I were in little danger. To these crazed creatures we were only impediments to their game. They were focused with single-minded intensity on the one quarry, Joachim, and we had to find him before they did.

Once in the wood again I was instantly lost. This time, though, the noise seemed to be concentrated in one direction, somewhere to the left. I pushed through the trees towards it, holding my bleeding arms up to shield my face from the whippy branches. My whole body hurt like hell but I didn't care. As single-mindedly as the boys I fought my way through the wood. 'Joachim!' I yelled, still hoping against hope for some kind of reply.

I was getting nearer all the time, that much I could tell. 'You bastards!' I screamed. 'If you hurt him I'll kill you, every single one of you!'

'Keep away!' Hanno yelled back.

But I was beyond listening, beyond caring what happened to me.

And then, suddenly, I was there, in a tiny clearing. The entire space was filled by the pack of boys and dogs, all of them flung in a heap on what could only be Joachim. At the same moment I reached the clearing, Hanno burst into it from the other side. There was no time for me even to feel relief at seeing him. We threw ourselves on to the pack, grabbing at the bodies and heaving them off. My own body no longer hurt, it had the strength of twenty as, crazy with anger, I grabbed at Joachim's tormentors.

There was a brief flash of light: a shred of moon shining off Joachim's bright blond hair. Then, in what must have been for him a monumental effort, he got to his feet, tumbling the last of the boys from him, and stumbled off into the wood.

I went after him, calling his name. Behind me was

Hanno, also calling. Why wouldn't Joachim stop, let us catch up with him and take him home? Surely he understood now that the worst of it was over? The baying had ceased and only a few yapping dogs showed that there was life other than ours in the wood. I had to hope that the loathsome children were making their way home, angry and disappointed in their defeat. Beyond that, I didn't dare think. All that mattered was to get to Joachim and take him back to his family.

I had lost sight of him. All I could do was continue in the same direction, down towards the riverside path which was clearly where Joachim was heading. I could hear Hanno behind me. I longed to turn round, just to glimpse his face, see something human and reassuring in this awful night, but I was still afraid the boys would return for one last attack.

The trees ended abruptly. To the left I could just see Joachim, running down the riverside path towards the bridge. I ran after him, Hanno still behind me, though further away than before. I looked back at him and saw him nearly fall. He was obviously hurt, perhaps badly. I stopped, my instinct to go back to him.

He waved me on with an impatient gesture. 'I'm all right! Get to Joachim before they find him! Get him back to the car! Don't stop!'

Blindly I obeyed, glancing back once or twice to see that he was following. Glancing, too, at the line of trees, terrified that at any moment the pack would return even more determined than ever to destroy its prey.

I'll never know what gave me the strength to go on, faster than I would have believed possible. The distance between Joachim and myself was shrinking with every step. Soon I would reach him, call out to him, let him know that everything would be all right. That's all I was thinking as I stormed along the muddy path. It never occurred to me that something might have snapped at last in Joachim's fragile mind.

The wood was silent. Only the river, swollen with rain, roared on the other side. Perhaps the boys had abandoned their game. Perhaps they were on their way home already, across the fields on the other side of the hill. How they would explain their state to their parents was their problem. I wanted revenge, oh yes, but not now. Now all I wanted was to get Joachim home.

I would have done it, too. I was nearly there, calling gently to him. Just a few yards separated us when it happened: one long eerie howl shattered the stillness. Whether dog or boy, whether near or far, I couldn't tell.

Joachim stopped as if turned to stone. Then, in a single motion of superhuman strength, he leapt towards the river. For a moment he was suspended above the turbulent water, and in that moment, it seemed to me that he had become the golden stag for one last time. The moon glittered off his rain-drenched clothes and his hair, turning him into a silvery-gold figure, flying, almost, for that heart-breaking moment free at last, his body a shining arc spanning the darkness of the sky and the darkness of the river. And then the arc descended.

I threw myself into the river so fast I must have hit the water at the same time as Joachim. When I shook the water out of my eyes, he was only a few feet away, his bright blond hair gleaming, his face radiant with happiness, his golden eyes fixed on the bank.

'Hanno!' he cried.

And then he was gone.

38

Darkness. And then light, the silvery-soft diffusion of moonlight through the leaded window. It fell directly on my face as I awoke, making me blink a little. All around was a silence so deep that I could hear my heart faintly keeping the time.

And then a second heartbeat, and the moon was eclipsed by his head. The light shone off its bright blondness in a gleaming aureole.

'Joachim?' I said.

The head moved slightly and a hand came to rest on my cheek. 'Hanno,' he said, very quietly, as if fearing to awake a sleepwalker too soon. 'How do you feel?'

I wasn't sure there was an 'I' to feel anything. 'Strange. Something missing.'

There was a long and rather odd pause. 'Yes,' he said at last. 'Something missing.' His voice had sunk to a whisper, leaving the silence almost intact.

'Joachim?' I said.

And now even our heartbeats seemed to stop. An owl hooted softly, a long way away, a long wavering *woo . . . ooo . . . ooo*. A gentle sound, not at all the night terror of myth.

Finally Hanno spoke again. 'Joachim is . . . gone.'

I didn't have to ask for explanations. I knew the meaning. Knew, too, that this was no euphemism he was using. The plain word for the final departure was inappropriate. Joachim was gone and yet here, his presence filling the house and the wood he had created outside the windows.

Hanno's hand slipped down to close over mine. We stayed like that for a long time, not speaking, not having to speak. Language had never been a part of Joachim's world.

Outside, a second owl answered the first with a bright metallic *kee . . . wick!* I smiled at its irreverence. That was Joachim's language. He would have known what they were saying. He would have known, too, the meaning of the scent drifting in through the open window. What to me was just the undifferentiated fragrance of green and growing things was for him a rich bouquet of a hundred individual plants, each different, each special. The little scrap of paradise he had created was paying its own tribute to him. It was more than we, bound tightly to our human lives, could do.

When the time came for words, few were needed. I remembered most of it and with a clarity that went beyond pain. Jumping into the river. Swimming clumsily towards Joachim through the turbulent water. Reaching him, grasping him just as he came up the second time. I think I'd known even then that it was too late. He didn't understand that water, which for him was what gave life to his trees, could also take life away. I think it took his quietly. I think there was no fear. Certainly there was none in his last inexplicable leap into the water, none in his voice as, jubilantly, he called his brother's name. Why he spoke that first and last time we'll never know, but I don't think he was calling for help; Hanno's own leap into the water had been spontaneous. I had kept Joachim's head above water all the time we swirled through the current towards the bridge. If he'd been alive, I would have saved him, but he wasn't. We had come to rest, all three of us, against a pillar of the bridge – in my case so hard I was knocked unconscious. Hanno had hauled us both out and somehow got us into the car and back to Joachim's Wood.

'Where is he?' I asked.

'The room next door. My parents are with him, and Christa.'

'May I see him?'

'Of course.'

Every inch of my body ached as I struggled out of bed. I hobbled painfully out of the room with Hanno. He was limping, too, one leg badly mangled by the dogs. I didn't want to think of that, of all the things that had preceded those last minutes in the water. I wanted the water to wash it all away, as it had done for Joachim.

Only when we reached the door of Joachim's room did I remember. 'Your parents,' I whispered. 'They . . . do they know? Will they mind if I . . . ?'

'They know everything. They've accepted. It's all right.'

We entered the room together. There was no light here either except the shaft of moonlight shining across the room and coming to rest on Joachim. As I approached the bed, Mrs Hirsch looked up at me. The awful face in the headlights was gone, in its place a mask of quiet grief. 'Please,' she said. 'Forgive me.'

There was nothing to forgive. I took her hand and we sat quietly through the night by Joachim's bed, all five of us mourning in our different ways. It was a wake, I suppose, though Joachim had no need of us to keep the evil spirits away. There had never been any evil spirits near him. There was no keening or any celebration of release, just a quiet watch.

Strangely enough, considering all that he'd been through, there were no marks on Joachim's face and nothing in his expression to speak of his ordeal. The moonlight fell on a face soft with peace and on the slightest hint of a smile.

If we'd been a normal family we would have phoned a doctor who in turn would have brought the police and set in motion all the sordid paraphernalia of death. But Joachim wasn't dead, not really, and none of us had ever lived a normal life. Even Christa had been so long with Joachim that to her he was the real world. There would be time enough in the morning. For now, in this as in so many things, we took our cue from Joachim and simply kept him company throughout the night. It was a peaceful night, one for healing. It was the last time he would be able to do this for us, and we treasured it.

We scattered his ashes in the little clearing which had been his favourite and Hanno's, where Hanno and I had first discovered our love and where he had told me of the link between himself and his brother. The link which had, perhaps, reached out to me in the identical clearing in Yorkshire when I'd first seen the vision of the golden stag.

Just the five of us again. No readings, no speeches, no music. Joachim didn't need any of that. Just a small plain stone flush with the ground and bearing his name and dates.

Hanno planted a silver birch beside it.

'Why did he do it?'

Three weeks had passed and Hanno and I were in the clearing. We came here often at weekends. Hanno had gone back to work – too many people depended on him to permit a long period of mourning. I had stayed behind with his parents and Christa, partly to deal with practicalities and partly, I hoped, to provide a little comfort. Hanno came down every weekend to be with us.

'I don't know,' he said. 'I don't think we ever will.'

It was the one question left unanswered, and if Hanno, who'd known him better than anyone, didn't know, then there was no answer.

'I just don't think it was suicide,' I said quietly.

'Neither do I. He didn't know what death was. He couldn't fear it or want it.'

Somewhere above us a blackbird sang lustily, very likely the last song of the season before he took himself off to the silent vigil of his mate's nest.

'Surely some of the things he planted died?'

'I suppose they must have, but I don't remember. All I remember is planting, helping him to plant, always planting.'

There was no death in the clearing. It was bursting into life. We'd been hard put to find a patch to sit on that wasn't aswarm with anemones and violets all trying to crowd out the tangle of wild bedstraw foliage. Above us the trees were greening up fast. Even the stone itself and the small circle containing the new birch had lost their rawness, the army of bedstraw marching steadily in from all sides to cover it with fresh soft colour.

'There was such joy in his face in those last seconds,' I said. 'And when he called your name. That's what I can't understand. As if he'd discovered something that night. Out of all that sordidness and horror, discovered some sense of freedom. That spectacular leap into the water. Freeing himself at last.'

'I know. He never should have been confined. We simply didn't know what else to do.'

'I wasn't criticising.'

'I know that. You understood why we lived as we did. But it wasn't enough and never could be. He had no place in the world.'

The song of an invisible wren trilled through the trees – high, unbelievably complex and so long that it was hard to imagine such tiny lungs holding so much air.

'Perhaps that's what he discovered that night,' I said. 'But instead of despair, it brought him a kind of liberation.'

A swathe of celandines cut across one corner of the clearing, their clear yellow petals so shiny they seemed to be varnished.

'Whatever; it was his choice,' said Hanno. 'We have no right to question it.'

No. And here amidst all the life he'd created, no need either.

A few months later we were married – on the same day as David and Charlotte, as it happened. My second wedding was, like the first, tiny and private. It had been Rhiannon's death all those years ago that had subdued the celebration. Now, although Joachim was always in our minds, there was no weight of mourning on us. We simply didn't want a fuss.

Hanno's parents were generous with their love. Joachim had liberated more than himself. In the aftermath of that night, his parents' long-held secret had lost much of its power, and when I accepted so naturally their extraordinary history, they accepted me. More than accepted. Welcomed. We had long talks in the days that followed, weaving through them the golden thread that had been Joachim. However tormented their lives had been, there had been brightness, too, and would be again. We talked until there was nothing left unsaid, until everything had been brought to the surface and laid to rest at last. There would be no more secrets left to fester unseen.

When those days were over, we emerged, like travellers long confined to subterranean passages, into the fresh light of day.

Summer was nearly over when we put Joachim's Wood up for sale. It hadn't been an easy decision. Part of us clung to the place he'd created and where his spirit was still strongest.

What finally prompted the decision was Christa. We'd asked her to stay on, no longer as Joachim's nurse but as companion and friend to Hanno's parents. She'd stayed on a while but she wasn't happy. She was highly trained, a specialist in nervous diseases. However difficult life had sometimes been with Joachim, the easy life of a companion was more difficult still. She felt she'd lost her purpose, and in a sense she was right. Her very special skills were being wasted.

In August she returned to Austria and to a new job at a tiny rural settlement formed to provide a home for brain-damaged children. It was a tearful farewell but a hopeful one, too.

After she left, Hanno's parents realised that their life at Joachim's Wood had come to its natural end. The idea of a new companion sharing a life set up for a Joachim who was no longer there distressed them. If a new start was necessary, it must be truly new.

I stayed on to supervise the sale myself, showing everyone around and watching their reactions carefully. The property was unique and worth a lot of money but that wasn't what we wanted. We were determined not to let it go to someone who saw the trees as nothing but a prestige setting for the house. However lovely the house, a house is just a house, a dead thing until someone lives in it. The woodland was different. It had its own life, and until we found someone who understood that, we would refuse all offers.

It took a long time, but finally they arrived, on a grey and rainy day in December: a lovely couple who stared in wonder at Joachim's creation. As the rain dripped off their hair, they talked of thinning this stand, coppicing the section over there – things Joachim himself had probably intended.

We dropped the price and sold it for half as much as had been offered by a smug executive wanting a country cottage. The estate agent was furious.

In February we left Joachim's Wood for the last time. It was late afternoon, one of those exquisite days when the sky was marbled in silvery-greys with the palest of pale gold suns lurking behind the filmy veils, just to hint at the cunning sunset it was designing. Beneath it was the subtle glow of bare bark in more shades of brown than one would think possible, with touches of green here and there from the multitude of different conifers that had been Joachim's special love. A band of early great tits, eager for spring, yelled loudly through the echo-chamber of the trees. Lusty, punchy, they strained their lungs in this battle of song. Comical, too. It's impossible to take a great tit seriously, unless you're another great tit.

And impossible to feel sadness at a send-off like that.

London seemed a foreign country when I returned. I'd grown so used to the natural rhythms of Joachim's Wood that I felt as dazzled as any provincial when the chaos of London folded round me again.

'Where are all these people going?' I said as my husband and I stood on the kerb waiting for a gap to appear in the river of cars streaming past.

'To work,' he said sternly. 'And you?'

Ah.

I'd wanted a long break from work after the fiasco of New York. Now I'd had it and more. I'd sold Joachim's Wood, I'd settled his parents into a lovely sheltered flat just a few streets away from us. I'd done everything that needed doing to clear the way for my return to the theatre. And still I waited. Hanno was fending off offers that no one in their right mind could refuse. And still I waited. Hanno was becoming impatient.

So was Jas. 'Rosie, sweet,' he said. 'You fall off a horse, you get on again. Otherwise, kaput – for ever. Okay, New York was a bummer, but that was centuries ago.'

'It's not that.'

'Then what? I could have *strangled* you when you turned down that Lady Macbeth. It's what we've been *panting* for all these years. He wrote it just for us, you know that, don't you? We would have turned that play upside-down and inside-out, we would have made the Dench/McKellen thing look like a couple of kids playing rainy-day theatricals, we would have –'

'Jas, please. It's not time yet.'

'Time! How much of that stuff do you think we have? A couple of years and you'll be playing Granny to Red Riding Hood.'

'Thanks.'

'Don't mention it.'

And still I waited. But the problem wasn't me. It was Hanno.

Almost the first thing I realised when Joachim died was that something of Hanno would die, too. It was inevitable. They'd shared an extraordinary closeness, far more than that of ordinary twins. There was no way of foreseeing what form the loss would take; there are no guide books to this territory.

When it came, it was worse even than I'd expected. Worse because subdued. There were no dramatics. No premature ageing ravaged the beloved face, though the vertical creases seemed a fraction deeper. No overnight greying of hair, no dulling of his gold-flecked eyes. The pall of the netherworld that hung over him was so faint that only those closest to him could sense it at all.

The only sphere in which it showed was in his work, and that was what made it so frightening. To everyone else, even his secretary, the Wigmore Street office seemed much the same. Hanno's desk was spread as always with a mass of papers, trade magazines, casting directors' lists. He took and made phone calls as usual. He even lunched once or twice with the rare director he deigned to meet personally. He scrutinised draft contracts as usual, and as usual struck out clauses and added his own with the same imperiousness which had formed his reputation.

And that was all. What had gone was the visionary, the Svengali who planned in detail every stage of an actor's career, who saw that career laid out before him in a single flash of inspiration as he had with me in Cambridge, who cunningly arranged the right succession of roles tailored to nurture that talent towards greatness. All gone. In its place, simply a good agent, a shrewd businessman. If I hadn't known that other brilliant Hanno, it would have been enough. But I had, and it wasn't.

'It was Joachim,' he said, when finally one evening I persuaded him to talk about it. 'It was he who told me what I needed to know.'

'That's not true. What you and Joachim had, you shared. You still have it.'

He shook his head.

'Hanno, what's happening is simply mourning. I appreciate that. But it won't last for ever, not like this. What you had, and still have, is special. Don't let it die. To let it fade away would be the worst thing you could do to Joachim. Don't destroy his memory like this.'

That shook him, but not enough.

When the miracle happened at last, it was in a setting so ludicrous I smile even now to remember it.

About a year after Joachim died, Hanno took a few days off and we went to Dorset. Just a short break. A bit of sea, fresh air, new surroundings, a little change to remind us we were still alive.

It rained every minute we were there. Not your cute little April showers but the real thing, tanksful of the stuff coming down and obliterating the sea, the sky, the land. Determined to have what we'd come for, we doggedly donned our weatherproofs every day and trudged out to be swallowed up by the soggy cotton wool. By night we made love to the accompaniment of our clothes drying out: drip, drip, drip. We didn't mind. It felt good, just to be somewhere new, to feel the clean cold wind in our faces and sense that there was life out there other than our own.

And then, our last night, the theatre came to town.

It must have been one of the most modest touring companies ever, just two men and a woman, all fresh from drama school and cobbling together a show with a tiny Arts Council grant and a heap of energy. If they were dismayed by their venue – a derelict ex-cinema with a leaky corrugated roof – they didn't show it. And if the audience was a let-down – a handful of soggy tourists and minor town worthies – they didn't show that either. They cavorted their way through the hand-made play with all the gusto of the RSC at full force.

But from the moment he first stepped on to the rickety stage, it was one person only who caught my breath and my wonder.

He wasn't Joachim, no. He didn't even look like Joachim, apart from perhaps the thickset body and the thatch of fair hair, though even that was sandy rather than gold. His eyes weren't gold-flecked either, but something in the animal warmth of their brown made me imagine just a glimmer. And of course he spoke, something Joachim had never done except for the final enigmatic cry to his brother. His voice was gentle but strong enough to ring out above the rain-drumming roof, even above the occasional crack of thunder as the storm swept towards the flimsy building.

And then, the inevitable. The stage was plunged into darkness. The audience gasped, then tittered nervously, not sure what to do in such untoward circumstances.

But he knew. Without even a pause to think, there burst from the darkened stage the most spectacular piece of ad-libbing I'd ever heard. Not just one or two apposite remarks to link the event to the play, but an entirely new scene being created out of nothing. It wasn't long before the others took their cue from him and began their own ad-libbing.

It all happened so naturally that it took me a while to see what that amazing actor had done. Step by easy step, he'd transformed a contemporary stage play into a 1940s radio play. At the same time, he'd transformed his audience from locals in a leaky theatre into a big family gathered round the Bakelite radio in their darkened sitting-room. Not a single murmur of discontent from the enthralled audience. We listened with the innocence of children to the world being created through voices alone, to the minor miracle taking place in the dark around us.

The lights came on again just as the play ended. I could almost believe he'd planned it that way, so clever was his ad-lib at that point. I glanced at the tatty typewritten programme: Michael McVie. I looked round at the audience. Every face aglow with excitement. In this absurd setting had taken place a theatrical event they would remember for ever.

Then I saw Hanno. His eyes, more golden than ever, were fixed on the bowed head of the actor now taking his curtain call. His own head was quivering with scarcely contained excitement. A kind of electricity crackled about him and transmitted itself to me. When, as we made our way up the gangway, he took my hand in his, I almost expected an electric shock to pass between us.

In the dreary space that passed as a foyer he spoke at last, his voice quiet but agitated. 'It's *him*, Rosalind.' I don't suppose it was entirely a coincidence that Joachim's image flitted through my mind, and I don't suppose he was so very far away when Hanno continued, 'That's him, the one I've been waiting for!'

He scrabbled about in a jacket pocket, at the same time

scanning the people around us. 'Can you see who's in charge?' he asked.

'That woman over there, I think.'

He nodded. 'Keep her in sight.' He turned away and, using a knobbly wall as a surface, scribbled something on a card.

That was when I understood. More than one miracle had taken place. Hanno had discovered the first of a brand-new generation of actors destined to be great. The year of mourning was over.

When he turned back to me I saw the cream-coloured card with the gold letters which I'd seen so many times before. Nothing fancy, just his name and address. On the back, a hastily written note which would certainly transform one life and, with a bit of luck and a great deal of hard work, do a little something for theatrical history, too.

The foyer was nearly empty now. Only a few people remained to see Hanno Hirsch walk across to the unsuspecting woman and press the card into her hand. Only a few people saw his happy smile and heard the words which might just revolutionise the theatre in the coming century. 'Please,' said my Svengali, 'I would be grateful if you would deliver this to Michael McVie.'

Epilogue

'Rosalind!' The voice, a little more imperious than it used to be, floated down the stairs of our Islington house. 'What have you done with my new shirt?'

'Hidden it,' I called up to him.

'Where?'

'On a hanger in your wardrobe.'

'Oh.'

The sound of the tiny disturbance faded away and in peace again I finished wrapping the present. As always, I'd left it till the last moment, never sure it was quite good enough, always hoping I might find something better.

I heard their footsteps and opened the door to Hanno's parents before they could knock. Behind them, Jas, who'd collected them on his way here. Jas would never marry, never have in-laws of his own. He'd appropriated mine.

Hugs all around. 'Hanno's late,' I said. 'He's hunting a shirt.'

When finally he made his appearance, I felt a foolish quickening of the pulse. I don't think it's just because he's my husband and I adore him. Some people are just like that: they give pleasure, fill a room with magic the moment they enter it.

Jas had good reason to be pleased, too. Hanno had decided it was time for an all-out effort to establish Rawlinson/Molyneux as the theatrical team of the century. He'd arranged a spectacular series of double billings: in the next two years Jas would be Claudius to my Gertrude, Lövborg to my Hedda Gabler, Aegisthus to my Clytemnestra, ending with, at long last, that charming Scottish couple, the Macbeths.

Right now, however, I had a more important role to play: mother to Matthew Farleton.

It was far too lovely a day to squeeze into a car and so we walked the few streets to Astrid's house, Jas rushing ahead from time to time to entertain us with some improvised foolery. Hanno's parents laughed a lot. They had taken to Jas in a big way. Sometimes the three of them went on outings together, Jas fussing over them like a solicitous son.

The Farleton Estate Land-Rover was parked in front of Astrid's house. I'd known David and Charlotte would be there, but I was surprised on entering to see Brendan and Belle too, deep in gossip with Astrid.

More hugs.

'How on earth did you persuade the tyrant to let you come?' I asked Brendan. David had never left his horses and forests to the care of anyone else.

'Truly the age of miracles has arrived,' he laughed.

'Force,' Belle explained. 'We just said we were leaving and if he didn't want to miss his son's birthday he'd have to learn to trust the students. By the way, can we camp out with you tonight? Char and David are staying here, but after that the inn's full. It was all very spur-of-the-moment. I tried to phone but you were out.'

'Of course – heaps of room. Stay as long as you like.'

Through the open french windows I could see Charlotte and David with Matti, the three of them grouped round the Norway maple which was the centrepiece of Astrid's garden. The tree wasn't as big as it should be by now, and I knew before I joined them that they were diagnosing the problem.

As I approached, I could see the looks of pleasure on all three faces. Yes, the age of miracles had truly arrived. Charlotte had long since forgiven me for my surly matchmaking. More amazing still, David had come to regard me not as the villainous ex-wife but as an old friend. I didn't even mind the 'old'. Whatever anxiety I'd had about middle-age had disappeared along with so many other demons of the night.

More hugs – we're a very physical family – and we returned to the house together.

In our brief absence the kitchen had filled with Astrid's music students. It was they who were organising the party. In an hour, Matti's schoolfriends would begin pouring into the house and garden and the ingenuity of the students would be more wickedly tried than on any concert platform of the future. Until then, it was family only.

Family? Oh, yes. However little we were related by blood, a bond that was featherlight and yet as strong as a piano wire knitted together the motley assortment that had through the years centred on Astrid's house.

The sleek roar of a Ferrari announced Hugh's arrival. I watched with amusement as he parked behind the mucky Land-Rover and opened the door for Natalie. A moment later they were in the house, being swallowed up by the throng. More miracles. Hugh and Astrid had slipped into a comfortable old friendship much as David and I had. He'd given up his ambition to marry into talent and settled for beauty instead. Natalie was his latest bimbo – her term, not ours – a sweet-natured model working her way up in the fashion world and not half so stupid as she pretended to be. We'd all grown very fond of her and hoped this time it would last.

Hugh was swinging a camera from his wrist. 'Thought we'd record the occasion for posterity,' he explained. 'It's not every day my only nephew reaches such an august age.' He began to shepherd us into the garden.

'We are not complete,' said Astrid serenely.

He scowled at her and drifted into the kitchen where the music students were finishing off the party table. He may have given up trying to marry talent but he hadn't given up ogling it.

At last Caroline and Michael arrived and our 'family' was complete. Michael was wearing the classic black sweater and trousers of a Hamlet. He'd been wearing this for several weeks now – 'Just getting myself into the role.' Persuading the RSC to take on the virtually unknown Michael had been one of Hanno's greatest triumphs. 'No

McVie, no Rawlinson or Molyneux,' he'd said, and threatened to hand over his trio to a rival production at the National. It was curious how something of Joachim's spirit seemed to have entered into Michael. We'd sensed it at that extraordinary little production in Dorset, and the feeling had grown steadily ever since. 'Michael is my posterity,' Hanno had once said.

'Michael is our photographer,' said Hugh now, as he fussed us into position around the Norway maple.

'No way!' 'Absolutely not!' 'Out of the question!' went up the cry from the photographees.

Hugh slunk through the house and out on to the street in search of the time-honoured stranger. It was a sunny Sunday, a good day to collar some unsuspecting stroller along the canal. It wasn't long before Hugh returned with a bemused American tourist in tow.

Whoever he was, I hope he became a professional photographer. An enlarged copy of the picture is now framed above our fireplace. It's brilliant. There we all are: Natalie stealing the show for beauty, with Hugh smirking beside her; David and Charlotte caught in some shared joke; Astrid, as serene as ever; Michael failing utterly to look the gloomy and introspective Hamlet; Brendan and Belle deep in conversation with Caroline and the music students, one of whom is clearly using the trunk of the tree as a cello to demonstrate some technique. Matti's face is split wide open in a grin, perhaps because the tree seems to be sprouting from his head. Ditto Jas. I make a passable picture as a doting mother. Ditto Hanno's parents as step-grandparents.

The only odd thing about the photograph is that some trick of the light casts a very faint shadow behind Hanno. No one else has one. But it's very faint indeed and doesn't detract from the tremendous exuberance which radiates from the photograph, making it the happiest group portrait I've ever seen.

LYDIA BENNETT

THE FOLLY

Buying a hill farm on impulse is not sensible behaviour, especially for a single woman, just turned thirty, with a well-paid City job. No wonder Charlotte Venables' friends think she's taken leave of her senses.

And life on the Yorkshire moors is not what she expects. There are rumours about the death of the previous owner, stories of strange rites in the ring of standing stones high on the moor.

Above all there is the brooding hostility of her nearest neighbour, David Farleton, the reclusive squire obsessed with forestry and transforming his neglected land into a strange new kind of forest.

But there are also rewards she could never have found in the City. If only she has the courage to stand her ground . . .

HODDER AND STOUGHTON PAPERBACKS